# THE MOOR'S LAST SIGH

Salman Rushdie is the author of six novels: *Grimus*, *Midnight's Children* (which was awarded the Booker Prize and the James Tait Black Prize), *Shame* (winner of the French Prix du Meilleur Livre Etranger), *The Satanic Verses* (winner of the Whitbread Prize for Best Novel), *Haroun and the Sea of Stories* (winner of the Writers' Guild Award), and *The Moor's Last Sigh* (winner of the Whitbread Novel of the Year Award). He has also published a collection of short stories, *East, West*; a book of reportage, *The Jaguar Smile: A Nicaraguan Journey*; a volume of essays, *Imaginary Homelands*; and a work of film criticism, '*The Wizard of Oz*'.

Salman Rushdie was awarded Germany's Author of the Year Award for his novel *The Satanic Verses* in 1989. In 1993, *Midnight's Children* was adjudged the 'Booker of Bookers', the best novel to have won the Booker Prize in its first 25 years. In the same year he was awarded the Austrian State Prize for European Literature. He is also an Honorary Professor in the Humanities at the Massachusetts Institute of Technology (MIT) and a Fellow of the Royal Society of Literature. His books have been published in more than two dozen languages.

## BY SALMAN RUSHDIE

Fiction

*Grimus*
*Midnight's Children*
*Shame*
*The Satanic Verses*
*Haroun And The Sea Of Stories*
*East, West*
*The Moor's Last Sigh*

Non-Fiction

*The Jaguar Smile:*
*A Nicaraguan Journey*
*Imaginary Homelands*
*'The Wizard Of Oz'*

Salman Rushdie

# THE MOOR'S
# LAST SIGH

VINTAGE CANADA

FIRST VINTAGE CANADA EDITION, 1996

Canadian Cataloguing in Publication Data

Rushdie, Salman

The Moor's last sigh

ISBN 0-394-28197-7

I. Title

PR9499.3.R8M6 1996  832'.914  C96-930457-9

10 9 8 7 6 5 4 3 2 1

Papers used by Random House UK Limited
are natural, recyclable products made from wood grown in
sustainable forests. The manufacturing processes conform to
the environmental regulations of the country of origin

Printed and bound in Great Britain by
Cox & Wyman Ltd, Reading, Berkshire

*For E.J.W.*

# Contents

## The Da Gama-Zogoiby Family Tree

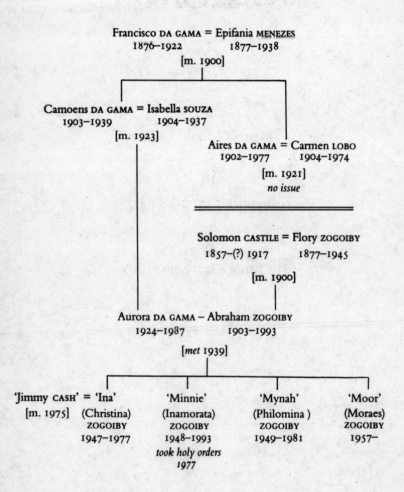

Francisco DA GAMA = Epifania MENEZES
1876–1922            1877–1938
[m. 1900]

Camoens DA GAMA = Isabella SOUZA
1903–1939            1904–1937
[m. 1923]

Aires DA GAMA = Carmen LOBO
1902–1977            1904–1974
[m. 1921]
*no issue*

Solomon CASTILE = Flory ZOGOIBY
1857–(?) 1917            1877–1945
[m. 1900]

Aurora DA GAMA – Abraham ZOGOIBY
1924–1987            1903–1993
[*met* 1939]

'Jimmy CASH' = 'Ina'
[m. 1975]     (Christina)
ZOGOIBY
1947–1977

'Minnie'
(Inamorata)
ZOGOIBY
1948–1993
*took holy orders*
*1977*

'Mynah'
(Philomina )
ZOGOIBY
1949–1981

'Moor'
(Moraes)
ZOGOIBY
1957–

# I
# A HOUSE DIVIDED

# 1

I HAVE LOST COUNT of the days that have passed since I fled the horrors of Vasco Miranda's mad fortress in the Andalusian mountain-village of Benengeli; ran from death under cover of darkness and left a message nailed to the door. And since then along my hungry, heat-hazed way there have been further bunches of scribbled sheets, swings of the hammer, sharp exclamations of two-inch nails. Long ago when I was green my beloved said to me in fondness, 'Oh, you Moor, you strange black man, always so full of theses, never a church door to nail them to.' (She, a self-professedly godly un-Christian Indian, joked about Luther's protest at Wittenberg to tease her determinedly ungodly Indian Christian lover: how stories travel, what mouths they end up in!) Unfortunately, my mother overheard; and darted, quick as snakebite: 'So full, you mean, of faeces.' Yes, mother, you had the last word on that subject, too: as about everything.

'Amrika' and 'Moskva', somebody once called them, Aurora my mother and Uma my love, nicknaming them for the two great super-powers; and people said they looked alike but I never saw it, couldn't see it at all. Both of them dead, of unnatural causes, and I in a far-off country with death at my heels and their story in my hand, a story I've been crucifying upon a gate, a fence, an olive-tree, spreading it across this landscape of my last journey, the story which points to me. On the run, I have turned the world into my pirate map, complete with clues, leading X-marks-the-spottily to the treasure of myself. When my pursuers have followed the trail they'll find me waiting, uncomplaining, out of breath, ready. *Here I stand. Couldn't've done it differently.*

(Here I sit, is more like it. In this dark wood – that is, upon this mount of olives, within this clump of trees, observed by the

3

quizzically tilting stone crosses of a small, overgrown graveyard, and a little down the track from the Ultimo Suspiro gas station – without benefit or need of Virgils, in what ought to be the middle pathway of my life, but has become, for complicated reasons, the end of the road, I bloody well collapse with exhaustion.)

And yes, ladies, much is being nailed down. Colours, for example, to the mast. But after a not-so-long (though gaudily colourful) life I am fresh out of theses. Life itself being crucifixion enough.

⤶

When you're running out of steam, when the puff that blows you onward is almost gone, it's time to make confession. Call it testament or (what you) will; life's Last Gasp Saloon. Hence this here-I-stand-or-sit with my life's sentences nailed to the landscape and the keys to a red fort in my pocket, these moments of waiting before a final surrender.

Now, therefore, it is meet to sing of endings; of what was, and may be no longer; of what was right in it, and wrong. A last sigh for a lost world, a tear for its passing. Also, however, a last hurrah, a final, scandalous skein of shaggy-dog yarns (words must suffice, video facility being unavailable) and a set of rowdy tunes for the wake. A Moor's tale, complete with sound and fury. You want? Well, even if you don't. And to begin with, pass the pepper.

– *What's that you say?* –

The trees themselves are surpriséd into speech. (And have you never, in solitude and despair, talked to the walls, to your idiot pooch, to empty air?)

I repeat: the pepper, if you please; for if it had not been for peppercorns, then what is ending now in East and West might never have begun. Pepper it was that brought Vasco da Gama's tall ships across the ocean, from Lisbon's Tower of Belém to the Malabar Coast: first to Calicut and later, for its lagoony harbour, to Cochin. English and French sailed in the wake of that first-arrived Portugee, so that in the period called Discovery-of-India – but how could we be discovered when we were not covered before? –

we were 'not so much sub-continent as sub-condiment', as my distinguished mother had it. 'From the beginning, what the world wanted from bloody mother India was daylight-clear,' she'd say. 'They came for the hot stuff, just like any man calling on a tart.'

⮌

Mine is the story of the fall from grace of a high-born cross-breed: me, Moraes Zogoiby, called 'Moor', for most of my life the only male heir to the spice-trade-'n'-big-business crores of the da Gama-Zogoiby dynasty of Cochin, and of my banishment from what I had every right to think of as my natural life by my mother Aurora, *née* da Gama, most illustrious of our modern artists, a great beauty who was also the most sharp-tongued woman of her generation, handing out the hot stuff to anybody who came within range. Her children were shown no mercy. 'Us rosary-crucifixion beatnik chicks, we have red chillies in our veins,' she would say. 'No special privileges for flesh-and-blood relations! Darlings, we munch on flesh, and blood is our tipple of choice.'

'To be the offspring of our daemonic Aurora,' I was told when young by the Goan painter V. (for Vasco )Miranda, 'is to be, truly, a modern Lucifer. You know: son of the blooming morning.' By then my family had moved to Bombay, and this was the kind of thing that passed, in the Paradise of Aurora Zogoiby's legendary salon, for a compliment; but I remember it as a prophecy, because the day came when I was indeed hurled from that fabulous garden, and plunged towards Pandaemonium. (Banished from the natural, what choice did I have but to embrace its opposite? Which is to say, *unnaturalism*, the only real ism of these back-to-front and jabber-wocky days. Placed beyond the Pale, would you not seek to make light of the Dark? Just so. Moraes Zogoiby, expelled from his story, tumbled towards history.)

– *And all this from a pepperpot!* –

Not only pepper, but also cardamoms, cashews, cinnamon, ginger, pistachios, cloves; and as well as spice'n'nuts there were coffee beans, and the mighty tea leaf itself. But the fact remains that, in Aurora's words, 'it was pepper first and onemost – yes, yes, onemost, because why say foremost? Why come forth if you can come first?' What was true of history in general was true of our family's fortunes in particular – pepper, the coveted Black Gold of Malabar, was the original stock-in-trade of my filthy-rich folks, the wealthiest spice, nut, bean and leaf merchants in Cochin, who without any evidence save centuries of tradition claimed wrong-side-of-the-blanket descent from great Vasco da Gama himself . . .

No secrets any more. I've already nailed them up.

# 2

A T THE AGE OF thirteen my mother Aurora da Gama took to wandering barefoot around her grandparents' large, odorous house on Cabral Island during the bouts of sleeplessness which became, for a time, her nightly affliction, and on these nocturnal odysseys she would invariably throw open all the windows − first the inner screen-windows whose fine-meshed netting protected the house from midges mosquitoes flies, next the leaded-glass casements themselves, and finally the slatted wooden shutters beyond. Consequently, the sixty-year-old matriarch Epifania − whose personal mosquito-net had over the years developed a number of small but significant holes which she was too myopic or stingy to notice − would be awakened each morning by itching bites on her bony blue forearms and would then unleash a thin shriek at the sight of flies buzzing around the tray of bed-tea and sweet biscuits placed beside her by Tereza the maid (who swiftly fled). Epifania fell into a useless frenzy of scratching and swatting, lunging around her curvaceous teak boat-bed, often spilling tea on the lacy cotton bedclothes, or on her white muslin nightgown with the high ruffled collar that concealed her once swan-like, but now corrugated, neck. And as the fly-swatter in her right hand thwacked and thumped, as the long nails on her left hand raked her back in search of ever more elusive mosquito-bites, so Epifania da Gama's nightcap would slip from her head, revealing a mess of snaky white hair through which mottled patches of scalp could (alas!) all too easily be glimpsed. When young Aurora, listening at the door, judged that the sounds of her hated grandmother's fury (oaths, breaking china, the impotent slaps of the swatter, the scornful buzzing of insects) were nearing peak volume, she would put on her sweetest smile and

7

breeze into the matriarch's presence with a gay morning greeting, knowing that the mother of all the da Gamas of Cochin would be pushed right over the edge of her wild anger by the arrival of this youthful witness to her antique helplessness. Epifania, hair a-straggle, kneeling on stained sheets, upraised swatter flapping like a broken wand, and seeking a release for her rage, howled like a weird sister, rakshasa or banshee at intruding Aurora, to the youngster's secret delight.

'Oho-ho, girl, what a shock you gave, one day you will killofy my heart.'

So it was that Aurora da Gama got the idea of murdering her grandmother from the lips of the intended victim herself. After that she began making plans, but these increasingly macabre fantasies of poisons and cliff-edges were invariably scuppered by pragmatic problems, such as the difficulty of getting hold of a cobra and inserting it between Epifania's bedsheets, or the flat refusal of the old harridan to walk on any terrain that, as she put it, 'tiltoed up or down'. And although Aurora knew very well where to lay her hands on a good sharp kitchen knife, and was certain that her strength was already great enough to choke the life out of Epifania, she nevertheless ruled out these options, too, because she had no intention of being found out, and too obvious an assault might lead to the asking of uncomfortable questions. The perfect crime having failed to make its nature known, Aurora continued to play the perfect granddaughter; but brooded on, privately, though it never occurred to her to notice that in her broodings there was more than a little of Epifania's ruthlessness:

'Patience is a virtue,' she told herself. 'I'll just bide-o my time.'

In the meanwhile she went on opening windows during those humid nights, and sometimes threw out small valuable ornaments, carved wooden trunk-nosed figures which bobbed away on the tides of the lagoon lapping at the walls of the island mansion, or delicately worked ivory tusks which naturally sank without trace. For several days the family was at a loss to understand these developments. The sons of Epifania da Gama, Aurora's uncle Aires-pronounced-Irish and her father Camoens-pronounced-

Camonsh-through-the-nose, would awake to find that mischievous night-breezes had blown bush-shirts from their closets and business papers from their pending trays. Nimble-fingered draughts had untied the necks of the sample-bags, jute sacks full of big and little cardamoms and karri-leaves and cashews that always stood like sentinels along the shady corridors of the office wing, and as a result there were fenugreek seeds and pistachios tumbling crazily across the worn old floor made of limestone, charcoal, egg-whites and other, forgotten ingredients, and the scent of spices in the air tormented the matriarch, who had grown more and more allergic with the passing years to the sources of her family's fortune.

And if the flies buzzed in through the opened netting-windows, and the naughty gusts through the parted panes of leaded glass, then the opening of the shutters let in everything else: the dust and the tumult of boats in Cochin harbour, the horns of freighters and tug-boat chugs, the fishermen's dirty jokes and the throb of their jellyfish stings, the sunlight as sharp as a knife, the heat that could choke you like a damp cloth pulled tightly around your head, the calls of floating hawkers, the wafting sadness of the unmarried Jews across the water in Mattancherri, the menace of emerald smugglers, the machinations of business rivals, the growing nervousness of the British colony in Fort Cochin, the cash demands of the staff and of the plantation workers in the Spice Mountains, the tales of Communist troublemaking and Congresswallah politics, the names *Gandhi* and *Nehru*, the rumours of famine in the east and hunger strikes in the north, the songs and drum-beats of the oral storytellers, and the heavy rolling sound (as they broke against Cabral Island's rickety jetty) of the incoming tides of history. 'This low-class country, Jesus Christ,' Aires-uncle swore at breakfast in his best gaitered and hatterred manner. 'Outside world isn't dirtyfilthy enough, eh, eh? Then what frightful bumbolina, what dash-it-all bugger-boy let it in here again? Is this a decent residence, by Jove, or a shithouse excuse-my-French in the bazaar?'

That morning Aurora understood that she had gone too far, because her beloved father Camoens, a little goateed stick of a man in a loud bush-shirt who was already a head shorter than his beanpole daughter, took her down to the little jetty, and positively capering in his emotion and excitement so that against the improbable beauty and mercantile bustle of the lagoon his silhouette seemed like a figure out of a fantasy, a leprechaun dancing in a glade, perhaps, or a benign djinni escaped from a lamp, he confided in a secret hiss his great and heartbreaking news. Named after a poet and possessed of a dreamy nature (but not the gift), Camoens timidly suggested the possibility of a haunting.

'It is my belief', he told his dumbstruck daughter, 'that your darling Mummy has come back to us. You know how she loved fresh breeze, how she fought with your grandmother for air; and now by magic the windows fly open. And, daughter mine, just look what-what items are missing! Only those she always hated, don't you see? *Aires's elephant gods*, she used to say. It is your uncle's little hobby-collection of Ganeshas that has gone. That, and ivory.'

*Epifania's elephant-teeth. Too many elephants sitting on this house.* The late Belle da Gama had always spoken her mind. 'I think so if I stay up tonight maybe I can look once more upon her dear face,' Camoens yearningly confided. 'What do you think? Message is clear as day. Why not wait with me? You and your father are in a same state: he misses his Mrs, and you are glum about your Mum.'

Aurora, blushing in confusion, shouted, 'But I at least don't believe in blooming ghosts,' and ran indoors, unable to confess the truth, which was that she was her dead mother's phantom, doing her deeds, speaking in her departed voice; that the night-walking daughter was keeping the mother alive, giving up her own body for the departed to inhabit, clinging to death, refusing it, insisting on the constancy, beyond the grave, of love – that she had become her mother's new dawn, flesh for her spirit, two belles in one.

(Many years later she would name her own home *Elephanta*; so matters elephantine, as well as spectral, continued to play a part in our saga, after all.)

↜

Belle had been dead for just two months. Hell's Belle, Aurora's Aires-uncle used to call her (but then he was always giving people names, imposing his private universe bully-fashion upon the world): Isabella Ximena da Gama, the grandmother I never knew. Between her and Epifania it had been war from the start. Widowed at forty-five, Epifania at once commenced to play the matriarch, and would sit with a lapful of pistachios in the morning shadow of her favourite courtyard, fanning herself, cracking nutshells with her teeth in a loud, impressive demonstration of power, singing the while in a high, implacable voice,

> *Booby Shafto's gone to sea-ea*
> *Silver bottles on his knee-ee . . .*

Ker-rick! Ker-rack! went the nutshells in her mouth.

> *He'll come back to bury me-ee*
> *Boney Booby Shafto.*

In all the years of her life only Belle refused to be scared of her. 'Four b-minuses,' the nineteen-year-old Isabella told her mother-in-law brightly the day after she entered the household as a disapproved-of but grudgingly accepted bride. 'Not booby, not bottles, not bury, not boney. So sweet you sing a love song at your age, but wrong words make it nonsense, isn't it.'

'Camoens,' said stony Epifania, 'inform your goodwife to shuttofy her tap. Some hot-water-trouble is leaking from her face.' In the days that followed she launched indomitably into a full medley of personalised shanties: *What shall we do with the shrunken tailor?* caused her new daughter-in-law much inadequately stifled merriment, whereupon Epifania, frowning, changed her tune: *Row, row, row your beau, gently down istream,* she sang, perhaps advising Belle to concentrate on her spousely duties, and then added the rather more metaphysical put-down: *Morally, morally, morally, morally . . .* ker-runch! *. . . wife is not a queen.*

Ah, the legends of the battling da Gamas of Cochin! I tell them as they have come down to me, polished and fantasticated by many re-tellings. These are old ghosts, distant shadows, and I tell their tales to be done with them; they are all I have left and so I set them free. From Cochin harbour to Bombay harbour, from Malabar

Coast to Malabar Hill: the story of our comings-together, tearings-apart, our rises, falls, our *tiltoings up and down*. And after that it's goodbye, Mattancherri, farewell, Marine Drive . . . at any rate, by the time my mother Aurora had arrived in that baby-starved household and grown into a tall and mutinous thirteen-year-old, the lines were clearly drawn.

'Too long for a girl,' was Epifania's disapproving verdict on her granddaughter as Aurora entered her teens. 'Trouble in her eye means devil in her heart. Shame on her front, also, as any eye can see. It stickofies too far out.' To which Belle angrily replied, 'And what so-so-perfect child has your darling Aires provided? At least one young da Gama is here, alive and kicking, and never mind her big booby-shaftoes. From Aires-brother and Sister Sahara, no sign of any produce: boobies or babies, both.' Aires's wife's name was Carmen, but Belle, mimicking her brother-in-law's fondness for inventing names, had named her after the desert, 'because she is barren-flat as sand and in all that waste ground I can't see any place to get a drink.'

Aires da Gama, brilliantine struggling to keep slicked-down his thick, wavy white hair (premature whitening has long been a family characteristic; my mother Aurora was snow-white at twenty, and what fairy-tale glamour, what icy *gravitas* was added to her beauty by the soft glaciers cascading from her head!): how my great-uncle postured! In the small, two-inch-by-two-inch mono-chrome photographs I remember, what a ludicrous figure he cut in his monocle, stiff collar, and three-piece suit of finest gabardine. There was an ivory-topped cane in one hand (*it was a swordstick*, family history whispers in my ear), a long cigarette-holder in the other; and he was also, I regret to mention, in the habit of wearing spats. Add height, and a pair of twirling moustachios, and the picture of a comic-opera villain would be complete; but Aires was as pocket-sized as his brother, clean-shaven and a little shiny of face, so that his look of a counterfeit Drone was, perhaps, more to be pitied than hissed at.

Here, too, on another page of memory's photograph album, is stooping, squint-eyed Great-Aunt Sahara, the Woman Without Oases, masticating betel-nut in those just-so-cameelious jowls and looking like she's got the hump. Carmen da Gama was Aires's first cousin, the orphan child of Epifania's sister Blimunda and a small-time printer named Lobo. Both parents had been carried away by a malaria epidemic, and Carmen's marriage prospects had been lower than zero, frozen solid until Aires amazed his mother by agreeing to the making of a match. Epifania in a torment of indecision suffered a week of sleepless nights, unable to choose between her dream of finding Aires a fish worth hooking and the increasingly desperate need to palm Carmen off on someone before it was too late. In the end her duty to her dead sister took precedence over her hopes for her son.

Carmen never looked young, never had children, dreamed of diddling Camoens's side of the family out of its inheritance by fair means or foul, and never mentioned to a living soul that on her wedding night her husband had entered her bedroom late, ignored his terrified and scrawny young bride who lay virginally quaking in the bed, undressed with slow fastidiousness, and then with equal precision slipped his naked body (so similar in proportions to her own) into the wedding-dress which her maidservant had left upon a tailor's dummy as a symbol of their union, and left the room through the latrine's outside door. Carmen heard whistles borne towards her on the water, and rising sheet-shrouded while the heavy knowledge of the future fell upon her shoulders and pushed them down into a stoop, she saw the wedding-dress gleaming in moonlight as a young man rowed it and its occupant away, in search of whatever it was that passed, among such occult beings, for bliss.

The story of Aires's gowned adventure, which left Great-Aunt Sahara abandoned in the cold dunes of her unbloodied sheets, has come down to me in spite of her silence. Most ordinary families can't keep secrets; and in our far-from-ordinary clan, our deepest mysteries usually ended up in oils-on-canvas, hanging on a gallery wall . . . but then again, perhaps the whole incident was invented, a fable the family made up to shock-but-not-too-much, to make more palatable – because more exotic, more *beautiful* – the fact of Aires's homosexuality? For while it's true that Aurora da Gama grew up to paint the scene – on her canvas the man in the moonlit dress sits primly, facing a bare perspiring oarsman's torso – it would be possible to argue that for all her bohemian credentials this double portrait was a domesticating fantasy, only conventionally outrageous: that the story, as told and painted, put Aires's secret wildness into a pretty frock, hiding away the cock and arse and blood and spunk of it, the brave determined fear of the runt-sized dandy soliciting hefty companions among the harbour-rats, the exalted terror of bought embraces, sweet alley-back and toddy-shack fondlings by thick-fisted stevedores, the love of the deep-muscled buttocks of cycle-rickshaw-youths and of the under-nourished mouths of bazaar urchins; that it ignored the fretful, argumentative, *amour fou* reality of his long, but by no means faithful liaison with the fellow in the wedding-night boat, whom Aires baptised 'Prince Henry the Navigator' . . . that it sent the truth offstage titillatingly dressed, and then averted its eyes.

No, sir. The painting's authority will not be denied. Whatever else may have happened between these three – the unlikely late-life intimacy between Prince Henry and Carmen da Gama will be recorded in its place – the episode of the shared wedding-dress was where it all began.

The nakedness beneath the borrowed wedding outfit, the bridegroom's face beneath the bridal veil, is what connects my heart to this strange man's memory. There is much about him that I do not care for; but in the image of his queenliness, where many back home (and not only back home) would see degradation, I see his courage, his capacity, yes, for glory.

'But if it wasn't prick in the bottom,' my dear mother, inheritor of her own mother's fearless tongue, used to say of life with her unloved Aires-uncle, 'then, darling, it was strictly pain in the neck.'

〜

And while we're getting down to it, to the root of the whole matter of family rifts and premature deaths and thwarted loves and mad passions and weak chests and power and money and the even more morally dubious seductions and mysteries of art, let's not forget who started the whole thing, who was the first one to go out of his element and drown, whose watery death removed the linch-pin, the foundation-stone, and began the family's long slide, which ended up by dumping me in the pit: Francisco da Gama, Epifania's defunct spouse.

Yes, Epifania too had once been a bride. She came from an old, but now much-reduced trader family, the Menezes clan of Mangalore, and there was great jealousy when, after a chance encounter at a Calicut wedding, she landed the fattest catch of all, against all reason, in the opinion of many disappointed mothers, because a man so rich ought to have been decently revolted by the empty bank accounts, costume jewellery and cheap tailoring of the little gold-digger's down-and-out clan. At the dawn of the century she came on Great-Grandfather Francisco's arm to Cabral Island, the first of my story's four sequestered, serpented, Edenic-infernal private universes. (My mother's Malabar Hill salon was the second; my father's sky-garden, the third; and Vasco Miranda's bizarre redoubt, his 'Little Alhambra' in Benengeli, Spain, was, is, and will in this telling become, my last.) There she found a grand old mansion in the traditional style, with many delightfully interlink-ing courtyards of greeny pools and mossed fountains, surrounded by galleries rich in woodcarving, off which lay labyrinths of tall rooms, their high roofs gabled and tiled. It was set in a rich man's paradise of tropical foliage; just what the doctor ordered, in Epifania's opinion, for though her early years had been relatively penurious she had always believed she had a talent for magnifi-cence.

However, a few years after the birth of their two sons, Francisco da Gama came home one day with an impossibly young and suspiciously winsome Frenchman, a certain M. Charles Jeanneret, who put on the airs of an architectural genius even though he was barely twenty years old. Before Epifania could blink, her gullible husband had commissioned the jackanapes to build not one but two new houses in her precious gardens. And what crazy structures they turned out to be! – The one a strange angular slabby affair in which the garden penetrated the interior space so thoroughly that it was often hard to say whether one was in or out of doors, and the furniture looked like something made for a hospital or a geometry class, you couldn't sit on it without bumping into some pointy corner; the other a wood and paper house of cards – 'after the style Japanese', he told an appalled Epifania – a flimsy fire-trap whose walls were sliding parchment screens, and in whose rooms one was not supposed to sit, but kneel, and at night one had to sleep on a mat on the floor with one's head on a wooden block, as if one were a servant, while the absence of privacy provoked Epifania into the observation that 'at least knowledge of stomach health of household members is no problem in a house with toilet-paper instead of bathroom walls'.

Worse still, Epifania soon discovered that once these madhouses were ready her husband frequently tired of their beautiful home, would smack his hand on the breakfast table and announce they were 'moving East' or 'going West'; whereupon the whole household had no choice but to move lock, stock and barrel into one or other of the Frenchman's follies, and no amount of protests made the slightest jot of difference. And after a few weeks, they moved again.

Not only was Francisco da Gama incapable of living a settled life like ordinary folks, but, as Epifania discovered despairingly, he was also a patron of the arts. Rum-and-whisky-drinking hemp-chewing persons of low birth and revolting dress-sense were imported for long periods and filled up the Frenchy's houses with their jangling music, poetry marathons, naked models, reefer-stubs, all-night card-schools and other manifestations of their in-all-ways-incorrect behaviour. Foreign artists came to stay and left behind strange mobiles that looked like giant metal coathangers twirling in the breeze, and pictures of devil-women with both eyes on the same side of their noses, and giant canvases that looked like an accident had befallen with the paint, and all these calamities Epifania was obliged to put on the walls and in the courtyards of her own beloved home, and look at every day, as if they were decent stuff.

'Your art-shart, Francisco,' she told her husband venomously, 'it will blindofy me with ugliness.' But he was immune to her poisons. 'Old beauty is not enough,' he told her. 'Old palaces, old behaviour, old gods. These days the world is full of questions, and there are new ways to be beautiful.'

Francisco was hero material from the day he was born, destined for questions and quests, as ill-at-ease with domesticity as Quixote. He was handsome as sin but twice as virtuous, and on the coir-matting cricket-pitches of the time he proved, when young, a devilish slow left arm tweaker and elegant number four bat. At college he was the most brilliant student physicist of his year, but was orphaned early and chose, after much reflection, to forgo the academic life, do his duty, and enter the family business. He grew up, becoming an adept of the age-old da Gama art of turning spice and nuts into gold. He could smell money on the wind, could sniff the weather and tell you if it was bringing in profit or loss; but he was also a philanthropist, funding orphanages, opening free health clinics, building schools for the villages lining the back-waterways, setting up institutes researching coco-palm blight, initiating elephant conservation schemes in the mountains beyond his spice-fields, and sponsoring annual contests at the time of the Onam flower festival to find and crown the finest oral storytellers in the region: so free with his philanthropy, in fact, that Epifania was driven to wailing (uselessly): 'And then, when funds are frittered, and children are cap-in-hand? Then can we eatofy your thisthing, your *anthropology*?'

She fought him every inch of the way, and lost every battle except the last. Francisco the modernist, his eyes fixed on the future, became a disciple first of Bertrand Russell – *Religion and Science* and *A Free Man's Worship* were his ungodly Bibles – and then of the increasingly fervent nationalist politics of the Theo-sophical Society of Mrs Annie Besant. Remember: Cochin, Travancore, Mysore, Hyderabad were technically not part of British India; they were Indian States, with their own princes. Some of them – like Cochin – could boast, for example, of educational and literacy standards far in excess of those prevailing under British direct rule, while in others (Hyderabad) there existed what Mr Nehru called a condition of 'perfect feudalism', and in Travancore even the Congress was declared illegal; but let us not confuse (Francisco did not confuse) appearance with reality; the fig-leaf is not the fig. When Nehru raised the national flag in Mysore, the local (Indian) authorities destroyed not only the flag but even the flagpole the moment he had left town, lest the event annoy the true rulers . . . Soon after the Great War broke out on his thirty-eighth birthday, something snapped inside Francisco.

'The British must go,' he announced solemnly at dinner beneath the oil-paintings of his suited-and-booted ancestors.

'O God, where are they going?' asked Epifania, missing the point. 'In such a bad moment they will abandon us to our fate and that boogyman, Kaiser Bill?'

Francisco exploded, and twelve-year-old Aires and eleven-year-old Camoens froze in their seats. 'The Kaiser is one bill we are already paying,' he thundered. 'Taxes doubled! Our youngsters dying in British uniform! The nation's wealth is being shipped off, madam: at home our people starve, but British Tommy is utilising our wheat, rice, jute and coconut products. I personally am required to send out goods below cost-price. Our mines are being emptied: saltpetre, manganese, mica. I swear! Bombay-wallahs getting rich and nation going to pot.'

'Too many crooks and books have filled your ears,' Epifania protested. 'What are we but Empire's children? British have given us everything, isn't it? – Civilisation, law, order, too much. Even your spices that stink up the house they buy out of their generosity, putting clothes on backs and food on children's plates. Then why speakofy such treason and filthy up my children's ears with what-all Godless bunk?'

After that day they had little to say to each other. Aires, defying his father, took his mother's side; Epifania and he were for England, God, philistinism, the old ways, a quiet life. Francisco was all bustle and energy, so Aires affected indolence, learned how to infuriate his father by the luxuriant ease of his lounging. (In my youth, for different reasons, I also was apt to lounge. But I was not seeking to annoy; my vain intent was to set my slowness against the accelerated rush of Time itself. This tale, too, will be revisited at its proper location.) It was in the younger boy, Camoens, that Francisco found his ally, inculcating in him the virtues of nationalism, reason, art, innovation, and above all, in those days,

18

of protest. Francisco shared Nehru's early contempt for the Indian National Congress – 'just a talk-shop for wogs' – and Camoens gave his grave assent. 'Annie this and Gandhi that,' Epifania scolded him. 'Nehru, Tilak, all these rogue gangsters from the North. Ignore your mother! Keep it up! Then it'll be the jailhouse for you, chop-chop.'

In 1916 Francisco da Gama joined the Home Rule campaign of Annie Besant and Bal Gangadhar Tilak, hitching his star to the demand for an independent Indian parliament which would determine the country's future. When Mrs Besant asked him to found a Home Rule League in Cochin and he had the nerve to invite dock-labourers, tea-pickers, bazaar coolies and his own workers to join as well as the local bourgeoisie, Epifania was quite overcome. 'Masses and classes in same club! Shame and scandal! Sense is gone from the man,' she expostulated faintly, fanning herself, and then lapsed into sullen silence.

A few days after the League was founded, there was a clash in the streets of the dockside Ernakulam district; a few dozen militant Leaguers managed to overpower a small detachment of lightly armed troops and sent them packing without their weapons. The next day the League was formally banned, and a motor-launch arrived at Cabral Island to place Francisco da Gama under arrest.

He was in and out of prison during the next six months, earning his elder son's contempt and the younger boy's undying admiration. Yes, a hero, absolutely. In those prison spells, and in his furious political activism between jail terms, when in accord with Tilak's instructions he deliberately courted arrest on many occasions, he acquired the credentials that made him a coming man, worth keeping an eye on, a fellow with a following: a star.

Stars can fall; heroes can fail; Francisco da Gama did not fulfil his destiny.

⌣

In prison he found time for the work that undid him. Nobody ever worked out where, in what reject-goods discount-store of the mind, Great-Grandfather Francisco got hold of the scientific theory that turned him from emerging hero into national laughing-stock, but in those years it came to preoccupy him more and more, eventually rivalling even the nationalist movement in his affections. Perhaps his old interest in theoretical physics had become confused with his newer passions, Mrs Besant's Theosophy, the Mahatma's insistence on the oneness of all India's widely differing millions, the search among modernising Indian intellectuals of the period for some secularist definition of the spiritual life, of that worn-out word, the soul; anyhow, towards the end of 1916 Francisco had privately printed a paper, which he then sent to all the leading journals of the time for their kind attention, entitled *Towards a Provisional Theory of the Transformational Fields of Conscience*, in which he proposed the existence, all around us, of invisible 'dynamic networks of spiritual energy similar to electro-magnetic fields', arguing that these 'fields of conscience' were nothing less than the repositories of the memory – both practical and moral – of the human species, that they were in fact what Joyce's Stephen had recently spoken (in the *Egoist* magazine) of wishing to forge in his soul's smithy: viz., the uncreated conscience of our race.

At their lowest level of operation, the so-called TFCs apparently facilitated education, so that what was learned anywhere on earth, by anyone, at once became more easily learnable by anyone else, anywhere else; but it was also suggested that on their most exalted plane, the plane that was admittedly hardest to observe, the fields acted ethically, both defining and being defined by our moral alternatives, being strengthened by each moral choice taken on the planet, and, conversely, weakened by base deeds, so that, in theory, too many evil acts would damage the Fields of Conscience beyond repair and 'humanity would then face the unspeakable reality of a universe made amoral, and therefore meaningless, by the destruction of the ethical nexus, the safety-net, one might even say, within which we have always lived'.

In fact, Francisco's paper propounded no more than the lower, educative functions of the fields with any degree of conviction, extrapolating the moral dimensions in one relatively short, and self-confessedly speculative passage. However, the derision it inspired was on the grand scale. A newspaper editorial in the Madras-based paper *The Hindu*, headed *Thunderbolts of Good and Evil*, lampooned him cruelly: 'Dr da Gama's fears for our ethical future are like those of a crackpot weatherman who believes our deeds control the weather, so that unless we act "clemently", so to speak, there will be nothing overhead but storms.' The satirical columnist 'Waspyjee' in the *Bombay Chronicle* – whose editor Horniman, a friend of Mrs Besant and the nationalist movement, had earnestly implored Francisco not to publish – inquired maliciously whether the famous Fields of Conscience were for human use alone, or if other living creatures – cockroaches, for example, or poisonous snakes – might learn to benefit from them; or whether, alternatively, each species had its own such vortices swirling around the planet. 'Should we fear contamination of our values – call it Gama Radiation – by accidental field collisions? Might not praying-mantis sexual mores, baboon or gorilla aesthetics, scorpion politics fatally infect our own poor psyches? Or, Heaven forfend – *perhaps they already have!!*'

It was these 'Gama rays' that finished Francisco off; he became a joke, light relief from the murderous war, economic hardship and the struggle for independence. At first he kept his nerve, and bloody-mindedly concentrated on thinking up experiments that could prove the first, lesser hypothesis. He wrote a second paper proposing that 'bols', the long strings of nonsense words used by Kathak dance instructors to indicate movements of feet arms neck, might be suitable bases for tests. One such sequence (*tat-tat-taa dreegay-thun-thun jee-jee-kathay to, talang, taka-thun-thun, tai! Tat tai!* &c.) could be used alongside four other strings of purposeless nonsense devised to be spoken in the same rhythmic pattern as the 'control'. Students in a country other than India, having no knowledge of Indian dance instructions, would be asked to learn all five; and, if Francisco's field theory held, the dance-class gobbledygook should prove much the easiest to memorise.

The test was never performed. And soon his resignation from the banned Home Rule League was requested and its leaders, who now included Motilal Nehru himself, stopped answering the increasingly plaintive letters with which my great-grandfather bombarded them. Arty types no longer arrived by the boatload to carouse in either of Cabral Island's follies, to smoke opium in papery East or drink whisky in pointy West, though from time to time, as the Frenchy's reputation grew, Francisco was asked if he had indeed been the first Indian patron of the young man who was now calling himself 'Le Corbusier'. When he received such an inquiry, the shattered hero would fire off a terse note in reply: 'Never heard of the fellow.' After a time these inquiries also stopped.

Epifania was exultant. As Francisco sank into introversion and despondency, his face acquiring the puckered look common in men convinced that the world has inexplicably done them a great and unjustified wrong, she moved in swiftly for the kill. (Literally, as it turned out.) I have come to the conclusion that the years of her suppressed discontents had bred in her a vindictive rage – rage, my true inheritance! – that was often indistinguishable from true, murderous hatred; although if you had ever asked her if she loved her husband, the very question would have shocked her. 'Ours was a love-match,' she told her dejected spouse during an interminable island evening with only the radio for company. 'For love or what else I gave in to your fancies? But see where they have brought you. Now for love you must give in to mine.'

The detested follies in the garden were locked up. Nor was politics to be mentioned in her presence again: when the Russian Revolution shook the world, when the Great War ended, when news of the Amritsar Massacre filtered down from the north and destroyed the Anglophilia of almost every Indian (the Nobel laureate, Rabindranath Tagore, returned his knighthood to the King), Epifania da Gama on Cabral Island stopped up her ears and continued to believe, to a degree that was almost blasphemous, in the omnipotent beneficence of the British; and her elder son Aires believed it along with her.

At Christmas, 1921, Camoens, eighteen, shyly brought the seventeen-year-old orphan Isabella Ximena Souza home to meet his parents (Epifania asked where they had met, was told with many blushes of a brief encounter at St Francis's Church, and with a disdain born of her great ability to forget everything inconvenient

about her own background, snorted, 'Hussy from somewhere!'
But Francisco gave the girl his blessing, stretching out a tired hand
at the to-tell-the-truth not-very-festive table and placing it on
Isabella Souza's lovely head). Camoens's future bride was characteristically outspoken. Her eyes shining with excitement, she
broke Epifania's five-year-old taboo and expressed delight at
Calcutta's virtual boycott of, and Bombay's large demonstrations
against, the visit of the Prince of Wales (the future Edward VIII),
praising the Nehrus, father and son, for the non-collaboration in
court that had sent them both to jail. 'Now the Viceroy will know
what's what,' she said. 'Motilal loves England, but even he has
preferred to go to lock-up.'

Francisco stirred, an old light dawning in those long-dulled eyes.
But Epifania spoke first. 'In this God-fearing Christian house,
British still is best, madder-moysselle,' she snapped. 'If you have
ambitions in our boy's direction, then please to mindofy your
mouth. You want dark or white meat? Speak up. Glass of imported
Dão wine, nice cold? You can have. Pudding-shudding? Why not.
These are Christmas topics, frawline. You want stuffing?'

Later, on the jetty, Belle was equally blunt about her findings,
complaining bitterly to Camoens that he had not stood up for her.
'Your family home is like a place lost in a fog,' she told her fiancé.
'Where is the air to breathe? Somebody there is casting a spell and
sucking life out of you and your poor Dad. As for your brother,
who cares, poor type is a hopeless case. Hate me don't hate me but
it is plain as the colours on your by-the-way-excuse-me too-
horrible bush-shirt that a bad thing is growing quickly here.'

'Then you won't come again?' Camoens wretchedly asked.

Belle got into the waiting boat. 'Silly boy,' she said. 'You are a
sweet and touching boy. And you have no idea at all of what I will
and will not do for love: to where I will come or not come, with
whom I will or will not fight, whose magic I will un-magic with
my own.'

In the following months it was Belle who kept Camoens
informed about the world, who recited to him Nehru's speech at
his re-sentencing to further imprisonment in May 1922. *Intimidation and terrorism have become the chief instruments of government. Do*

*they imagine that they will thus instil affection for themselves? Affection and loyalty are of the heart. They cannot be extorted at the point of a bayonet.* 'Sounds like your parents' marriage to me,' Isabella cheerily said; and Camoens, his nationalist zeal rekindled by his adoration of his beautiful, loudmouthed girl, had the grace to blush.

Belle had made him her project. In those days he had begun to sleep badly and, asthmatically, to wheeze. 'It's all that bad air,' she told him. 'So, so. I must save one da Gama at least.'

She ordered changes. Under her instructions – and to Epifania's rage: 'Don't think-o for two secs I will cut out chicken in this house because your little chickie, that little floozy-fantoozy, wants you to eat beggar-people's food' – he became a vegetarian, and learned to stand on his head. Secretly, too, he broke a window-frame and climbed into the spider-webbed West house where his father's library languished, and began to devour the books along with the bookworms. Attar, Khayyam, Tagore, Carlyle, Ruskin, Wells, Poe, Shelley, Raja Rammohun Roy. 'You see?' Belle encouraged him. 'You can do it; you can become a person, too, instead of a doormat in an ugly-bug shirt.'

They didn't save Francisco. One night after the rains he dived off the island and swam away; perhaps he was trying to find some air beyond the island's enchanted rim. The rip-tide took him; they found his bloated body five days later, bumping up against a rusty harbour buoy. He should have been remembered for his part in the revolution, for his good works, for his progressivism, for his mind; but his true legacies were trouble in the business (which had been badly neglected these past years), sudden death, and asthma.

Epifania swallowed the news of his death without a tremor. She ate his death as she had eaten his life; and grew.

# 3

O N THE LANDING OF the wide, steep staircase leading to Epifania's bedroom was the private family chapel, which Francisco had in the old days permitted one of his 'Frenchies' to redecorate in spite of Epifania's piercing protests. Out had gone the gilded altarpiece with the little inset paintings in which Jesus worked his miracles against a background of coco-palms and tea-plantations, and the china dolls of the apostles, and the golden cherubs posing on teak pedestals and blowing their trumpets, and the candles in their glass bowls the shape of giant brandy glasses, and the imported Portuguese lace on the altar, and even the crucifix itself, 'all the quality stuff,' Epifania complained, 'and Jesus and Mary lockofied in the box-room along-with,' and not content with these desecrations the blasted fellow had gone and painted the whole place white as if it were a hospital ward, furnished it with the least comfortable wooden pews in Cochin, and then, in that windowless interior room, fixed giant paper cut-outs to the walls, imitations of stained-glass windows, 'as if we can not put proper windows if we want,' Epifania moaned, 'see how cheap it makes us look, paper windows in the house of God,' and the windows didn't even have decent pictures on them, just slabs of colour in crazy-paving patterns, 'like a child's party décor,' Epifania sniffed. 'In such a room one should not keep-o blood and body of Our Saviour, but only birthday cake.'

Francisco had rejoined, in defence of his protégé's work, that in it shape and colour not only took the place of content but demonstrated that, properly handled, they could in fact *be* content: provoking Epifania's contemptuous reply, 'So maybe we have no need of Jesus Christ, because just shape of cross will do, why bother with any crucifixion, isn't it? What a blasphemy your Frenchy type has made: a church that lettofies off the Son of God from dying for our sins.'

The day after her husband's funeral Epifania had it all burned, and back came the cherubs, lace and glass, the thickly padded chapel chairs covered in dark red silk and the matching cushions edged in golden braid upon which a woman of her position in the world might decently kneel before her Lord. Antique tapestries from Italy depicting kababed saints and tandooried martyrs were restored to the walls and surrounded by ruched and gathered drapes, and soon the disconcerting memory of the Frenchy's austere novelties had been obliterated by the familiar mustinesses of devotion. 'God's in his heaven,' the brand-new widow announced. 'All is tip-top with the world.'

'From now on,' Epifania determined, 'it is the simple life for us. Salvation is not to be found in Little Man Loincloth and his ilks.' And indeed the simplicity she sought was anything but Gandhian, it was the simplicity of rising late to a tray of strong, sweet bed-tea, of clapping her hands for the cook and ordering the day's repasts, of having a maid come in to oil and brush her still-long but quickly greying and thinning hair, and of being able to blame the maid for the increasing quantities left each morning in the brush; the simplicity of long mornings scolding the tailor who came over to the house with new dresses, and knelt at her feet with mouthfuls of pins which he removed from time to time to unloose his flatterer's tongue; and then of long afternoons at the fabric stores, as bolts of magnificent silks were flung across a white-sheeted floor for her delight, cloth after cloth flowing thrillingly through the air to settle in soft fold-mountains of brilliant beauty; the simplicity of gossip with her few social equals, and of invitations to the 'functions' of the British in the Fort district, their Sunday cricket, their dancing teas, the seasonal carolling of their plain heat-beaten children, for they were Christian after all, even if it was only the Church of England, never mind, the British had her respect though they would never have her heart, which belonged to Portugal, of course, which dreamed of walking beside the Tagus, the Douro, of sashaying through the streets of Lisbon on the arm of a grandee. It was the simplicity of daughters-in-law who would attend to most of her needs while she made their lives a living hell, and of sons who would keep the money supply flowing as freely as was required; of everything-in-its-place, of being, at long last, at the heart of the web, the top of the heap, of lounging dragonwise upon a pile of gold and letting loose, when it pleased her, a burst of cleansing, terrorising flame. 'It will cost a fortune to keep your Mama in her simplicity,' Belle da Gama, prefiguring a remark often made about M. K. Gandhi, complained to her husband (she married Camoens early in 1923). 'And if she has her way it will cost-o us our youth as well.'

What ruined Epifania's dreams: Francisco left her nothing except her clothes, her jewellery and a modest allowance. For the rest, she learned to her fury, she would be dependent upon the goodwill of her sons, to whom everything had been bequeathed on a fifty-fifty basis, with the proviso that the Gama Trading Company should not be broken up 'unless business circumstances dictated otherwise', and that Aires and Camoens 'should seek to work together lovingly, lest the family's assets be damaged by disharmony or discord'.

'Even after death,' Great-Grandmother Epifania wailed at the reading of the will, 'he slaps me on both sides of the face.'

This, too, is part of my inheritance: the grave settles no quarrels.

The Menezes family lawyers failed to find a loophole, much to the widow's dismay. She wept, tore her hair, pounded her tiny bosom, and ground her teeth, which produced an alarmingly piercing noise; but the lawyers continued doggedly to explain that the matrilinear principle, for which Cochin, Travancore and Quilon were famous, and according to which the disposition of family property would have been a matter for Mme Epifania to decide rather than the late Dr da Gama, could by no stretch of the law be held to apply to the Christian community, being part of Hindu tradition alone.

'Then bring me a Shiva lingam and a watering-can,' Epifania, according to legend, was heard to say, though she afterwards denied it. 'Bring me to River Ganges and I will jump in double-quick. *Hai Ram!*'

(I should comment that in my view Epifania's willingness to

perform puja and pilgrimage sounds unconvincing, apocryphal; but wailing, gnashing of teeth, rending of hair and beating of bosom there most certainly was.)

The sons of the late magnate neglected business affairs, it must be admitted, being too often distracted by worldly matters. Aires da Gama, more distressed than he cared to reveal by his father's suicide, sought solace in promiscuity, provoking a deluge of correspondence – letters on cheap paper, written in a barely legible, semi-literate script. Love letters, messages of desire and anger, threats of violence if the beloved persisted in his too-hurtful ways. The author of this anguished correspondence was none other than the boy in the wedding-night rowing-boat: Prince Henry the Navigator himself. *Do not think I do not hear what all you do. Give me heart or I will cut it from your body. If love is not whole world and sky above then it is nothing, worse than dirt.*

If love is not all, then it is nothing: this principle, and its opposite (I mean, infidelity), collide down all the years of my breathless tale.

Aires, out tom-catting all night, as often as not spent the daylight hours sleeping off the effects of hashish or opium, recovering from his exertions, and, not infrequently, needing attention for various minor wounds; Carmen, without a word, applied medication and drew hot baths to soothe his bruises; and, when he fell into snoring sleep in that bathwater drawn from the deep well of her grief, if she ever thought about pushing his head below the surface, then she did not give in to temptation. Soon there would be another outlet for her rage.

As for Camoens, in his timid, soft-spoken way he was his father's son. Through Belle, he fell in with a group of young nationalist radicals who, impatient with talk of non-violence and passive resistance, were intoxicated by the great events in Russia. He began to attend, and later to deliver, talks with titles like *Forward!* and *Terrorism: Does End Justify This Means?*

'Camoens, who wouldn't say booski to a mouseski,' Belle laughed. 'What a big bad redski you will make.'

It was Grandfather Camoens who found out about the fake Ulyanovs. In late 1923 he informed Belle and their friends that an élite group of Soviet actors had been given exclusive rights to the rôle of V. I. Lenin: not only in specially prepared touring productions which told the Soviet people about their glorious revolution, but also at the thousands upon thousands of public functions at which the leader was unable to be present owing to the pressures on his time. The Lenin-thesps memorised, and then delivered, the speeches of the great man, and when they appeared in full make-up and costume people shouted, cheered, bowed and quaked as if they were in the presence of the real thing. 'And now,' Camoens excitedly concluded, 'applications from foreign-language actors are being solicited. We can have our personal Lenins right here, properly accredited, speaking Malayalam or Tulu or Kannada or any damn thing we please.'

'So they are reproducing the big boss in the See See See Pee,' Belle told him, placing his hand on her belly, 'but, husband, see see see please, you have already begun a little reproduction of your own.'

It is a demonstration of the ludicrous – yes! I dare to use that word – the *ridiculous and ludicrous* perversity of my family that – in a period when the country and indeed the planet was engaged in such momentous affairs – and when the family business needed the most scrupulous attention, because in the aftermath of Francisco's death the lack of leadership was becoming alarming, there was discontent in the plantations and slackness at the two Ernakulam godowns, and even the Gama Company's long-term customers had begun to listen to the siren voices of its competitors – and when, to crown it all, his own wife had announced her pregnancy, and was bearing what turned out to be not only their firstborn but also their only child, the only child, what is more, of her generation, my mother Aurora, the last of the da Gamas – my grandfather became increasingly obsessed with this question of counterfeit Lenins. With what zeal he scoured the locality to discover men with the necessary acting skill, memory capacity and interest in his plan! With what dedication he worked, getting copies of the latest statements of the illustrious leader, finding translators, acquiring the services of make-up artists and costumiers, and rehearsing his little troupe of seven whom Belle, with her customary brutality, had dubbed the Too-Tall Lenin, the Too-

Short Lenin, the Too-Fat Lenin, the Too-Skinny Lenin, the Too-Lame Lenin, the Too-Bald Lenin, and (this was a misfortunate fellow with gravely defective orthodonture) Lenin the Too-Thless ... Camoens corresponded feverishly with contacts in Moscow, cajoling and persuading; certain Cochinian authorities, both pale- and dark-skinned, were likewise persuaded and cajoled; and finally, in the hot season of 1924, he had his reward. When Belle was bursting with child, there arrived in Cochin a genuine, card-carrying member of the Special Lenin Troupe, a Lenin First Class, with the power to approve and further instruct the members of the Troupe's new Cochin Branch.

He came by ship from Bombay and when he walked down the gangway in character there were little gasps and shrieks from the dockside, to which he responded with a series of magnanimous bows and waves. Camoens noticed that he was perspiring freely in the heat; little rivulets of dark hair-dye ran down his forehead and neck and had constantly to be mopped.

'How may I address you?' asked Camoens, blushing politely as he met his guest, who was travelling with an interpreter.

'No formality, Comrade,' said the interpreter. 'No honorifics! A simple Vladimir Ilyich will suffice.'

A crowd had gathered at the dockside to watch the arrival of the World Leader and now Camoens, in a little theatrical gesture of his own, clapped his hands, and out of the arrivals shed came the seven local Lenins in their beards. They stood shuffling their feet on the dockside, grinning sweetly at their Soviet colleague; who burst, however, into long fusillades of Russian.

'Vladimir Ilyich asks what is the meaning of this outrage,' the interpreter told Camoens as the crowd around them enlarged. 'These persons have blackness of skin and their features are not his. Too tall, too short, too fat, too skinny, too lame, too bald, and that one has no teeth.'

'I was informed', said Camoens, unhappily, 'that we were permitted to adapt the Leader's image to local needs.'

More barrages of Russian. 'Vladimir Ilyich opines that this is not adaptation but satirical caricature,' the interpreter said. 'It is insult and offence. See, two beards at least are improperly affixed in spite of the admonishing presence of the proletariat. A report will be made at the highest level. Under no circumstances do you have authority to proceed.'

Camoens's face fell; and seeing him on the point of tears, his dreams in ruins, his actors – his *cadres* – leapt forward; eager to demonstrate the care with which they had learned their rôles, they began to strike attitudes and declaim. In Malayalam, Kannada, Tulu, Konkani, Tamil, Telugu and English they proclaimed the revolution, they demanded the immediate departure of the revanchist poodles of colonialism, the blood-sucking cockroaches of imperialism, to be followed by the common ownership of assets and annual over-fulfilment of rice quotas; their right-hand index fingers stabbing towards the future while their left fists rested magisterially against their hips. Babeling Lenins, their beards coming loose in the heat, addressed the now-enormous crowd; which began, little by little at first, and then in a great swelling tide, to guffaw.

Vladimir Ilyich turned purple. Leninist vituperations issued from his mouth and hung in the air above his head in Cyrillic script. Then, spinning on his heel, he stalked back up the gangway and disappeared below decks.

'What did he say?' Camoens disconsolately asked the Russian interpreter.

'This country of yours,' the interpreter replied, 'Vladimir Ilyich tells frankly that it gives to him the shits.'

A small woman pushed her way through the triumphant hilarity of the People, and through the moist curtain of his misery Grandfather Camoens recognised his wife's maid Maria. 'Better you come, sir,' she shouted over the People's mirth. 'Your good madam has given you a girl.'

∽

After his dockside humiliation, Camoens turned away from Communism, and became fond of saying that he had learned the hard way that it was not 'the Indian style'. He became a Congresswallah, a Nehru man, and followed from a distance all the great events of the ensuing years: from a distance, because although he spent hours each day absorbed in the subject, to the exclusion of most other things, reading and talking and writing voluminously on the subject, he never again took an active part in the movement, never published a word of his passionate scribblings ... let us contemplate, for a moment, the case of my maternal grandfather. How easy to dismiss him as a butterfly, a lightweight, a dilettante! A millionaire flirting with Marxism, a timid soul who could only be a revolutionary firebrand in the company of a few friends, or in the privacy of his study, in the writing of secret papers which – perhaps fearing a repeat of the jeers that had finished off Francisco – he could not bring himself to print; a nationalist whose favourite poets were all English, a professed atheist and rationalist who could bring himself to believe in ghosts, and who could recite from memory, and with deep sentiment, the whole of Marvell's 'On a Drop of Dew':

> So the Soul, that Drop, that Ray
> Of the clear Fountain of Eternal Day,
> Could it within the humane flow'r be seen,
>   Remembering still its former height,
>   Shuns the sweet leaves and blossoms green;
>   And, recollecting its own Light,
> Does, in its pure and circling thoughts, express
> The greater Heaven in an Heaven less.

Epifania, most severe and least forgiving of mothers, dismissed him as a confused fool of a boy; but, influenced by the more loving views of him that have come down to me through Belle and Aurora, I make a different estimation. To me, the doublenesses in Grandfather Camoens reveal his beauty; his willingness to permit the coexistence within himself of conflicting impulses is the source of his full, gentle humaneness. If you pointed out the contradictions between, for example, his egalitarian ideas and the olympian reality of his social position, he would answer with no more than an owning-up smile and a disarming shrug. 'Everyone should live well, isn't it,' he was fond of saying. 'Cabral Island for all, that is my motto.' And in his fierce love of English literature, his deep friendships with many Cochin English families, and his equally fierce determination that the British *imperium* must end and the rule of princes along with it, I see that hate-the-sin-and-love-the-sinner sweetness, that historical generosity of spirit, which is one of the true wonders of India. When empire's sun set, we didn't slaughter our erstwhile masters, saving that privilege for one another ... but the notion is too cruel to have occurred to Camoens, who was baffled by evil, calling it 'inhuman', an absurd notion, as even his loving Belle pointed out; and, luckily-unluckily for him, he didn't live to see the Partition massacres in the Punjab. (Sadly, he also died long before the election, after independence, in the new state of Kerala forged from old Cochin-Travancore-Quilon, of the first Marxist government in the sub-continent, the vindication of all his broken hopes.)

He lived to see trouble enough, for the family was already plunging towards that catastrophic conflict, the so-called 'battle of the in-laws', which would have wiped out many a lesser house, and from which our family fortunes took a decade to recover.

The women are now moving to the centre of my little stage. Epifania, Carmen, Belle, and the newly arrived Aurora – they, not the men, were the true protagonists in the struggle; and inevitably, it was Great-Grandmother Epifania who was the troublemaker-in-chief.

She declared war the day she heard Francisco's will, summoning Carmen to her boudoir for a pow-wow. 'My sons are useless playboys,' she announced with a wave of her fan. 'From now on, better us ladies should call-o the tune.' She would be the commander-in-chief and Carmen, her niece as well as her daughter-in-law, was to be her lieutenant, general factotum and dogsbody. 'It is your duty not only to this house but to Menezes family also. Never forget that till I saved your skin you were sittoed on a shelf and would have rottofied till Kingdom Come.'

Epifania's first order was the most ancient wish of dynasts: that Carmen must conceive a male child, a king-in-waiting through whom his loving mother and grandmother would rule. Carmen, realising in her bitter consternation that this very first instruction would have to be disobeyed, lowered her eyes, muttered, 'Okay, Epifania Aunty, wish is my command,' and fled the room.

(When Aurora was born the doctors said that owing to an unfortunate occurrence Belle would be unable to conceive again. That night Epifania read the riot act to Carmen and Aires. 'See that Belle, what she popped out with! But a girl child and no more kiddies is some luck from God for you. Buck up! Make a boy, or maybe the whole kit-cat-caboodle will be hers: the whole hang shoot.')

⟿

On Aurora da Gama's tenth birthday a barge came across the harbour to Cabral Island, bearing a Northern fellow, a U.P. type with a great pile of wooden planks which he assembled into a simplified giant wheel, fixing wooden seats to each end of the arms of a wooden X. From a green velvet box he produced an accordion and launched into a jolly medley of fairground tunes. When Aurora and her friends had had their fill of whirling through the sky on what the accordionist called a *charrakh-choo*, he put on a scarlet cape and made fish swim out of the young girls' mouths and drew live snakes from beneath their skirts, to the horror of Epifania, much tut-tutting from the still-childless Carmen and Aires, and the giggling delight of Belle and Camoens. After Aurora saw the Northerner she understood that a personal magician was what she needed most in life, someone who could make her wishes come true, who could magic her grandmother away for ever and make cobras bite Aires-uncle and Carmen-aunty to death and enable Camoens to live happily-ever-after; for this was in the time of the divided house, which had chalk lines drawn across its floors, like frontiers, and spice-sacks piled up across courtyards, forming little walls, as though they were defences against the risk of floods, or sniper fire.

It had all started when Epifania, using her sons' wandering attention as an excuse, invited her relatives to Cochin. She chose the moment for her coup expertly; this was at the time of Aires's post-Francisco promiscuity, and Camoens's hunt for Lenins, and

Belle's pregnancy, so there were few protests. In fact, the most vociferous objections came from Carmen, who had never been kindly treated by her 'mother's side' and found her Lobo hackles rising at the advent of so many Menezeses. When she made her feelings known to Epifania, haltingly, and with much circumlocution, that lady replied with a calculated use of coarseness, 'Missy, your future prospects are right there between your legs, so kindly concentrate on making your husband interested, and buttofy out of your elders' business.'

Bees-to-honey Menezes men arrived from Mangalore by the boatload, nor were their womenfolk and children far behind. Further Menezeses poured out of the bus depot, and yet more members of the clan were believed to be trying to get down by train, but had been delayed on account of the eccentricities of the railway service. By the time Belle had recovered from Aurora's birth, and Camoens from his Lenin fiasco, Epifania's people had got in everywhere, they were twining themselves around the Gama Trading Company like pepper-creepers around coco-palms, bullying the plantation overseers, nosing into the accounts, meddling with procedures at the godowns; it was an invasion all right, but it is never easy for conquerors to be loved, and no sooner was Epifania certain of her power than she started making mistakes. Her first error was to be too Machiavellian, for even though Aires was her favourite son she could not deny that Camoens had produced the only heir, and therefore could not be entirely excluded from her calculations. She began to flirt clumsily with Belle, who did not respond because of her growing anger at the behaviour of the numberless Menezeses; however, Epifania's too-obvious efforts to seduce her alienated Carmen to a considerable degree. Then Epifania made an even bigger error: on account of her worsening allergy to the spices that were the mainstay of the family's wealth – yes, even to pepper, to pepper most of all! – she let it be known that in future the Gama Trading Company would be developing a fragrance business, 'so that, in quick time, good perfume can take the place of these stuffs that maddofy my nose'.

Carmen lost patience. 'Menezeses were always small fry,' she railed at Aires. 'Will you let your mother turn big business into bottled smells?' But in those days Aires da Gama's over-indulgences had instilled a torpor that all Carmen's cajolings could not dispel. 'Then if you will not take up your rightful place in this house,' she cried, 'at least have the goodness to permit that Lobo family members may help us instead of these Menezes fellows crawling everywhere like white ants and eating up our cash.' Great-Uncle Aires readily agreed. Belle, who was equally agitated, had less success (and no relatives); Camoens was not a warrior by nature, and argued that since he had no head for business he should not stand in the way of his mother. But then the Lobos arrived.

∽

What started with perfume ended with a very big stink indeed . . . there is a thing that bursts out of us at times, a thing that lives in us, eating our food, breathing our air, looking out through our eyes, and when it comes out to play nobody is immune; possessed, we turn murderously upon one another, thing-darkness in our eyes and real weapons in our hands, neighbour against thing-ridden neighbour, thing-driven cousin against cousin, brother-thing against brother-thing, thing-child against thing-child. Carmen's Lobos headed for the da Gama estates in the Spice Mountains, and things began to stir.

The Jeep-road to the Spice Mountains bumps & grinds past rice-paddies, red-plantain trees, and roadside carpets of green and red capsicums laid out to dry in the sun; through cashew and areca-nut orchards (Quilon is cashewtown, just as Kottayam is rubberville); and up, up to the kingdoms of cardamom and cumin, to the shadow of young coffee plants in flower, to the terraces of tea that look like giant green tiled roofs, and to the empire of Malabar pepper above all. Early in the morning the bulbuls sing, working elephants amble past, munching amiably at the vegetation, an eagle circles in the sky. Cyclists come, riding four abreast, arms on one another's shoulders, defying the thundering trucks. See: one cyclist has rested a foot against the back of his friend's saddle. Idyllic, no? But within days of the coming of the Lobos there were rumours of trouble in the mountains, Lobos and Menezeses jostling for power, there were stories of arguments and blows.

As for the house on Cabral Island, it was full-to-overflowing; you fell over the Lobos lining the stairs, and the toilets were blocked by Menezeses. Lobos angrily refused to budge when Menezeses tried to ascend or descend 'their' staircases, and such was the Menezes's monopoly of hygiene facilities that Carmen's people were reduced to performing their natural functions in the open air, in full view of the inhabitants of the nearby island of Vypeen with its fishing villages and its ruined Portuguese fort ('o-ou, aa–aa,' sang the fisherfolk as they rowed past Cabral Island, and Lobo women blushed deeply and competed for the shelter of the bushes), and of the workers in the not-so-far-away coir doormat factory on Gundu Island, and of decaying princelings in their launches, passing by on a spree. There was much bumping and shoving in the queues that formed at mealtimes, and harsh words were spoken in the courtyards beneath the neutral gaze of carved wooden leogryphs.

Fights started to break out. The two Corbusier follies were opened up to cope with the overcrowding problem, but they proved unpopular with the in-laws; there were fisticuffs over the increasingly vexed question of which family members should be granted the supposedly higher status of sleeping in the main house. Lobo women started pulling Menezes pigtails and Menezes children started grabbing, and ripping apart, the Lobo kiddies' dolls. The da Gama household servants complained of the high-handed attitude of the in-laws, of bad language and other injuries to staff pride.

Things were coming to a head. One night rival gangs of Menezes and Lobo teenagers clashed violently in the Cabral Island gardens; there were broken arms and cracked heads and knife-wounds, two of them serious. The gangs had ripped the paper walls of the Corbusier's East folly-in-the-style-Japanese, and damaged its wooden structure so gravely that it had to be demolished soon afterwards; they had broken into the West folly and destroyed much of the furniture and many of the books. On the night of the gang violence of the in-laws Belle shook Camoens out of sleep and said, 'It is time you paid attention, or all will be lost.' At that moment a flying cockroach fluttered into her face, and she screamed. The scream brought Camoens to his senses. He jumped out of bed, killed the cockroach with a rolled newspaper, and when he went to shut the window there was a smell on the breeze that told him the real trouble had already started: the unmistakable odour of burning spices, cumin coriander turmeric, red-pepper-black-pepper, red-chilli-green-chilli, a little garlic, a little ginger, some sticks of cinnamon. It was as if some mountain giant were preparing, in a monstrous pan, the largest, hottest dish of curry ever cooked.

'We can't live all together like this any more,' Camoens said. 'Belle, we are burning up our own house.'

Yes, the big stink came rolling down from the Spice Mountains to the sea, *the da Gama in-laws are firing the spice-fields*, and that night, when Belle saw Carmen *née* Lobo standing up for the first time in her life to her mother-in-law Epifania *née* Menezes, when she saw them in their nighties, loose-haired, like witches, howling accusations and blaming each other for the catastrophe of the burning plantations, then, with great deliberation, she settled little Aurora in her cot, filled a bowl with cold water, carried it down into the moonlit courtyard where Epifania and Carmen were going at it hammer-and-tongs, took careful aim and drenched them both to the skin. 'Since you could start-o these evil fires with your scheming,' she said to them, 'then it is with you that we must begin to put them out.'

After that the scandal and family's disgrace deepened. The malevolent flames drew more than fire-fighters. Policemen came to Cabral Island, and after policemen there were soldiers, and then Aires and Camoens da Gama were taken, manacled and under armed escort, not directly to prison, but to the beautiful Bolgatty Palace on the island of the same name, where in a high cool room they were made to kneel on the floor at gunpoint while a cream-suited, balding Englishman with thick, pebbly eye-glasses and a walrus moustache stared out of the window at Cochin harbour with his hands clasped lightly behind his back, and talked, as it seemed, to himself.

'No one, not even the Supreme Government, knows everything about the administration of the Empire. Year by year England sends out fresh drafts for the first fighting-line, which is officially called the Indian Civil Service. These die, or kill themselves by overwork, or are worried to death, or broken in health and hope in order that the land may be protected from death and sickness, famine and war, and may eventually become capable of standing alone. It will never stand alone, but the idea is a pretty one, and men are willing to die for it, and yearly the work of pushing and coaxing and scolding and petting the country into good living goes forward. If an advance be made all credit is given to the native, while the Englishmen stand back and wipe their foreheads. If a failure occurs the Englishmen step forward and take the blame. Overmuch tenderness of this kind has bred a strong belief among many natives that the native is capable of administering the country, and many devout Englishmen believe this also, because the theory is stated in beautiful English with all the latest political colours.'

'Sir, you can have no doubt of my personal gratitude,' Aires began, but a sepoy, a common Malayali, slapped him across the face, and he fell silent.

'We shall administer the country, whatever you say now,' shouted Camoens, defiantly. He, too, was slapped: once, twice, thrice. Blood trickled from his mouth.

'There are other men who hope to administer the country in their own way,' said the man at the window, still addressing his remarks to the harbour. 'That is to say, with a garnish of Red Sauce. Such men must exist among three hundred million people, and, if they are not attended to, may cause trouble and even break the great idol called *Pax Britannica*, which, as the newspapers say, lives between Peshawur and Cape Comorin.'

The man turned to face them, and of course he was a man well known to them: a well-read man with whom Camoens had enjoyed discussing Wordsworth's views on the French Revolution, Coleridge's 'Kubla Khan', and Kipling's almost schizophrenic early stories of the Indiannesses and Englishnesses that struggled within him; with whose daughters Aires had danced at

39

the Malabar Club on Willingdon Island; whom Epifania had entertained at her table; but who wore, now, an oddly absent look.

He said, 'This Resident, this Englishman, at least, is disinclined
on this occasion to take the blame. Your clans are guilty of arson,
riot, murder and bloody affray and therefore, in my view,
though you took no direct part, so are you. We – by which
pronoun you will naturally understand me to be referring to your
own local authorities – are going to make sure that you suffer for it.
You will be spending very little time with your families for the
next many years.'

⌒

In June 1925 the da Gama brothers were sentenced to fifteen years'
imprisonment. The unusual severity of the judgment led to some
speculation that the family was being paid back for Francisco's
involvement with the Home Rule Movement, or even Camoens's
comic-opera efforts at importing the Soviet Revolution; but for
most people such speculations had been rendered superfluous,
even offensive, by the hideous discoveries at the Gama Trading
Company estates in the Spice Mountains, the unarguable evidence
that the Menezes and Lobo gangs had lost their heads completely.
In a torched cashew orchard the bodies of the (Lobo) overseer, his
wife and daughters were found, tied to trees with barbed wire:
burned, like heretics, at the stake. And in the smouldering ruins of a
fertile cardamom grove, the charred corpses of three Menezes
brothers were also found on fire-eaten trees. Their arms were
outstretched, and through the centre of each of their six palms an
iron nail had been driven.

I say these things baldly because they make me shake with
shame.

My family has been under many clouds. What sort of family is
this? Is this *normal*? Is this what we are all like?

We are like this; not always, but potentially. This, too, is what
we are.

Fifteen years: Epifania fainted in the courtroom, Carmen wept,
but Belle was dry-eyed and hard-faced, with Aurora similarly silent

and grave upon her lap. Many Menezes and Lobo men, and some women, were jailed or condemned; the survivors melted away, returning ash-stained to Mangalore. When they had gone the house on Cabral Island became very quiet, but the walls, the furniture, the rugs were still a-crackle with the electricity generated by the recently departed; there were parts of the house so highly charged that just to enter them made your hair stand on end. The old place released the memory of the mob slowly, slowly, as if it half-expected the bad times to return. But in the end it relaxed, and peace and silence began to think about moving back in.

Belle had her own ideas about how civilisation should be restored, and she wasted no time. Ten days after the jailings of Aires and Camoens, as an afterthought, the authorities ordered the arrest of Epifania and Carmen as well; but a week later, just as whimsically, they released them again. During those seven days, with Camoens's written authorisation – as a Grade A prisoner, he was allowed to receive daily meals from home, as well as writing materials, books, newspapers, soap, towels, fresh clothes, and could send out dirty laundry and letters – Belle went to see the lawyers of the Gama Trading Company, the appointed trustees of Francisco da Gama's last testament, and persuaded them of the immediate necessity of dividing the business in two. 'The conditions of the will are clearly met,' she said. 'Disharmony and discord have been introduce-o'ed everywhere by appointees of Aires, whether direct or indirect does not signify; business circumstances plainly dictate that company integrity is impossible to maintain. If the Gama Company remains a single cell, then the shame of these atrocities will finish it off. Divide, and maybe the sickness can be contained in one half only. If we do not live separately then we will die together.'

While lawyers were busying themselves with a proposal for the halving of the family business, Belle went back to Cabral Island and divided the grand old house itself, from deepest-bottom to highest-top; the old family sets of linen, cutlery, crockery were all summarily divorced, down to the last tea spoon, pillow-slip and quarter-plate. With the one-year-old Aurora on her hip she directed the household staff; almirahs, tallboys, poufs, long-armed cane chairs, bamboo poles for mosquito-nets, summer charpoys for those who preferred to sleep in the open air during the hot season, spittoons, thunderbox pots, hammocks, wine-glasses were all moved around; even the lizards on the walls were captured, and evenly distributed on both sides of the great divide. Studying the house's crumbling old ground plans, and paying scrupulous attention to exact allocation of floor-space windows balconies, she split the mansion, its contents, courtyards and gardens, right down the middle. She had sackfuls of spices piled high along her newly established frontiers and where such barriers were inappropriate – for example on the main staircase – she drew white lines down the centre and demanded that these demarcations be respected. In the kitchen she parted the pots and pans, and put up a chart of hours on the wall that bisected the week, day by day. The domestic servants were divided too, and even though almost all of them pleaded to be allowed to remain under her command she insisted on scrupulous fairness, one maid here, another there, one kitchen boy on this side, another across the cease-fire line. 'As for the chapel,' she told a stunned Epifania and Carmen when they returned to the *fait accompli* of a newly segregated universe, 'along with ivory teeth and Ganesha gods, you are welcome to it. On our side we have no plans to collect elephants, or to pray.'

⌒

Neither Epifania nor Carmen had the strength, after recent events, to stand against the fury of Belle's unleashed will. 'Two of you have brought Hell-fire down on this family,' she told them. 'Now I do not want to see your ugly mugs again. Keep to your fifty per cent! Employ your own in-charges, or let the whole she-bang go to pot, or sell up, I don't care! I just will see to it that my Camoens's fifty will survive'n'thrive.'

'You came from nowhere,' said Epifania, sneezing, across a wall of cardamom-sacks, 'and, madam, nowhere is your fate,' but it didn't sound convincing, and neither she nor Carmen argued when Belle told them that the destroyed fields were part of their allocated fifty, and Aires da Gama sent a defeated note from prison: 'Chop it up, blast it! Slice up the whole demnition affair, why not.'

So it was that Belle da Gama, at the age of twenty-one, took charge of her jailed husband's fortunes; and, though there were many vicissitudes in the following years, husbanded them well. After the jailing of Camoens and Aires, the Gama Company's lands and godowns had been placed under public administration: while lawyers drew up the deeds of separation, the reality was that armed sepoys patrolled the Spice Mountains, and public officers sat in the company's high chairs. It took Belle months of haranguing, wheedling, bribing and flirtation to get the business back. By this time many clients, shocked by the scandal, had taken their business elsewhere, or else, when they learned that a *chit of a girl* was now in charge, had demanded new terms of business that placed further burdens on the company's already tottering finances. There were many offers to buy her out for a tenth or at best an eighth of the business's real value.

She didn't sell. She started dressing in men's trousers, white cotton shirts and Camoens's cream fedora. She went to every field, every orchard, every plantation under her control and won back the confidence of the terrified employees, many of whom had bolted for their lives. She found managers whom she could trust and whom the work-force would follow with respect but without fear. She charmed banks into lending her money, bullied departed clients into returning, and became a mistress of small print. And for the rescue of her fifty per cent of the Gama Trading Company she earned a respectful nickname: from Fort Cochin's salons to the Ernakulam dockside, from the British Residency in old Bolgatty Palace to the Spice Mountains, there was only one Queen Isabella of Cochin. She did not like the nickname, though the admiration behind it made her hot with pride. 'Call me Belle,' she would insist. 'Plain Belle is fine for me.' But she was never plain; and, more than any local princess, had earned her royalty.

After three years Aires and Carmen surrendered, because their fifty per cent had by this time come to the point of collapse. Belle could have bought them out for next to nothing, but because Camoens would not do such a thing to his brother, she paid out twice as much. And in the years that followed she worked as feverishly on saving the Aires Fifty as she had on rescuing her own. The company name was changed, however; the Gama Trading Company was gone for good. In its place stood the restored edifice of the so-called C-50, the Camoens Fifty Per Cent Corp. (Private) Limited. 'Just goes to show,' she liked to say, 'how, in this life, fifty plus fifty equals fifty.' Meaning that the business might be re-united by Queen Isabella's *reconquista* but the rift in the family remained unbridged; the sack-barricades remained in place. And would remain for many long years.

~

She wasn't perfect; perhaps it's time that was said. She was tall, beautiful, brilliant, brave, hard-working, powerful, victorious, but, ladies and gents, Queen Isabella was no angel, no wings or halo in her wardrobe, no sir. In those years of Camoens's jail sentence she smoked like a volcano, grew increasingly foul-mouthed and failed to restrain her language in front of her growing child, went in for occasional drinking sprees that would leave her unconscious, sprawled like a tart on a mat in some backwoods shebeen; she became the toughest of nuts, and there were hints that her business methods extended at times to a little intimidation, a little strong-arming of suppliers, contractors, rivals; and she was frequently, casually, shamelessly unfaithful, unfaithful without discrimination or restraint. She would step out of her working attire into a beaded flapper dress and cloche hat, practise the Charleston, wide-eyed and pout-lipped, in front of her dressing-room mirror, and then, leaving Aurora with her ayah, head off for the Malabar Club. 'See you later, chickadee,' she'd say in her deep, smoke-shattered voice. 'Mummy's hunting tigers tonight.' Or, again, kicking up her heels and coughing profoundly: 'Sweet dreams, honeybunch; Mummy needs lion meat to munch.'

In later years my mother Aurora da Gama told this story to her circle of bohemian chums. 'You know, I was five-six-seven-eight years old, a proper little madam. If the phone rang, I would pick it up and say, "I'm *so* sorry, but Daddy and Aires-uncle are both in prison, Carmen-aunty and Granny are on the other side of the smelly sacks and aren't allowed to come over, and Mummy will be out tiger-shooting all night; may I take a message?"

While Belle was on the razzle, little Aurora, this solitary child, left to her own devices in her surreally cloven home, turned upon that inward eye which is the bliss of solitude; and, according to legend, found her gift. When she had grown up and was enclosed within the cult of herself, her admirers liked to linger upon the image of the little girl alone in the big house, throwing open the windows and allowing the torrential reality of India to awaken her soul. (You will notice that two episodes from Aurora's early life have been conflated to form this image.) It was said of her, in awe, that even as a child she never drew childishly; that her figures and landscapes were adult from the first. This was a myth she did nothing to discourage; indeed, she may even have fostered it, by backdating certain drawings and destroying other pieces of juvenilia. What is probably true is that Aurora began her life in art during those long motherless hours; that she had a talent for drawing and as a colourist, perhaps even one that an expert eye could have recognised; and that she pursued her new interest in deadly secret, hiding her tools and her work, so that Belle never knew about it all the days of her life.

She got her materials from school, she spent every penny of her pocket-money on crayons and papers and calligraphy pens and China ink and children's watercolour sets, she used wood-charcoal from the kitchen, and her ayah Josy, who knew everything, who helped her conceal her sketch-pads, never betrayed her confidence. It was only after her imprisonment by Epifania . . . but I am getting ahead of my tale. And, anyway, there are minds better equipped than mine to write about my mother's genius, eyes that see more clearly what she achieved. What absorbs me when I contemplate the after-image of the little, lonely girl who grew up to be my immortal mother, my Nemesis, my foe beyond the grave, is that she never seemed to hold her isolation against the father who was absent throughout her childhood, locked away in jail, or the mother who spent her days running a business and her nights in search of wildlife; rather, she worshipped them both, and refused

45

to hear a word of criticism, for example from me, about their skill as parents.

(But she kept her true nature secret from them. She hugged it to herself; until it burst out of her, as such truth always will: because it must.)

～

Epifania, at prayer,

and ageing, because when her sons were jailed she was forty-eight, but she was fifty-seven by the time they were released after serving nine years of their sentence, *the years drifting by like lost boats, Lord, as if we had time to waste,* entered into a kind of ecstasy, an apocalyptic frenzy in which guilt and God and vanity and the end of the world, the destruction of the old shapes by the hated advent of the new, were all jumbled up, *it wasn't meant to be this way, Lord, I wasn't meant to be banished in my own home behind a pile of sacks, forbidden to cross that madwoman's white lines,* she scratched at the wounds of the present and the past, *my own servants, Lord, they keep-o me in my place, for I am in prison too and they are my warders, I cannot dismiss them because I do not pay their wages, she she she, everywhere and evermore she, but I can wait, see, patience is a virtue, I'll just bide-o my time,* Epifania in her orisons called down curses on Lobos, *and why do you tormentofy me, sweet Jesus, holy Mary, by making me live with the daughter of that cursed house, that barren thing I tried in my generosity to befriend, see how she repays me, how that household of printers came and smashed my life,* but at other times the memory of the dead rose up and accused her, *Lord, I have sinned, I should be scalded with hot oils and burned with cold ice, have mercy on me Mother of God for I am the lowest of the low, save me if it be your will from the chasm the bottomless pit, for in my name and by my doing was great and murderous evil unloosed upon the earth,* she chose punishments for herself, *Lord, today I decided to sleep without mosquito-nets, let them come, Lord, the stings of Thy retribution, let them needle-o me in the night and suckofy my blood, let them infect me, Mother of God, with the fevers of Thy wrath,* and this penance was to continue after the release of her sons when she forgave herself her sins and once again draped around herself that protective billow of nocturnal mist, blindly refusing to concede that in their years of disuse the already-perforated mosquito-nets had been eaten full of moth-holes, *Lord, my hair is falling out, the world is broken, Lord, and I am old.*

∽

And Carmen, in her solitary bed,

her fingers reaching down for solace below her waist, entwined herself in herself, drank her own bitterness and called it sweet, walked in her own desert and called it lush, excited herself with fantasies of seductions by dark sailors in the back of the family's black-and-gold, wood-panelled Lagonda, of seducing Aires's lovers in the family Hispano-Suiza, *O God think how many new men he will find is finding has found in jail,* and lying sleepless night after night she caressed her bony body while her youth slipped away, twenty-one when Aires went to jail, thirty when he came out, *and still untouched, untouchable, never to be touched, not by others, but these fingers know, oh they know oh oh;* and soap-slippery in the bath and sweat-moistened in the bazaar she sought her daily joy, *it wasn't meant to be like this, Aires-husband, Epifania-mother-in-law, it was meant to be beautiful; and there is beauty all around me, the infinite power of Belle, the whimsicality and possibilities of her beauty. But I, I, I am* unbeauty. *In this house in thrall to the beautiful I have been shown myself, and lo, sirs, I am beastly, oho-ho, ladies and ladahs, yes indeed,* and closing her misfortunate eyes and arching her back she gave in to the pleasure of disgust, *flay me flay my skin from my body whole entire and let me start again let me be of no race no name no sex oh let the nuts rot in the shells oh oh the spices wither in the sun oh let it burn oh let it burn let it burn, ohh,* and collapsing afterwards in tears she cowered in her sheets while the inflamed dead closed in on her and howled *revenge.*

∽

On her tenth birthday Aurora da Gama was asked by the Northern fellow with the *charrakh-choo,* the accordion, the U.P. accent and the magic tricks, 'What do you want most in the world?' – and

47

before she answered he had granted her wish. A motor-launch sounded its siren in the harbour and came in towards the jetty on Cabral Island, and there on the deck, paroled six years before the end of their sentences, were Aires and Camoens, *all-thin-and-bone*, as their mother cried out in delight. Home they came, weakly waving, identically smiling: the just-freed prisoner's tentative, greedy smile.

Grandfather Camoens and Grandmother Belle embraced on the jetty. 'I have for you your most hideous bush-shirt ironed and ready,' she said. 'Go get gift-wrapped and then give yourself to that birthday girl with the big grin twisting all over her face. See her, already tall as a tree, and trying to recognise her dad.'

I feel their love washing down towards me across the years; how great it was, how little time they had together. (Yes, in spite of all her screwing around, I insist; what existed between Belle and Camoens was the real McCoy.) I hear Belle coughing even as she brought Camoens to Aurora, I feel the deep raw coughs tear at me, as if they were my own. 'Too many cigarettes,' she choked. 'Bad habit.' And, lying, so as not to cast a shadow over the homecoming: 'I'll give it up.'

At Camoens's soft request – 'this family has been through too much, now we must start to heal' – she agreed to the dismantling of the barriers that had kept Epifania and Carmen out of sight. For Camoens, she gave up, overnight and for ever, her dissolute, philandering ways. Because Camoens requested it, she allowed Aires to join them on the board of the family business, though the question of his buying back a share did not, in his impecunious circumstances, arise. I think, I hope, that they were wonderful lovers, Belle and Camoens, that his shy gentleness and her voluptuary hunger made a perfect pairing; that, for those so-brief-too-brief three years after Camoens was freed, they satisfied one another, and lay happily in each other's arms.

But for three years she coughed, and though the aftershock of everything that had happened made the reunited house a cautious place in those years, her growing daughter was not fooled. 'And even before I heard death in Belle's lungs, they knew, those witches,' my mother told me. 'I knew those bastards were just waiting on. Once divided, always divided; in that household it was a fight to the bloody finish.'

When, one evening not long after the brothers' return, the family gathered at Camoens's request in the long-disused grand dining hall, beneath the portraits of the ancestors, to eat a meal of reconciliation, it was Belle's chest that ruined it all, it was Belle hawking bloody sputum into a chrome spittoon that roused Epifania, who presided at the head of the table in a black lace mantilla, to remark, 'I suppose so now you've hookoed the money you don't need the manners,' and there were recriminations and stormings-out and then the uneasy truce settled down again, but there were no more gatherings at mealtimes.

She awoke coughing, and coughed frighteningly before going to sleep. Coughs would wake her up in the night and she would wander the old house, throwing open the windows . . . but two months after his return it was Camoens who awoke to find her coughing in a feverish sleep and dribbling blood from her mouth. Tuberculosis was diagnosed, it had settled on both lungs, it was much more dangerous then than it is now, and she was told by the doctors that the battle would be hard and she must cut back drastically on her professional activities. 'Damn it, Camoens,' she growled. 'If you fuck up what I unfucked for you once, you better hope on I'm around to unfuck it for you twice.' At which that gentle soul, beside himself with anxiety, burst into tears boiling with his love.

And Aires, returning, had also encountered an altered wife. She came into his bedroom on the night of his release and said, 'If you do not give up your shame and scandal then, Aires, I will kill you while you sleep.' He bowed to her deeply in acknowledgment, the bow of a Restoration dandy, the right hand spiralling foppishly outwards, the right foot extended, its toe deliciously cocked, and she left. He did not give up his adventures; but became more circumspect, snatching afternoon hours in a rented Ernakulam apartment with a slow ceiling fan, powder-blue walls, unadorned and peeling, an attached bathroom with a pump-handle shower and a squatting toilet, and a large low charpoy bed whose puttees he had renewed, for hygiene, and for strength. Through the chick-blinds thin blades of daylight fell across his body and another's, and the cries of the market rose up to him and mingled with his lover's moans.

In the evenings he played bridge at the Malabar Club, where his presence could be vouched for, or else stayed modestly at home. He bought padlocks for the bolts on his door and acquired a British bulldog which, to provoke Camoens, he named Jawaharlal. He had emerged from prison as opposed as ever to the Congress and its demands for independence, and now he became an ardent letter-writer, filling newspaper columns with his advocacy of the so-called Liberal alternative. 'This misguided policy of ejection of our rulers,' he thundered. 'Suppose it succeeds; then what will become? Where in this India are the democratic institutions to replace the British Hand, which is, I can personally avow, benevolent even when it chastises us for our infantile misdeeds.' When the Liberal editor of the *Leader* paper, Mr Chintamani, suggested that India had 'better submit to the present unconstitutional government rather than to the more reactionary and furthermore unconstitutional government of the future', Great-Uncle Aires wrote to say 'Bravo!' and when another Liberal, Sir P. S. Sivaswamy Iyer, argued that 'in advocating the convention of a constituent assembly, Congress places too much faith in the wisdom of the multitude, and does too little justice to the sincerity and ability of men who have taken part in various Round Table Conferences. I very much doubt whether the constituent assembly would have done better,' then Aires da Gama penned his congratulations: 'I *heartily* concur! Common man in India has always bowed his knee to the counsels of his betters – of persons of education and breeding!'

Belle confronted him on the jetty the next morning. Pale of face and red of eye, she was wrapped in shawls, but insisted on seeing Camoens off to work. As the brothers stepped into the family launch she waved the morning paper in Aires's face. 'In this house there is education and breeding,' Belle said loudly, 'and we have behaved like dogs.'

'Not we,' said Aires da Gama. 'Our pig-ignorant poor relations, for whom I have suffered enough, dash it, and on whose behalf I accept no further blame. Oh, do stop barking now, Jawaharlal; down, boy, down.'

Camoens reddened, but held his tongue, thinking of Mr Nehru in Alipore prison, of so many good men and women in far-off lock-ups. At night he sat with Belle and her cough, wiping her eyes and lips, putting cold compresses on her brow, and he would whisper to her about the *dawning of a new world, Belle, a free country, Belle, above religion because secular, above class because socialist, above caste because enlightened, above hatred because loving, above vengeance because forgiving, above tribe because unifying, above language because many-tongued, above colour because multi-coloured, above poverty because victorious over it, above ignorance because literate, above stupidity because brilliant, freedom, Belle, the freedom express, soon soon we will stand upon that platform and cheer the coming of the train*, and while he told her his dreams she would fall asleep and be visited by spectres of desolation and war.

When she fell asleep he would recite poetry to her sleeping form,

> *Absent thee from felicity awhile,*
> *And for a season draw thy breath in pain,*

and he was whispering to the imprisoned as well as to his wife, to the whole captured land, he bent in terror over her sickened, sleeping body and sent his anguished hope and love upon the wind,

> *When all its work is done, the lie shall rot;*
> *The truth is great and shall prevail,*
> *When none cares whether it prevails or not.*

It wasn't tuberculosis, or not only tuberculosis. In 1937 Isabella Ximena da Gama, *née* Souza, aged only thirty-three, was found to be suffering from a cancer of the lung, which had reached an advanced – a terminal – stage. She went quickly, in great pain, railing against the enemy in her body, savagely angry with death for arriving too soon and behaving so badly. One Sunday morning when there was a sound of church bells across the water and woodsmoke on the air and when Aurora and Camoens were at her side she said, turning her face to the streaming sunlight, *remember the story of El Cid Campeador in Spain, he also loved a woman called Ximena.*

Yes we remember.

*And when he was mortally wounded he told her to tie his dead body to his horse and send him back into battle, so the enemy would see he was still alive.*

Yes mother. My love yes.

*Then tie my body to a bloody rickshaw or whatever damn mode of transport you can find, camel-cart donkey-cart bullock-cart bike, but for godsake not a bloody elephant; okay? Because the enemy is close and in this sad story Ximena is the Cid.*

Mother, I will.

[*Dies.*]

# 4

I N MY FAMILY WE'VE always found the world's air hard to breathe; we arrive hoping for somewhere better.

Speaking for myself, at this late hour? Just about managing, thanks for asking; though old, old, old before my time. You could say I lived too fast, and like a marathon runner collapsing because he failed to pace himself, like a suffocating astronaut who danced too merrily on the Moon, in my overheated years I used up a full lifespan's air-supply. O wastrel Moor! To spend, in just thirty-six years, your allotment of threescore-and-twelve. (But let me say, in mitigation, that I didn't have much choice.)

So: there is difficulty, but I surmount it. Most nights there are noises, the croaks and honks of fantastic beasts, issuing from the jungles of my lungs. I awake gasping and, sleep-heavy, grab fistfuls of air and stuff them uselessly into my mouth. Still, it is easier to breathe in than out. As it is easier to absorb what life offers than to give out the results of such absorption. As it is easier to take a blow than to hit back. Nevertheless, wheezing and ratchety, I eventually exhale, I overcome. There is pride to be taken in this; I do not deny myself a pat on my aching back.

At such times I become my breathing. Such force of self as I retain focuses upon the faulty operations of my chest: the coughing, the fishy gulps. I am what breathes. I am what began long ago with an exhaled cry, what will conclude when a glass held to my lips remains clear. It is not thinking makes us so, but air. *Suspiro ergo sum.* I sigh, therefore I am. The Latin as usual tells the truth: *suspirare* =*sub*, below,+*spirare*, verb, to breathe.

*Suspiro*: I under-breathe.

In the beginning and unto the end was and is the lung: divine afflatus, baby's first yowl, shaped air of speech, staccato gusts of laughter, exalted airs of song, happy lover's groan, unhappy lover's lament, miser's whine, crone's croak, illness's stench, dying whisper, and beyond and beyond the airless, silent void.

A sigh isn't just a sigh. We inhale the world and breathe out meaning. While we can. While we can.

– *We breathe light* – the trees pipe up. Here at journey's end in this place of olive-trees and tombstones the vegetation has decided to strike up a conversation. *We breathe light*, indeed; most informative. They are 'El Greco' cultivars, these chatty oliviers; well-named, one might remark, after that light-breathing God-ridden Greek.

Henceforth I'll turn a deaf ear to prattling foliage with its arboreal metaphysics, its chlorophyllosophy. My family tree says all I need to hear.

⌒

I have been living in a folly: Vasco Miranda's towered fortress in Benengeli village, which looks down from a brown hill to a plain dreaming, in glistening mirages, of being a medi-terranean sea. I, too, have been dreaming, and through a narrow slit-window of my habitation I have seen not Spain's, but India's South; seeking, in spite of distances in space and time, to re-enter that Dark Age between Belle's death and my father's arrival on the scene. Here, filtering through this slender portal, this narrow crack in time, was Epifania Menezes da Gama, kneeling, at prayer, her chapel like a golden pool in the dark of the great stairwell. I blinked, and there came a memory of Belle. One day soon after his release from jail Camoens arrived at breakfast in simple khaddar clothes; Aires, a dandy once again, laughed into his kedgeree. After breakfast Belle took Camoens aside. 'Darling, get out of fancy-dress,' she said. 'Our national effort is to run a good business and look after our workers, not to dress like errand boys.' But this time Camoens was unshakable. Like her, he was for Nehru, not Gandhi – for business and technology and progress and modernity, for the city, and against all that sentimental clap-trap of spinning your own cotton and travelling third-class on the train. But wearing homespun pleased him. To change your masters, change your clothes. 'Okay,

Bapuji,' she teased him. 'But don't think you'll get me out of trousers, unless into a sexy dancing dress.'

I watched Epifania praying and gave thanks that somehow, by some great fluke that seemed at the time the most ordinary thing in the world, my parents had been cured of religion. (Where's their medicine, their priest-poison-beating anti-venene? Bottle it, for pity's sake, and send it round the world!) I looked at Camoens in his khaddar jibba and remembered that he once went, without Belle, all the way across the mountains to the small town of Malgudi on the river Sarayu, just because Mahatma Gandhi was to speak there: this, in spite of being a Nehru man. He wrote about it in his journal:

*In that huge gathering sitting on the sands of Sarayu I was a tiny speck. There were a lot of volunteers clad in white khaddar moving around the dais. The chromium stand of the microphone gleamed in the sun. Police stood about here and there. Busybodies were going round asking people to remain calm and silent. People obeyed them . . . the river flowed, the leaves of the huge banyan and peepul trees on the banks rustled; the waiting crowd kept up a steady babble, constantly punctuated by the pop of soda-water bottles; longitudinal cucumber slices, crescent-shaped, and brushed up with the peel of a lime dipped in salt, were disappearing from the wooden tray of a vendor who was announcing in a subdued tone (as a concession to the coming of a great man), 'Cucumber for thirst, the best for thirst.' He had wound a green Turkish towel around his head as a protection from the sun.*

Then Gandhi came and made everyone clap hands in rhythm over their heads and chant his favourite *dhun*:

> *Raghupati Raghava Raja Ram*
> *Patitha pavana Sita Ram*
> *Ishwara Allah tera nam*
> *Sabko Sanmati dé Bhagwan.*

And there was *Jai Krishna, Hare Krishna, Jai Govind, Hare Govind*, there was *Samb Sadashiv Samb Sadashiv Samb Sadashiv Samb Shiva Har Har Har Har*. 'After all that,' Camoens told Belle on his return, 'I heard nothing. I had seen India's beauty in that crowd with its soda-water and cucumber but with that God stuff I got scared. In the city we are for secular India but the village is for Ram. And they

55

say *Ishwar and Allah is your name* but they don't mean it, they mean only Ram himself, king of Raghu clan, purifier of sinners along with Sita. In the end I am afraid the villagers will march on the cities and people like us will have to lock our doors and there will come a Battering Ram.'

# 5

A FEW WEEKS AFTER his wife's death, mysterious scratches began to appear on Camoens da Gama's body during his sleep. First there was one on his neck, round at the back where it had to be pointed out to him by his daughter of all people, then three long raking lines on his right buttock and after that one on his cheek right down the edge of his goatee. At the same time Belle started coming to him in his dreams, naked and demanding, so that he would wake up weeping, because even as he made love to her dream-image he knew it wasn't real. But the scratches were real enough and even though he didn't say so to Aurora his feeling that Belle had returned had as much to do with these love-marks as with the open windows and the missing elephant items.

His brother Aires took a simpler approach to the riddle of the lost ivory-tusks and Ganeshas. He assembled the staff in the main courtyard under the peepul tree with the lower part of its trunk painted white, and in the afternoon heat he strutted up and down before them in a straw panama, collarless shirt and white duck pants held up by red braces, icily bellowing out his certain-sure conviction that one of them was a thief. The domestic servants, gardeners, boatmen, sweepers, latrine-cleaners, all faced him in a sweating, terror-stricken line, wearing the ingratiating smile of their fear while Jawaharlal the bulldog emitted a low menacing rumble and his master Aires taunted them with nicknames.

'Who will speak up here?' he demanded. '*Gobbledy*gokhale, you? Nallappa*boomdiay*? Karampal*stiltskin*? Out with it, pronto!' And the houseboys were *Tweedlydum and Tweedlydee* as he slapped them once each on the face, and the gardeners were nuts and spices as he poked them in the chest, *Cashew, Pista, Big and Little*

*Cardamom*, and the latrine-cleaners whom of course he would not touch were *Number One and Number Two*.

Aurora came running when she heard what was happening, and for the first time in her life the presence of the servants filled her with shame, she couldn't meet their eyes, she turned to the assembled family (for impassive Epifania, Carmen with the ice-splinter in her heart and even Camoens – squirming but not, it must be pointed out, interrupting – had come out to study Aires's interrogation technique) and in a high ascending shriek confessed, *it-wasn't-them-it-was-ME*.

'What?' Aires screeched back, mocking, annoyed: a tormentor deprived of his pleasure. 'Speak up can't hear a word.'

'Stop bullying them,' Aurora howled. 'They did nothing; they didn't touch your something something elephants and their blankety blank teeth. I did it all.'

Her father paled. 'Baby, for what?' The bulldog, snarling, bared his gums.

'Don't call me baby,' she answered, defying even him. 'It is what my mother always wanted to do. You will see: from now I am in her place. And Aires-uncle, you should lock up that crazy dog, by the way, I've got a pet-name for *him* that he *really* deserves: call him *Jaw-jaw*, that all-bark-no-bite mutt.' And turned, head held high, and marched off, leaving her family open-mouthed in wonder: as if they had truly seen an avatar, a reincarnation, her mother's living ghost.

～

But it was Aurora who was locked up; as a punishment, she was banished to her room on a rice-and-water diet for a week. However, food and drink – *idli* and *sambar*, but also mince-and-potato 'cutlets', pomfret fried in breadcrumbs, spicy prawn plates, banana jelly, crème caramel, soda-pop – were smuggled up to her by doting Josy; and the old ayah also covertly brought her the instruments – charcoal, brushes, paints – through which Aurora chose, at this true moment of her coming-of-age, to make public her inner self. All that week she worked, hardly pausing for sleep.

When Camoens came to the door she told him to go away, she would endure her sentence by herself and had no need of an ex-jailbird father who would not fight to keep his own daughter out of the lock-up, and he hung his head and obeyed.

At the end of her period of house arrest, however, Aurora invited Camoens inside, making him the second person on earth to see her work. Every inch of the walls and even the ceiling of the room pullulated with figures, human and animal, real and imaginary, drawn in a sweeping black line that transformed itself constantly, that filled here and there into huge blocks of colour, the red of the earth, the purple and vermilion of the sky, the forty shades of green; a line so muscular and free, so teeming, so violent, that Camoens with a proud father's bursting heart found himself saying, 'But it is the great swarm of being itself.' As he grew accustomed to his daughter's newly revealed universe he began to see her visions: she had put history on the walls, King Gondophares inviting St Thomas the Apostle to India; and from the North, Emperor Asoka with his Pillars of Law, and the lines of people waiting to stand with their backs against the pillars to see if they could join their hands behind them for good luck; and her versions of erotic temple-carvings, whose explicit details made Camoens blanch, and of the building of the Taj Mahal, after which, as she unflinchingly showed, its great masons were mutilated, their hands cut off, so that they could never build anything finer; and from her own South she had chosen the battle of Srirangapatnam and the sword of Tipu Sultan and the magic fortress of Golconda where a man speaking normally in the gatehouse may be heard clearly in the citadel and the coming long ago of the Jews. Modern history was there too, there were jails full of passionate men, Congress and Muslim League, Nehru Gandhi Jinnah Patel Bose Azad, and British soldiers whispering rumours of an approaching war; and beyond history were the creatures of her fancy, the hybrids, half-woman half-tiger, half-man half-snake, there were sea-monsters and mountain ghouls. In an honoured place was Vasco da Gama himself, setting his first foot on Indian soil, sniffing the air, and seeking out whatever was spicy and hot and made money.

Camoens began to pick out family portraits, portraits not only of the dead and living but even of the never-born – of, for example, her unborn siblings grouped gravely around her dead mother beside a grand piano. He was startled to find an image of Aires da Gama stark naked in a dockyard, light glowing from him while dark shapes closed in all around, and shaken by the parody of the Last Supper in which the family servants caroused wildly at the dining-table while their raggedy ancestors stared down from the portraits on the wall and the da Gamas served as waiters, bringing food and pouring wine and being treated badly, Carmen having her bottom pinched, Epifania's rump being kicked by a drunken gardener; but then the rapid rush of the composition drew him onwards, away from the personal and into the throng, for beyond and around and above and below and amongst the family was the crowd itself, the dense crowd, the crowd without boundaries; Aurora had composed her giant work in such a way that the images of her own family had to fight their way through this hyper-abundance of imagery, she was suggesting that the privacy of Cabral Island was an illusion and this mountain, this hive, this endlessly metamorphic line of humanity was the truth; and wherever Camoens looked he saw the rage of the women, the tormented weakness and compromise in the faces of the men, the sexual ambivalence of the children, the passive uncomplaining faces of the dead. He wanted to know how she knew these things, with the bitter taste on his tongue of his own failure as a father he wondered that at her tender age she could have heard so much of the world's anger and pain and disappointment and tasted so little of its delight, *when you have learned joy*, he wanted to say, *then only then your gift will be complete*, but she knew so much already that it scared the words away and he did not dare to speak.

Only God was absent, for no matter how carefully Camoens peered at the walls, and even after he climbed a step-ladder to stare at the ceiling, he was unable to find the figure of Christ, on or off the cross, or indeed any other representation of any other divinity, tree-sprite, water-sprite, angel, devil or saint.

And it was all set in a landscape that made Camoens tremble to see it, for it was Mother India herself, Mother India with her garishness and her inexhaustible motion, Mother India who loved and betrayed and ate and destroyed and again loved her children, and with whom the children's passionate conjoining and eternal quarrel stretched long beyond the grave; who stretched into great mountains like exclamations of the soul and along vast rivers full of mercy and disease, and across harsh drought-ridden plateaux on which men hacked with pickaxes at the dry infertile soil; Mother India with her oceans and coco-palms and rice-fields and bullocks at the water-well, her cranes on treetops with necks like coat-hangers, and high circling kites and the mimicry of mynahs and the yellow-beaked brutality of crows, a protean Mother India who could turn monstrous, who could be a worm rising from the sea with Epifania's face at the top of a long and scaly neck; who could turn murderous, dancing cross-eyed and Kali-tongued while thousands died; but above all, in the very centre of the ceiling, at the point where all the horn-of-plenty lines converged, Mother India with Belle's face. Queen Isabella was the only mother-goddess here, and she was dead; at the heart of this first immense outpouring of Aurora's art was the simple tragedy of her loss, the unassuaged pain of becoming a motherless child. The room was her act of mourning.

Camoens, understanding, held her, and they wept.

∽

Yes, mother; once you were a daughter, too. You were given life, and you took it away . . . Mine is a tale of much mayhem, many sudden deaths, *felos* of other fellows as well as *de se*. Fire, water and disease must play their part alongside – no, *around and within* – the human beings.

On Christmas Eve, 1938, seventeen Christmases after the young Camoens had brought seventeen-year-old Isabella Souza home to meet the family, their daughter, my mother Aurora da Gama, was woken by period pains and couldn't get back to sleep. She went to the bathroom and attended to herself as old Josy had taught her to, with cotton-wool and gauze and a long pyjama-cord to hold everything in place . . . thus trussed, she coiled up on the white-tiled floor and fought against the pain. After a time it subsided. She

61

decided to go out into the gardens and bathe her aching body in the shining, the insouciant miracle of the Milky Way. *Star light, star bright* . . . we look up and we hope the stars look down, we pray that there may be stars for us to follow, stars moving across the heavens and leading us to our destiny, but it's only our vanity. We look at the galaxy and fall in love, but the universe cares less about us than we do about it, and the stars stay in their courses however much we may wish upon them to do otherwise. It's true that if you watch the sky-wheel turn for a while you'll see a meteor fall, flame and die. That's not a star worth following; it's just an unlucky rock. Our fates are here on earth. There are no guiding stars.

More than a year had passed since the incident of the open windows, and the house on Cabral Island slumbered that night under a kind of truce. Aurora, too old for Father Christmas, put a light shawl around her night-dress, stepped around the sleeping figure of Josy-ayah on her mat by the door, and went barefoot down the hall.

(Christmas, that Northern invention, that tale of snow and stockings, of merry fires and reindeer, Latin carols and *O Tannenbaum*, of evergreen trees and Sante Klaas with his little piccaninny 'helpers', is restored by tropical heat to something like its origins, for whatever else the Infant Jesus may or may not have been, he was a hot-weather babe; however poor his manger, it wasn't *cold*; and if Wise Men came, following (unwisely, as I've indicated) yonder star, they came, let's not forget it, from the East. Over in Fort Cochin, English families have put up Christmas trees with cotton wool on the branches; in St Francis's Church – Anglican in those days, though no longer – the young Rev. Oliver D'Aeth has already held the annual carol service; and there are mince pies and glasses of milk waiting for Santa, and somehow there will be turkey on the table tomorrow, yes, and two kinds of stuffing, and even brussels sprouts. But there are many Christian-ities here in Cochin, Catholic and Syriac Orthodox and Nestorian, there are midnight masses where incense chokes the lungs, there are priests with thirteen crosses on their caps to symbolise Jesus and the Apostles, there are wars between the denominations, R.C. v. Syriac, and *everyone* agrees the Nestorians are no sort of Christians, and all these warring Christmases, too, are being prepared. In the house on Cabral Island it is the Pope who rules. There are no trees here; instead there is a crib. Joseph could be a carpenter from Ernakulam, and Mary a woman from the tea-fields, and the cattle are water-buffalo, and the skin of the Holy Family (gasp!) is rather dark. There are no presents. For Epifania da Gama, Christmas is a day for Jesus. Presents – and even this somewhat unloving family makes an exchange of gifts – are for Twelfth Night, the night of gold frankincense myrrh. Nobody is shinning down a chimney in *this* house . . . )

Aurora reached the top of the great staircase and saw that the chapel doors were open; the chapel itself was illuminated, and the light emanating from the doorway made a little golden sun in the stairwell dark. Aurora crept forward, peered in. A small figure, head covered by a black lace mantilla, knelt at the altar. Aurora could hear the tiny click of Epifania's ruby rosary beads. The young girl, not wishing the matriarch to become aware of her presence, began to back out of the room. Just then, in complete silence, Epifania Menezes da Gama fell sideways and lay still.

'*One day you will killofy my heart.*'

'*Patience is a virtue. I'll just bide-o my time.*'

How did Aurora approach her fallen grandmother? Did she, like a loving child, run forward, raising a stricken hand to her lips?

*She approached slowly, circling along the walls of the chapel, moving in towards the immobile form in gradual, deliberate steps.*

Did she cry out, beat a gong (there was a gong in the chapel) or in other ways do her level best to sound the alarm?

*She did not.*

Perhaps there was no point in doing so; perhaps it was plain that Epifania was already beyond help: that death had been swift and merciful?

*When Aurora reached Epifania, she saw that the hand that held the rosary was still twitching feebly at the beads; that the old woman's eyes were open, and met hers with recognition; that the old woman's lips moved faintly, though no audible word emerged.*

And on seeing her grandmother still alive, did she then act to save her life?

*She paused.*

And, after pausing? Granted, she was young; a certain paralysis can be attributed to youthful panic, and forgiven, but, after pausing, she quickly summoned the household, so that help could be provided . . . did she not?

*After pausing, she took two steps backwards; and sat down, cross-legged, on the floor; and watched.*

Did she feel no pity, no shame, no fear?

*She was worried, it's true. If Epifania's seizure proved to be less than fatal, then her own behaviour would count against her; even her father would be angry. She knew that.*

No more than that?

*She worried about discovery; and so she went and closed the chapel doors.*

Why not go the whole hog, in that case; why not blow out the candles and turn out the electric lights?

*All must be left as Epifania left it.*

This was cold-blooded murder, then. Calculations were being made.

*If murder can be committed by inaction, then yes. If Epifania had suffered so great a blow that she could not have survived, then no. The point is moot.*

Did Epifania die?

*After an hour, her mouth moved one last time; her eyes turned again to her grandchild. Whose ear, placed against dying lips, heard her grandmother's curse.*

And the murderess? Or, in fairness: the maybe-murderess?

*Left the chapel doors wide open, as she found them; and went back to sleep . . .*

. . . Surely she could not . . . ?

*. . . and slept, as soundly as a child. And woke up on Christmas morn.*

⤳

One hard truth must be spoken: after Epifania died, life increased. Some long-sequestered sprite, of gaiety perhaps, returned to Cabral Island. It was obvious to everyone that the quality of the light had changed, as if some filter had been removed from the air;

brightness burst out, like a birth. In the new year the gardeners reported unprecedented levels of growth, along with a marked decline in infestations, and even the least horticultural of eyes could see the great cascades of bougainvillaea, even the least sensitive of noses could smell the newly resplendent growths of jasmine and lily-of-the-valley and orchids and queen-of-the-night. The old house itself seemed to be humming with a new excitement, a new sense of possibility; a certain morbidity had departed from its courts. Even Jawaharlal the bulldog seemed to mellow in this new age.

Visitors became as frequent as they had been during Francisco's glory days. Boatloads of young people came over to marvel at Aurora's Room and to spend the evenings in the surviving Corbusier house, which with the zeal of youth they quickly set to rights; once again there was music on the island, and the latest dance crazes. Even Great-Aunt Sahara, Carmen da Gama, got into the mood, and under the pretext of acting as the young folks' chaperone she assisted at these gatherings, until at length she was tempted by a handsome youth to cut a pshawing, tut-tutting but surprisingly limber figure on the dance-floor. It turned out Carmen had rhythm, and in the evenings that followed, as Aurora's young fellows queued up to ask her to dance, it was possible to see the masquerade of antiquity dropping away from Mrs Aires da Gama, to see the stoop straightening and the eyes ceasing to squint and the hangdog expression being replaced by a tentative suggestion of pleasure. She was not yet thirty-five years old, and for the first time in an eternity she looked younger than her years.

As Carmen began to shimmy, so Aires began to look on her with something like interest, and said, 'It's time we adults had some people over so we can show you off a little bitsy bit.' It was the kindest thing he had ever said to her, and Carmen spent the next weeks in a frenzy of invitation-cards and Chinese lanterns for the gardens and menus and trestle tables and the sweet, sweet agony of deciding what to wear. On the night of the party there was an orchestra on the main lawn and phonograph records in the Corbusier gazebo, and women in jewels and men in white-tie finery came over by the launch-load, and if some of them gazed too deeply into her husband's eyes then Carmen on her night of nights was disposed not to notice.

One member of the family had remained unaffected by the general lightening of spirits: in the midst of the ball on Cabral Island, Camoens could only think of Belle, whose beauty on such a great night would have dimmed the stars. He no longer awoke with love-scratches on his body, and now that he could no longer cling to the forlorn hope that she might come back to him from beyond the grave, something holding him to life had come loose; there were days and nights when he could not bear to look at his daughter, because her mother's presence in her was so strong. He even felt, at times, a kind of anger towards her, for possessing more of Belle than he would ever have again.

He stood alone on the jetty with a glass of pomegranate juice in his hand. A young woman, more than slightly drunk, with her hair in black ringlets and too much scarlet lipstick on her mouth, came leaning towards him in a billowing puff-sleeved frock. 'Snow White!' she declared tipsily.

Camoens, his thoughts far away, failed to reply.

'You didn't see that picture?' the young woman angrily slurred. 'It finally came out in town, I saw it eleven-twelve times.' Then, indicating her dress, 'Just like in the fillum! I made my tailor make her outfit, same to same. I can name the seven dwarfs,' she went on without stopping for a response. 'Sneezysleepyhappydopeygrumpybashfuldoc. You are which one, please?'

Miserable Camoens could find no answer; simply shook his head.

Boozy Snow White was undaunted by his silence.'Not Sneezy, not Happy, not Doc,' she said. 'So Sleepydopeygrumpybashful which? — You don't admit so I am guessing. Sleepy no, Dopey don't think so, Grumpy maybe, but Bashful yes. Hi-ho, Bashful! Whistle while you work!'

'Miss,' Camoens attempted, 'perhaps it would be better if you rejoined the party. I, sorry to say, am not in party mood.'

Snow White stiffened, disappointed. 'Mr Big Shot Jailbird Camoens da Gama,' she snapped. 'Can't keep a civil tongue for any lady, still pining for your late wife, isn't it, and never mind that she fooled with half the town, rich man poor man beggar man thief. O God listen to me I am not supposed to say.' She turned to go; Camoens caught her by the upper arm. 'God, men, let off, you are leaving a bruise!' Snow White exclaimed. But the demand in Camoens's face could not be denied. 'You are scaring,' Snow White said, wrenching her arm away. 'You look raving mad or what. Are you drunk? Maybe you are too much drunk. So. I am sorry I said but everybody knows, and some time it had to come out, isn't it? Now enough, tata-bata, you are not Bashful but Grumpy and I think so there must be some other dwarf for me.'

The next morning Snow White with a murderous headache was visited by two police officers and asked to reconstruct the above scene. 'What are you talking, men, I left him on the jetty and that's it, finish, nothing more to add.' She was the last person ever to see my grandfather alive.

Water claims us. It claimed Francisco and Camoens, father and son. They dove into the black night-harbour and swam out to the mother-ocean. Her rip-tide bore them away.

# 6

IN AUGUST 1939 AURORA da Gama saw the cargo vessel *Marco Polo* still at anchor in Cochin harbour and flew into a rage at this sign that, in the interregnum between the deaths of her parents and her own arrival at full adulthood, her unbusinesslike uncle Aires was letting the reins of commerce slip through his indolent fingers. She directed her driver to 'go like clappers' to C-50 (Pvt) Ltd Godown No.1 at Ernakulam dock, and stormed into that cavernous storehouse; where she momentarily stalled, unnerved by the cool serenity of its light-shafted darkness, and by its blasphemous atmosphere of a gunny-sack cathedral, in which the scents of patchouli oil and cloves, of turmeric and fenugreek, of cumin and cardamom hung like the memory of music, while the narrow passages vanishing into the gloom between the high stacks of export-ready produce could have been roads to hell and back, or even to salvation.

(Great family trees from little 'corns: it is appropriate, is it not, that my personal story, the story of the creation of Moraes Zogoiby, should have its origins in a delayed pepper shipment?)

There were clergy in this temple too: shipping clerks bent over clipboards who went worrying and scurrying between the coolies loading their carts and the fearsomely emaciated trinity of comptrollers – Mr Elaichipillai Kalonjee, Mr V. S. Mirchandal-chini and Mr Karipattam Tejpattam – perching like an inquisition on high stools in pools of ominous lamplight and scratching with feathered nibs in gigantic ledgers which tilted towards them on desks with long, stork-stilty legs. Below these grand personages, at an everyday sort of desk with its own little lamp, sat the godown's duty manager, and it was upon him that Aurora descended, upon recovering her composure, to demand an explanation of the pepper shipment's delay.

'But what is Uncle thinking?' she cried, unreasonably, for how could so lowly a worm know the mind of the great Mr Aires himself? 'He wants family fortunes to drownofy or what?'

The sight at close quarters of the most beautiful of the da Gamas and the sole inheritrix of the family crores – it was common knowledge that while Mr Aires and Mrs Carmen were the in-charges for the time being, the late Mr Camoens had left them no more than an allowance, albeit a generous one – struck the duty manager like a spear in the heart, rendering him temporarily dumb. The young heiress leaned closer towards him, grabbed his chin between her thumb and forefinger, transfixed him with her fiercest glare, and fell head over heels in love. By the time the man had conquered his lightning-struck shyness and stammered out the news of the declaration of war between England and Germany, and of the skipper of the *Marco Polo*'s refusal to sail for England – 'Possibility of attacks on merchant fleet, see' – Aurora had realised, with some anger at the treachery of her emotions, that on account of the ridiculous and inappropriate advent of passion she would have to defy class and convention by marrying this inarticulately handsome family employee at once. 'It's like marrying the dratted driver,' she scolded herself in blissful misery, and for a moment was so preoccupied by the sweet horror of her condition that she did not take in the name painted on the little block of wood on his desk.

'My God,' she burst out when at last the white capitals insisted on being seen, 'it isn't disgraceful enough that you haven't got a bean in your pocket or a tongue in your head, you had to be a Jew as well.' And then, aside: 'Face facts, Aurora. Thinkofy. You've fallen for a bloody godown Moses.'

Pedantic white capitals corrected her (the object of her affections, thunderstruck, moon-struck, dry of mouth, thumping of heart, incipiently fiery of loin, was unable to do so, having been deprived anew of the power of speech by the burgeoning of feelings not usually encouraged in members of staff): Duty Manager Zogoiby's given name was not Moses but Abraham. If it is true that our names contain our fates, then seven capital letters confirmed that he was not to be a vanquisher of pharaohs, receiver of commandments or divider of waters; he would lead no people towards a promised land. Rather, he would offer up his son as a living sacrifice on the altar of a terrible love.

And 'Zogoiby'?

~

'Unlucky.' In Arabic, at least according to Cohen the chandler and Abraham's maternal family's lore. Not that anyone had even the most rudimentary knowledge of that faraway language. The very idea was alarming. 'Just look at their writing,' Abraham's mother Flory once remarked. 'Even that is so violent, like knife-slashes and stab-wounds. Still and all: we also have come down from martial Jews. Maybe that's why we kept on this wrong-tongue Andalusian name.'

(You ask: But if the name was his mother's, then how come the son . . . ? I answer: Control, please, your horses.)

'You are old enough to be her father.' Abraham Zogoiby, born in the same year as deceased Mr Camoens, stood stiffly outside the blue-tiled Cochin synagogue – *Tiles from Canton & No Two Are Identical*, said the little sampler on the ante-room wall – and, smelling strongly of spices and something else, faced his mother's wrath. Old Flory Zogoiby in a faded green calico frock sucked her gums and heard her son's stumbling confession of forbidden love. With her walking-stick she drew a line in the dust. On one side, the synagogue, Flory and history; on the other, Abraham, his rich girl, the universe, the future – all things unclean. Closing her eyes, shutting out Abrahamic odour and stammerings, she summoned up the past, using memories to forestall the moment at which she would have to disown her only child, because it was unheard-of for a Cochin Jew to marry outside the community; yes, her memory and behind and beneath it the longer memory of the tribe . . . the White Jews of India, Sephardim from Palestine, arrived in numbers (ten thousand approx.) in Year 72 of the Christian Era, fleeing from

70

Roman persecution. Settling in Cranganore, they hired themselves out as soldiers to local princes. Once upon a time a battle between Cochin's ruler and his enemy the Zamorin of Calicut, the Lord of the Sea, had to be postponed because the Jewish soldiers would not fight on the Sabbath day.

O prosperous community! Verily, it flourishéd. And, in the year 379 CE, King Bhaskara Ravi Varman I granted to Joseph Rabban the little kingdom of the village of Anjuvannam near Cranganore. The copper plates upon which the gift was inscribed ended up at the tiled synagogue, in Flory's charge; because for many years, and in defiance of gender prejudices, she had held the honoured position of caretaker. They lay concealed in a chest under the altar, and she polished them from time to time with much enthusiasm and elbow-grease.

'A Christy wasn't bad enough, you had to pick the very worst of the bunch,' Flory was muttering. But her gaze was still far away in the past, fixed upon Jewish cashews and areca-nuts and jack-fruit trees, upon the ancient waving fields of Jewish oilseed rape, the gathering of Jewish cardamoms, for had these not been the basis of the community's prosperity? 'Now these come-latelies steal our business,' she mumbled. 'And proud of being bastards and all. Fitz-Vasco-da-Gamas! No better than a bunch of Moors.'

If Abraham had not been knocked sideways by love, if the thunderbolt had been less recent, he would in all probability have held his tongue out of filial affection and the knowledge that Flory's prejudices could not be argued away. 'I gave you a too-modern brought-up,' she went on. 'Christies and Moors, boy. Just hope on they never come for you.'

But Abraham was in love, and hearing his beloved under attack he burst out with the observation that 'in the first place if you look at things without cock-eyes you'd see that you also are a come-lately Johnny', meaning that Black Jews had arrived in India long before the White, fleeing Jerusalem from Nebuchadnezzar's armies five hundred and eighty-seven years before the Christian era, and even if you didn't care about them because they had intermarried with the locals and vanished long ago, there were, for example, the Jews who came from Babylon and Persia in 490–518

CE; and many centuries had passed since Jews started setting up shop in Cranganore and then in Cochin Town (a certain Joseph Azaar and his family moved there in 1344 as everybody knew), and even from Spain the Jews started arriving after their expulsion in 1492, including, in the first batch, the family of Solomon Castile . . .

Flory Zogoiby screamed at the mention of the name; screamed and shook her head from side to side.

'Solomon Solomon Castile Castile,' thirty-six-year-old Abraham taunted his mother with childish vengefulness. 'From whom descends at least this one *infant* of Castile. You want I should begat? All the way from Señor Leon Castile the swordsmith of Toledo who lost his head over some Spaini Princess Elephant-and-Castle, to my Daddyji who also must have been crazy, but the point is the Castiles got to Cochin twenty-two years before any Zogoiby, so *quod erat demonstrandum* . . . And in the second place Jews with Arab names and hidden secrets ought to watch who they're calling Moors.'

Elderly men with rolled trouser-legs and women with greying buns emerged into the shady Jewish alley outside the Mattancherri synagogue and gave solemn witness to the quarrel. Above angry mother and retaliating son blue shutters flew open and there were heads at windows. In the adjoining cemetery Hebrew inscriptions waved on tombstones like half-mast flags at twilight. Fish and spices on the evening air. And Flory Zogoiby, at the mention of secrets of which she had never spoken, dissolved abruptly into stutters and jerks.

'A curse on all Moors,' she rallied. 'Who destroyed the Cranganore synagogue? Moors, who else. Local-manufacture made-in-India Othello-fellows. A plague on their houses and spouses.' In 1524, ten years after Zogoibys arrived from Spain, there had been a Muslim-Jewish war in these parts. It was an old quarrel to revive, and Flory did so in the hope of turning her son's thoughts away from hidden matters. But oaths should not be lightly uttered, especially before witnesses. Flory's curse flew into the air like a startled chicken and hovered there a long while, as if uncertain of its intended destination. Her grandson Moraes

Zogoiby would not be born for eighteen years; at which time the chicken came home to roost.

(And what did Muslims and Jews fight over in the *cinquecento*? – What else? The pepper trade.)

'Jews and Moors were the ones who went to war,' old Flory grunted, goaded by misery into speaking a sentence too many, 'and now your Christian Fitz-Vascos have gone and pinched the market from us both.'

'You're a fine one to talk about bastards,' cried Abraham Zogoiby who bore his mother's name. 'Fitz she says,' he addressed the gathering crowd. 'I'll show her Fitz.' Whereupon with furious intent he strode into the synagogue with his mother scrambling after him, bursting into dry and shrieky tears.

ᔕ

About my grandmother Flory Zogoiby, Epifania da Gama's opposite number, her equal in years although closer to me by a generation: a decade before the century's turn Fearless Flory would haunt the boys' school playground, teasing adolescent males with swishings of skirts and sing-song sneers, and with a twig would scratch challenges into the earth – *step across this line*. (Line-drawing comes down to me from both sides of the family.) She would taunt them with nonsensical, terrifying incantations, 'making like a witch':

> *Obeah, jadoo, fo, fum,*
> *chicken entrails, kingdom come.*
> *Ju-ju, voodoo, fee, fi,*
> *piddle cocktails, time to die.*

When the boys came at her she attacked them with a ferocity that easily overcame their theoretical advantages of strength and size. Her gifts of war came down to her from some unknown ancestor; and though her adversaries grabbed her hair and called her jewess they never vanquished her. Sometimes she literally rubbed their noses in the dirt. On other occasions she stood back, scrawny arms folded in triumph across her chest, and allowed her stunned victims to back unsteadily away. 'Next time, pick on

73

someone your own size,' Flory added insult to injury by inverting the meaning of the phrase: 'Us pint-size jewinas are too hot for you to handle.' Yes, she was rubbing it in, but even this attempt to make metaphors of her victories, to represent herself as the champion of the small, of the Minority, of *girls*, failed to make her popular. Fast Flory, Flory-the-Roary: she acquired a Reputation.

The time came when nobody would cross the lines she went on drawing, with fearsome precision, across the gullies and open spaces of her childhood years. She grew moody and inward and sat on behind her dust-lines, besieged within her own fortifications. By her eighteenth birthday she had stopped fighting, having learned something about winning battles and losing wars.

The point I'm leading up to is that Christians had in Flory's view stolen more from her than ancestral spice fields. What they took was even then getting to be in short supply, and for a girl with a Reputation the supply was even shorter . . . in her twenty-fourth year Solomon Castile the synagogue caretaker had stepped across Miss Flory's lines to ask for her hand in marriage. The act was generally thought to be one of great charity, or stupidity, or both. Even in those days the numbers of the community were decreasing. Maybe four thousand persons living in the Mattancherri Jewtown, and by the time you excluded family members and the very young and the very old and the crazy and infirm, the youngsters of marriageable age were not spoiled for choice of partners. Old bachelors fanned themselves by the clocktower and walked by the harbour's edge hand in hand; toothless spinsters sat in doorways sewing clothes for non-existent babies. Matrimony inspired as much spiteful envy as celebration, and Flory's marriage to the caretaker was attributed by gossip to the ugliness of both parties. 'As sin,' the sharp tongues said. 'Pity the kids, my *God*.'

(*Old enough to be her father*, Flory scolded Abraham; but Solomon Castile, born in the year of the Indian Uprising, had been twenty years her senior, *poor man probably wanted to get married while he was still capable*, the wagging tongues surmised . . . and there is one more fact about their wedding. It took place on the same day in 1900 as a much grander affair; no newspapers recorded the Castile-Zogoiby nuptials in their social-register columns, but there were many photographs of Mr Francisco da Gama and his smiling Mangalorean bride.)

The vengefulness of the spouseless was finally satisfied: because after seven years and seven days of explosive wedlock, during which Flory gave birth to one child, a boy who would perversely grow up to be the most handsome young man of his dwindling generation, caretaker Castile at nightfall on his fiftieth birthday walked over to the water's edge, hopped into a rowing-boat with half a dozen drunken Portuguese sailors, and ran away to sea. 'He should have known better'n to marry Roary Flory,' according to contented bachelor-spinster whispers, 'but wise man's brain don't come automatic along with wise man's name.' The broken marriage came to be known in Mattancherri as the Misjudgment of Solomon; but Flory blamed the Christian ships, the mercantile armada of the omnipotent west, for tempting her husband away in search of golden streets. And at the age of seven her son was obliged to give up his father's name; unlucky in fathers, he took his mother's unlucky Zogoiby for his own.

After Solomon's desertion, Flory took over as caretaker of blue ceramic tiles and Joseph Rabban's copper plates, claiming the post with a gleaming ferocity that silenced all rumbles of opposition to her appointment. Under her protection: not only little Abraham, but also the parchment Old Testament on whose ragged-edged leathery pages the Hebrew letters flowed, and the hollow golden crown presented (Christian Era 1805) by the Maharaja of Travancore. She instituted reforms. When the faithful came to worship she ordered them to remove their shoes. Objections were raised to this positively Moorish practice; Flory in response barked mirthless laughs.

'What devotion?' she snorted. 'Caretaking you want from me, better you take some care too. Boots off! Chop chop! Protectee Chinee tiles.'

*No two are identical.* The tiles from Canton, 12″ × 12″ approx., imported by Ezekiel Rabhi in the year 1100 CE, covered the floors, walls and ceiling of the little synagogue. Legends had begun to stick to them. Some said that if you explored for long enough you'd find your own story in one of the blue-and-white squares, because the pictures on the tiles could change, were changing, generation by generation, to tell the story of the Cochin Jews. Still others were convinced that the tiles were prophecies, the keys to whose meanings had been lost with the passing years.

Abraham as a boy crawled around the synagogue bum-in-air with his nose pressed against antique Chinese blue. He never told his mother that his father had reappeared in ceramic form on the synagogue floor a year after he decamped, in a little blue rowing-boat with blue-skinned foreign-looking types by his side, heading off towards an equally blue horizon. After this discovery, Abraham periodically received news of Solomon Castile through the good offices of the metamorphic tiles. He next saw his father in a cerulean scene of Dionysiac willow-pattern merrymaking amid slain dragons and grumbling volcanoes. Solomon was dancing in an open hexagonal pavilion with a carefree joy upon his blue-tile face which utterly transformed it from the dolorous countenance which Abraham remembered. If he is happy, the boy thought, then I'm glad he went. From his earliest days Abraham had instinctive knowledge of the paramountcy of happiness, and it was this same instinct which, years later, would allow the grown-up duty manager to seize the love offered with many blushes and sarcasms by Aurora da Gama in the chiaroscuro of the Ernakulam godown . . .

Over the years Abraham found his father wealthy and fat in one tile, seated upon cushions in the Position of Royal Ease and waited upon by eunuchs and dancing-girls; but only a few months later he was skinny and mendicant in another twelve-by-twelve scenario. Now Abraham understood that the former caretaker had left all restraints behind him, and was oscillating wildly through a life that had deliberately been allowed to go out of control. He was a Sindbad seeking his fortune in the oceanic happenstance of the earth. He was a heavenly body which had managed by an act of will to wrench itself free of its fixed orbit, and now wandered the galaxies accepting whatever destiny might provide. It seemed to Abraham that his father's breakaway from the gravity of the everyday had used up all his reserves of will-power, so that after that initial and radical act of transformation he was broken-ruddered, at the mercy of the winds and tides.

As Abraham Zogoiby neared adolescence, Solomon Castile began to appear in semi-pornographic tableaux whose appropriateness for a synagogue would have been the subject of much controversy had they come to anyone else's notice but Abraham's. These tiles cropped up in the dustiest and murkiest recesses of the building and Abraham preserved them by allowing mould to form and cobwebs to gather over their more reprehensible zones, in which his father disported himself with startling numbers of individuals of both sexes in a fashion which his wide-eyed son could only think of as educational. And yet in spite of the salacious gymnastics of these activities the ageing wanderer had regained his old lugubriousness of mien, so that, perhaps, all his journeys had done no more than wash him up at the last on the same shores of discontent whence he had first set forth. On the day Abraham Zogoiby's voice broke he was gripped by the notion that his father was about to return. He raced through the alleys of the Jewish quarter down to the waterfront where cantilevered Chinese fishing nets were spread out against the sky; but the fish he sought did not leap out of the waves. When he returned in despondency to the synagogue all the tiles depicting his father's odyssey had changed, and showed scenes both anonymous and banal. Abraham in a feverish rage spent hours crawling across the floor in search of magic. To no avail: for the second time in his life his unwise father Solomon Castile had vanished into the blue.

∽

I no longer remember when I first heard the family story which provided me with my nickname and my mother with the theme of her most famous series of paintings, the 'Moor sequence' that reached its triumphant culmination in the unfinished, and subsequently stolen masterpiece, *The Moor's Last Sigh*. I seem to have known it all my life, this lurid saga from which, I should add, Mr Vasco Miranda derived an early work of his own; but in spite of long familiarity I have grave doubts about the literal truth of the story, with its somewhat overwrought Bombay-talkie *masala* narrative, its almost desperate reaching back for a kind of authentification, for *evidence* . . . I believe, and others have since confirmed, that simpler explanations can be offered for the transaction between Abraham Zogoiby and his mother, most particularly for what he did or did not find in an old trunk underneath the altar; I will offer one such alternative version by and by. For the moment, I present the approved, and polished, family yarn; which, being so profound a part of my parents' pictures of themselves – and so significant a part of contemporary Indian art history – has, for those reasons if no other, a power and importance I will not attempt to deny.

We have reached a key moment in the tale. Let us return briefly to young Abraham on hands and knees, frantically searching the synagogue for the father who had just abandoned him again, calling out to him in a cracked voice swooping from bulbul to crow; until at length, overcoming an unspoken taboo, he ventured for the first time in his life behind & beneath the pale blue drape with golden hem that graced the high altar . . . Solomon Castile wasn't there; the teenager's flashlight fell, instead, upon an old box marked with a Z and fastened with a cheap padlock, which was soon picked; for schoolboys have skills which adults forget as surely as lessons learned by rote. And so, despairing of his absconded father, he found his mother's secrets out instead.

What was in the box? – Why, the only treasure of any value: viz., the past, and the future. Also, however, emeralds.

～

And so to the day of crisis, when the adult Abraham Zogoiby charged into the synagogue – *I'll show her Fitz*, he cried – and dragged the trunk out from its hiding-place. His mother, pursuing him, saw her secrets coming out into the open and felt her legs give way. She sat down on blue tiles with a thump, while Abraham opened the box and drew out a silver dagger, which he stuck in his trouser-belt; then, breathing in short gasps, Flory watched him remove, and place upon his head, an ancient, tattered crown.

*Not the nineteenth-century circlet of gold donated by Maharaja Travancore, but something altogether more ancient* was the way I heard it. A dark green turban wound in cloth rendered illusory by age, so delicate that even the orange evening light filtering into the synagogue seemed too fierce; so provisional that it might almost have disintegrated beneath Flory Zogoiby's burning gaze . . .

And upon this phantasm of a turban, the family legend went, hung age-dulled chains of solid gold, and dangling off these chains were emeralds so large and green that they looked like toys. *It was four and a half centuries old, the last crown to fall from the head of the last prince of al-Andalus; nothing less than the crown of Granada, as worn by Abu Abdallah, last of the Nasrids, known as 'Boabdil'.*

'But how did it get there?' I used to ask my father. How indeed? This priceless headgear – this royal Moorish hat – how did it emerge from a toothless woman's box to sit upon the head of Abraham, future father, renegade Jew?

'It was', my father answered, 'the uneasy jewellery of shame.'

I continue, for the moment, without judging his version of events: When Abraham Zogoiby as a boy first discovered the hidden crown and dagger he replaced the treasures in their hiding-place, fastened the padlock tight and spent a night and a day fearing his mother's wrath. But once it became clear that his inquisitiveness had gone unnoticed his curiosity was reborn, and again he drew forth the little chest and again picked the lock. This time he found, wrapped in burlap in the turban-box, a small book made up of handwritten parchment pages crudely sewn together and bound in hide. It was written in Spanish, which the young Abraham did not understand, but he copied out a number of the names therein, and over the years that followed he unlocked their meanings, for instance by asking innocent questions of the crotchety and reclusive old chandler Moshe Cohen who was at that time the appointed head of the community and the keeper of its lore. Old Mr Cohen was so astonished that any member of the younger generation should care about the old days that he had talked freely, pointing towards distant horizons while the handsome young man sat wide-eyed at his feet.

Thus Abraham learned that, in January 1492, while Christopher Columbus watched in wonderment and contempt, the Sultan Boabdil of Granada had surrendered the keys to the fortress-palace of the Alhambra, last and greatest of all the Moors' fortifications, to the all-conquering Catholic Kings Fernando and Isabella, giving up his principality without so much as a battle. He departed into exile with his mother and retainers, bringing to a close the centuries of Moorish Spain; and reining in his horse upon the Hill of Tears he turned to look for one last time upon his loss, upon the palace and the fertile plains and all the concluded glory of al-Andalus . . . at which sight the Sultan sighed, and hotly wept – whereupon his mother, the terrifying Ayxa the Virtuous, sneered at his grief. Having been forced to genuflect before an omnipotent queen, Boabdil was now obliged to suffer a further humiliation at the hands of an impotent (but formidable) dowager. *Well may you weep like a woman for what you could not defend like a man*, she taunted him: meaning of course the opposite. Meaning that she despised this blubbing male, her son, for yielding up what she would have fought for to the death, given the chance. She was Queen Isabella's equal and opposite; it was *reina Isabel's* good fortune to have come up against the mere cry-baby, Boabdil . . .

Suddenly, as the chandler spoke, Abraham curled upon a coil of rope felt all the mournful weight of Boabdil's coming-to-an-end, felt it as his own. Breath left his body with a whine, and the next breath was a gasp. The onset of asthma (more asthma! It's a wonder I can breathe at all!) was like an omen, a joining of lives across the centuries, or so Abraham fancied as he grew into his manhood and the illness gained in strength. *These wheezing sighs not only mine, but his. These eyes hot with his ancient grief. Boabdil, I too am thy mother's son.*

Was weeping such a weakness? he wondered. Was defending-to-the-death such a strength?

After Boabdil handed over the keys to the Alhambra, he diminished into the south. The Catholic Kings had allowed him an estate, but even this was sold out from under his feet by his most trusted courtier. Boabdil, the prince turned fool. He eventually died in battle, fighting under some other kingling's flag.

Jews, too, moved south in 1492. Ships bearing banished Jews into exile clogged the harbour at Cádiz, obliging the year's other voyager, Columbus, to sail from Palos de Moguer. Jews gave up the forging of Toledo steel; Castiles set sail for India. But not all Jews left at once. The Zogoibys, remember, were twenty-two years behind those old Castiles. What happened? Where did they hide?

'All will be told in good time, my son; all in own good time.'

Abraham in his twenties learned secrecy from his mother, and to the annoyance of the small band of eligible women of his generation kept himself to himself, burrowing into the heart of the city and avoiding the Jewish quarter as much as possible, the synagogue most of all. He worked first for Moshe Cohen and then as a junior clerk for the da Gamas, and although he was a diligent worker and gained promotion early he wore the air of a man in waiting for something, and on account of his abstraction and beauty it became commonplace to say of him that he was a genius in the making, perhaps even the great poet that the Jews of Cochin had always yearned for but never managed to produce. Moshe Cohen's slightly too hairy niece Sara, a large-bodied girl waiting like an undiscovered sub-continent for Abraham's vessel to sail into her harbour, was the source of much of this speculative adulation. But the truth was that Abraham utterly lacked the artistic spark; his was a world of numbers, especially of numbers in action – his literature a balance-sheet, his music the fragile harmonies of manufacture and sale, his temple a scented warehouse. Of the crown and dagger in the wooden box he never spoke, so nobody knew that that was why he wore the look of a king in exile, and privily, in those years, he learned the secrets of his lineage, by teaching himself Spanish from books, and so deciphering what a twine-bound notebook had to say; until at last he stood crown-on-head in an orange evening and confronted his mother with his family's hidden shame.

～

Outside in the Mattancherri alley the enlarging crowd grew murmurous. Moshe Cohen, as community leader, took it upon himself to enter the synagogue, to mediate between the warring mother and son, for a synagogue was no place for such a quarrel; his

81

niece Sara followed him in, her heart slowly cracking beneath the weight of the knowledge that the great country of her love must remain virgin soil, that Abraham's treacherous infatuation with Aurora the infidel had condemned her for ever to the dreadful inferno of spinsterhood, the knitting of useless bootees and frockies, blue and pink, for the children who would never fill her womb.

'Going to run off with a Christian child, Abie,' she said, her voice loud and harsh in the blue-tiled air, 'and already you're dressing up like a Christmas tree.'

But Abraham was tormenting his mother with old papers bound up 'twixt twine and hide. 'Who is the author?' he asked, and, as she remained silent, answered himself: 'A woman.' And, continuing with this catechism: 'What was her name? – Not given. – What was she? – A Jew; who took shelter beneath the roof of the exiled Sultan; beneath his roof, and then between his sheets. Miscegenation,' Abraham baldly stated, 'occurred.' And though it would have been easy enough to feel compassion for this pair, the dispossessed Spanish Arab and the ejected Spanish Jew – two powerless lovers making common cause against the power of the Catholic Kings – still it was the Moor alone for whom Abraham demanded pity. 'His courtiers sold his lands, and his lover stole his crown.' After years by his side, this anonymous ancestor crept away from crumbling Boabdil, and took ship for India, with a great treasure in her baggage, and a male child in her belly; from whom, after many begats, came Abraham himself. *My mother who insists on the purity of our race, what say you to your forefather the Moor?*

'The woman has no name,' Sara interrupted him. 'And yet you claim her tainted blood is yours. Have you no shame to make your mummy weep? And all for a rich girl's love, Abraham, I swear. It stinks, and by the way, so do you.'

From Flory Zogoiby came a thin assenting wail. But Abraham's argument was not complete. *Consider this stolen crown, wrapped in rags, locked in a box, for four hundred years and more. If it was stolen for simple gain, would it not have been sold off long ago?*

'Because of secret pride in the royal link, the crown was kept; because of secret shame, it was concealed. Mother, who is worse?

My Aurora who does not hide the Vasco connection, but takes delight; or myself, born of the fat old Moor of Granada's last sighs in the arms of his thieving mistress – Boabdil's bastard Jew?'

'Evidence,' Flory whispered in reply, a mortally wounded adversary pleading for the death-blow. 'Only supposition has been given; where are hard-fast facts?' Inexorable Abraham asked his penultimate question.

'Mother, what is our family name?'

When she heard this, Flory knew the coup-de-grâce was near. Dumbly, she shook her head. To Moshe Cohen, whose old friendship he would, that day, forsake for ever, Abraham threw down a challenge. 'The Sultan Boabdil after his fall was known by one sobriquet, and she who took his crown and jewels in a dark irony took the nickname also. Boabdil the Misfortunate: that was it. Anyone here can say that in the Moor's own tongue?'

And the old chandler was obliged to complete the proof. '*El-zogoybi.*'

Gently, Abraham set down the crown beside defeated Flory; resting his case.

'At least he fell for a pushy girl,' Flory said emptily to the walls. 'I had that much influence while he was still my son.'

'Better you go now,' said Sara to pepper-odorous Abraham. 'Maybe when you marry you should take the girl's name, why not? Then we can forget you, and what difference between a bastard Moor and a bastard Portugee?'

'A bad mistake, Abie,' old Moshe Cohen commented. 'To make an enemy of your mother; for enemies are plentiful, but mothers are hard to find.'

෴

Flory Zogoiby, alone in the aftermath of one catastrophic revelation was granted another. In the sunset's vermilion afterglow she saw the Cantonese tiles pass before her eyes one by one, for had she not been their servitor and their student, cleaning and buffing them these many years; had she not many times attempted

83

to enter their myriad worlds, those universes contained within the uniformity of twelve-by-twelve and held captive on so-neatly-grouted walls? Flory who loved to draw lines was enthralled by the serried ranks of the tiles, but until this moment they had not spoken to her, she had found there neither missing husbands nor future admirers, neither prophecies of the future nor explanations of the past. Guidance, meaning, fortune, friendship, love had all been withheld. Now in her hour of anguish they unveiled a secret.

Scene after blue scene passed before her eyes. There were tumultuous marketplaces and crenellated fortress-palaces and fields under cultivation and thieves in jail, there were high, toothy mountains and great fish in the sea. Pleasure gardens were laid out in blue, and blue-bloody battles were grimly fought; blue horsemen pranced beneath lamplit windows and blue-masked ladies swooned in arbours. O, and intrigue of courtiers and dreams of peasants and pigtailed tallymen at their abacuses and poets in their cups. On the walls floor ceiling of the little synagogue, and now in Flory Zogoiby's mind's eye, marched the ceramic encyclopaedia of the material world that was also a bestiary, a travelogue, a synthesis and a song, and for the first time in all her years of caretaking Flory saw what was missing from the hyperabundant cavalcade. 'Not so much what as who,' she thought, and the tears dried in her eyes. 'In the whole place, no trace.' The orange light of evening fell on her like thunderous rain, washing away her blindness, opening her eyes. Eight hundred and thirty-nine years after the tiles came to Cochin, and at the beginning of a time of war and massacres, they delivered their message to a woman in pain.

'What you see is what there is,' Flory mumbled under her breath. 'There is no world but the world.' And then, a little louder: 'There is no God. Hocus-pocus! Mumbo-jumbo! *There is no spiritual life.*'

⌒

It isn't hard to demolish Abraham's arguments. What's in a name? The da Gamas claimed descent from Vasco the explorer, but claiming isn't proving, and even about that ancestry I have my serious doubts. But as for this Moor-stuff, this Granada-yada, this incredibly *loose* connection – a surname that sounds like a nickname, for Pete's sake! – it falls down even before you blow on it. Old leather-bound notebook? Gas! Never seen it. Not a trace. As for the emerald-laden crown, I don't buy that, either; it's a fairy tale of the sort we folks love to tell ourselves about ourselves, and, gents & gentesses, it does not wash. Abraham's had never been a wealthy family, and if you believe that a boxful of gems would have remained untouched for four centuries, then, busters and busterinas, you'll believe anything. Oh, but they were *hair-looms*? Well, roll my eyes and strike my brow! What a blank-blank joke! Who in the whole of India cares two paisa about heirlooms if he's given the choice between old stuff and money in the bank?

Aurora Zogoiby painted some famous pictures, and passed away in horrific circs. Reason requires that we put the rest down to the self-mythologising of the artist, to which, in this instance, my dear father lent more than just a hand . . . you want to know what was in the box? Listen: forget about jewelled turbans; but emeralds, yes. Sometimes more, sometimes less. – Not heirlooms, though. – What then? – Hot rocks, that's what. Yes! Stolen goods! Contraband items! Loot! You want family shame, I'll tell you its true name: my granny, Flory Zogoiby, was a crook. For many years she was a valued member of a successful gang of emerald smugglers; for who would ever look under the synagogue altar for boodle? She took her cut of the proceeds, kept it safe, and was not so foolish as to spend spend spend. Nobody ever suspected her; and the time came when her son Abraham came to claim his illegal inheritance . . . it's illegitimacy you want? Never mind about genetics; just follow the cash.

The above is my understanding of what lay behind the stories I was told; but there is also a confession I must make. In what follows you will find stranger tales by far than the one I have just attempted to debunk; and let me assure you, let me say to-whom-it-may-concern, that of the truth of these further stories there can be no doubt whatsoever. So finally it is not for me to judge, but for you.

And as for the yarn of the Moor: if I were forced to choose

between logic and childhood memory, between head and heart, then sure; in spite of all the foregoing, I'd go along with the tale.

❧

Abraham Zogoiby walked out of Jewtown and towards St Francis's Church, where Aurora da Gama was waiting for him by Vasco's tomb with his future in the palm of her hand. When he reached the waterfront he looked back for a moment; and thought he saw, silhouetted against the darkening sky, the impossible figure of a young girl capering upon the roof of a storehouse painted in gaudy horizontal stripes, can-canning her skirt and petticoat and uttering familiar sorceries as she challenged him to fight: *Step across this line.*

> *'Obeah, jadoo, fo, fum,*
> *chicken entrails, kingdom come.'*

Tears filled his eyes; he pushed them away. She was gone.

# 7

CHRISTIANS, PORTUGUESE AND JEWS; Chinese tiles promoting godless views; pushy ladies, skirts-not-saris, Spanish shenanigans, Moorish crowns . . . can this really be India? *Bharat-mata, Hindustan-hamara*, is this the place? War has just been declared. Nehru and the All-India Congress are demanding that the British must accept their demand for independence as a precondition for Indian support in the war effort; Jinnah and the Muslim League are refusing to support the demand; Mr Jinnah is busily articulating the history-changing notion that there are two nations in the sub-continent, one Hindu, the other Mussulman. Soon the split will be irreversible; soon Nehru will be back in Dehra Dun jail, and the British, having imprisoned the Congress leadership, will turn to the Leaguers for support. At such a time of upheaval, of the ruinous climax of divide-and-rule, is this not the most eccentric of slices to extract from all that life – a freak blond hair plucked from a jet-black (and horribly unravelling) plait?

No, sahibzadas. Madams-O: no way. Majority, that mighty elephant, and her sidekick, Major-Minority, will not crush my tale beneath her feet. Are not my personages Indian, every one? Well, then: this too is an Indian yarn. That's one answer; but here's another: *everything in its place*. Elephants are promised for later. Majority and Major-Minority will have their day, and much that has been beautiful will be tusked & trampled by their flap-eared, trumpeting herds. Until then, I continue to guzzle this last supper; to exhale, albeit wheezily, this aforementioned *dernier soupir*. To hell with high affairs of state! I have a love story to tell.

In the perfumed half-light of C-50 Godown No.1, Aurora da Gama grabbed Abraham Zogoiby by the chin and looked deep into his eyes . . . no, men, I can't do this stuff. This is my mother and father I'm talking about, and even though Aurora the Great was the least bashful of women I guess on this matter I am in possession of her share of bash as well as my own. Did you ever see your father's cock, your mother's cunt? Yes or no, doesn't matter, the point is these are mythical locations, surrounded by taboo, put off thy shoes for it is holy ground, as the Voice said on Mount Sinai, and if Abraham Zogoiby was playing the part of Moses then Aurora my mother sure as eggs was the Burning Bush. Handing down commandments, pillar of fire, *I am that I am* . . . yes, indeed, she had made a study of the Old Testament god. Sometimes I think she practised partings of waters in the bath.

'I couldn't wait-o,' that is how Aurora herself used to tell it. In her gold-and-orange drawing-room full of cigarette-smoke, with young beauties stretched out on sofas while men sat on Isfahani rugs and pressed their ankle-braceleted, mauve-nailed feet, and while her ageing husband leaned in a corner in a business suit, mouth twitching in an embarrassed smile, hands flapping helplessly until at last they settled around my young ears, Aurora drank champagne from an opalescent glass like an opening flower and was casually explicit about her own deflowering, laughing lightly at her youthful audacity. 'By the chin, I swear. I just pulled at him and he followed, popped right up out of his chair like a cork from a bottle, and I led him on. My very own *yahoody*. My in-those-days beloved Jew.'

*In-those-days* . . . there will be more to say about the cruelty of that phrase, so easily tossed out with a little wave of the hand, a dismissive little bangle-jingle. But right now we are indeed in those days, we are *on that very day*, and so: by the chin she led him, and he followed; abandoning his post, and disapprovingly watched, I have no doubt, by the ledger-inscribing high trinity of clerks, Kalonjee, Mirchandalchini and Tejpattam, he pursued his chin, surrendering himself to his fate. Beauty is destiny of a sort, beauty speaks to beauty, it recognises and assents, it believes it can excuse everything, so that even though they knew no more about each other than the words *Christian heiress* and *Jewish employee*, they had already made the most important decisions of all. Throughout her life Aurora Zogoiby was quite clear about the reason why she led her duty manager into the murky depths of the godown, and why, motioning him to follow, she climbed a long and bouncy ladder to the highest level of the most remote stacks. Resisting all efforts at psychological analysis, she angrily rejected the theory that in the aftermath of too-many-deaths-in-the-family she had been vulnerable to the charms of an older man, that she had been first held, then captured, by Abraham's look of wounded kindness: that it had been a simple case of innocence being drawn towards experience. 'In the first place,' she would argue, to cheers and applause, while Daddy Abraham earned my contempt by skulking shamefacedly away, 'excuse me, but who drewofied whom towards where? Seems to me I was the puller, not the pulled. Seems to *me* that Abie was the know-nothing and I was one smart fifteen-year-old cookie. And in the second place, I always was a sucker for a *heero*, a *loverboy*, a hunk.'

Way up there near the roof of Godown No.1, Aurora da Gama at the age of fifteen lay back on pepper sacks, breathed in the hot spice-laden air, and waited for Abraham. He came to her as a man goes to his doom, trembling but resolute, and it is around here that my words run out, so you will not learn from me the bloody details of what happened when she, and then he, and then they, and after that she, and at which he, and in response to that she, and with that, and in addition, and for a while, and then for a long time, and quietly, and noisily, and at the end of their endurance, and at last, and after that, until . . . phew! Boy! Over and done with! – No. There's more. The whole thing must be told.

This I will say: what they had was certainly hot & hungry. Mad love! It drove Abraham back to confront Flory Zogoiby, and then it made him walk away from his race, looking back only once. *That for this favour, He presently become a Christian*, the Merchant of Venice insisted in his moment of victory over Shylock, showing only a limited understanding of the quality of mercy; and the Duke agreed, *He shall do this, or else I do recant The pardon that I late pronounced here* . . . What was forced upon Shylock would have been freely chosen by Abraham, who preferred my mother's love to God's. He was prepared to marry her according to the laws of Rome – and O, what a storm that statement conceals! But their love was strong enough to withstand all the buffetings, to survive the full force of the scandal; and it was my knowledge of their strength that would give me the strength, when I, in my turn, – when my beloved and I, – but on that occasion she, my mother, – instead of, – when I fully expected, – she turned on me, and, just when I needed her most, she, – against her own flesh and blood . . . you see that I am not able, as yet, to tell this story either. Once again, the words have let me down.

Pepper love: that's how I think of it. Abraham and Aurora fell in pepper love, up there on the Malabar Gold. They came down from those high stacks with more than their clothes smelling of spice. So passionately had they fed upon one another, so profoundly had sweat and blood and the secretions of their bodies mingled, in that foetid atmosphere heavy with the odours of cardamom and cumin, so intimately had they conjoined, not only with each other but with what-hung-on-the-air, yes, and with the spice-sacks themselves – some of which, it must be said, were torn, so that peppercorns and *elaichees* poured out and were crushed between legs and bellies and thighs – that, for ever after, they sweated pepper'n'spices sweat, and their bodily fluids, too, smelled and even tasted of what had been crushed into their skins, what had mingled with their love-waters, what had been breathed in from the air during that transcendent fuck.

There; keep worrying at a subject for long enough, and in the end some words do come. But Aurora on the same topic was never one to be shy. 'Ever since then, let me tell you, I have had to keep-o old Abie here away from the kitchen, because that stink of grinding spices, my *dears*, it makes him paw the ground. Speaking for myself, however, I tubbofy, I scrubbofy, I brush, I groom, I fill-o the room with fine perfume, and that is why, as all can see, I'm just as sweet as I can be.' O, father, father, why did you let her do it to you, why were you her daily-nightly butt? Why were we all? Did you really still love her so much? Did we really love her at all in those days, or was it just her long dominance over us, and our passive acceptance of our enslavement, that we mistook for love?

⮑

'From now on I will always look after you,' my father told my mother after the first time they made love. But she was beginning to be an artist, she answered, and so 'the most important part of me, I can take care of by myself'.

'Then,' said Abraham, humbly, 'I will look after the less important part, the part that needs to eat, enjoy, and rest.'

⮑

Men in conical Chinese hats punted slowly across the darkening lagoon. Red-and-yellow ferryboats made the day's last journeys, moving stolidly between the islands. A dredger stopped work, and with the halting of its *boom-yacka-yacka-yacka-boom* a silence fell over the harbour. There were yachts at anchor and little boats with patchwork leather sails making their way home to Vypeen village for the night; there were rowboats and motor-boats and tugs. Abraham Zogoiby, leaving behind the phantom of his mother capering on a Jewtown roof, was on his way to meet his darling at St Francis's Church. The Chinese fishing-nets had been hauled up for the night. Cochin, city of nets, he thought, and I have been netted just like any fish. Twin-stacked steamers, the cargo ship *Marco Polo*, and even a British gunboat hung out there in the last light, like ghosts. Everything looks normal, Abraham marvelled. How does the world manage to preserve this illusion of sameness when in fact everything has been changed, irreversibly transformed, by love?

Perhaps, he thought, because strangeness, the idea of difference, is a thing to which we react with unease. The newly besotted lover makes us wince, if we are truthful; he is like the pavement-sleeper talking to an invisible companion in an empty doorway, the rummy woman staring out to sea with, in her lap, an enormous ball of string; we see them and pass on by. And the colleague at work of whom we learn, by chance, that he has unusual sexual preferences,

91

and the child preoccupied by uttering repeated sequences of sounds without any apparent meaning, and the beautiful woman seen by chance at a lighted window, allowing her nipples to be licked by her lap-dog; oh, and the brilliant scientist who spends his time at parties in corners, scratching at his posterior and then carefully examining his fingernails, and the one-legged swimmer, and . . . Abraham stopped in his tracks and blushed. How his thoughts were running on! Until this morning he had been the most methodical and ordered of men, a man of ledgers and columns, and here, Abie, just listen to yourself, all this airy-fairy tommyrot, pick up your pace now, the lady will already be in church, for the rest of your life you must do your level best not to keep your young Mrs waiting . . .

. . . Fifteen years old! Okay, okay. In our part of the world that's not so young.

↜

At St Francis's: Who's this, moaning softly in church? This short-arsed ginger-haired paleface scratching wildly at the backs of his hands? This bucktooth cherub with sweat running down his trouser-leg? – a priest, sirs. What should one expect to find in churchy surroundings if not a dog-collar? In this case, the Reverend Oliver D'Aeth, a young dog of fine Anglican pedigree, not long off the boat, and suffering, in Indian heat, from photophobia.

Like werewolves, he shunned the light. The sun's rays sought him out, however; they dogged him, no matter how doggedly he hunted for shadows. Tropical sundogs caught him unawares, they pounced, they licked him all over while he uselessly protested; whereupon the tiny champagne-bubbles of his allergy burst through the surface of his skin, and, like a mangy dog, he began uncontrollably to itch. A hangdog priest indeed, hounded by the unfailing brilliance of the days. At night he dreamed of clouds, of his faraway homeland where the sky rested cosily, in soft greys, just above his head; of clouds, but also – for though it was getting dark the tropic heat still clutched at his loins – of girls. Of, to be specific,

92

a tall girl entering St Francis's church in a floor-length red velvet skirt with her head wreathed in a distinctly un-Anglican white lace mantilla, a girl to make a lonely young priest perspire like a burst water-tank, to make him turn a most ecclesiastical shade of purple with desire.

⌒

She would come in once or twice a week to sit for a while beside da Gama's vacant tomb. The very first time she swept past D'Aeth, like an empress or a grand tragedienne, he was done for. Even before he saw her face the purpling of his own was well advanced. Then she turned towards him and it was as if he had drowned in sunlight. At once the violence of perspiration and itching assailed him; inflammations erupted on his neck and hands in spite of the cooling sweeps of the great punga fans that brushed the churchy atmosphere in long, slow strokes, as if it were a woman's hair. As Aurora approached him, it worsened: the dreadful allergy of desire. 'You look', she said sweetly, 'like a lobster quadrille. You look like a flea-ring circus after all the fleas escapofied. And what water-works, sir! Let Bombay keep its Flora Fountain because here, Reverend, we got you.'

She had him indeed. Palm of her hand. From that day on, the pain of his allergy was as nothing as compared to the pain of his unspoken, impossible love. He waited for her contempt, longed for it, for it was all she gave him. But slowly it changed something in him. Earnest and deliquescent and tongue-tied and Englishy-schoolboy as he was, a joke figure even for his own kind, teased for his inarticulacy by Emily Elphinstone the coir merchant's widow who gave him steak and kidney pud on Thursdays and hoped for (but had not yet received) something in return, he turned, behind his façade of a churchy joke, into something else entirely; his fixation darkened slowly towards hate.

Perhaps it was her attachment to the empty grave of the Portuguese explorer that made him begin to hate her, because of his own fears of dying, because how could she come by just to sit beside the tomb of Vasco da Gama and talk to it so softly, how, when the living were hanging on her every gesture, her every movement and syllable, could she prefer a morbid intimacy with a hole in the ground whence Vasco had been removed no more than fourteen years after being placed there, returning in death to the Lisbon which he left so long ago? Just once D'Aeth made the mistake of approaching Aurora and saying, is there some help you seek, daughter; at which she turned on him with all the haughty rage of the infinitely wealthy and told him, 'This is family business; go and boilofy your head.' Then, relenting slightly, she told him she came to make confession, and the Reverend D'Aeth was shaken by the blasphemy of seeking absolution from an empty grave. 'We're Church of England here,' he limply said, and that brought her to her feet, she unfurled herself and dazzled him, Venus rising in red velvet, and then she shrivelled him with her scorn. 'Soon,' she said, 'we will drive you into the sea, and you can take along this Church that only startofied because some Piss-in-Boots old king wanted a sexy younger wife.'

She eventually asked him his name. When he told her she laughed and clapped her hands. 'O, too much,' she said. 'Reverend Allover Death.' After that he couldn't talk to her any more, because she had touched a raw spot. India had unnerved Oliver D'Aeth; his dreams were either erotic fantasies of nude teas with the Widow Elphinstone on prickly brown lawns of coir matting, or else torture-nightmares in which he found himself in a place in which he was invariably beaten, like a carpet, like a mule; also kicked. Men with hats that were flat at the back so that they could stand with their backs to walls and prevent their enemies from creeping up behind them, hats made of a stiff and shiny black substance, these men waylaid him on rocky hillside paths. They pummelled him but did not speak. He, however, cried out loudly, giving up his pride. It was humiliating to be made to cry out, but he could not prevent the cries from escaping. Yet he knew, in his dreams, that this place was and would continue to be his home; he would continue to walk along this hillside path.

After he saw Aurora in St Francis's Church she started appearing in these terrible, pummelling dreams. *A man's choices are unfathomable*, she said to him once, seeing him dragging himself along after a particularly violent thrashing. Did she judge him? Sometimes he thought she must find him contemptible for putting up with such degradation. But at other times he detected the beginnings of wisdom in her eyes, in the solid musculature of her upper arms, in the birdlike angle of her head. If a man's choices are unfathomable, she seemed to be saying, then they are also beyond judgment, beyond contempt. 'I am being flayed,' he told her in his dream. 'It is my holy calling. We will never gain our humanity until we lose our skins.' When he woke he was not sure whether the dream had been inspired by his faith in the oneness of mankind, or by the photophobia that made his skin torment him so: whether it was a heroic vision, or a banality.

India was uncertainty. It was deception and illusion. Here at Fort Cochin the English had striven mightily to construct a mirage of Englishness, where English bungalows clustered around an English green, where there were Rotarians and golfers and tea-dances and cricket and a Masonic Lodge. But D'Aeth could not help seeing through the conjuring trick, couldn't help hearing the false vowels of the coir traders lying about their education, or wincing at the coarse dancing of their to-tell-the-truth-mostly-rather-common wives, or seeing the bloodsucker lizards beneath the English hedges, the parrots flying over the rather un-Home-Counties jacaranda trees. And when he looked out to sea the illusion of England vanished entirely; for the harbour could not be disguised, and no matter how Anglicised the land might be, it was contradicted by the water; as if England were being washed by an alien sea. Alien, and encroaching; for Oliver D'Aeth knew enough to be sure that the frontier between the English enclaves and the surrounding foreignness had become permeable, was beginning to dissolve. India would reclaim it all. They, the British, would – as Aurora had prophesied – be driven into the Indian Ocean – which, by an Indian perversity, was known locally as the Arabian Sea.

Still, he thought, standards must be upheld, continuity must be maintained. There was the right way and the wrong, God's road and the Left-Hand Path. Though obviously these were but metaphors, and it would not do to interpret them too literally, to sing too loud of Paradise or damn too many sinners to Hell. He added this codicil with a kind of ferocity, because India had been nibbling away at the edges of his mildness; India, where Doubting Thomas had established what one might have thought would be a Christianity of Uncertainty, in fact met the gentle reasonableness of the Church of England with great clouds of fervent incense and blasts of religious heat . . . he looked at the walls of St Francis's, at the memorials to the young English dead, and became afraid. Eighteen-year-old girls came over with the man-hunting 'fishing fleet', set foot on Indian soil, and seemed to dive straight into the ground. Nineteen-year-old scions of great families had the earth rattling on their coffin-lids within months of arriving. Oliver D'Aeth, who wondered daily when the mouth of India would gobble him down as well, found Aurora's joke about his name as tasteless as her chats with da Gama's empty grave. He didn't say so, of course. Wouldn't be right. Besides, her beauty seemed to thicken his tongue; it increased his hot confusion – for when she transfixed him with her scornful, amused gaze, he *wished the ground would swallow him up* – and it also made him itch.

↬

Aurora, with lace-covered head, and smelling strongly of sex and pepper, awaited her lover by Vasco's tomb; Oliver D'Aeth, bursting with lusts and resentments, skulked in the shadows. The only other occupants of the darkening church, in which a few yellow wall-lamps did little to lift the gloom, were three English mem-sahibs, the sisters Aspinwall, who had clucked disapprovingly when Catholic Aurora swaggered past them in scarlet – one of them went so far as to raise a perfumed handkerchief to her nose – and had at once been rewarded with the rough edge of her tongue. 'Who are you making chicken-noises at?' Aurora had demanded. 'Like chickens you don't look. More like fishes with fishbones stuck in their throat.'

And the young priest, unable to approach her, unable to leave her be, driven half-mad by her powerful odour, felt the Widow Elphinstone recede to the back of his mind, even though, at only twenty-one, she was a handsome woman, by no means without admirers. *We may not have much but we are choosy*, she had told him. Many men knocked at a young widow's door, not all of them with gentlemanly intentions. *Many call but few are answered*, she said. *A line must be drawn that is not easy to cross*. Emily Elphinstone, an upstanding young woman and a poisonously vile cook, would be at her stove, expecting Oliver D'Aeth to happen by; and so he would, so he would. In the meanwhile, however, he stayed where he was, even though his stolen glances at the woman of his dreams felt like a kind of infidelity.

Abraham arrived in a rush, and all but ran to Vasco's tomb. When Aurora clasped his hands between her own, and the two of them began to speak in urgent whispers, Oliver D'Aeth felt a surge of anger. He turned abruptly and walked away, the heels of his black boots clicking on the stone floor, the yellow pools of light revealing, to the watching Aspinwall sisters, that the young man's fists were clenched. They rose, and intercepted him at the door: had he smelled what, fanned across the church by the long, slow pungas, was unmistakable and could not be denied? – Ladies, he had. – And had he observed her, the Papist hussy, making love before their very eyes? – And perhaps he did not know, being so recently arrived, that the fellow pawing at her in God's house was not only her family's lowly employee, but, in addition, it has to be said, of the Jewish faith? – Ladies, he did not know, he was most grateful for the information. – But it was not to be tolerated, he was not to stand for it, and did he intend to act? – Ladies, he would; not at this moment, there must be no ugly scene here, but action would certainly be taken, most decisively, they need have no fear on that account. – Well! He should see to it that it was. They were returning to Ooty in the morning, but would certainly wish to see progress by their next descent. 'You samjao that baysharram pair', said the eldest sister Aspinwall, 'that this sort of tamasha is simply not the cheese.' – Ladies, your humble servant.

Later that night, Oliver D'Aeth, while taking a little port wine with the young widow, and recovering from the heaped platefuls of burned and leathery corpses which she had set before him, mentioned the evening's events in St Francis's Church. But no sooner had he spoken Aurora da Gama's name than the sweating and itches returned, even her name had the power to inflame him, and Emily burst out in shocking and uncharacteristic rage: 'Those people don't belong here any more than we do, but at least we can go home. One day India will turn against them, too, and they'll have to sink or swim.' No, no, D'Aeth demurred, here in the South there was little communal trouble of that sort, but she rounded on him ferociously. They were *outcasts*, she shouted, these peculiar Christians with their unrecognisable hobson-jobson services, not to mention these dying-out Jews, they were the least important people in the world, the tiniest of the tiny, and if they wanted to, to *rut*, then it was the least interesting thing on Earth, certainly not a thing she wished to ruin such an agreeable evening thinking about, and even if those old gargoyles from snooty Ootacamund, those *tea-ladies*, were raising a hue and cry she had no intention of spending another instant on the subject, and she was bound to say that he, Oliver, had gone down in her estimation, she would have thought he would have had the delicacy not to raise such a topic, let alone turn bright red and start *dripping* when he spoke that person's name. 'The late Mr Elphinstone', she said, her voice unsteady, 'had a weakness for chhi-chhi women. But he did me the politeness of keeping his nautch-girl infatuations to himself; whereas you, Oliver – a man of the cloth! – you sit at my table and *drool*.'

Oliver D'Aeth, having been informed by the Widow Elphinstone that he need no longer trouble to call upon her, took his leave; and vowed revenge. Emily had put it well. Aurora da Gama and her Jew were no more than flies upon the great diamond of India; how dare they so shamelessly challenge the natural order of things? They were asking to be squashed.

                      ⌣

By the empty grave of the legendary Portuguese, Abraham Zogoiby placed his hands between his young beloved's and confessed: quarrel, chucking-out, homelessness. Tears, once again, were brimming. But he had left his mother for an even tougher cookie; Aurora took charge at once. She spirited Abraham away and installed him in the refurbished Western-style Corbusier folly on Cabral Island. 'Unfortunately you are too tall and broad in the shoulder,' she told him, 'so my poor dead Daddy's little suits won't fitto on you. Tonight, but, you will not require suits.' Both of my parents would afterwards call this their true wedding night, in spite of earlier events on high among sacks of Malabar Gold, because of what happened,

after the fifteen-years-young spice-trade heiress entered the bedchamber of her lover the twenty-one-years-older duty manager dressed in nothing but moonlight, with garlands of jasmine and lily-of-the-valley plaited (by old Josy) in and out of the loose black hair which hung down behind her like a monarch's cloak, reaching almost to the cool stone floor over which her bare feet moved so lightly that for a moment the awestruck Abraham thought she was flying;

after their second spice-fragrant love-making, in which the older man surrendered completely to the will of the younger woman, as though his ability to make choices had been exhausted by the consequences of the act of choosing her;

after Aurora murmured her secrets in his ear, *because for many years I have confessed only to a hole, but now, my husband, I can tell you everything*, the murder of her grandmother, the old woman's dying curse, everything, and Abraham without flinching accepted his fate; banished from the fellowship of his own people, he took upon himself the matriarch's last malediction, which Epifania whispered into Aurora's ear and whose sweet poison the young woman now dropped into his: *a house divided against itself cannot stand*, that's what she said, my husband, *may your house be for ever partitioned, may its foundations turn to dust, may your children rise up against you, and may your fall be hard*;

after Abraham comforted Aurora by vowing to disprove the curse, to stand beside her, shoulder to shoulder, through the worst life had to offer;

and after he said, yes, to marry her he would take the great step, he would accept instruction and enter the Church of Rome, and in the presence of her naked body which inspired in him a kind of religious awe the thing did not seem so difficult to say, in this matter too he would surrender to her will, her cultural conventions, even though she had less faith than a mosquito, even though there was a voice within him uttering a command he did not repeat aloud, a voice which told him that he must guard his Jewishness in the innermost chamber of his soul, that at the core of his being he must build a room nobody could enter and keep his truth there, his secret identity, and only then could he give up the rest of himself for love:

then,

the door of their nuptial chamber flew open, and there, in pyjamas with a lantern and a Wee Willie Winkie nightcap, was Aires da Gama looking like a storybook picture except for his expression of counterfeit wrath; and in one of Epifania's old muslin mob-caps and ruffled-neck nighties, Carmen Lobo da Gama, doing her best to look horrified but failing to push the envy off her face; and slightly behind them was the avenging angel, the traitor, bright pink and sweating profusely: of course, Oliver D'Aeth. But Aurora was not able to contain herself, would not behave according to the rules of this tropicalised Victorian melodrama. 'Aires-uncle! Aunty Sahara!' she cried, gaily. 'But where have you dumpoed dear Jaw-jaw? Won't he be upset? Because tonight you are taking for a walk a dog of a different collar.' At which Oliver D'Aeth grew even redder.

'Whore of Babylon,' Carmen roared, attempting to get things back on track. 'Harlot's seed is harlot indeed!' Aurora under a white linen bedsheet stretched her long body for maximum provocation; a breast burst into view, caused a sharp ecclesiastical gasp, and obliged Aires to address his remarks to the Telefunken radiogram. 'Zogoiby, for God's sake. Do you lack all common decency, man?'

' "*That, sir, is my niece!*" Waugh-waugh-waugh! So pompous, with his track record!' my mother guffawed when the story was told on Malabar Hill. 'Folks, I split my sides. "*What is the meaning of this?*" Stupid ass. I told him straight. The meaning of this is marriage, I told him. "Look," I said, "here is a priest, and close family members are present, and you are cho chweetly giving me

100

away. Turn on the radiogram and maybe they'll play a wedding march." '

Aires ordered Abraham to dress and leave; Aurora countermanded the order. Aires threatened the lovers with police intervention; Aurora replied, 'And, Aires-uncle, is there nothing for you to fear from nosy cops?' Aires coloured deeply, and with a muttered *we'll discuss this further in the a.m.* beat a retreat, followed hastily by Oliver D'Aeth. Carmen stood in the doorway for a moment, with her mouth hanging open. Then she also staged her exit: slamming the door. Aurora rolled over to Abraham, who had covered his face with his hands. 'Here I come, ready or not,' she whispered. 'Mister, here comes the bride.'

⌐

Abraham Zogoiby covered his face that night in August 1939 because he had been assailed by fear; not fear of Aires or Carmen or the photophobic priest, but a sudden terrible apprehension that the ugliness of life might defeat its beauty; that love did not make lovers invulnerable. Nevertheless, he thought, even if the world's beauty and love were on the edge of destruction, theirs would still be the only side to be on; defeated love would still be love, hate's victory would not make it other than it was. 'Better, however, to win.' He had promised Aurora looking-after, and he would be as good as his word.

⌐

My mother painted *The Scandal*, I don't need to tell any art-lovers, since the huge canvas is right there in the National Gallery of Modern Art in New Delhi, filling up a whole wall. Go past Raja Ravi Verma's *Woman Holding a Fruit*, that young bejewelled temptress whose sidelong gaze of open sensuality reminds me of pictures of the young Aurora herself; turn the corner at Gaganendranath Tagore's spooky water-colour *Jadoogar (Magician)*, in which a monochrome Indian version of the distorted world of *The Cabinet of Dr Caligari* stands upon a shocking orange carpet (and, I confess, I am reminded of the house on Cabral Island by the harsh shadows, skulking figures and shifting perspectives of this picture, to say nothing of the strange, half-screened figure, at its heart, of a gowned'n'crowned giantess); and – turn away quickly now! This is not the moment to get into the arch-cosmopolitan Aurora Zogoiby's contemptuous opinion of the work of her older, and determinedly village-oriented rival for the title of Greatest Woman Painter! – facing Amrita Sher-Gil's masterpiece *The Ancient Story-Teller*, there it is: Aurora at her best, in my humble or maybe not-so-humble opinion the equal for colour and movement of any Matisse dance-circle, only in this densely crowded picture with its deliberately garish magentas, its scandalous neon greens, the dance is not of bodies but of tongues, and all the tongues of the highly coloured figures whispering *lick-lick-lick* into one another's ears are black, black, black.

I will not speak here of the picture's painterly qualities, but simply point out some of its thousand-and-one anecdotes, for as we know Aurora had learned much from the narrative-painting traditions of the South: see, here is the repeated and cryptic figure of a ginger-coloured, sweating priest with the head of a dog, and we can agree, I hope, that this is, in many ways, the figure which orchestrates the action of the painting. Look! There he is, a splash of ginger lurking in the blue tiles of the synagogue; and again, at the Santa Cruz Cathedral, painted from top to bottom with fake balconies, fake garlands and of course the Stations of the Cross, there! You can see the dog-vicar whispering in the ear of a shocked Catholic Bishop, represented as a Fish, in full regalia.

The scandal – I should say *The Scandal* – is a great spiral of a scene, into which Aurora has woven both the scandals that enveloped the da Gamas of Cochin, both the burning spice-fields and the lovers whose smell of spices gave their game away. Warring Lobo and Menezes clans can be spotted on the mountains that form the backdrop for the spiralling throng: the Menezes people all have serpents' heads and tails and the Lobos, of course, are wolves. But in the foreground are the streets and waterways of Cochin, and they teem with scandalised congregations: fish-Catholics, dog-Anglicans, and the Jews all painted Delft blue, like figures in Chinese tiles. The Maharaja, the Resident, various officers of law are shown receiving petitions; action of various sorts is being demanded. *Lick-lick-lick!* Placards are carried, burning torches raised. There are armed men defending godowns against the righteous arsonists of the town. Yes, tempers are running high in this painting: as in life. Aurora always said that the picture had its origins in her family history, irritating those critics who objected to such historicising, which reduced art to mere 'gossip' . . . but she never denied that the figures at the heart of the angrily swirling spiral were based upon Abraham and herself. They are the still heart of the whirlwind, asleep on a peaceful island at the centre of the storm; they lie with their bodies entwined in an open pavilion set in a formal garden of waterfalls and willow-trees and flowers, and if you look closely at them, for they are small, you will see that they have feathers instead of skin: and their heads are the heads of eagles, and their eagerly licking tongues are not black, but juicy, plump, and red. 'The storm died down,' my father told me when he took me to see this picture as a boy. 'But we soared above it, we defied the lot of them, and we endured.'

～

I want – finally! – to say something good at this point about Great-Uncle Aires and his wife, Carmen/Sahara. I want to offer arguments in extenuation of their behaviour: that in fact they had been genuinely worried on Aurora's behalf when they burst in on her little love-nest, that after all it is no simple matter for a penniless thirty-six-year-old man to deflower a fifteen-year-old millionairess. I want to say that Aires and Carmen's lives were painful and twisted, because they were living out a lie, and so sometimes their behaviour came out twisted, too. Like Jaw-jaw-Jawaharlal, they made plenty of noise but didn't draw much blood. Above all, I want to emphasise that they very quickly regretted their brief alliance with the Angel Allover-Death, and when the scandal was at its height, when mobs came within feet of destroying their warehouses, when there was talk of lynching the Jew and his child-whore, when the dwindling population of the Mattancherri Jewtown had for a few days to fear for their lives and the news from

Germany didn't sound as if it came from very far away, Aires and Carmen stood by the lovers: they closed ranks, defended family interests. And if Aires had not stood before the godown-threatening throng and shouted down its leaders – an act of immense personal courage – and if he and Carmen had not personally visited all the city's religious and secular authorities and insisted that what had happened between Abraham and Aurora was a love-match, and that as her legal guardians they made no objection to it, then perhaps things would have spiralled out of control. As it was, however, the scandal fizzled out in a few short days. At the Masonic Lodge (Aires had recently become a Freemason), local worthies congratulated Mr da Gama on his sensitive handling of the affair. The sisters Aspinwall, returning too late from 'Snooty Ooty', missed all the fun.

No victory is ever complete. The Bishop of Cochin refused to countenance the idea of Abraham's conversion, and Moshe Cohen the leader of the Cochin Jews declared that under no circumstances could any Jewish marriage be performed. This is why – I now reveal for the first time – my parents were so keen to speak of the event in the Corbusier chalet as their wedding night. When they went to Bombay, they would call themselves Mr and Mrs, and Aurora took the name Zogoiby and made it famous; but, ladies and gents, there were no wedding bells.

I salute their unmarried defiance; and note that Fate so arranged matters that neither of them – irreligious as they were – needed to break confessional links with the past, after all. I, however, was raised neither as Catholic nor as Jew. I was both, and nothing: a jewholic-anonymous, a cathjew nut, a stewpot, a mongrel cur. I was – what's the word these days? – *atomised*. Yessir: a real Bombay mix.

*Bastard*: I like the sound of the word. *Baas*, a smell, a stinky-poo. *Turd*, no translation required. Ergo, *Bastard*, a smelly shit; like, for example, me.

⌒

Two weeks after the end of the scandal he had unleashed against my future parents, Oliver D'Aeth was visited by a particularly nasty anopheles mosquito, which crawled, while he slept, through a hole in his mosquito-net. Soon after this visit by the mosquito of poetic justice, he contracted the malaria of just desserts, and in spite of being nursed night and day by the Widow Elphinstone, who mopped his brow with the cold compresses of dashed hopes, he sweated mightily, and died.

Man, but I'm in a compassionate sort of mood today. What do you know? I feel sorry for that poor bugger, too.

# 8

THE THIRD, AND MOST shocking, of our family scandals never became public knowledge, but now that my father Abraham Zogoiby has given up the ghost at ninety years of age I no longer feel any compunction about letting his skeletons out of the cupboard . . . *it's better to win* was his unchanging motto, and from the moment he entered Aurora's life she understood that he meant what he said; because no sooner had the hullabaloo about their love affair died down than, with a chug of smoke from its funnels and a loud *whom whom whom* from its horn, the cargo ship *Marco Polo* set off for the London Docks.

That evening Abraham returned to Cabral Island after a whole day's absence, and when he went so far as to pat the bulldog Jawaharlal on the head it was plain that he was bursting with delight. Aurora, at her most imperious, demanded to know where he'd been. In reply he pointed at the departing boat and made, for the first of many times in their life together, the sign that meant *don't ask*: he drew an imaginary needle and thread through his lips, as if to sew them shut. 'I told you', he said, 'that I would take care of the unimportant things: but to do it, sometimes I must go quietly to Thread-Needle Street.'

At that time the newspapers, the radio, the gossip in the streets spoke of nothing but war – to be frank, Hitler and Churchill did as much as anyone to prevent my scandalous parents' goose from being cooked; the outbreak of World War II was a pretty effective diversionary tactic – and the prices of pepper and spices had grown unstable on account of the loss of the German market, and the growing number of stories about the risks to cargo vessels. Particularly persistent were the rumours about German plans to paralyse the British Empire by sending warships and submarines –

people were starting to learn the term *U-boats* – into the shipping lanes of the Indian Ocean as well as the Atlantic, and trading vessels (so everybody believed) would be as high-priority a target as the British Navy; on top of which there would be mines. In spite of all this, Abraham had worked his magic trick, and the *Marco Polo* was even now disappearing out of Cochin harbour and heading West. *Don't ask*, his lip-stitching fingers warned; and Aurora, my empress of a mother, put up her hands, brought them together for a little round of applause, and asked no more. 'I always wanted a magician,' was all she said. 'Looks like I found one after all.'

I marvel at my mother when I think of it. How did she stifle her curiosity? Abraham had done the impossible, and she was content not to know how: she was prepared to live in ignorance, as the Young Lady of Thread-Needle Street. And in the years that followed, as the family business diversified triumphantly in a hundred and one directions, as the treasure-mountains grew from mere Gama-Ghats into Zogoiby-Himalayas, did she never imagine – did she never think for one moment – but of course, she must have; hers was a chosen blindness, her complicity the complicity of silence, of don't-tell-me-things-I-don't-want-to-know, of quiet-I-am-busy-with-my-Great-Work. And such was the force of her not-seeing that none of us looked either. What a cover she was for Abraham Zogoiby's operations! What a brilliant, legitimising façade . . . but I must not run ahead of my story. For the present, it is necessary only to reveal – no, it is *high time* that somebody revealed it! – that my father, Abraham Zogoiby, turned out to have a genuine talent for changing reluctant minds.

I have it from the horse's mouth: he spent most of his missing hours among the dock-workers, drawing aside the largest and strongest of those known to him, and pointing out that if the Nazis' attempt at a blockade succeeded, if businesses like the da Gamas' Camoens Fifty Per Cent Corp. (Private) Limited were to go under, then they, the stevedores, and their families, too, would quickly sink into destitution. 'That *Marco Polo* captain,' he murmured contemptuously, 'by his cowardice in refusing to sail, is snatching food from your kiddies' plates.'

Once he had succeeded in building an army strong enough to

overpower the ship's crew, should the need arise, Abraham went by himself to see the chief clerks. Messrs Tejpattam, Kalonjee and Mirchandalchini met him with ill-concealed distaste, for had he not been their humble minion until very recently, theirs to command as they pleased? Whereas – thanks to his seduction of that cheap hussy, the Proprietor – he now had the effrontery to come laying down the law like a boss of bosses ... however, having no option, they followed his instructions. Urgent and insistent telegraphic messages were sent to the owners and the master of the *Marco Polo*, and a short while after that Abraham Zogoiby, still unaccompanied, was taken out to the cargo-boat by the harbour pilot himself.

The meeting with the ship's captain didn't take long. 'I laid out the total situation frankly,' my father told me in his great old age. 'Necessity of prompt action to corner the British market as compensation for loss of German income, so on so forth. I was generous, that is always wise in negotiation. Because of his courage, I said, we would make him a rich man just when he reached East India Dock. This he liked. This made him well disposed.' He paused, gasping, trying to fill the tattered remnant of his lungs. 'Naturally, there was not only this bowl of carrot-*halva* but a big *bumboo*-stick as well. I informed Skipper that if there was no compliance by sunset then to my great regret, speaking as a colleague, his ship would go to the bottom of the harbour and he personally would, alas, be required to accompany the same.'

Would he have carried out his threat? I asked him. For a moment I thought he was going to reach for his invisible needle and thread; but then a coughing fit seized him, he hacked and hawked, his milky old eyes streamed. Only when the convulsions subsided a little did I understand that my father had been laughing. 'Boy, boy,' croaked Abraham Zogoiby, 'never try an ultimatum unless'n'until you are ready and willing to have the ultimatee call your bluff.'

The master of the *Marco Polo* did not dare call the bluff; but someone else did. The cargo ship journeyed across the ocean, travelling beyond rumour, beyond calculation, until the German cruiser *Medea* holed her when she was no more than a few hours away from the island of Socotra off the tip of the Horn of Africa. She sank quickly; all hands, and the full cargo, were lost.

'I played my ace,' my antique father reminisced. 'But, damme, it got trumped.'

~

Who could blame Flory Zogoiby for going a little loco after her only child walked out on her? Who could begrudge her the hours upon hours she had begun to spend straw-hatted, sucking her gums on a bench in the synagogue entrance-hall, slapping down patience cards or clicking away with mah-jong tiles, and delivering herself of a non-stop tirade against 'Moors', a concept which had by now expanded to include just about everyone? And who would not have forgiven her for thinking she was seeing things, when prodigal Abraham marched up to her, bold as brass, one fine day in the spring of 1940, grinning sweetly all over his face as if he'd just located some rainbow-end pot of gold?

'So, Abie,' she said slowly, not looking directly at him in case she found she could see through him, which would prove that she had finally cracked into little pieces. 'You want to play a game?'

His smile widened. He was so handsome that it made her angry. What business did he have coming here, pouring his good looks all over her without any warning? 'I know you, Abie boy,' she said, still staring at her cards. 'When you got that smile on, you're in trouble, and the wider the smile, the deeper the mud. Looks to me like you can't handle what you got, so you came running to mother. I never in all my days saw you smile so big. Sit! Play one-two hands.'

'No games, mother,' Abraham said, his smile almost touching his ear-lobes. 'Can we go inside or does the whole of Jewtown have to know our business?'

Now she looked him in the eye. 'Sit,' she said. He sat; she dealt for nine-card rummy. 'You think you can beat me? Not me, son. You never had a chance.'

A ship sank. Abraham's new trader family's fortunes were placed once more in crisis. I am pleased to say that this led to no unseemly squabbling on Cabral Island – the truce between old and new clan members held firm. But the crisis was real enough; after much cajoling, and other, less, mentionable tactics from the depths of Thread-Needle Street, a second and then a third da Gama shipment had been sent on their way, going the long way round via Good Hope to avoid North African dangers. In spite of this precaution and the British Navy's efforts to police all vital sea-routes – though it must be said, and Pandit Nehru said it from jail, that the British attitude to Indian shipping was, to understate matters, more than a little lax – these two ships also ended up adding spice to the ocean-bed; and the C-50 condiment empire (and, who knows, perhaps also the heart of Empire itself, deprived of peppery inspiration) began to totter and sway. Overheads – wage-bills, maintenance costs, interest on loans – mounted. But this is not a company report, and so you must simply take it from me: things had reached a sorry pass when beaming Abraham, latterly a powerful merchant of Cochin, returned to Jewtown. *Hath all his ventures failed? What, not one hit?* – Not one. Okay-fine? Then let's get on. I want to tell you a fairy-tale.

In the end, stories are what's left of us, we are no more than the few tales that persist. And in the best of the old yarns, the ones we ask for over'n'over, there are lovers, it's true, but the parts we go for are the bits where shadows fall across the lovers' path. Poisoned apple, bewitched spindle, Black Queen, wicked witch, baby-stealing goblins, that's the stuff. So: once upon a time, my father Abraham Zogoiby gambled heavily, and lost. But he had made a vow: *I'll take care of things.* And accordingly, when all other devices failed, his desperation was so great that he was obliged to come, grinning mightily, to plead with his maddened mother. – For what? – What else? Her treasure chest.

～

Abraham swallowed his pride and came a-begging, which in itself told Flory all she needed to know about the strength of her hand. He had made a boast he could not make good; spinning-straw-into-gold, that kind of old-time stuff; and was too proud to admit his failure to his in-laws, to tell them they must mortgage or sell off their great estate. *They gave you your head, Abie, and see, here it is on a plate.* She made him wait a little, but not too long; then agreed. Capital needed? Jewels from an old box? Then OK, he could take. All speeches of gratitude, explanations of temporary cash-flow problems, disquisitions upon the especially persuasive properties of jewels when sailors are being requested to risk their lives, all offers of interest and pecuniary profit were waved away. 'Jewels I am giving,' Flory Zogoiby said. 'A greater jewel must be my reward.'

Her son failed to grasp her meaning. Certainly, he radiantly vowed, she would receive full recompense for her loan, once their ship came in; and if she preferred to receive her share in the form of emeralds, then he would undertake to select the finest stones. Thus he babbled; but he had entered darker waters than he knew, and beyond them lay a black forest in which, in a clearing, a little mannikin danced, singing *Rumpelstiltskin is my name* . . . 'This is by-the-by,' Flory interrupted. 'Return of loan I do not doubt. But for so risky an investment only the greatest jewel can be my prize. You must give me your firstborn son.'

(Two origins have been suggested for Flory's box of emeralds, family heirloom and smugglers' hoard. Setting sentiment aside, reason and logic recommend the latter; and if they are right, if Flory was speculating with the gangsters' stockpile, then her own survival was in doubt. Does it make her demand less shocking that she risked herself to gain the human life for which she asked? Was it, in fact, heroic?)

*Bring me your firstborn* . . . A line from legends hung between this mother and this son. Abraham, aghast, told her it was out of the question, it was evil, unthinkable. 'Wiped that stupid smile off your mouth, Abie, didn't I?' Flory grimly asked. 'And don't think you can grab the box and run. It is in another cache. You need my stones? Give me your eldest boy; his flesh'n'skin'n'bones.'

O mother you are mad, mother. O my ancestor I am much afeared that thou art stark raving nuts. 'Aurora is not expecting as yet,' Abraham muttered weakly.

'Oho-ho Abie,' giggled Flory. 'You think I'm crazy, boy? I'll kill and eat him up, or drink his blood, or what? I am not a rich woman, child, but there is enough food on my table without consuming family members.' She grew serious. 'Listen: you can see him when-when you want. Even the mother can come. Outings, holidays, these also are OK. Only send him to live with me so I can do my level best to bring him up as the thing you have ceased to be, that is, a male Jew of Cochin. I lost a son; I'll save a grandson at least.' She did not add her secret prayer: *And maybe, in saving him, rediscover a God of my own.*

As the world fell back into place, Abraham, in the dizziness of his relief, the great hunger of his need, and the absence of an actual pregnancy, acquiesced. But Flory was implacable, wanted it in writing. 'To my mother, Flory Zogoiby, I hereby promise my firstborn male child, to be raised in the Jewish ways.' Signed, sealed, delivered. Flory, snatching the paper, waved it above her head, picked up her skirt and capered in a circle by the synagogue door. *An oath, an oath, I have an oath in heaven . . . I stay here on my bond.* And for these promised pounds of unborn flesh she delivered Abraham her wealth; and, paid and bribed by jewels, his last-chance argosy set sail.

Of these privy matters, however, Aurora was not informed.

⤶

And it came to pass that the ship was brought safely to port, and after it another, and another, and another. While the world's fortunes worsened, the da Gama-Zogoiby axis prospered. (How did my father ensure his cargo's protection by the British Navy? Surely it is not being suggested that emeralds, contraband or heirloom, found their way into Imperial pockets? What a bold stroke that would have been, what an all-or-nothing throw! And how implausible to suggest that such an offer might have been accepted! No, no, one must just put what happened down to naval diligence – for the marauding *Medea* was finally sunk – or to the Nazis' preoccupations in other theatres of the war; or call it a miracle; or blind, dumb luck.) At the earliest opportunity, Abraham had paid off the jewel-money borrowed from his mother, and offered her a generous additional sum by way of profit. However, he left brusquely, without answering, when she refused the bonus with a plaintive call: 'And the jewel, my contracted reward? And when will that be paid?' *I crave the law, the penalty and the forfeit of my bond.*

Aurora continued to be without child: but knew nothing of a signed paper. The months lengthened towards a year. Still Abraham held his tongue. By now he was the sole in-charge of the family business; Aires never really had the heart for it, and after his new nephew-in-law had performed his triumphant rescue act the surviving da Gama brother retired gracefully – as they say – into private life . . . on the first of every month Flory sent her son the great merchant a message. 'I hope you are not slacking off; I want my precious stone.' (How strange, how *fated*, that in those blazing days of their hot-pepper love Aurora conceived no child! Because had there been a boy, and here I speak as my parents' sole male issue, then the bone of contention – the *flesh'n'skin'n'bones* – could have been me.)

Again he offered her money; again, she refused. At one point he pleaded; how could he ask his young wife to send a newborn son away, to be cared for by one who hated her? Flory was implacable. 'Should've thought before.' Finally his anger took control, and he defied her. 'Your piece of paper buys nothing,' he shouted down the telephone. 'Wait on and see who can pay more for a judge.' Flory's green stones could not match the family's renewed affluence; and if indeed they were hot rocks, she'd think twice before showing them to court officers, even those willing to feather their nests. What were her options? She had lost her belief in divine retribution. Vengeance was for this world.

Another avenger! Another ginger dog, or murderous mosquito! What an epidemic of getting-even runs through my tale, what a malaria cholera typhoid of eye-for-tooth and tit-for-tat! No wonder I have ended up . . . But my ending up must not be told before my starting out. Here's Aurora on her seventeenth birthday in the spring of 1941, visiting Vasco's tomb alone; and here, waiting in the shadows, is an old crone . . .

When she saw Flory dart towards her out of the shadows of the

church, Aurora thought for a startled moment that her grandmother Epifania had risen from the grave. Then she collected
herself with a little smile, remembering how she had once ridiculed
her father's ghostly notions; no, no, this was just some hag, and
what was that paper she was thrusting out? Sometimes beggar-
women gave you such papers, *Have mercy in the name of God, cannot
speak, and 12 kiddies to support.* 'Forgive me, sorry,' Aurora said
perfunctorily, and began to turn away. Then the woman spoke her
name. 'Madam Auroral' (Loudly.) 'My Abie's Roman whore! This
paper you must read.'

She turned back; took the document Abraham's mother
proffered; and read.

~

Portia, a rich girl, supposedly intelligent, who acquiesces in her late
father's will – that she must marry any man who solves the riddle of
the three caskets, gold silver lead – is presented to us by
Shakespeare as the very archetype of justice. But listen closely;
when her suitor the Prince of Morocco fails the test, she sighs:

> *A gentle riddance. Draw the curtains: go.*
> *Let all of his complexion choose me so.*

No lover then, of Moors! No, no; she loves Bassanio, who by a
happy chance picks the right box, the one containing Portia's
picture (*'thou, thou meagre lead'*). Lend an ear, therefore, to this
paragon's explanation of his choice.

> *. . . ornament is but the guilèd shore,*
> *To a most dangerous sea; the beauteous scarf*
> *Veiling an Indian beauty; in a word,*
> *The seeming truth which cunning times put on . . .*

Ah, yes: for Bassanio, Indian beauty is like a 'dangerous sea'; or,
analogous to 'cunning times'! Thus Moors, Indians, and of course
'the Jew' (Portia can only bring herself to use Shylock's name on
two occasions; the rest of the time she identifies him purely by his

race) are waved away. A fair-minded couple, indeed; a pair of Daniels, come to judgment . . . I adduce all this evidence to show why, when I say that our tale's Aurora was no Portia, I do not mean it wholly as a criticism. She was rich (like Portia in this), but chose her own husband (unlike in this); she was certainly intelligent (like), and, at seventeen, near the height of her very Indian beauty (most unlike). Her husband was – as Portia's could never have been – a Jew. But, as the maid of Belmont denied Shylock his bloody pound, so my mother found a way, with justice, of denying Flory the child.

'Tell your mother', Aurora commanded Abraham that night, 'that there will be no children born in this house while she remains alive.' She moved him out of her bedroom. 'You do your work and I'll do mine,' she said. 'But the work Flory is waiting for, that she never will see.'

⤳

She, too, had drawn a line. That night she scrubbed her body until the skin was raw and not a trace of love's peppery perfume remained. ('*I scrubbofy and tubbofy* . . .') Then she locked and bolted her bedroom door, and fell into a deep and dreamless sleep. In the following months, however, her work – drawings, paintings, and terrible little skewered dolls moulded in red clay – grew full of witches, fire, apocalypse. Later she would destroy most of this 'Red' material, with the consequence that the surviving pieces have gained greatly in value; they have rarely been seen in the saleroom and when they were, a fevered excitement prevailed.

For several nights Abraham mewled piteously at her locked door, but was not admitted. At length, Cyrano-fashion, he hired a local accordionist and ballad-singer who serenaded her in the courtyard below her window, while he, Abraham, stood idiotically beside the music-man and mouthed the words of the old love-songs. Aurora opened her shutters, and threw flowers; then the water from the flower-vase; and finally the vase itself. All three scored direct hits. The vase, a heavy piece of stoneware, struck Abraham on his left ankle, breaking it. He was taken, wet and yowling, to hospital, and thereafter did not try to change her mind. Their lives moved along diverging paths.

After the episode of the stone vase, Abraham always walked with a slight limp. Misery was etched in every line of his face, misery dragged down the corners of his mouth and damaged his good looks. Aurora continued, contrastingly, to blossom. Genius was being born in her, filling the empty spaces in her bed, her heart, her womb. She needed no-one but herself.

❧

She was absent from Cochin from most of the war years, at first on long visits to Bombay, where she met, and was taken up by, a young Parsee, Kekoo Mody, who had begun dealing in contemporary Indian artists – not, at the time, a very lucrative field – from his home on Cuffe Parade. Limping Abraham did not accompany her on these trips; and when she left, her invariable parting words were, 'Okay, fine, Abie! Mindofy the store.' So it was in his absence, away from his lamed, hangdog expression of unbearable longing, that Aurora Zogoiby grew into the giant public figure we all know, the great beauty at the heart of the nationalist movement, the loose-haired bohemian marching boldly alongside Vallabh-bhai Patel and Abul Kalam Azad when they took out processions, the confidante – and, according to persistent rumours, mistress – of Pandit Nehru, his 'friend of friends', who would later vie with Edwina Mountbatten for his heart. Distrusted by Gandhiji, loathed by Indira Gandhi, her arrest after the Quit India resolution of 1942 made her a national heroine. Jawaharlal Nehru was jailed, too, in Ahmadnagar Fort, where in the *cinquecento* the warrior-princess Chand Bibi had resisted the armies of the Mughal Empire – of the Grand Mughal Akbar himself. People began saying that Aurora Zogoiby was the new Chand Bibi, standing up against a different and even more powerful Empire, and her face began to appear everywhere. Painted on walls, caricatured in the papers, the maker of images became an image herself. She spent two years in Dehra Dun District Jail. When she emerged she was twenty years old, and her hair was white. She returned to Cochin, translated into myth.

Abraham's first words to her were: 'Store is in good shape.' She nodded briefly, and went back to work.

Some things had changed on Cabral Island. During Aurora's jail term, Aires da Gama's long-time lover, the man known to us as Prince Henry the Navigator, had fallen seriously ill. He was found to be suffering from a particularly pernicious strain of syphilis, and it soon became clear that Aires, too, had been infected. Syphilitic eruptions on his face and body made it impossible for him to leave home; he became gaunt of body and hollow of eye and looked two decades older than his forty-odd years. His wife Carmen, who had long ago threatened to kill him for his infidelities, came instead to sit beside his bedside. 'Look what happened to you, my Irish-man,' she said. 'You're going to die on me or what?' He turned his head on the pillow and saw nothing but compassion in her eyes. 'We better get you well,' she said, 'or who am I going to dance with the rest of my life? You,' and here she made the briefest of pauses, and her colour heightened dramatically, 'and your Prince Henry, too.'

Prince Henry the Navigator was given a room in the house on Cabral Island, and in the months that followed Carmen, with an inexhaustible determination, supervised the two men's treatment by the finest and most discreet – because most highly paid – specialists in town. Both patients slowly recovered; and the day came when Aires, sitting out in the garden in a silk dressing-gown with Jawaharlal the bulldog and drinking a fresh lime-water, was visited by his wife, who suggested, quietly, that there was no need for Prince Henry to move out. 'Too many wars in this house and outside it,' she told him. 'Let us make at least this one three-cornered peace.'

In the middle of 1945, Aurora Zogoiby reached adulthood. She spent her twenty-first birthday in Bombay, without Abraham, at a party given for her by Kekoo Mody and attended by most of the city's artistic and political luminaries. At that time the British had released the Congress prisoners, because new negotiations were in the air; Nehru himself had been freed, and sent Aurora a long letter from a house called Armsdell in Simla, apologising for his absence from her celebrations. 'My voice is very hoarse,' he wrote. 'I can't make out why I attract these crowds. Very gratifying, no doubt, but also very trying and often irritating. Here in Simla I have had to go out to the balcony and verandah frequently to give *darshan*. I doubt if I shall ever be able to go out for a walk because of crowds following, except at dead of night . . . You should be grateful that I have spared you this experience by staying away.' As a birthday present, he sent her Hogben's *Science for the Citizen* and *Mathematics for the Million*, 'to leaven your artistic spirit with a little of the other side of the mind'.

She immediately gave the books to Kekoo Mody, with a little grimace. 'Jawahar is keen on all this boffin-shoffin. But I am a single-minded girl.'

⤚

As for Flory Zogoiby: she was still alive, but had grown a little strange of late. Then, one day near the end of July, she was found crawling around the Mattancherri synagogue floor on her hands and knees, claiming that she could see the future in the blue Chinese tiles, and prophesying that very soon a country not far from China would be eaten up by giant, cannibal mushrooms. Old Moshe Cohen had the sad duty of relieving her of her duties. His daughter Sara – still a spinster – had heard of a church near the sea in Travancore where mentally troubled people of all religions had started going, because it was thought to have the power of curing madness; she told Moshe she wanted to take Flory there, and the chandler agreed to pay all the expenses of the trip.

Flory spent her first day sitting in the dust of the compound outside the magic church, drawing lines in the dirt with a twig, and talking volubly to the invisible, because non-existent, grandson by her side. On the second day of their stay, Sara left Flory alone for an hour while she walked along the beach and watched the fishermen in their longboats come and go. When she returned there was pandemonium in the church compound. One of the madmen assembled there had committed fiery suicide by pouring petrol over himself at the foot of the life-sized figure of Christ crucified. When he struck the fatal match the *whoosh* of flame had licked murderously at the hem of an old lady's floral-printed skirt, and she, too, had been engulfed. It was my grandmother. Sara brought the body home, and it was laid to rest in the Jewtown cemetery. Abraham remained by her graveside for a long time after the funeral, and when Sara Cohen took his hand, he did not draw it away.

A few days later a giant mushroom cloud ate the Japanese city of Hiroshima, and on hearing the news Moshe Cohen the chandler burst into hot, bitter tears.

⌒

They have almost all gone now, the Jews of Cochin. Less than fifty of them remaining, and the young departed to Israel. It is the last generation; arrangements have been made for the synagogue to be taken over by the government of the State of Kerala, which will run it as a museum. The last bachelors and spinsters sun themselves toothlessly in the childless Mattancherri lanes. This, too, is an extinction to be mourned; not an extermination, such as occurred elsewhere, but the end, nevertheless, of a story that took two thousand years to tell.

By the end of 1945, Aurora and Abraham had left Cochin and bought a sprawling bungalow set amid tamarind, plane and jack-fruit trees on the slopes of Malabar Hill, Bombay, with a steeply terraced garden looking down on Chowpatty Beach, the Back Bay and Marine Drive. 'Cochin is finished, anyway,' Abraham reasoned. 'From a strictly business point of view the move makes complete sense.' He left hand-picked men in charge of the operation down South, and would continue to make regular inspection trips over the years . . . but Aurora needed no reasoned arguments. On the day they moved in she went to the look-out point where the garden's terracing ended in a vertiginous drop towards black rocks and foaming sea; and at the top of her voice she out-screamed the wheeling *chils* for joy.

Abraham shyly waited some yards back, hands clasped before him, looking for all the world like the duty manager he once was. 'I hope so that the new locale will prove beneficial to your creative process,' he said with painful formality. Aurora came running towards him and leapt into his arms.

'Creative process you're after, is it?' she demanded, looking at him as she had not looked for years. 'Then come on, mister, let's go indoors and create.'

# II
# MALABAR MASALA

# 9

ONCE A YEAR, MY mother Aurora Zogoiby liked to dance higher than the gods. Once a year, the gods came to Chowpatty Beach to bathe in the filthy sea: fat-bellied idols by the thousand, papier-mâché effigies of the elephant-headed deity Ganesha or Ganpati Bappa, swarming towards the water astride papier-mâché rats – for Indian rats, as we know, carry gods as well as plagues. Some of these tusk'n'tail duos were small enough to be borne on human shoulders, or cradled in human arms; others were the size of small mansions, and were pulled along on great-wheeled wooden carts by hundreds of disciples. There were, in addition, many Dancing Ganeshas, and it was these wiggle-hipped Ganpatis, love-handled and plump of gut, against whom Aurora competed, setting her profane gyrations against the jolly jiving of the much-replicated god. Once a year, the skies were full of Color-by-DeLuxe clouds: pink and purple, magenta and vermilion, saffron and green, these powder-clouds, squirted from re-used insecticide guns, or floating down from some bursting balloon-cluster wafting across the sky, hung in the air above the deities 'like aurora-not-borealis-but-bombayalis', as the painter Vasco Miranda used to say. Also sky-high above crowds and gods, year after year – for forty-one years in all – fearless upon the precipitous ramparts of our Malabar Hill bungalow, which in a spirit of ironic mischief or perversity she had insisted on naming *Elephanta*, there twirled the almost-divine figure of our very own Aurora Bombayalis, plumed in a series of dazzle-hued mirrorwork outfits, outdoing in finery even the festival sky with its hanging gardens of powdered colour. Her white hair flying out around her in long loose exclamations (O prophetically premature white hair of my ancestors!), her exposed belly not old-bat-fat but fit-cat-flat, her bare feet stamping, her ankles a-jingle with silver jhunjhunna bell-bracelets, snapping her neck from side to side, speaking incomprehensible volumes with her hands, the great painter danced her defiance, she danced her contempt for the perversity of humankind, which led these huge crowds to risk death-by-trampling 'just to dumpofy their dollies in the drink,' as she liked incredulously, and with much raising of eyes to skies and wry twisting of the mouth, to jeer.

'Human perversity is greater than human heroism' – jingle-*jangle!* – 'or cowardice' – th-th-*thump!* – 'or art,' my dancing mother declaimed. 'For there are limits to these things, there are points beyond which we will not go in their name; but to perversity there is no limit set, no frontier that anyone has found. Whatever today's excess, tomorrow's will exceed-o it.'

As if to prove her belief in the polymorphous power of the perverse, dancing Aurora became, over the years, a star attraction of the event she despised, a part of what she had been dancing against. The crowds of the devout – wrongly but incorrigibly – saw their own devotion mirrored in her swirling (and faithless) skirts; they assumed she, too, was paying homage to the god. *Ganpati Bappa morya*, they chanted, jigging, amid the blaring of cheap trumpets and giant conches and the hammer-blows of drug-speedy drummers with egg-white eyes and mouths stuffed with the appreciative banknotes of the faithful, and the more scornfully the legendary lady danced on her high parapet, the further above it all she seemed to herself to be, the more eagerly the crowds sucked her down towards them, seeing her not as a rebel but as a temple dancer: not the scourge, but rather the groupie, of the gods.

(Abraham Zogoiby, as we shall see, had other uses for temple dancers.)

Once, in a family quarrel, I reminded her angrily of the many newspaper reports of her assimilation by the festival. By that time Ganesha Chaturthi had become the occasion for fist-clenched, saffron-headbanded young thugs to put on a show of Hindu-fundamentalist triumphalism, egged on by bellowing 'Mumbai's Axis' party politicos and demagogues such as Raman Fielding, a.k.a. *Mainduck* ('Frog'). 'You're not just a tourist sight now,' I gibed. 'You're an advert for the Beautification Programme.' This attractively-named MA policy involved, to put it simply, the elimination of the poor from the city's streets; but Aurora Zogoiby's armour-plating was too strong to be pierced by so crude a thrust.

'You think I can be squashed by gutter pressure?' she howled, dismissively. 'You think I can be dirtified by your black tongue? What is this Mumbo's Jumbos fundo foolery to me? I-tho am up against a greater opponent: Shiva Nataraja himself, yes, and his big-nosed holy-poly disco-baby too – for years I have been dancing them off the stage. Watch on, blackfellow. Maybe even you will learn how to whirl-up a whirlwind, how to hurry-up a hurricane – yes! How to dance up a storm.' Thunder, right on cue, rolled overhead. Fat rain would soon start tumbling from the sky.

Forty-one years of dancing on the day of Ganpati: she danced without a care for the danger of it, without a downward glance towards the barnacled, patient boulders gnashing below her like black teeth. The very first time she emerged from *Elephanta* in full regalia and began her cliff-edged pirouettes, Jawaharlal Nehru himself begged her to desist. This was not long after the anti-British strike by the navy in Bombay harbour, and the supporting shut-down in the city, the *hartal*, had ended at Gandhiji and Vallabhbhai Patel's joint request, and Aurora did not fail to get in her little dig. 'Panditji, Congress-tho is always chickening out in the face of radical acts. No soft options will be takeofied round here.' When he continued to plead with her she set him a forfeit, saying she would only descend if he recited from memory the whole of 'The Walrus and the Carpenter'; which, to general admiration, he did. As he helped her down from her dizzy balustrade, he said, 'The strike was a complex matter.'

'I know what I think about the strike,' she retorted. 'Tell me about the poem.' At which Mr Nehru flushed heavily and swallowed hard.

'It is a sad poem,' he said after a moment, 'because the oysters are so young; a poem, one could say, about the eating of children.'

'We all eat children,' my mother rejoined. This was about ten years before I was born. 'If not other people's, then our own.'

She had four of us. Ina, Minnie, Mynah, Moor; a four-course meal with magic properties, because no matter how often and how heartily she tucked in, the food never seemed to run out.

For four decades, she ate her fill. Then, dancing her Ganpati dance for the forty-second time at the age of sixty-three, she fell. A thin, salivating tide washed over her body, as the black jaws went to work. By that time, however, although she was still my mother, I was no longer her son.

~

At the gate to *Elephanta* stood a man with a wooden leg, propped against a crutch. If I close my eyes it is still easy to conjure him up: that simple Peter at the doors of an earthly Paradise, who became my personal cut-price Virgil, leading me down to Hell – to the great city of Hell, Pandaemonium, that dark-side, through-the-looking-glass evil twin of my own and golden city: not Proper, but Improper Bombay. Beloved monopod guardian! The parents in their lingo-garbling way called him Lambajan Chandiwala. (It seems they had become infected by Aires da Gama's habit of nicknaming the world.) In those days many more people would have understood the inter-lingual joke: lamba, long; jan, sounds like John, chandi, silver. Long John Silverfellow, terrifyingly hairy-faced but literally and metaphorically as toothless as the day he was born, grinding paans between his betel- or blood-red gums. 'Our private pirate,' Aurora called him, and yes, you guessed it, there was normally a green clipped-winged Totah squawking obscenities on his shoulder. My mother, a perfectionist in all things, arranged for the bird; would settle for nothing less.

'So *what* point in a pirate if no parrot?' she'd inquire, arching her eyebrows and twisting her right hand as if it held an invisible doorknob; adding, lightly, and scandalously (for it was not done to make lewd jokes about the Mahatma): 'Might as well have had the little man without the loincloth.' She tried hard to teach the parrot pirate-speak, but it was a stubborn old Bombay bird. 'Pieces of eight! Me hearties!' my mother shrieked, but her pupil maintained a mutinous silence. However, after years of such persecution

Totah gave in and snapped, bad-temperedly: 'Peesay – saféd – hathi!' This remarkable utterance, translating approximately as *mashed white elephants*, became the family's oath of choice. I was not present at the occasion of Aurora Zogoiby's last dance, but many who were later testified that the parrot's magnificent curse trailed after her, *diminuendo*, as she plummeted to her doom: 'Ohhh . . . *Mashed* White Elephants,' my mother howled before hitting the rocks. Next to her body, borne towards her on the tide, was a broken effigy of Dancing Ganesha. But that was not what she had meant at all.

Totah's utterance had a profound effect upon Lambajan Chandiwala also, for he – like so many of us – was a man with elephants on the brain; after the parrot spoke up, Lamba recognised the presence upon his shoulder of a kindred spirit, and opened up his heart thereafter to that intermittently oracular, but more often taciturn and (if the truth be told) irascible and fucking awful bird.

Of what isles of treasure did our parroted pirate dream? Chiefly and most often he spoke of the real Elephanta. To the Zogoiby children, who were being educated beyond the point at which it was possible to see visions, Elephanta Island was nothing, a hilly lump in the Harbour. Before Independence – before Ina, Minnie and Mynah – people could go out there if they got hold of a boat and were willing to brave the possibility of snakes &c.; by the time I arrived, however, the island had long been tamed and there were regular motor-launch excursions from the Gateway of India. My three big sisters were bored by the place. So for my child-self as it squatted beside Lambajan in the afternoon heat Elephanta was anything but a fantasy island; but for Lambajan, to hear him tell it, it was the land of milk and honey itself.

'Once in that place there were elephant kings, baba,' he confided. 'Why do you think-so god Ganesha is so popular in Bombay City? It is because in the days before men there were elephants sitting on thrones and arguing philosophy, and it was the monkeys who were their servants. It is said that when men first came to Elephanta Island in the days after the elephants' fall they found statues of mammoths higher than the Qutb Minar in Delhi, and they were so afraid that they smashed up the whole lot. Yes, men wiped away the memory of the great elephants but still not all of us have forgotten. Up there in Elephanta in the hills is the place where they buried their dead. No? Head is shaking? See, he does not believe us, Totah. Okay, baba. Forehead is frowning? Then look at this!'

And here to much parroty noising he produced – what else, what else, O my nostalgic heart? – a crumple of cheap paper, which even the boy Moor could see was not in the least bit ancient. It was, of course, a map.

'One great elephant, maybe *the* Great Elephant, hides up there still, baba. I have seen what I have seen! Who else do you think bit away my leg? And then in his grandness and his scorn he let me crawl bleeding down the jungly hill and into my little boat. What-what I saw! Jewels he guards, baba, a hoard greater than the khazana of the Nizam of Hyderabad himself.'

Lambajan accommodated our piratical fantasy of him – for naturally my mother the great explainer had made sure he understood his nickname – and in doing so constructed a dream of his own, an Elephanta for *Elephanta*, in which, as the years passed, he appeared more and more deeply to believe. Without knowing it, he connected himself to the legends of the da Gama-Zogoibys, in which hidden jewel-boxes were a prominent feature. And thus Malabar Coast masala found its yet-more-fabulous counterpart on Malabar Hill, as was perhaps inevitable, because no matter what pepper'n'spices goings-on there might be or have been in Cochin, this great cosmopolis of ours was and is the Central Junction of all such tamashas, and the hottest tales, the juiciest-bitchiest yarns, the most garish and lurid not-penny-but-paisa-dreadfuls, are the ones walking our streets. In Bombay you live crushed in this crazy crowd, you are deafened by its blaring horns of plenty, and – like the figures of family members in Aurora's Cabral Island mural – your own story has to shove its way through the throngs. Which was fine by Aurora Zogoiby; never one for a quiet life, she sucked in the city's hot stenches, lapped up its burning sauces, she gobbled its dishes up whole. Aurora came to think of herself as a corsair, as the city's outlaw queen. 'In this residence it's the Jolly Roger we flyofy,' she declared repeatedly, to her children's embarrassment and ennui. She actually had one made up by her tailor and handed it to the chowkidar. 'Come on quick, Mister Lambajan! Run-o it up the flagstaff and let's see who-who salutes.'

As for me, I did not salute Aurora's skull-and-crossbones; was not, in those days, at all the piratical type. Besides, I knew how Lambajan had really lost his leg.

~

The first point to note is that people's limbs got detached more easily in those days. The banners of British domination hung over the country like strips of flypaper, and, in trying to unstick ourselves from those fatal flags, we flies – if I may use the term 'we' to refer to a time before my birth – would often leave legs or wings behind, preferring freedom to wholeness. Of course, now that the sticky paper is ancient history, we find ways of losing our limbs in the struggle against other equally lethal, equally antiquated, equally adhesive standards of our own devising. – Enough, enough; away with this soap-box! Unplug this loud-hailer, and be still, my wagging finger! – To continue: the second essential piece of info in the matter of Lambajan's leg concerns my mother's window-curtains; the fact, I mean to say, that there were gold-and-green curtains, kept permanently closed, on the rear windscreen and back windows of her American motor car . . .

In February 1946, when Bombay, that super-epic motion picture of a city, was transformed overnight into a motionless tableau by the great naval and landlubber strikes, when ships did not sail, steel was not milled, textile looms neither warped nor woofed, and in the movie studios there was neither turnover nor cut – the twenty-one-year-old Aurora began to zoom around the paralysed town in her famous curtained Buick, directing her driver Hanuman to the heart of the action, or, rather, of all that grand inaction, being set down outside factory gates and dockyards, venturing alone into the slum-city of Dharavi, the rum-dens of Dhobi Talao and the neon fleshpots of Falkland Road, armed only with a folding wooden stool and a sketchbook. Opening them both up, she set about capturing history in charcoal. 'Ignore-o me,' she commanded the open-mouthed strikers whom she sketched at high speed as they picketed, whored and drank. 'I-tho am here just-like-that; like a lizard on the wall; or call me a doodling bug.'

'Crazy woman,' Abraham Zogoiby marvelled many years later. 'Your mother, my boy. Crazy as a monkey in a monkey-puzzle tree. God only knows what she thought. Even in Bombay it is no small thing for unaccompanied ladies to sit in the public thoroughfare and stare men in the face, to go into bad-area gambling dens and get out a portrait pad. And a doodle-bug, remember, was a bomb.'

It was no small thing. Burly goldtooth stevedores accused her of trying to steal their souls by literally *drawing them out of their bodies*, and striking men of steel suspected that in another, secret, identity she might be a police spy. The sheer strangeness of the activity of art made her a questionable figure; as it does everywhere; as it always has and perhaps always will. All this and more she overcame: the jostlings, the sexual menace, the physical threats were all stared down by that level, unyielding gaze. My mother always possessed the occult power of making herself invisible in the pursuit of her work. With her long white hair twisted up into a bun, dressed in a cheap floral-print dress from Crawford Market, she quietly and indomitably returned day after day to her chosen scenes, and in slow steps the magic worked, people stopped noticing her; they forgot that she was a great lady descending from a car that was as big as a house and even had curtains over its windows, and allowed the truth of their lives to return to their faces, and that was why the charcoal in her flying fingers was able to capture so much of it, the face-slapping quarrels of naked children at a tenement standpipe, the grizzled despair of idling workers smoking beedis on the doorsteps of locked-up pharmacies, the silent factories, the sense that the blood in men's eyes was just about to burst through and flood the streets, the toughness of women with saris pulled over their heads, squatting by tiny primus stoves in pavement-dwellers' jopadpatti shacks as they tried to conjure meals from empty air, the panic in the eyes of lathi-charging policemen who feared that one day soon, when freedom came, they would be seen as oppression's enforcers, the elated tension of the striking sailors at the gates to the naval yards, the guilty-kiddie pride on their faces as they munched channa at Apollo Bunder and stared out at the immobilised ships flying red flags in praise of revolution as they lay at anchor in the Harbour, the shipwrecked arrogance of the English officers from whom power was ebbing like the waves, leaving them beached, with no more than the strut and posture of their old invincibility, the rags of their imperial robes; and beneath all this was her own sense of the inadequacy of the world, of its failure to live up to her expectations, so that her own disappointment with reality, her anger at its wrongness, mirrored her subjects', and made her sketches not merely reportorial, but personal, with a violent, breakneck passion of line that had the force of a physical assault.

Kekoo Mody hastily rented a hall in the Fort district and put up these sketches, which came to be known as her 'Chipkali' or lizard pictures, because at Mody's suggestion – the pictures were clearly subversive, clearly pro-strike and therefore a challenge to British authority – Aurora did not sign them but simply placed a tiny drawing of a lizard in a corner of each sketch. Kekoo himself fully expected to be arrested, had decided he was happy to take the fall on Aurora's behalf (for he had been under her spell from their first meeting) and when he was not – when, in fact, the British chose to ignore the exhibition entirely – he took it as a further indication of the waning not only of their power but of their will. Tall, pale, awkward and majestically short-sighted, his round glasses almost thick-lensed enough to be bullet-proof, he paced around the Chipkali show waiting for the arrest that never came, took too many sips from an innocent-looking thermos flask which he had filled with cheap rum that was the same colour as strong tea, and buttonholed visitors to the gallery to expatiate at inordinate length on the Empire's imminent demise. Abraham Zogoiby – visiting the exhibition alone one afternoon, behind Aurora's back – took a different view. 'You art-wallahs,' he told Kekoo. 'Always so certain-sure of your impact. Since when do the masses come to such shows? And as for the Britishers, just now, kindly permit me to inform, pictures are not their problem.'

For a time Aurora was proud of her alias, because she had indeed made of herself what she had wanted to be, an unblinking lizard on the wall of history, watching, watching; but when her pioneering work spawned followers, when other young artists began to act as public recorders and even began calling themselves the 'Chipkalist Movement', then, characteristically, my mother publicly disowned her disciples. In a newspaper article entitled 'I Am The Lizard' she admitted her authorship, defying the British to move against her (they did not) and dismissing her imitators as 'cartoonists and photographers'.

'The grand manner is all very well,' my father, reminiscing, commented in his old age. 'But it makes for a lonely life.'

∽

When Aurora Zogoiby heard that the Naval Strike Committee had been persuaded by the Congress leadership to call off the stoppage, and that it had convoked a meeting of the sailors to order them back to their posts, her disappointment with the world as it was burst its banks. Without thinking, without waiting for her driver Hanuman, she leapt into the curtained Buick and took off for the naval base. By the time she reached the Afghan Church in the Colaba Cantonment, however, the bubble of her invulnerability had burst, and she was beginning to have second thoughts about the wisdom of her journey. The road to the base was thick with defeated sailors, frustrated young men in clean uniforms and filthy moods, young men swirling listlessly like fallen leaves. Crows jeered in a plane-tree; a sailor picked up a stone and hurled it in the direction of the noise. Black forms fluttered contemptuously, circled, settled down, resumed their taunts. Police officers in short trousers muttered anxiously in small knots, like children afraid of punishment, and even my mother began to see that this was no place for a lady with a sketchbook and folding stool, let alone a gleaming Buick without so much as the protective presence of a chauffeur. It was a hot, humid, ill-tempered afternoon. A child's lilac kite, its string cut in some other lost battle, fell pathetically from the sky.

Aurora did not need to lower her window to ask what was on the sailors' minds, because she was thinking the same things – that the Congress were acting like chamchas, toadies; that even now, when the British were too unsure of the army to send it in against the sailors, they could be sure that Congresswallahs would spare them the trouble of having to do so. When the masses actually do rise up, she thought, the bosses turn tail. Brown bosses, white bosses, it was the same thing. 'This strike has scare-o'ed our lot as much as theirs.' Aurora, too, was in a mutinous mood; but she was not a sailor, and knew that to those angry boys she would look like a rich bitch in a fancy car – as, perhaps, the enemy.

The sullen, aimless thickening of the crowd had forced her to slow the Buick to walking pace, and when, with a gesture whose swift casualness concealed a frightening strength, one scowling young giant twisted the chrome housing of the Buick's wing-mirror until it hung uselessly off the car like a broken limb, she felt her heart begin to pound, and decided it was time to leave. Unable to turn round, she put the car into reverse; and realised, as she pushed the accelerator, that without the wing-mirror she was unable to check her rear on account of the intervening presence of green-and-gold cloth; that some sailors, in a final show of defiance, had suddenly decided to sit down in the road; and that, thanks to her growing, thumping feeling of alarm, she had accelerated harder than she intended, and was going much, much too fast.

As she braked, she felt a small bump.

Stories of Aurora Zogoiby being gripped by panic are rare, but this is one such tale: feeling the bump, my horrified mother, who had at once understood that someone had been staging a sit-down protest behind her car, column-shifted the Buick into first. The car leapt forward a few feet, thus passing bumpily over the stricken sailor's outstretched leg for a second time. At this moment several policemen, waving sticks and blowing whistles, raced towards the Buick, and Aurora, acting now in a kind of dream, motivated by some disoriented notion of guilt and escape, jerked the car into reverse once more. There was a third bump, although this time it was less noticeable than on the previous occasions. Shouts of rage mounted behind her, and, completely unhinged by the situation, she lurched forward again in a wild response to the cries – barely feeling the fourth bump – and knocked at least one policeman flat on his back. At this point, mercifully, the Buick stalled.

What puzzled me most when I heard the story as a boy, what continues to perplex, is how, having more or less cut a man in two, she managed to get out of there in one piece. Aurora herself varied her explanations with each telling, attributing her escape, variously, to the disorientation of those unhappy sailors; or to some residue of naval discipline, which prevented them from becoming a lynch mob; or to the innate chivalry and sense of hierarchy of Indian men, which kept them from harming a lady, especially a grand one. Or, again, it might have been on account of her deep and evident concern – no grand manner there! – for the injured man, whose leg had taken on an upsetting resemblance to her dangling wing-mirror; or the result of the speed and habit of command with which she had him scooped up and placed on the Buick's back seat, where he was shielded from angry eyes by green-and-gold cloth while she pointed out to the assembled gathering that the injured man needed transport, and hers was the most readily available vehicle. The truth was that she had no idea why she was spared by that increasingly ugly crowd, but in her dark moments she perhaps came closest to the truth, admitting that she had been saved by fame; for her image was everywhere still, and with her beautiful young face and long white hair she wasn't hard to recognise. 'Tell your Congress friends they let us down,' someone shouted, and she shouted back, 'I will'; and then they let her go. (Some months later, pirouetting on the ramparts of her home, she kept her word, and let Jawaharlal Nehru have it straight. Soon after that, the Mountbattens arrived in India, and Nehru and Edwina fell in love. Is it too much to suppose that Aurora's plain speaking in the matter of the great naval strike turned Panditji away from her and towards the Last Viceroy's possibly less disputatious mame?)

Abraham's version – Abraham, who had promised to look after her always – was different. Long after she died he confided in me. 'Back then I kept a top team secretly on her tail, and she led us a merry dance. I don't say it was so hard keeping your fool mummy safe when she went off on her madcap ventures, but I had to stay on my toes. Wherever that Buick turned up, my boys were also there. How could I inform her? If she knew she would have chewed me out.'

It is difficult for me, after all these years, to know what to believe. How could Abraham have known that Aurora was going to dash off as she did? — But maybe it is her version that is suspect — perhaps her departure was not so precipitate, after all. The old biographer's problem: even when people are telling their own life stories, they are invariably improving on the facts, rewriting their tales, or just plain making them up. Aurora needed to seem independent; her version followed from that desire, just as Abraham's derived from his need to make the world think — to make *me* think — her safety depended on his care. The truth of such stories lies in what they reveal about the protagonists' hearts, rather than their deeds. In the case of the amputated sailor, however, the truth is simpler to establish: the poor fellow lost his leg.

⌐

She brought him home and changed his life. She had diminished him, subtracting a leg and therefore his future in the navy; and now she sought fiercely to enlarge him again, providing him with a new uniform, a new job, a new leg, a new identity and a grumpy parrot to go with it all. She had ruined his life, but she saved him from the worst, gutter-dwelling, begging-bowl consequences of that ruination. As a result, he fell in love with her, what else; he became Lambajan Chandiwala as she desired, and the fabulous elephant-tales he told were his way of expressing his love, which was the impossible dog-devoted love of a slave for his queen, and which disgusted our sour and bony ayah and housekeeper Miss Jaya Hé, who became his bride and the bane of his life. 'Baap-ré!' she berated him. 'Why not go on a salt march and don't stop when you reach the sea?'

Lambajan at Aurora's gates — at the gates, as Vasco Miranda called them, of dawn — guarded his mistress from the coarse world outside, but he was also, in a way, protecting others against her. Nobody entered until he knew their business; but Lamba also made it his own business to give visitors the benefit of his advice. 'Today speak soft only,' he might say. 'Today her head is full of whispers.' Or else: 'Dark thoughts are on her. You must tell good joke.' Thus forewarned, my mother's guests could (if they were wise enough to obey Lambajan's tips) avoid the supernova detonations of her legendary – and highly artistic – rage.

~

My mother Aurora Zogoiby was too bright a star; look at her too hard and you'd be blinded. Even now, in the memory, she dazzles, must be circled about and about. We may perceive her indirectly, in her effects on others – her bending of other people's light, her gravitational pull which denied us all hope of escape, the decaying orbits of those too weak to withstand her, who fell towards her sun and its consuming fires. Ah, the dead, the unended, endlessly ending dead: how long, how rich is their story. We, the living, must find what space we can alongside them; the giant dead whom we cannot tie down, though we grasp at their hair, though we rope them while they sleep.

Must we also die before our souls, so long suppressed, can find utterance – before our secret natures can be known? To whom it may concern, I say No, and again I say, No Way. When I was young I used to dream – like Carmen da Gama, but for less masochistic, masturbatory reasons; like photophobic, God-bothered Oliver D'Aeth – of peeling off my skin plantain-fashion, of going forth naked into the world, like an anatomy illustration from *Encyclopaedia Britannica*, all ganglions, ligaments, nervous pathways and veins, set free from the otherwise inescapable jails of colour, race and clan. (In another version of the dream I would be able to peel away more than skin, I would float free of flesh, skin and bones, having become simply an intelligence or a feeling set loose in the world, at play in its fields, like a science-fiction glow which needed no physical form.)

So, in writing this, I must peel off history, the prison of the past. It is time for a sort of ending, for the truth about myself to struggle out, at last, from under my parents' stifling power; from under my own black skin. These words are a dream come true. A painful dream, that I do not deny; for in the waking world a man's not as easy to flay as a banana, no matter how ripe he be. And Aurora and Abraham will take some shaking off.

Motherness – excuse me if I underline the point – is a big idea in India, maybe our biggest: the land as mother, the mother as land, as the firm ground beneath our feet. Ladies-O, gents-O: I'm talking *major* mother country. The year I was born, Mehboob Productions' all-conquering movie *Mother India* – three years in the making, three hundred shooting days, in the top three all-time mega-grossing Bollywood flicks – hit the nation's screens. Nobody who saw it ever forgot that glutinous saga of peasant heroinism, that super-slushy ode to the uncrushability of village India made by the most cynical urbanites in the world. And as for its leading lady – O Nargis with your shovel over your shoulder and your strand of black hair tumbling forward over your brow! – she became, until Indira-Mata supplanted her, the living mother-goddess of us all. Aurora knew her, of course; like every other luminary of the time the actress was drawn towards my mother's blazing flame. But they didn't hit it off, perhaps because Aurora could not refrain from raising the subject – how close to my own heart! – of mother-son relations.

'The first time I saw that picture', she confided to the famous movie star on the high terrace at *Elephanta*, 'I took one look at your Bad Son, Birju, and I thought, O boy, what a handsome guy – too much sizzle, too much chilli, bring water. He may be a thief and a bounder, but that is some A-class loverboy goods. And now look – you have gone and marry-o'ed him! What sexy lives you movie people leadofy: to marry your own son, I swear, wowie.'

The film actor under discussion, Sunil Dutt, stood stiffly beside his wife and sipped lemonade, flushing. (In those days Bombay was a 'dry' state, and even though whisky-soda was plentiful at *Elephanta*, the actor was making a moral point.) 'Auroraji, you are mixing truth and make-believe,' he said pompously, as if it were a sin. 'Birju and his mother Radha are fictions only, in two dimensions on the silver screen; but we are flesh and blood, available in full 3D – as guests in your fine home.' Nargis, sipping nimbu-pani, smiled a thin smile at the rebuke hidden in the last phrase.

'Even in the picture, but,' Aurora went relentlessly on, 'I knew right off that bad Birju had the hots for his gorgeous ma.'

Nargis stood speechless, open-mouthed. Vasco Miranda, who could never resist a bit of trouble-making, saw the storm brewing and made haste to join in. 'Sublimation', he offered, 'of mutual parent-child longings, is deep-rooted in the national psyche. The use of names in the picture makes the meaning clear. This "Birju" moniker is also used by God Krishna, isn't it, and we know that milky "Radha" is the blue chap's one true love. In the picture, Sunil, you are made up to look like the god, and you even fool with all the girls, throwing your stones to break their womby water-pots; which, admit it, is Krishna-esque behaviour. In this interpretation,' and here clowning Vasco attempted unsuccessfully to convey a certain scholarly *gravitas*, '*Mother India* is the dark side of the Radha-Krishna story, with the subsidiary theme of forbidden love added on. But what the hell; Oedipus-schmoedipus! Have another chhota peg.'

'Dirty talk,' said the Living Mother Goddess. 'Filthy-dirty, chhi. I heard tell that depraved artists and beatnik intellectuals came up here, but I gave you all benefit of doubt. Now I observe that I am among the blaspheming scum of the earth. How you people wallow-pollow in negative images! In our picture we put stress on the positive side. Courage of the masses is there, and also dams.'

'Bad language, eh?' mused Vasco, innocently. 'Good for you! But in the final cut the censor must have removed it.'

'*Bewaqoof!*' shouted Sunil Dutt, provoked beyond endurance. 'Bleddy dumbo! Not oathery, but new technology is being referred to: to wit, the hydro-electric project, as inaugurated by my goodwife in the opening scene.'

'And when you say your wife,' ever-helpful Vasco clarified, 'you mean, of course, your mother.'

'Sunil, come,' said the legend, sweeping away. 'If this godless anti-national gang is the world of art, then I-tho am happy to be on commercial side.'

In *Mother India*, a piece of Hindu myth-making directed by a

Muslim socialist, Mehboob Khan, the Indian peasant woman is idealised as bride, mother, and producer of sons; as long-suffering, stoical, loving, redemptive, and conservatively wedded to the maintenance of the social status quo. But for Bad Birju, cast out from his mother's love, she becomes, as one critic has mentioned, 'that image of an aggressive, treacherous, annihilating mother who haunts the fantasy life of Indian males'.

I, too, know something about this image; have been cast as a Bad Son in my turn. My mother was no Nargis Dutt – she was the in-your-face type, not serene. Catch her hauling a shovel on her shoulder! *I am pleased to say that I have never seen a spade.* Aurora was a city girl, perhaps *the* city girl, as much the incarnation of the smartyboots metropolis as Mother India was village earth made flesh. In spite of this I have found it instructive to compare and contrast our families. Mother India's movie-husband was rendered impotent, his arms crushed by a rock; and ruined limbs play a central rôle in our saga, too. (You must judge for yourselves whether Abraham was a potent fellow or im-.) And as for Birju and Moor: dark skins and crookery were not all we had in common.

I have been keeping my secret for too long. High time I spilt my beans.

⌒

My three sisters were born in quick succession, and Aurora carried and ejected each of them with such perfunctory attention to their presence that they knew, long before their births, that she would make few concessions to their post-partum needs. The names she gave them confirmed these suspicions. The eldest, originally called Christina in spite of her Jewish father's protests, eventually had her name sliced in half. 'Stop sulking, Abie,' Aurora commanded. 'From now on she's plain Ina without the Christ.' So poor Ina grew up with only half a handle, and when the second child was born a year later matters were made worse because this time Aurora insisted on 'Inamorata'. Abraham protested again: 'People will confuse,' he said plaintively. 'And with this *Ina-more* it is like saying she is Ina-plus . . .' Aurora shrugged. 'Ina was a ten-pound baby, the little so-and-so,' she reminded Abraham. 'Head like a cannonball, hips like a ship's behind. How can this little pocket mousey be anything but Ina-minus?' Within a week, she had decided that Baby Inamorata, the five-pound mouse, bore a close resemblance to a famous cartoon rodent – 'all big ears, wide eyes and polka dots' – and my middle sister was always Minnie after that. When Aurora announced, eighteen months later, that her newborn third daughter would be Philomina, Abraham tore his hair. 'Now comes this *Minnie-'meena* mix-up,' he groaned. 'And another *-ina*, too.' Philomina, listening in on this dispute, began to cry, a fat tuneless roar of a noise that convinced everyone except her mother of the comical inappropriateness of naming her after the nightingale. When the child was three months old, however, Miss Jaya Hé the ayah heard a series of alarming caws and piercing trills emanating from the nursery and rushed in to find the baby lying contentedly in her cot with bird-song pouring from her lips. Ina and Minnie stared at their sister through the bars of the cot with expressions of terror and awe. Aurora was summoned and, with an unfazed casualness that instantly normalised the miracle, nodded brusquely and gave judgment: 'So if she can mimic like this she is not a bulbul but a mynah,' and from then on it was Ina, Minnie, Mynah, except that at Walsingham House School on Nepean Sea Road they became Eeny Meeny Miney, three quarters of an unfinished line followed by a hollow beat, a silent space where a fourth word should be. Three sisters waiting – and they had a long wait of it, because between Mynah and me there was an eight-year gap – to catch a brother by his toe.

The male child for which old, cursing Flory Zogoiby had intrigued in vain continued to prove elusive, and it must be recorded to the honour of my father's memory that he always professed himself satisfied with his daughters. As the girls grew, he proved himself the most doting of fathers; until one day – it was in 1956, during the long school holidays after the rains – when the family had gone for an outing to see the two-thousand-year-old Buddhist cave-temples at Lonavla, he clutched gasping at his heart half-way up the steep stairway cut into the hillside that led to the dark mouth of the biggest cave, and as the breath rattled in his throat and his eyes blurred he reached uselessly out towards the three girls, then aged nine, eight and almost-seven, who failed to notice his distress and scampered, giggling, up and away from him with all the insouciant speed and immortality of the young.

Aurora caught him before he fell. An old mushroom-selling crone had appeared beside them and helped Aurora sit Abraham down with his back against the rock, his straw hat falling forward over his brow and cold sweat pouring down his neck.

'Don't croak-o, damn it,' Aurora shouted, cupping his face in her hands. 'Breathe! You are not allowed to die.' And Abraham, obeying her as always, survived. The breathing eased, the eyes cleared, and he rested for long minutes with bowed head. The girls came running goggle-eyed down the stairs with their fingers jammed into their mouths.

'You see the problems of being an old father,' fifty-three-year-old Abraham muttered to Aurora before their daughters came into earshot. 'See how fast they are growing, and how fast I am cracking up, too. If I had my wish all this growing – up and old, both – would stop for ever right now.'

Aurora made herself speak lightly as the worried children arrived. 'You-tho will be around for ever,' she told Abraham. 'I've got no worries about *you*. And as for these savage creatures, they can't growofy fast enough for me. God! How long this childhood business draggoes on! Why couldn't I have kids – why not even *one* child – who grew up *really* fast.'

A voice behind her said a few words, almost inaudibly. *Obeah, jadoo, fo, fum.* Aurora whirled around. 'Who said that?'

There were only the children. Other visitors, some of them carried in sedan chairs (Abraham had spurned this soft option), were making their way to and from the caves, but they were all too far away, above and below.

'Where's that woman?' Aurora asked her children. 'The mushroom woman who helped me. Where has she disappeared?'

'We didn't see anybody,' Ina answered. 'It was just the two of you.'

⌇

Mahabaleshwar, Lonavla, Khandala, Matheran . . . O cool beloved hill-stations I will never see again, whose names echo for Bombay folk with the memory of childhood laughter, sweet love-songs, and days and nights in cool green forests, spent in walking and repose! In the dry season before the rains these blessed hilltops seem to float lightly on a shimmering magic haze; after the monsoon, when the air is clear, you can stand, for example, on Matheran's Heart Point or One Tree Hill, and sometimes in that supernatural clarity you can see, if not for ever, then at least a little way into the future, maybe one or two days ahead.

On the day of Abraham's collapse, however, the hill-stations' quaint slow ways were not what the doctor ordered. The family was booked in for the season at the Lord's Central House in Matheran, which meant that after Abraham's collapse they had to drive over twenty miles on a slow untended road, and then, at the road's end, leave Hanuman in charge of the Buick and take the toy train up the hill from Neral through the One Kiss Tunnel and beyond, a crawling two-hour journey during which Aurora relaxed her usual ironclad rules and stuffed the girls with pieces of sugar-and-nut chikki-toffee to keep them quiet, while Miss Jaya wet handkerchiefs from a water surahi so that Aurora could spread them on Abraham's weakened brow. 'Takes longer to gettofy to this Lord's House', Aurora complained, 'than to Paradise itself.'

But at least the Lord's Central House was real, it had an empirically provable basis in fact, whereas heavenly Paradise has never been something by which my family set much store . . . the narrow-gauge train puffed up the hill, pink curtains flapping at the first-class windows, and finally it stopped, and monkeys swung down from its roof and tried to steal the chikki from the Zogoiby girls' startled hands. It was the end of the line; and that night, in a room in the Lord's House newly heavy with odours of spice, and while lizards watched from the walls, Aurora Zogoiby on a noisy spring bed under a slow-moving ceiling fan caressed her husband's body until his return to life was complete; and *four and a half months later*, on New Year's Day, 1957, she gave birth to their fourth and final child.

Ina, Minnie, Mynah, and at last Moor. That's me: the end of the line. And something else. I'm something else as well: call it a wish come true. Call it a dead woman's curse. I am the child the lack of whom Aurora Zogoiby lamented on the steps to the Lonavla caves. This is my secret, and after all these years all I can do is say it, straight out, and to hell with how it sounds.

*I am going through time faster than I should.* Do you understand me? Somebody somewhere has been holding down the button marked 'FF', or, to be more exact, 'x2'. Reader, listen carefully, take in every word, for what I write now is the simple and literal truth. I, Moraes Zogoiby, known as Moor, am – for my sins, for my many and many sins, for my fault, for my most grievous fault – a man living double-quick.

And the mushroom seller? Aurora, inquiring into the matter the next morning, was informed by the hotel desk clerk that mushrooms had never to his knowledge been grown or sold in the region of the Lonavla caves. And the old woman – *chicken entrails, kingdom come* – was never seen again.

(*I see the morning appearing; and fall silent, discreetly.*)

# 10

I'LL SAY IT AGAIN. from the moment of my conception, like a visitor from another dimension, another time-line, I have aged twice as rapidly as the old earth and everything and everyone thereupon. Four and a half months from conception to birth: how could my two-timing evolution have given my mother anything but the most difficult of pregnancies? As I see, in fancy's vision, the accelerated swelling of her womb, it resembles nothing so much as a movie special effect, as if under the influence of some twice-pushed genetic button her biochemical pixels had gone loco and begun to morph her protesting body so violently that the speeded-up outward effects of my gestation actually became visible to the naked eye. Engendered on one hill, born on another, I attained mountainous proportions when I should still have been at the minor molehill stage . . . the point I am making is that, while there can be no disputing that I was conceived in the Lord's Central House, Matheran, it is also unarguably the case that when Baby Gargantua Zogoiby drew his first, surprising breath at the élite private nursing home-cum-nunnery of the Sisters of Maria Gratiaplena on Altamount Road, Bombay, his physical development was already so advanced – a generous erection serving somewhat to impede his passage down the birth canal – that nobody in their right mind would have thought of calling him half-formed.

Premature? Post-mature is much more like it. Four and a half months in the wet and slimy felt much too long to me. From the beginning – from before the beginning – I knew I had no time to waste. Passing from lost waters towards necessary air, jammed solid in Aurora's lower passages by my soo-soo's rather military decision to salute the moment by standing at attention, I decided to let people know about the urgent nature of my problem, and unleashed a mighty bovine groan. Aurora, hearing my first sound emerging from inside her body (and getting a sense, too, of the immense size of what was waiting to be born), was at once appalled and impressed; but not, naturally, lost for words. 'After our Eeny-Meeny-Miney,' she gasped at the frightened ecclesiastical midwife, who was looking as if she'd heard a hound from Hell, 'I think, Sister, here comes Moo.' From Moo to Moor, from first groan to last sigh: on such hooks hang my tales.

How many of us feel, these days, that something that has passed too quickly is ending: a moment of life, a period of history, an idea of civilisation, a twist in the turning of the unconcerned world. *A thousand ages in Thy sight*, they sing in St Thomas's Cathedral to their no-doubt-nonexistent god, *are like an evening gone*; so might I just point out, O my omnipotent reader, that I have been passing too quickly, too. A double-speed existence permits only half a life. *Short as the watch that ends the night, Before the morning sun.*

No need for supernatural explanations; some cock-up in the DNA will do. Some premature-ageing disorder in the core programme, leading to the production of too many short-life cells. In Bombay, my old hovel'n'highrise home town, we think we're on top of the modern age, we boast that we're natural techno fast-trackers, but that's only true in the high-rises of our minds. Down in the slums of our bodies, we're still vulnerable to the most disorderly disorders, the scurviest of scurvies, the plaguiest of plagues. There may be pet pussies prowling around our squeaky-clean, sky-high penthouses, but they don't cancel out the rat-infested corruption in the sewers of the blood.

If a birth is the fall-out from the explosion caused by the union of two unstable elements, then perhaps a half-life is all we can expect. From Bombay nunnery to Benengeli folly, my life's journey has taken just thirty-six calendar years. But what remains of the tender young giant of my youth? The mirrors of Benengeli reflect an exhausted gent with hair as white, as thin, as serpentine as his great-grandmother Epifania's long-gone chevelure. His gaunt face, and in his elongated body no more than a memory of an old, slow grace of movement. The aquiline profile is now merely beaky, and the womanly full lips have thinned, like the dwindling corona of hair. An old brown leather greatcoat, worn over paint-spattered check shirt and shapeless corduroy trousers, flaps behind him like a broken wing. Chicken-necked and pigeon-chested, this bony, dusty old-timer still manages an admirable erectness of bearing (I could always walk with a pitcher of milk balanced comfortably on my head); but if you could see him, and had to guess his age, you'd say he was fit for rocking-chairs, soft food and rolled trousers, you'd put him out to pasture like an old horse, or – if by chance you were not in India – you might pack him off to a retirement home. Seventy-two years old, you'd say, with a deformed right hand like a club.

~

'Nothing that grew-o'ed so fast could have grown right,' Aurora thought (and later, when our troubles came, said aloud, right into my face). Filled with revulsion at the sight of my deformity, she tried in vain to console herself: 'Lucky it's only a hand.' The midwife, Sister John, was bemoaning the tragedy on my mother's behalf, because to her way of thinking (which was not so very different from my mother's own) a physical abnormality was only one notch lower than mental illness on the scale of family shame. She swaddled the baby in white, concealing the good hand as well as the bad; and when my father came in, she offered him the astonishingly outsized bundle with a muffled – and perhaps only half-hypocritical – sob. 'Such a beautiful baby from a so-fine household,' she snuffled. 'Rejoice humbly, Mr Abraham, that Lord God Almighty hath inflicted upon your son His tough-tough wound of love.'

That was too much for Aurora, of course; my right hand, however revolting, was not a matter to be intruded upon by non-family members or gods. 'Get that woman out of here, Abie,' my mother roared from her bed, 'before I inflictofy some tough-tough wounds myself.'

My right hand: the fingers welded into an undifferentiated chunk, the thumb a stunted wart. (To this day, when I shake hands,

I offer my unexceptional left, inverted, the thumb pointing towards the floor.) 'Hello, boxer,' Abraham greeted me miserably as he examined the ruined limb. 'Hiya, champion. Take my word for it: you're going to knock the whole world flat with a fist on you like that.' Which fatherly effort to make the best of a bad business, spoken through a misery-twisted mouth, turned out to be nothing less than a prophecy, nothing more than the simple truth.

Not to be outdone in bright-side-lookery, Aurora – who did not intend to allow her first-ever difficult pregnancy to end in anything less than triumph – put away her horror and disgust, locking it away in a dank basement of her soul until the day of our final quarrel, when she set it free, grown monstrous and slavering, and allowed the beast-within to have its way at last ... for the moment, however, she chose to stress the miracle of my life, of my extraordinary more-than-full-grown size, of the astounding gestational speed which had given her such 'gyp' but which also proved that I must be a child in a million. 'That damn fool Sister John was right about one thing,' she said, taking me in her arms. 'He is the most beautiful of our kids. And this, what is it? Nothing, na? Even a masterpiece can have a little smudge.'

With these words she took an artist's responsibility for her handiwork; my messed-up mitt, this lump as misshapen as modern art itself, became no more than a slip of the genius's brush. Then, in a further act of generosity – or was it a mortification of the flesh, a self-inflicted punishment for her instinctual revulsion? – Aurora gave me an even greater gift. 'Miss Jaya's bottle was okay for the girls,' she announced. 'But as for my son, I will feed-o him myself.' I wasn't arguing; and clamped myself firmly to her breast.

'See, how beautiful,' Aurora determinedly purred. 'Yes, drink your fill, my little peacock, my *mór.*'

᠗

One day in early 1947 an etiolated young fellow, a certain Vasco Miranda of Loutulim in Goa, had arrived penniless at Aurora's gates, identified himself as a painter, and demanded to be admitted to the presence of 'the only Artist in this artless Dumpistan whose greatness approaches my own'. Lambajan Chandiwala took one look at the thin, weak line of the moustache above the small-time confidence man's smile, the backwoods quiff-and-sideburns hairdo dripping with coconut oil, the cheap bush-shirt, trousers and sandals, and began to laugh. Vasco laughed right back, and soon it was getting pretty hilarious out there at the gates of dawn, the two men were a-wiping of their eyes and a-slapping of their thighs – only the parrot, Totah, remained unamused, and concentrated on clutching anxiously at the chowkidar's heaving shoulders – until at length Lambajan spluttered, 'Do you know whose house this is?' and at once, to Totah's discomfiture, unleashed a new shoulder-quake of giggles. 'Yes,' sobbed Vasco through tears of laughter, whereupon Lambajan's mirth grew so great that the parrot flew off and settled morosely atop the gates themselves. 'No,' wept Lambajan, and began to beat Vasco violently with a long wooden crutch, 'no, mister badmash, you don't know whose house this is. Understand me? You have never known, you don't know now, and tomorrow you won't know even better.'

So Vasco ran away down Malabar Hill to whatever hole he was living in at that time – some rickety Mazagaon chawl, I think – where, bruised but undaunted, he sat right down and wrote Aurora a letter, which achieved what he had failed to do in person: it sneaked past the chowkidar into the great lady's hands. This letter was an early expression of the New Cheekiness – *Nayi Badmashi* – with which Vasco would afterwards make his name, though it was little more than a spiced-up rehash of the European surrealists; he even made a short film called *Kutta Kashmir Ka* ('A Kashmiri' – rather than Andalusian – 'Dog'). But Vasco's career would not tarry long on these kooky, derivative shores; he soon discovered that his genuine gift was for the kind of bland, inoffensive concepts for which the owners of public buildings would pay truly surrealist sums, and after that his reputation – never very serious – declined as rapidly as his bank-balance increased.

In the letter he announced himself as Aurora's unsuspected soul-mate. Both 'Southern Stars', both 'Anti-Christians', both exponents of an 'Epico-Mythico-Tragico-Comico-Super-Sexy-

High-Masala-Art' in which the unifying principle was 'Techni-color-Story-Line', they would strengthen each other's work '. . . like Frenchy Georges and Spanish Pablo, only better, because of the difference in Gender. Also, I perceive that you are Public Spirited, and interested in many Topics of the Moment; whereas I, I fear, am completely Frivolous – when the Political Sphere bounces into view I become a malevolent and untamable child, and with a good sharp kick I despatch the said Sphere out of my Zone of Operations. You are a Hero, and I am a spineless Jellyfish; how can we fail to sweep all before us? It will be a union of dreams – for you are Right, while I, unfortunately, am Wrong.'

When Lambajan Chandiwala at the gates of *Elephanta* heard his mistress's peals of laughter, her banshee howls of merriment, wafting towards him on the breeze, he understood that Vasco had outsmarted him, that comedy had vanquished security, and the next time that cheap clown came up the hill he would have to stand to attention and salute. 'I'll be watching him, but,' the chowkidar muttered to his ever-taciturn parrot, 'one day the stupid lafanga will slip up and when I catch him let's see on what side of the face is his laugh.'

On an Isfahani rug in the chhatri at the corner of the high terrace, Aurora Zogoiby was reclining in an approximation of the clothed-Maja position when Vasco was brought before her at sunset the next day. She was sipping French champagne and smoking an imported cigarette through a long amber holder, with her Ina-swollen belly propped up on silken cushions. He fell in love with her before she had spoken, fell for her as he had meant never to fall for any woman, and in his falling set in motion a great deal of what would follow. As a spurned lover, he became a darker man.

'I've been look-o'ing for a painter,' Aurora told him.

'I am he,' began Vasco, striking an attitude, but Aurora cut him short.

'House painter,' she said, a little brutally. 'Nursery requires to be decoratoed in no time flat. Are you up to it? Speak up! Pay is generous in this house.'

Vasco Miranda was deflated, but also broke. After a few seconds he flashed her his most dazzling smile and inquired, 'Your preferred subjects, madam?'

'Cartoons,' she told him, looking vague. 'You go to the pictures? You read comic-cuts? Then, that mouse, that duck, and what is the name of that bunny. Also that sailor and his saag saga. Maybe the cat that never catchoes the mouse, the other cat that never catchoes the bird, or the other bird that runs too fast for the coy-oat. Give me boulders that only temporarily flattofy you when they drop down on your head, bombs that give black faces only, and running-over-empty-air-until-you-looko-down. Give me knottofied-up rifle-barrels, and bathfuls of big gold coins. Never mind about harps and angels, forget all those stinking gardens; for my kiddies, this is the Paradise I want.'

Autodidact Vasco, just up from Goa, knew next to nothing about wicked woodpeckers or pesky wabbits. In spite of having no idea what Aurora was talking about, however, he grinned and bowed. 'Madam, money talks. You have the hit-fortune to be addressing the absolutely-greatest number-one-in-the-parade Paradise-painter in Bombay.'

'Hit-fortune?' Aurora wondered.

'Like hit-take, hit-alliance, hit-conception, hit-terious,' Vasco explained. 'Opposite of mis-.'

∽

Within days he had moved in; no formal invitation was ever issued, but one way and another he stuck around for thirty-two years. Aurora treated him, at first, like a sort of pet. She unhicked his hairstyle and convinced him to stop trimming his moustache, and, when it grew luxuriant and long, to wax it until it looked like a hairy Cupid's-bow. She got her tailor to run up outfits for him: broad-striped silk suits and huge floppy bow-ties that convinced *le tout* Bombay that Aurora Zogoiby's new discovery must be a raving queen (in fact he was a genuine fifty-fifty bisexual, as many young men and women in the *Elephanta* circle would learn over the years). She was attracted to his huge appetite for information, food, work, and above all pleasure; and for the nakedness with which, smiling his Binaca smile, he went after what he wanted. 'Let him stay,' she pronounced when Abraham wondered mildly if the fellow showed any sign of ever pushing off. 'I like having him around. After all, as he said, he is my hit-fortune; think-o of him as a good-luck charm.' When he had finished decorating the nursery, she gave him his own studio, and equipped it with easels, crayons, a chaise-longue, brushes, paints. Abraham Zogoiby like a sceptical parrot tucked his head into a doubtful shoulder; but let the matter rest. Vasco Miranda kept this studio long after he became rich, and had an American dealer and work-places scattered across the Western world. He spoke of it as his 'roots'; and it was Aurora's decision to uproot him that finally drove him over the edge . . .

Vasco-speak quickly became Zogoiby-chat. Ina, Minnie and Mynah grew up dividing their teachers at Walsingham House School into 'hits' and 'misses'. At home in *Elephanta*, nothing was turned on or off any more; telephones, light-switches, radiograms were always 'opened' or 'closed'. Unaccountable gaps in the language were filled in: if the opposed answer-and-question pairs *there/where, then/when, that/what, thither/whither, thence/whence* all existed, then, Vasco argued, 'every *this* must also have its *whis*, every *these* its *whese*, every *those* its *whoase*.'

As for the nursery, he was as good as his word. In a large light room with a sea view, he created what my sisters and I would always think of as the closest we ever came to an earthly (though mercifully non-horticultural) Eden. For all his Bombay-talkie bendy-cane-twirling comic-uncle antics he was a diligent worker, and within days of his appointment had acquired a knowledge of his subject that far exceeded Aurora's requirements. On the nursery walls he first painted a series of trompe-l'oeil windows, Mughal-palatial, Andalusian Moorish, Manueline Portuguese, roseate Gothic, windows great and small; and then, through these magic casements, which were windows both of and on the world of make-believe, he gave us glimpses of his fabulous throngs. Early-period Mickey on his steamboat, Donald fighting the hands of Time, Unca Scrooge with $ signs in his eyes. Huey-Dewey-Louie. Gyro Gearloose, Goofy, Pluto. Crows, chipmunks, and other couples that have passed beyond my recollection:

Heckle'n'Jeckle, Chip'n'Dale, What'n'Not. He also gave us Looney Tunes: Daffy, Porky, Bugs and Fudd; and in the air above this two-dimensional portrait gallery he hung their cacophonetic expostulations – hahahaHAha, thuffering thuccotash, tawt-I-taw, beep-beep, what's-up-Doc and wak. There were talking roosters, booted pussies and flying, red-caped Wonder Dogs; also great galleries of more local heroes, for he gave us more than we had bargained for, adding djinns on carpets and thieves in giant pitchers and a man in the claws of a giant bird. He gave us story-oceans and abracadabras, Panchatantra fables and new lamps for old. Most important of all, however, was the notion he implanted in all of us through the pictures on our walls: the notion, that is, of the secret identity.

*Who was that masked man?* It was from the walls of my childhood that I first learned about the wealthy socialite Bruce Wayne and his ward Dick Grayson, beneath whose luxury residence lurked the secrets of the Bat-Cave, about mild-mannered Clark Kent who was the space-immigrant Kal-El from the planet Krypton who was Superman, about John Jones who was the Martian J'onn J'onzz and Diana King who was Wonder Woman the Amazon Queen. It was from these walls that I learned how profoundly a super-hero could yearn for normality, that Superman who was brave as a lion and could see through anything except lead wanted more than life itself that Lois Lane should love him as a meek wimp in specs. I never thought of myself as a super-hero, don't get me wrong; but with my hand like a club and my personal calendar losing pages at super-speed I was exceptional all right, and had no desire to be. Learning from the Phantom and the Flash, from Green Arrow and Batman and Robin, I set about devising a secret identity of my very own. (As had my sisters before me; my poor, damaged sisters.)

By the age of seven-and-a-half I had entered adolescence, developing face-fuzz, an adam's apple, a deep bass voice and fully-fledged male sexual organs and appetites; at ten, I was a child trapped in the six-foot-six body of a twenty-year-old giant, and possessed, from these early moments of self-consciousness, by a terror of running out of time. Cursed with speed, I put on slowness the way the Lone Ranger wore a mask. Determined to decelerate my evolution by sheer force of personality, I became ever more languid of body, and my words learned how to stretch themselves out in long sensual yawns. For a time I affected the drawling-aristo speech-mannerisms of Billy Bunter's Indian chum, Hurree Jamset Ram Singh, the Dusky Nabob of Bhanipur: I was never merely thirsty in that period, but 'the thirstfulness was terrific'. My sister Mynah the mimic cured me of what she called 'being in a hurree' by becoming my ridiculing echo, but even after I left the Dusky Nabob behind she continued to convulse the family with slow-motion, moon-walking impersonations of my half-paced manner-isms; but this 'Slomo' – her name for me – was only one of my secret identities, only the most visible of my layers of disguise.

Southpaw, sinister, cuddy-wiftie, keggy-fistie, corrie-paw: what a vocabulary of denigration clusters around left-handedness! What an infinity of small humiliations await the non-dextrous round every corner! Where, pray, is one to find a left-handed trouser-fly, chequebook, corkscrew, or flatiron (yes, an iron; imagine how awkward for a lefty that the flex always emerges from the right)? A left-handed cricketer, being a valued member of any middle order, will have no trouble finding a bat to suit him; but in all the hockey-mad land of India there's no such creature as a wrong-way hockey-stick. Of potato peelers and cameras I will not deign to speak . . . and if life is hard for 'natural' left-handers, how much harder it was for me – for it turned out that I was a right-handed entity, a dexter whose right hand just happened to be a wreck. It was as hard for me to learn to write with my left as it would be for any righty in the world. When I was ten, and looked twenty, my handwriting was no better than a toddler's early scrawls. This, too, I overcame.

What was hard to overcome was the feeling of being in that house of art, surrounded by makers of beauty, both resident and visiting, and knowing that in my life such making must remain a closed book; that where my mother (and Vasco too) went for their greatest joy, there I could not follow. What was harder still was the feeling of being ugly; malformed, wrong, the knowledge that life had dealt me a bad hand, and a freak of nature was obliging me to play it out too fast. What was hardest of all was the sense of being an embarrassment, a shame.

All this, too, I concealed. The first lessons of my Paradise were educations in metamorphosis and disguise.

When I was very young (though not so small), Vasco Miranda would creep into my bedroom while I slept and change the pictures on the walls. Certain windows would shut, others would open; mouse or duck or cat or rabbit would change position, would move from one wall, and one adventure, to the next. For a long time I believed that I did indeed inhabit a magic room, that the fantasy-creatures on the walls came to life after I fell asleep. Then Vasco gave me a different explanation.

'You are changing the room,' he whispered to me one night. 'It is you. You do it in your sleep, with this third hand.' He pointed in the general direction of my heart.

'Whis third hand?'

'Why, this one here, this invisible hand, with these invisible fingers on which are those rough-rough, those badly bitten nails . . . '

'Whese? Whoase?'

' . . . the hand you can only see clearly in your dreams.'

No wonder I loved him. I would have loved him for the gift of the dream-hand alone; but as soon as I was old enough to understand he whispered an even greater secret into my nocturnal ear. He told me that as a result of a botched appendix operation many years ago there was a needle lost inside him. It gave him no trouble but one day it would reach his heart and he would die instantly, speared from within. This was the secret of his hyperactive personality – he slept no more than three hours a night, and when awake, was incapable of sitting still even for three minutes. 'Until the day of the needle I have much to do,' he confided. 'Live until you die, that is my creed.'

*I'm like you.* That was his kind, fraternal message. *I also am short of time.* And maybe he was just trying to reduce my feeling of being alone in the universe, because as I grew I found his story harder to believe, I could not understand how a man so outrageous and unconventional as the famous V. Miranda could accept such a

dreadful fate so passively, why he did not seek to have the needle
traced and then removed; so I came to think of the needle as a
metaphor – as, perhaps, the prick of his ambitions. But that
childhood night, when Vasco tapped at his chest and made
wincing faces, when he rolled his eyes and fell to the floor with his
feet in the air, playing dead for my entertainment – then, then I
believed him utterly; and, recalling this absolute belief in later years
(recalling it even now, after finding him again in Benengeli, in
thrall to other needles, his youthful slenderness swollen into old-
aged obesity, his lightness grown dark, his openness slammed shut,
the wine of love spoiled in him long ago, and turned into the
vinegar of hate), I was able – I am able – to find a different meaning
in his secret. Perhaps the needle, if indeed it really was in there, lost
in the haystack of his body, was in truth the source of his whole self
– perhaps it was his soul. To lose it would be to lose his life at once,
or at least its meaning. He preferred to work, and wait. 'A man's
weakness is his strength, and vercy visa,' he told me once. 'Would
Achilles have been a great warrior without his heel?' and
remembering that I can almost envy him his sharp, wandering,
enabling angel of death.

In the well-known Hans Andersen story the young Kay,
escaping the Snow Queen, is left with a splinter of ice in his veins, a
splinter that pains him for the rest of his life. My whitehair mother
had been Vasco's Snow Queen, whom he loved, and from whom,
in the grip of an enraging humiliation, he finally fled, with the cold
splinter of bitterness in his blood; which continued to ache, to
lower his body temperature, and to chill that once-warm heart.

$\backsim$

Vasco with his silly clothes and verbal inventions, with his
frivolous disrespect of all shibboleths, conventions, sacred cows,
pomposities and gods, and with, above all, his legendary inexhaustibility, as effective in the pursuit of commissions, bed-mates and
squash-balls as of love, became my first hero. When I was four years
old, the Indian Army entered Goa, ending 451 years of Portuguese
colonial rule, and Vasco was plunged for weeks into one of his

black–dog depressions. Aurora encouraged him to see the event as a liberation, as many Goans did, but he was inconsolable. 'Up to now I had only three Gods and the Virgin Mary to disbelieve in,' he complained. 'Now I have three hundred million. And what Gods! For my taste, they have too many heads and hands.' He bounced back soon enough, and spent days in the kitchens of *Elephanta*, winning over our at-first-outraged old cook Ezekiel by teaching him the secrets of Goan cuisine and entering them in a new green copybook of recipes which he hung by the kitchen door on a length of wire; and for weeks after that it was all pork, we were obliged to eat Goan chourisso sausage and pig's liver sarpotel and pork curries with coconut milk until Aurora complained that we were all starting to turn into pigs; whereupon Vasco returned grinning from market bearing immense claw-clacking baskets of shellfish and finny-toothy packets of shark, and when our sweeper-woman caught sight of him she threw down her stick-broom and ran out of the gates, informing Lambajan that she would not return to her sweeping job so long as those 'unclean' monsters were in residence.

Nor was his counter-revolution confined to the dining table. Our days grew full of tales of the heroism of Alfonso de Albuquerque who conquered Goa from the Sultan of Bijapur, one Yusuf Adilshah, on St Catherine's Day, 1510; and of Vasco da Gama, too. 'A pepper-spice family like yours should understand how I feel,' he told Aurora, plaintively. 'Ours is a common history; what do these Indian soldiers know about it?' He sang us mando love songs and served the adults contraband cashew and coconut feni liquor and at night I would sit with him in the room of magic casements while he told me his fishy Goan tales. 'Down with Mother India,' he cried dismissively, striking an attitude, while I giggled under my sheet. 'Viva Mother Portugoose!'

After forty days Aurora put an end to our very own Goan invasion. 'Mourning period is over,' she announced. 'Henceforth history will proceedofy.'

'Colonialist,' complained Vasco dolefully. 'Cultural suprema-cist, plus.' But – as we all did when Aurora issued a command – he obediently complied.

I loved him; but for a long time I did not see – how could I? – the crossfire within him, the battle between his rage-to-become and his shallowness, between loyalty and careerism, between ability and desire. I did not understand the price he had paid on his way to our gates.

He had no friends who preceded our knowledge of him; at least, none was ever mentioned or produced. He never spoke about his family, and rarely about his early life. Even his village of origin, Loutulim with its houses of red laterite stone and its windows with panes of oyster-shell, was a fact we had to take on trust. He did not speak of it, though he did let slip a reference to a period as a market porter in the north Goan town of Mapusa, and at another time there was some mention made of a casual job in the port of Marmagoa. It seemed that in the pursuit of his chosen future he had shed all affiliations of blood and place, a decision which implied a certain ruthlessness, and hinted, too, at instability. He was his own invention, and it should have occurred to Aurora – as it occurred to Abraham and to many members of their circle, as it occurred to my sisters but not to me – that the invention might not work, that in the end it might fall apart. For a long time, however, Aurora refused to hear the slightest criticism of her pet; as, afterwards, in the matter of Uma Sarasvati, another self-inventor, I refused in my turn. When a mistake of the heart is revealed as folly, we think of ourselves as fools, and ask our near-and-dear why they failed to save us from ourselves. But that is an enemy against whom no-one can defend us. Nobody could save Vasco from himself; whatever that was, whoever he might have been, or have become. Nobody could save me.

⌖

In April 1947, when my sister Ina was just three months old and Aurora's pregnancy with the future Minnie-the-mouse had been confirmed, Abraham Zogoiby, proud husband and father, approached Vasco Miranda in a gruff, awkward attempt at friendliness. 'So, if you are supposed to be a proper painter, why not make a portrait of my carrying wife and child?'

This portrait was Vasco's first work on canvas, which Abraham bought for him and Aurora showed him how to prime. His early work had been done on board or paper, for economic reasons; and soon after he moved into his *Elephanta* studio he destroyed everything he had done before that date, declaring himself to be a new man who was only now making his real start in life; only now, as he put it, being born. The Aurora portrait was that new beginning.

I say 'the Aurora portrait' because, when Vasco finally unveiled it (he had refused to let anyone view the work in progress), Abraham discovered, to his fury, that Baby Ina had been wholly ignored. Having already lost half her name, my poor eldest-sister had succeeded in vanishing completely from the work of which she was a principal subject, and which had been commissioned as a direct result of her recent arrival on the scene. (New Minnie-the-bump was omitted too, but at that early stage in Aurora's second pregnancy this was more easily excused.) Vasco had depicted my mother sitting cross-legged on a giant lizard under her chhatri, cradling empty air. Her full left breast, weighty with motherhood, was exposed. 'What in tarnation?' Abraham roared. 'Miranda, men, you got eyes in your head or stones?' But Vasco waved away all naturalistic criticisms; when Abraham pointed out that his wife had at no time posed with uncovered bosom, and that the obliterated Ina was not being breast-fed anyway, the painter's face grew heavy with disdain. 'Next you will be telling me there is no outsize chipkali kept upon the premises as a pet,' he sighed. When Abraham heatedly reminded Vasco who was paying the bills, however, the artist lifted a haughty nose into the air. 'Genius is no rich man's slave,' he averred. 'A canvas is not a mirror to reflect a goo-goo smile. I have seen what I have seen: a presence, and an absence. A fullness, and an emptiness. You wanted a double portrait? Behold. He who hath eyes to see, let him see.'

'So now that you have completed your reflections,' said Abraham in a voice like a knife, 'we also have much upon which we must reflect.'

Was Vasco summarily expelled from the premises for his outrageous slur on the character of Baby Ina? Did the infant's mother fall upon him with bared fang and claw? Reader, he was not; she did not. Aurora Zogoiby as a mother was always a supporter of the Hard Knock schooling system, and saw no need to defend her children against the buffetings of life (was it, I wonder, because she had to collaborate with Abraham to create us that Aurora, a natural soloist, placed us firmly among her lesser works?) . . . However, two days after the unveiling of my mother's portrait, Abraham summoned the painter to his office premises in Cashondeliveri Terrace – named after the nineteenth-century Parsi grandee and cut-throat moneylender Sir Duljee Duljeebhoy Cashondeliveri – to inform him that the picture was 'surplus to requirements' and that it was only on account of the extreme clemency and good nature of Mrs Zogoiby that he was not being thrown back into the street, 'where,' Abraham balefully concluded, 'in my personal opinion, you belong.'

After the rejection of his portrait of my mother, Vasco ceased to wax his moustache and locked himself in his studio for three days, emerging haggard and dehydrated with the canvas, wrapped in gunny sacking, under his arm. He walked out of *Elephanta* past the hostile stares of chowkidar and parrot and did not return for a week. Lambajan Chandiwala had just begun to allow himself to believe that the scoundrel had gone for good when he came back in a yellow-and-black taxicab, wearing a fancy new suit, and completely restored to his old, flamboyant good humour. It turned out that in his three days' sequestration he had painted over my mother's image, hiding it beneath a new work, an equestrian portrait of the artist in Arab attire, which Kekoo Mody – who knew nothing about the rejected painting underneath this strange new depiction of Vasco Miranda in fancy dress, weeping on a great white horse – had managed to sell almost instantly, to no less a personage than the steel billionaire, the crorepati C. J. Bhabha, for a surprisingly high price that enabled Vasco to repay Abraham for the canvas and to order several more. Vasco had discovered that his work was commercial. It was the launch of that extraordinary – and in many ways meretricious – career during which it would seem, at times, that no new hotel lobby or airport terminal was complete until it had been decorated with a gigantic V. Miranda mural that managed, somehow, to be at once pyrotechnic and banal . . . and in every picture Vasco painted, in every triptych and mural and fresco and glass-painting, he never failed to include a small, immaculate image of a cross-legged woman with one exposed breast, sitting on a lizard with her arms cradling nothing, unless of course they were cradling the invisible Vasco, or even the whole world; unless by seeming to be nobody's mother she indeed became the mother of us all; and when he had finished this small detail, on which it often seemed that he lavished more attention than on the rest of the work, he would invariably obliterate it beneath the broad, sweeping brush-strokes by which his work came increasingly to be defined – those famous, phoney marks which looked so flamboyant and in which he could work so prolifically and so fast.

'Did you hate-o me so much to blottofy me out?' cried Aurora, bursting into his studio, both contrite and distraught. 'It was impossible to wait-o five minutes till I could calm old Abie down?' Vasco pretended not to understand. 'But of course little Ina was not the problem,' Aurora went on. 'You made me look too-much sexy, and Abraham was jealous.'

'So now he has nothing to be jealous about,' Vasco said, smiling a bitter, but also flirtatious smile. 'Or maybe he has even more cause; because now, Auroraji, you must lie buried for ever under me. Mr Bhabha will hang us on his bedroom wall, visible Vasco with invisible Aurora beneath, and even more invisible Ina in your hands. In its way, it has become a kind of family group.'

Aurora shook her head. 'What nonsense, I swear. You men. Nonsensical from beginning to end. And a weeping Arab on a horse! It serves that no-taste Bhabha right. Even a bazaar painter would not make such a stupid picture.'

'I have called it *The Artist as Boabdil, the Unlucky (el-Zogoybi), Last Sultan of Granada, Seen Departing from the Alhambra,*' said Vasco with a straight face. '*Or, The Moor's Last Sigh.* I trust this choice of title will not give Abie-ji any further cause for taking offence. Appropriation of surname and family tall-stories and such-much personal material. Without, I regret, asking a by-your-leave.'

Aurora Zogoiby stared at him in wonderment; then began, in

loud and possibly Moorish sobs, to laugh. 'Oh you naughty Vasco,' she said at length, wiping her eyes. 'Oh you bad, black man. How to stoppo my husband from breakofying your wicked neck, that is what I must work out.'

'And you?' Vasco asked. 'Did you like the unlucky, rejected painting?'

'I liked the unlucky, rejected painter,' she said softly, and kissed his cheek, and was gone.

⸻

Ten years later the Moor found his next incarnation in me; and the time came when Aurora Zogoiby, following in V. Miranda's footsteps, also made a picture which she called *The Moor's Last Sigh* . . . I have lingered on these old tales of Vasco because the telling of my own story obliges me to face again, and reconquer, my fear. How am I to explain the wild, stomach-dropping-away, white-knuckle-ride scariness of living an over-accelerated life – of being forced, against my will, to live out the literal truth of the metaphors so often applied to my mother and her circle? In the fast lane, on the fast track, ahead of my time, a jet-setter right down to my genes, I burned – having no option – the candle at both ends, even though by inclination I was of the careful-conservation-of-candlewax brigade. How to communicate the werewolf-movie terror of feeling my rapidly-enlarging feet pushing against the insides of my shoes, of having hair that grew almost fast enough to see; how to make you feel the growing pains in my knees that often made it impossible for me to run? It was a kind of miracle that my spine grew straight. I have been a hothouse plant, a soldier on a perpetual forced march, a traveller caught in a flesh-and-blood time machine, perpetually out of breath, because I've been running faster than the years, in spite of painful knees.

Please understand that I am not claiming to have been a prodigy of any kind. I had no early genius for chess or mathematics or the sitar. Yet I have always been, if only in my uncontrollable increases, prodigious. Like the city itself, Bombay of my joys and sorrows, I mushroomed into a huge urbane sprawl of a fellow, I expanded without time for proper planning, without any pauses to learn from my experiences or my mistakes or my contemporaries, without time for reflection. How then could I have turned out to be anything but a mess?

Much that was corruptible in me has been corrupted; much that was perfectible, but also capable of being demolished, has been lost.

'*See how beautiful, my peacock, my mór* . . . ' my mother sang as she suckled me at her breast, and I may say without false modesty that, for all my South Indian dark skin (*so* unattractive to society matchmakers!), and with the exception of my crippled hand, I did indeed grow up good-looking; but for a long time that right hand made me unable to see anything but ugliness in myself. And to blossom into a handsome young man when in reality I was still a child was in fact a double curse. It first denied me the natural fruits of childhood, the smallness, the *childishness* of being a child, and then departed, so that by the time I had indeed become a man I no longer possessed the golden-apple beauty of youth. (By the age of twenty-three my beard had turned white; and other things, too, had ceased to function as well as they once did.)

My inside and outside have always been out of sync; you will appreciate, then, that what Vasco Miranda once called my 'movie star hit-shapenness' has been of little value in my life.

I will spare you the doctors; my medical history would fill a half a dozen volumes. The tree-stump hand, the super-speed ageing, the astonishing size of me, six foot six in a country where the average male rarely grows above five foot five: all these were subjected to repeated scrutiny. (To this day the words 'Breach Candy Hospital' conjure up, for me, the memory of a sort of house of correction, a benevolent torture chamber, a zone of infernal torments run by well-meaning demons who mortified me – who *roasted* me – who *tikka-kababed and Bombay-ducked* me – for my own good.) And in the end, after every effort, the slow inevitable shaking of the eminent stethoscoped head of some boss-devil, the upturned-palm gestures of helplessness, the murmurs about karma, kismet, Fate. As well as medical practitioners, I was taken to see Ayurvedic specialists, Tibia College professors, faith-healers, saints. Aurora was a thorough and determined woman, and was accordingly prepared – again, in my best interests! – to expose me to all manner of guru-fakery which she herself both despised and abhorred. 'Just in case,' I heard her say to Abraham more than once. 'I swear, if one of these ju-ju guys can fix the poor boy's clock, then I will convertofy in one tick flat.'

Nothing worked. That was the time of the emergence of the boy-mahaguru Lord Khusro Khusrovani Bhagwan, who acquired a following of millions in spite of the persistent rumours that he was the wholly spurious creation of his mother, a certain Mrs Dubash. One day, when I was about five (and looked ten), Aurora Zogoiby swallowed her scruples – *for my sake*, naturally – and (for a high price) arranged a private audience with the magic child. We visited him aboard a luxury yacht anchored in Bombay harbour, and in his chooridar pajamas, gold skirt and turban he struck my parents as a frightened child obliged to live his whole life trapped in wedding-party fancy-dress; in spite of this, my mother gritted her teeth, explained my problems and asked for his help. The boy Khusro looked at me with grave, sad, intelligent eyes.

'Embrace your fate,' he said. 'Rejoice in what gives you grief. That which you would flee, turn and run towards it with all your heart. Only by becoming your misfortune will you transcend it.'

'Too much wisdom,' exclaimed Mrs Dubash, who lay munching mangoes messily on a divan. 'Wah-wah! Rubies, diamonds, pearls! Now, please,' she added, concluding our audience, 'account may kindly be settled. Cash rupees only, unless foreign currency is available, in which event fifteen per cent discount may be given for cash dollars or pounds sterling.'

For a long time I remembered those days with bitterness, the useless doctors, the even more useless quacks. I resented my mother for the hoops she put me through, for being the hypocrite these genuflections to the guru industry seemed to reveal her to be. I don't resent her any more; I have learned to see the love in what she did, learned to see that her humiliation at the hands of all the mango-sticky Mrs Dubashes we encountered was at least as great as mine. Also, I must admit, Lord Khusro taught me a lesson that I have often, in my life, been obliged to learn again. And on each of these occasions, the cost has been high, and no foreign-currency discount has been offered.

By embracing the inescapable, I lost my fear of it. I'll tell you a secret about fear: it's an absolutist. With fear, it's all or nothing. Either, like any bullying tyrant, it rules your life with a stupid blinding omnipotence, or else you overthrow it, and its power vanishes in a puff of smoke. And another secret: the revolution against fear, the engendering of that tawdry despot's fall, has more or less nothing to do with 'courage'. It is driven by something much more straightforward: the simple need to get on with your life. I stopped being afraid because, if my time on earth was limited, I didn't have seconds to spare for funk. Lord Khusro's injunction echoed Vasco Miranda's motto, another version of which I found, years later, in a story by J. Conrad. *I must live until I die.*

I inherited the family's gift for sleep. All of us slept like babies when sadness or trouble loomed. (Not always, it's true: the thirteen-year-old Aurora da Gama's window-opening, ornament-tossing insomnia was an old, but important, exception to this rule.) So on days when I felt badly I would lie down and switch myself off, 'close' myself, as Vasco would put it, like a light; and hope to 'open' in a better frame of mind. This didn't always work. Sometimes in the middle of the night I would awake and weep, I would cry out pitifully for love. The shakes, the sobs came from a place too deep within to be identifiable. In time I accepted these nocturnal tears, too, as the penalty I had to pay for being exceptional; though, as I have said, I had no desire for exceptionality – I wanted to be Clark Kent, not any kind of Superman. In our fine mansion I would happily have lived out my days as a wealthy socialite like Bruce Wayne, with or without benefit of a 'ward'. But no matter how hard I wished, my secret, essential bat-nature could not be denied.

⤳

Permit me to clarify a point about Vasco Miranda: from the very start, there were frightening signs that not all the bats in his belfry were harmless. We who loved him would gloss over the times when an aggressive fury would pour out of him, when he seemed to crackle with such a current of dark, negative electricity that we feared to touch him lest we stuck to him and burned up. He went on dreadful benders and, like Aires (and Belle) da Gama in another time and place, would turn up unconscious in some Kamathipura gutter or wandering dazed around the Sassoon fish dock, drunk, drugged, bruised, bleeding, robbed, and giving off a terrible fishy stench, which could not be washed off him for days. When he became successful, the darling of the international moneyed establishment, it took a lot of hush-money to keep these episodes out of the newspapers, especially because there were indications that many of the partners he found on these bisexual orphic sprees were afterwards less than happy about their experiences. There was a Hell in Vasco, born of whatever devil-deal he had done to shed his past and be born again through us, and at times he seemed capable of bursting into flames. 'I am the Grand Old Duke of York,' he would say when he was better. 'When I am up I am up, and when I am down I am down. Also, by the way, I have had ten thousand men; and ten thousand women, too.'

On the night of India's independence, the red mist came over him in a rush. The contradictions of that high moment tore him apart. That celebration of freedom whose engulfing emotions he could not avoid even though, as a Goan, he was technically not involved, and which, to his horror, was taking place while great blood-rivers were still flowing in the Punjab, destroyed the fragile equilibrium at the heart of his invented self, and set the madman free. That was the way my mother told it, anyhow, and no doubt that version contained some of the truth, but I know that there was also the matter of his love for her, the love he could not openly declare, which filled him up and boiled over, turning to rage. He sat at the foot of Aurora and Abraham's long and glittering table, glaring at the many distinguished and excited guests, and drank vinho verde in quantity and at speed, sunk in darkness. As midnight burst in showers of light across the sky, his mood grew ever blacker; until, deeply drunk, he rose unsteadily to his feet and showered the guests with blurry, spittle-flecked abuse.

'What are you all so pleased about?' he shouted, swaying. 'This isn't your night. Bleddy Macaulay's minutemen! Don't you get it?

Bunch of English-medium misfits, the lot of you. Minority group members. Square-peg freaks. *You don't belong here.* Country's as alien to you as if you were what's-the-word *lunatics*. *Moon-men*. You read the wrong books, get on the wrong side in every argument, think the wrong thoughts. Even your bleddy dreams grow from foreign roots.'

'Stop making a fool of yourself, Vasco,' said Aurora. 'Everybody here is shocked by the Hindu-Muslim killings. You have no monopoly on that pain, only on vinho verde and on being a righteous bum.'

Which would have stopped most people: but it didn't stop poor, driven Vasco, crazed by history, love and the torment of keeping up the great pretence of himself. 'Useless fucking art-johnny clever-dicks,' he jeered, leaning sideways at a dangerous angle. 'Circular sexualist India my *foot*. No. Bleddy tongue twister came out wrong. Secular-socialist. That's it. Bleddy *bunk*. Panditji sold you that stuff like a cheap watch salesman and you all bought one and now you wonder why it doesn't work. Bleddy Congress party full of bleddy fake Rolex salesmen. You think India'll just roll over, all those bloodthirsty bloodsoaked gods'll just roll over and *die*. Our great hostess, Aurora, great lady, great artist, thinks she can dance the gods away. *Dance!* Tat-tat-taa-dreegay-thun-thun! Tai! Tat-tai! Tat-tai! Jesus Christ.'

'Miranda,' said Abraham, rising, 'that's enough.'

'And I'll tell *you* something, Mr Big Businessman Abie,' Vasco said, beginning to giggle. 'Let me give you a tip. Only one power in this damn country is strong enough to stand up against those gods and it isn't blankety blank sockular specialism. It isn't blankety blank Pandit Nehru and his blankety blank protection-of-minorities Congress watch-wallahs. You know what it is? I'll tell you what it is. Corruption. You get me? Bribery, and.'

He lost his balance and fell backwards. Two bearers in gold-buttoned white Nehru jackets held him, preparing to remove him from the party at Abraham's signal. But Abraham Zogoiby paused, and allowed the scene to play itself out.

'Jolly old damn fine bribery and grease,' said Vasco, in tearful tones, as if speaking of an old and beloved dog. 'Backhanders, payoffs, sweeteners. You follow me? Abie-ji: are you with me? V. Miranda's definition of democracy: one man one bribe. That's the way. That's the big secret. That's it.' His hands rushed to his mouth in sudden alarm. 'Oh. Oh. Stupid me. Stupid, stupid Vasco. It's no secret. Abie-ji being such a bleddy big shot, of course he knows it all. Such a bleddy big grandmother sucking so many bleddy big eggs. Apologies. Please to excuse.'

Abraham nodded; the white jackets hooked their arms under his armpits and began to drag him backwards.

'One more thing,' Vasco roared, so loudly that the bearers faltered. He hung in their arms like a stuffed doll, waving an insane finger. 'Piece of good advice for you all. Get on the boats with the British! Just get on the bleddy boats and *buggeroff*. This place has no use for you. It'll beat you and eat you. Get out! Get out while the getting's good.'

'And you,' Abraham asked, standing with steely courtesy in the shocked silence. 'You, Vasco. What advice do you have for yourself?'

'Oh, *me*,' he sang out as the white coats bore him away. 'Don't worry about *me*. I'm *Portuguese*.'

# 11

NOBODY EVER MADE A movie called *Father India*. 'Bharat-pita?' Sounds all wrong. 'Hindustan-ké-Bapuji'? Too specifically Gandhian. 'Valid-e-Azam'? Overly Mughal. 'Mr India', however, perhaps the crudest of all such nationalistic formulations, that we did latterly get. The hero was a slick young loverboy trying to convince us of his super-heroic powers: no paternal connotations there, neither bouncy India–Abba–man nor patriarchal Indodaddy. Just a made-in–India runty-bodied imitation Bond. The great Sridevi, at her voluptuous-siren best in the wettest of wet saris, stole the movie with contemptuous ease . . . but I remember the picture for another reason. It seems to me that maybe, in this trashy extravaganza, as worthless in its gaudy colours as the old Nargis mother-vehicle was sombre and worthy, the producers did unintentionally provide us with an image of the National Father after all. There he sits, like a dragon in his cave, like a thousand-fingered puppet-master, like the heart of the heart of darkness; commander of uzied legions, fingertip-controller of pillars of diabolic fire, orchestrator of all the secret music of the under-spheres: the arch-villain, the dark capo, Moriartier than Moriarty, Blofelder than Blofeld, not just Godfather but Gone-farthest, the dada of all dadas: *Mogambo*. His name, filched from the title of an old Ava Gardner vehicle, a forgettable piece of African hokum, is carefully chosen to avoid offending any of the country's communities; it's neither Muslim nor Hindu, Parsi nor Christian, Jain nor Sikh, and if there's an echo in it of the bongo-bongo *Sanders-of-the-River* caricatures inflicted by post-war Hollywood on the people of the 'Dark Continent', well, that's a brand of xenophobia unlikely to make many enemies in India today.

In Mr India's struggle against Mogambo I recognise the life-

and-death oppositions of many movie fathers and sons. Here is *Blade Runner*'s tragic replicant crushing his creator's skull in a lethal filial embrace; and *Star Wars*'s Luke Skywalker in his ultimate duel with Darth Vader, as champions of the light and dark sides of the Force. And in this junk drama with its cartoon villain and gimcrack hero, I see a lurid mirror-image of what was never, will never be a movie: the story of Abraham Zogoiby and myself.

⌒

On the face of it he was the very antithesis of a demon king. The Abraham Zogoiby I first came to know, sixtyish, with his stone-vase limp accentuated by age, seemed a weak, diminished figure, whose breaths came raspingly and whose right hand rested lightly against his chest, in a gesture at once self-protective and obeisant. Not much left there (except duty-managerish deference) of the fellow with whom the heiress Aurora had fallen so swiftly and deeply into pepper love! In my childhood memory of him he is a rather colourless phantom hanging around the edges of tumultu-ous Aurora's court, hesitant, slightly stooped, frowning the vague frown with which servitors indicate their anxiety to please. In the forward tilt of his body there appeared to be something unpleas-antly over-eager, something ingratiating. 'Here's a tautology,' sharp-tongued Aurora was fond of saying to raise a laugh. ' "*Weak man.*" ' And I, as Abraham's son, could not help despising Abraham for being the butt of the joke, and feeling that his weakness demeaned us all – by which I meant, of course, all men.

In accordance with some strange logic of the heart, Aurora's great passion for 'her Jew' had cooled rapidly after my birth. Characteristically, she announced the cooling of her ardour to anyone within earshot. 'When I see him coming at me, on heat and smellofying of curry,' she'd laugh, 'baap-ré! Then I hide-o behind my kids and hold my nose.' These humiliations, too, he suffered without protest. 'Men in our part of the world!' Aurora would hold forth in the famous orange and gold drawing-rooms. 'All are either peacocks or shabbies. But even a peacock like my *mór* is as nothing compared to us ladies, who live-o in a blaze of glory. Look out for the shabbies, I say! They-tho are our jailers. They are the ones holding the cash-books and the keys to the gilded cage.'

This was the closest she came to thanking Abraham for the uncomplaining inexhaustibility of his cheques, for the city of gold he had so quickly built from her family's wealth, which for all its old-money graciousness had been no more than, as it were, a village, a country estate, or a small provincial town, compared to the great metropolis of their present fortune. Aurora was not unaware that her lavishness required maintenance, so that she was bound to Abie by her own needs. Sometimes she came close to admitting this, even to worrying that the scale of her spending, or the looseness of her tongue, might bring the house down. Always fond of macabre bedtime stories, she would tell me the parable of the scorpion and the frog, in which the scorpion, having hitched a ride across a stretch of water in return for a promise not to attack his mount, breaks his vow and administers a potent and fatal sting. As the frog and scorpion are both drowning, the murderer apologises to his victim. 'I couldn't help it,' says the scorpion. 'It's in my nature.'

Abraham, it took me a long time to see, was tougher than any frog; she stung him, for it was in her nature to do so, but he did not drown. How easy was my scorn for him, how long it took me to understand his pain! For he had never ceased to love her as fiercely as on the day of their first meeting; and everything he did, he did for her. The greater, the more public her betrayals, the more overarching, and secret, grew his love.

(And when I learned the things he had done, things for which it might be said that despising was an inadequate response, I found it hard to summon back that youthful disgust; for by then I had fallen under the power of a frog of a different water, and my own deeds had taken from me the right to be my father's judge.)

When she abused him in public, she did so with a diamond smile that suggested she was only teasing, that her constant belittlements were no more than a way of concealing an adoration too enormous to express; it was an ironising smile that sought to put her behaviour into quotes. This act was never completely convincing. Often, she drank – the anti-alcohol regulations came and went, paralleling Morarji Desai's political fortunes, and after the partition of the State of Bombay into Maharashtra and Gujarat, they disappeared from the city for good – and when she drank, she cursed. Confident of her genius, armed with a tongue as merciless as her beauty and as violent as her work, she excluded nobody from her colaratura damnations, from the hawk-swoops and rococo riffs and great set-piece ghazals of her cursing, all delivered with that cheery stone-hard smile that sought to anaesthetise her victims as she ripped out their innards. (Ask me how it felt! I was her only son. The closer to the bull you work, the likelier you are to be gored.)

It was Belle all over again, of course; Belle, returning, as foretold, to occupy her daughter's body. *You will see*, Aurora had said. *From now on I am in her place.*

Imagine: in a cream silk sari edged with a golden geometric design intended to call to mind a Roman senator's toga – or perhaps, if the tide of her ego is running especially high, in an even more resplendent sari of imperial purple – she lounges on a chaise and stinks out her drawing-rooms with dragon-clouds of cheap beedi smoke, presiding over one of her occasional notorious nights loosened by whisky and worse, nights whose socialite licentiousness sharpens the city's many wagging tongues; although she herself has never been seen acting improperly, neither with men nor with women nor, it should be said, with needles . . . and in the small hours of the debauch, she strides around like an inebriated prophetess, and launches into a savage parody of what booze unleashed in Vasco Miranda on Independence Night; without troubling to acknowledge his copyright, so that the assembled company has no idea that she is offering up the most ferocious of lampoons, she details the coming destruction of her guests – painters, models, 'middle cinema' auteurs, thespians, dancers, sculptors, poets, playboys, sporting heroes, chess masters, journalists, gamblers, antique-smugglers, Americans, Swedes, freaks, *demi-mondaines*, and the loveliest and wildest of the city's gilded young – and the parody is so convincing, so convinced, its irony so profoundly concealed, that it is impossible not to believe in her lip-smacking *schadenfreude*, or – for her moods are swinging rapidly – in her Olympian, immortal unconcern.

'Imitations of life! Historical anomalies! Centaurs!' she declaims. 'Will you not be blownofied to bits by the coming storms? Mixtures, mongrels, ghost-dancers, shadows! Fishes out of water! Bad times are coming, darlings, don't think they won't, and then all ghosts will go to Hell, the night will blot out shadows, and mongrel blood will run-o, as thin and free as water. I, but, will survive' – this, at the height of her peroration, delivered with back arched and finger stabbing at the sky like Liberty's candle – 'on account, you miserable wretches, of my Art.' Her guests lie in heaps, too far gone to listen, or to care.

For her offspring, too, she foretells tragedies. 'Poor kids are such a bungle, seems like they are doomed to tumble.'

. . . And we spent our lives living up, down and sideways to her predictions . . . did I mention that she was irresistible? Listen: she was the light of our lives, the excitement of our imaginations, the beloved of our dreams. We loved her even as she destroyed us. She called out of us a love that felt too big for our bodies, as if she had made the feeling and then given it to us to feel – as if it were a work. If she trampled over us, it was because we lay down willingly beneath her spurred-and-booted feet; if she excoriated us at night, it was on account of our delight at the sweet lashings of her tongue. It was when I finally realised this that I forgave my father; for we were all her slaves, and she made our servitude feel like Paradise. Which is, they say, what goddesses can do.

And in the aftermath of her fatal plunge into rocky water, it occurred to me that the fall she had been predicting, with that superb and ice-hard smile, with the irony that everybody missed, had perhaps always been her own.

⌒

I forgave Abraham, too, because I began to see that even though they no longer slept in the same bed each of them was still the one whose good opinion the other needed most; that my mother needed Abraham's approval as much as he longed for hers.

He was always the first to see her work (closely followed by Vasco Miranda, who invariably contradicted everything my father had said). In the decade after Independence, Aurora fell into a deep creative confusion, a semi-paralysis born of an uncertainty not merely about realism but about the nature of the real itself. Her small output of paintings from this period is tortured, unresolved, and with hindsight it is easy to see in these canvases the tension between Vasco Miranda's playful influence, his fondness for imaginary worlds whose only natural law was his own sovereign whimsicality, and Abraham's dogmatic insistence on the importance, at that historical juncture, of a clear-sighted naturalism that would help India describe herself to herself. The Aurora of those days – and this was in part why she indulged on occasion in nights of intoxicated shallow ranting – veered uneasily between clumsily revisionist mythological paintings and an uncomfortable, even stilted return to the lizard-signed documentary pictures of her Chipkali work. It was easy for an artist to lose her identity at a time when so many thinkers believed that the poignancy and passion of the country's immense life could only be represented by a kind of selfless, dedicated – even patriotic – mimesis. Abraham was by no means the only advocate of such ideas. The great Bengali film director Sukumar Sen, Aurora's friend and, of all her contemporaries, perhaps her only artistic equal, was the best of these realists, and in a series of haunting, humane films brought to Indian cinema – Indian cinema, that raddled old tart! – a fusion of heart and mind that went a long way towards justifying his aesthetic. Yet these realist movies were never popular – in a moment of bitter irony they were attacked by Nargis Dutt, Mother India herself, for their Westernised élitism – and Vasco (openly) and Aurora (secretly) preferred the series of films for children in which Sen let his fantasy rip, in which fish talked, carpets flew and young boys dreamed of previous incarnations in fortresses of gold.

And apart from Sen there was the group of distinguished writers who gathered for a time under Aurora's wing, Premchand and Sadat Hasan Manto and Mulk Raj Anand and Ismat Chughtai, committed realists all; but even in their work there were elements of the fabulous, for example in *Toba Tek Singh*, Manto's great story of the partition of the sub-continent's lunatics at the time of the larger Partition. One of the crazies, formerly a prosperous landlord, was caught in a no-man's land of the soul, unable to say whether his Punjabi home town lay in India or Pakistan, and in his madness, which was also the madness of the time, he retreated into a kind of celestial gibberish, with which Aurora Zogoiby fell in love. Her painting of the tragic final scene of Manto's story, in which the hapless loony is stranded between two stretches of barbed wire, behind which lie India and Pakistan, is perhaps her finest work of the period, and his piteous gibberish, which represents not only his personal communications breakdown but our own, forms the picture's long and wonderful title: *Uper the gur gur the annexe the bay dhayana the mung the dal of the laltain.*

The spirit of the age, and Abraham's own preferences, dragged Aurora towards naturalism; but Vasco reminded her of her instinctive dislike of the purely mimetic, which had led her to reject her Chipkalist disciples, and tried to turn her back towards the epic-fabulist manner which expressed her true nature, encouraging her to pay attention once again not only to her dreams but to the dream-like wonder of the waking world. 'We are not a nation of "averagis",' he argued, 'but a magic race. Will you spend your life painting boot-polish boys and air-hostesses and two acres of land? Is it to be all coolies and tractor-drivers and Nargis-y hydro-electric projects from now on? In your own family you can see the disproof of such a world-view. Forget those damnfool realists! The real is always hidden – isn't it? – inside a miraculously burning bush! Life is fantastic! Paint that – you owe it to your fantastic, un-real son. What a giant he is, this beautiful child-man, your human time-rocket! "Chipko" to his incredible truth – stick to that, to him, not to that used-up lizard shit.'

Because of her desire for Abraham's good opinion, Aurora for a time put on artistic clothes that looked unnatural upon her; because Vasco was the voice of her secret identity she forgave him every excess. And because of her confusion, she drank, grew raucous, hostile and obscene. Finally, however, she took Vasco's tip; and made me, for a long while, the talisman and centrepiece of her art.

As for Abraham, I often saw a melancholy shadow of puzzlement crossing his face. He was certainly mystified by me. Realism

174

confused him, so that, after one of his long absences, on his return from business trips to Delhi or Cochin or other destinations whose identity remained secret for many years, he would either bring me absurdly tiny clothes that were appropriate for a child my age, but much too small for me; or else he would offer me books that a young man my size might enjoy, books that utterly baffled the child who dwelt within all my outsized flesh. And he was bewildered, too, by his wife, by the change in her feelings towards him, by the darkening violence within her, and by her self-destructive gifts, which had never been more fully demonstrated than on her last meeting with the Prime Minister of India, nine months before I was born . . .

⌒

. . . Nine months before I was born, Aurora Zogoiby travelled to Delhi to receive, from the President's hands and in the presence of her good friend the Prime Minister, a State Award – the so-called 'Esteemed Lotus' – for her services to the arts. By an unfortunate coincidence, however, Mr Nehru had only just returned from a trip to England, during the course of which he had spent most of his private time in the company of Edwina Mountbatten. Now it was a much-observed (though little-commented-on) fact of our family life that the mere mention of the name of that distinguished lady was enough to send Aurora into vituperative apoplexies. The intimate details of the friendship between Pandit Nehru and the last Viceroy's wife have long been a matter for speculation; my own speculations linger, more and more, on the similar rumours about the PM and my mother. Certain chronological verities cannot be denied. Turn back the clock four and a half months from my birth, and you return to the events at the Lord's Central House, Matheran, and what may have been the last occasion on which my parents made love. But let the clock travel a further four and a half months in reverse and there is Aurora Zogoiby in Delhi, entering a ceremonial hall in Rashtrapati Bhavan, and being received by Panditji himself; there is Aurora Zogoiby creating a scandal, by giving in to what the newspapers would call 'an unseemly display of artistic temperament', and saying loudly into Nehru's appalled face: 'That chicken-breasted mame! Edweenie Mount-teenie! If Dickie was the -roy then my dear she was certainly the Vice-. God knows why you go keep on going sucking back like a beggar at her gate. If it's white meat you want, ji, you won't find-o much on her.'

After which, leaving the assembled company open-mouthed and the President waiting with the Esteemed Lotus in his hand, she spurned the award, turned on her heel, and went back to Bombay. That, at least, was the version published in the nation's horrified press the following day; but two details nag at me, the first of which is the interesting point that when Aurora went north, Abraham went south. Mysteriously failing to accompany his beloved wife at this moment of her high recognition, he went instead to check on business interests back home. On some days I can't help but see this – hard as it is to believe! – as the behaviour of a complaisant husband. . . and the second detail has to do with the copybooks of Ezekiel, our cook.

Ezekiel, my Ezekiel: eternally ancient, egg-bald, his three canary-yellow teeth bared in a permanent cackling grin, he squatted beside a traditional open stove, waving the charcoal fumes away with a shell-shaped fan of straw. He was an artist in his own right, and recognised as such by all who ate the food whose secret recipes he recorded, in a slow, shaky hand, in the green-jacketed copybooks which he kept in a padlocked box: like emeralds. Quite an archivist, our Ezekiel; for in his hoard of copybooks were not only recipes but records of meals – a full account, made over all the long years of his service, of what was served to whom on which occasion. During my sequestered childhood years (of which more anon) I spent long hours of apprenticeship at his side, learning how to do with one hand what he did with two; and learning, too, our family's history of food, divining moments of stress by the margin-notes which told me that very little had been eaten, guessing at the angry scenes behind the laconic entry 'spilled'. Happy moments were evoked also; by the frill-less references to wine, or cake, or other special requests – favourite dishes for a child who had done well at school, celebratory banquets marking some triumph in business or in painting. It is true, of course, that in food as in other matters there is much about our personalities that remains opaque. What is one to make of my sisters' united hatred for aubergines, or of my passion for the selfsame brinjal? What is revealed by my father's preference for mutton or chicken on the bone, and my mother's insistence on nothing but bone-free flesh? I set such mysteries aside to record that when I consulted the copybook relating to the period under discussion, it revealed that Aurora did not return to Bombay for three nights after the uproar in Delhi. I am too familiar with the Delhi–Bombay Frontier Mail down-train to need to check: the journey took two nights and a day, leaving one night unaccounted for. 'Madam probably stopped on in Delhi to eat some other khansama's dish,' was Ezekiel's mournful comment on her absence. He sounded like a betrayed man trying to forgive his errant, unfaithful lover.

*Some other khansama* . . . what spicy dish kept Aurora Zogoiby away from home? What, to put it bluntly, was cooking? It was one of my mother's weaknesses that her grief and pain so often came out as anger; it was, in my view, a further weakness that once she had permitted herself the luxury of letting rip, she felt a huge rush of apologetic affection for the people she hurt. As if good feelings could only swell up in her in the aftermath of a ruinous flood of bile.

Nine months to the day before I arrived, there was a missing night. But innocent-till-proven-otherwise is an excellent rule, and neither Aurora nor that late great leader have any proof of impropriety to answer. Probably there are perfectly good explanations for all these matters. Children never understand why parents act as they do.

How vain it would be of me baselessly to claim descent – even illegitimate descent – from so great a line! Reader: I have sought only to express a certain head-shaking puzzlement, but rest assured, I make no allegations. I stick to my story, namely, that I was conceived at the hill-station that I have previously specified; and that certain biological norms were diverged from thereafter. Permit me to insist: this is not some sort of cover-up.

Jawaharlal Nehru was sixty-seven years old in 1957; my mother was thirty-two. They never met again; nor did the great man ever again travel to England, to meet another great man's wife.

Public opinion – not for the last time – swung against Aurora. Between Delhi-folk and Bombay types there has always been a measure of mutual contempt (I am speaking, of course, of the bourgeoisie); Bombay-wallahs have tended to dismiss Delhiites as the fawning lackeys of power, as greasy-pole-climbers and placemen, while the capital's citizens have sneered at the superficiality, the bitchiness, the cosmopolitan 'Westoxication' of my home-town's business babus and lacquered, high-gloss femmes. But in the furore over Aurora's refusal of the Lotus, Bombay was as scandalized as Delhi. Now, the many enemies her high-handed style had made saw their opportunity and struck. Scoundrelly patriots called her a traitress, the godly called her godless, self-styled spokesmen for the poor berated her for being rich. Many artists failed to defend her: the Chipkalists remembered her attack on them, and were silent; those artists who were truly in thrall to the West, and spent their careers imitating, to dreadful effect, the styles of the great figures of the United States and France, now abused her for 'parochialism', while those other artists – and there were many of these – who floundered about in the dead sea of the country's ancient heritage, producing twentieth-century versions of the old miniature art (and often, secretly, making pornographic fakes of Mughal or Kashmiri art on the side), reviled her just as loudly for 'losing touch with her roots'. All the old family scandals were raked up, except for the Rumpelstiltskin firstborn-son business between Abraham and his mother Flory, which had never become public property; the newspapers printed with relish every available detail of the disgrace of old Francisco with his 'Gama rays', and the absurd efforts of Camoens da Gama to train a troupe of South Indian Lenins, and the murderous war between the Lobos and Menezeses as a result of which the da Gama brothers were sent to jail, and the suicide-by-drowning of poor heartbroken Camoens, and, of course, the great scandal of the coming together, out of wedlock, of the poor, no-account Jew and his filthy-rich Christian whore. When questions about the legitimacy of the Zogoiby children began to be hinted at, however, it seems that on a certain day the editors of all the major newspapers received quiet visits from emissaries of Abraham Zogoiby, who had a word-to-the-wise in their ears; and after that the press campaign stopped instantly, as if it had had a heart attack and died of fright.

Aurora retreated somewhat from public life. Her salon continued to glitter, but the more conservative elements in high society and in the country's artistic and intellectual life dropped her for good. She herself remained, more and more, inside the walls of her personal Paradise, and turned, once and for all, in the direction Vasco Miranda had been urging upon her, the true direction of her heart: that is to say, inwards, to the reality of dreams.

(It was at this time, when language riots prefigured the division of the state, that she announced that neither Marathi nor Gujarati would be spoken within her walls; the language of her kingdom was English and nothing but. 'All these different lingos cuttofy us off from one another,' she explained. 'Only English brings us together.' And to prove her point she would recite, with a doleful expression that could not fail to provoke wicked thoughts in her audience, the popular rhyme of those days: 'A-B-C-D-E-F-G, out of this came Panditji.' To which only her trusted ally V. Miranda had the nerve to reply, 'H-I-J-K-L-M-N, and now he's buggered off again.')

I, too, was obliged to lead a relatively sheltered life; and it must be stressed that the two of us were thrown together more than most mothers and sons, because soon after I was born, she began the series of major canvases with which she is most strongly associated; those works whose name ('the Moor paintings') is the same as mine, in which my growing-up is more meaningfully documented than in any photograph album, and which will keep us joined to each other for ever and a day, no matter how far, and how violently, our lives drove us apart.

❧

The truth about Abraham Zogoiby was that he had put on a disguise; had created a mild-mannered secret identity to mask his covert super-nature. He had deliberately painted the dullest possible picture of himself – not for him the kitsch excess of Vasco Miranda's lachrymose self-portrait *en arabe*! – over the thrilling but unacceptable reality. The deferential, complaisant surface was what Vasco would have called his 'overneath'; underneath it, he ruled a Mogambo-ish underworld more lurid than any masala-movie fantasy.

Soon after he settled in Bombay he had made a pilgrimage of respect to old man Sassoon, head of the great Baghdadi-Jewish family which had hobnobbed with English kings, intermarried with the Rothschilds, and dominated the city for a hundred years. The patriarch agreed to receive him, but only in the Sassoon & Co offices in the Fort; not at home, not as an equal, but as a johnny-come-lately supplicant from the provinces did Abraham come into the Presence. 'The country may be about to become free,' the old gentleman told him, smiling benignly, 'but you must appreciate, Zogoiby, that Bombay is a closed town.'

Sassoon, Tata, Birla, Readymoney, Jeejeebhoy, Cama, Wadia, Bhabha, Goculdas, Wacha, Cashondeliveri – these great houses had their grip on the city, on its precious and industrial metals, on its chemicals, textiles and spices, and they weren't about to let go. The da Gama-Zogoiby enterprise had a solid foothold in the last of these areas; and everywhere he went, Abraham received tea or 'cold-drink', sweetmeats, warm welcomes, and, lastly, a series of unfailingly courteous but icily serious warnings to keep off any other patches over which he might have been running an entrepreneurial eye. A mere fifteen years later, however, when official sources revealed that just one and a half per cent of the country's companies owned over half of all private capital, and that even within this élite one and a half per cent, just twenty companies dominated the rest, and that within these twenty companies there were four super-groups who controlled, between them, one quarter of all the share capital in India, the da Gama-Zogoiby C-50 Corporation had already risen to number five.

He had begun by studying history. There is a certain endemic vagueness in Bombay on the subject of time past; ask a man how long he's been in business and he'll answer, 'Long.' – Very well, Sir, and how old is your house? – 'Old. From Old Time.' – I see;

and your great-grandfather, when was he born? – 'Some time back. What are you asking? Such dead letters are lost in the ancient mists.' Records are kept tied up with ribbon in dusty box-rooms and nobody ever looks at them. Bombay, a relatively new city in an immensely ancient land, is not interested in yesterdays. 'So if today and tomorrow are competitive areas,' Abraham reasoned, 'let me make my first investment in what nobody values: i.e., what is gone.' He devoted much time and many resources to a close study of the great families, unearthing their secrets. From the history of the Cotton Mania, or Bubble, of the 1860s he learned that many grandees had been badly damaged, almost ruined, by that time of wild speculation, and that after it their dealings were marked by a profound caution and conservatism. 'Therefore a gap may exist', Abraham hypothesised, 'in the area of risk. None but the brave deserves the prize.' He traced the great houses' networks of connections and understood how they pulled the strings; and he discovered, too, which empires were built on sand. So when, in the mid-Fifties, he made his spectacular reverse takeover of the House of Cashondeliveri, which had begun as a firm of money-lenders and grown over the course of a century into a giant enterprise with extensive holdings in banking, land, ships, chemicals and fish, it was because he had discovered that the old Parsi family at its heart was in a state of terminal decline, 'and when decay is so advanced,' he noted in his private journal, 'then the rotten teeth must be yanked out double-quick, or the whole body may suffer infection and die.' With each Cashondeliveri genera-tion the level of business acumen had declined sharply and the present generation of playboy brothers had incurred colossal gambling losses in the casinos of Europe, and, in addition, had been foolish enough to become involved in a hushed-up bribery scandal resulting from their efforts to export Indian business methods somewhat too crudely into Western financial markets that required rather more subtle treatment. All these skeletons Abra-ham's staff assiduously extracted from their cupboards; and then one fine morning Abraham simply walked into the inner sanctum of the House of Cashondeliveri and quite straightforwardly and in broad daylight blackmailed the two pale not-quite-youths he found there into submitting instantly to his many and precise demands. The once-great clan's weakling scions, Lowjee Lowerjee Cashondeliveri and Jamibhoy Lifebhoy Cashondeliveri, seemed, as they sold their birthright, almost happy to be free of the responsibilities they were so ill-equipped to shoulder, 'the way the decadent Persian Emperors must have felt when the armies of Islam thundered in,' as Abraham liked to say.

But Abraham was no holy warrior, no sir. That man who in his domestic life exuded an air of ineffectuality, even weakness, made of himself, in reality, a veritable czar, a mughal of human frailty. Would it shock you to know that within months of his arrival in Bombay he had begun to trade in human flesh? Reader: it shocked me. My father, Abraham Zogoiby? – Abraham, whose love-story had been a thing of such high passion, such romance? – I fear so; the same. My unforgivable father, whom I forgave . . . I have said many times already that as well as the loving husband, the uncomplaining protector of our greatest modern artist, there had from the beginning been a darker Abraham; a man who had made his way by threats and coercion, of reluctant ship's-captains and press barons, too. This Abraham invariably sought out, and came to mutually satisfactory arrangements with, those personages – call them *black merchants* – who purveyed menace, and bootleg whisky, and also sex, as devotedly as the Tatas and Sassoons plied their more respectable, 'white market' trades. Bombay in those days was, Abraham discovered, quite unlike the 'closed town' that old man Sassoon had described. For a man prepared to take risks, to give up scruple – for, in short, a black merchant – it was wide, wide open, and the only limit to the money that could be made was the boundary of your imagination.

More will be said later of the feared Muslim gang-boss, 'Scar', whose real name I will not make so bold as to set down here, contenting myself with that terrifying cliché of a sobriquet by which he was known throughout the city's underworld, and finally – as we shall see – beyond it. For the moment I will content myself with recording that as a result of an alliance with this gentleman Abraham gained the 'protection' which was from the beginning such a feature of his preferred mode of operation; and in return for this protection my father became, and covertly remained throughout his long and wicked life, the prime supplier of new young girls to the houses which Scar's people so efficiently maintained, the Grant Road-Falkland Road-Foras Road-Kamathipura fleshpots of Bombay.

– What's that? – 'Where did he get them from?' – Why, from the temples of South India, I regret to say, especially from those shrines dedicated to the worship of a certain Karnataka goddess, Kellamma, who seemed incapable of protecting her poor young 'disciples' . . . it is a matter of record that in our sorry age with its prejudice in favour of male children many poor families donated to their favoured cult-temple the daughters they could not afford to marry off or feed, in the hope that they might live in holiness as servants or, if they were fortunate, as dancers; vain hopes, alas, for in many cases the priests in charge of these temples were men in whom the highest standards of probity were mysteriously absent, a failing which laid them open to offers of cash on the nail for the young virgins and not-quite-virgins and once-again-virgins in their charge. Thus Abraham the spice merchant was able to use his widespread Southern connections to harvest a new crop, entered in his most secret ledgers as 'Garam Masala Super Quality', and also, I note with some embarrassment, 'Extra Hot Chilli Peppers: Green.'

And it was in secret partnership with 'Scar', too, that Abraham Zogoiby went into the talcum-powder industry.

~

Crystallised hydrated magnesium silicate, $Mg_3Si_4O_{10}(OH)_2$: talc. When Aurora asked him over breakfast why he was going into the baby-bottom business, he cited the twin advantages of a protectionist economy, which imposed prohibitive tariffs on imported talcum brands, and a population explosion, which guaranteed a 'bum boom'. He spoke enthusiastically of the product's global potential, characterising India as the one Third World economy capable of rivalling the First World in its sophistication and growth without necessarily becoming enslaved by the almighty US dollar, and suggested that many other Third World countries would leap at the chance to buy a high-quality talcum powder for which no greenback payments were required. By the time he had begun to speculate on the very real short-term possibility of his 'Baby Softo' brand taking on Johnson & Johnson in their home markets, Aurora had stopped listening. When he began to sing the advertising jingle with which he proposed to launch his new wheeze, with lyrics personally composed by himself and set to the maddening tune of *Bobby Shafto*, my mother covered her ears.

'Baby Softo, sing it louder,/Softo-pofto talcum powder,' carolled Abraham.

'Talcum you can make or don't make,' cried Aurora, 'but this racket must stoppo pronto. It is crackofying the shell of my egg.'

As I write this I wonder again at Aurora's unwillingness to see how often and how casually Abraham deceived her, I marvel at the things she accepted without questioning, because of course he was lying, and the white powder he was interested in did not come from quarries in the Western Ghats, but found its way into selected Baby Softo canisters by a highly unusual route involving nocturnal lorry convoys from unknown places of origin, and extensive and systematic bribery of policemen and other officials manning octroi posts along the sub-continent's trunk roads; and these relatively few canisters produced, for several years, an export-based income which far outstripped the rest of the company's profits, and made possible a broad-based corporate diversification – an income which was never declared, however, which appeared in no ledger save the secret encoded book of books which Abraham kept profoundly hidden, perhaps in some dark recess of his corrupted soul.

The city itself, perhaps the whole country, was a palimpsest, Under World beneath Over World, black market beneath white; when the whole of life was like this, when an invisible reality moved phantomwise beneath a visible fiction, subverting all its meanings, how then could Abraham's career have been any different? How could any of us have escaped that deadly layering? How, trapped as we were in the hundred per cent fakery of the real, in the fancy-dress, weeping-Arab kitsch of the superficial, could we have penetrated to the full, sensual truth of the lost mother below? How could we have lived authentic lives? How could we have failed to be grotesque?

It is clear to me now, as I look back, that the only thing wrong with Vasco Miranda's Independence Night gag about the power of corruption being equal to that of the gods was the excessive mildness of its formulation. And of course Abraham Zogoiby must have known very well that the painter's boozy attempt at flamboyant cynicism was in fact an understatement of the case.

'Your mother and her art crowd were always complaining what tough times they had *making something out of nothing*,' Abraham confessing his crimes in his great old age remembered, with more than a little amusement. 'What did they make? Pictures! But I, I, I- tho brought a whole new city out of nowhere! Now you judge: which is the harder magic trick? From your dear mother's conjuring hat came many fine creatures; but from mine, mister – King Kong!'

During the first twenty or so years of my life, new tracts of land – 'something out of nothing' – were reclaimed from the Arabian Sea at the southern end of the Bombay peninsula's Back Bay, and Abraham invested heavily in this reverse-Atlantis rising from the waves. In those days there was much talk of relieving the pressure on the overcrowded city by limiting the extent and height of new buildings in the Reclamation area, and then constructing a second city centre on the mainland across the water. It was important for Abraham that this scheme should fail – 'how could I maintain the value of the property in which I had sunk so many assets, if not?' he asked me, spreading his skeletal arms wide and baring his teeth in what would once have been a disarming smile, but now, in the semi-darkness of his office high above the city streets, gave my nonagenarian father the appearance of a voracious skull.

He found an ally when Kiran ('K.K.' or 'Kéké') Kolatkar, a little pop-eyed black cannonball of a politico from Aurangabad, and the toughest of all the hard men who have bossed Bombay over the years, rose to dominate the Municipal Corporation. Kolatkar was a man to whom Abraham Zogoiby could explain the principles of invisibility, those hidden laws of nature that could not be overturned by the visible laws of men. Abraham explained how invisible funds could find their way through a series of invisible bank accounts and end up, visible and clean as a whistle, in the account of a friend. He demonstrated how the continued invisibility of the dream-city across the water would benefit those friends who might have, or by chance acquire, a stake in what had until recently been invisible but had now risen up like a Bombay Venus from the sea. He showed how easy it would be to persuade those worthy officers whose job it was to monitor and control the number and height of new buildings in the Reclamation that they would be much advantaged were they to lose the gift of sight – 'metaphorically, of course, boy – it was only a figure of speech; don't think we wanted to put out anybody's eyes, not like Shah Jehan with that peeping Tom who wanted a sneak preview of the Taj'– so that great crowds of new edifices could actually remain invisible to public scrutiny, and soar into the sky, as high as anyone could wish. And, once again, hey presto, the invisible buildings would generate mountains of cash, they would become some of the most valuable real-estate on earth; something out of nothing, a miracle, and all the friends who had helped make it so would be well rewarded for their pains.

Kolatkar was a quick learner, and even came up with an inspiration of his own. Suppose these invisible buildings could be built by an invisible work-force? Would that not be the most elegant and economic of results? 'Naturally, I agreed,' old Abraham confessed. 'That little bullet-head Kéké was getting into the swing.' Soon after that the city authorities decreed that any persons who had settled in Bombay subsequent to the last census were to be deemed not to exist. Because they had been cancelled, it followed that the city bore no responsibility for their housing or welfare, which came as a welcome relief to those honest, and actually-existing citizens who paid taxes for the upkeep of the messy, dynamic burg. However, it cannot be denied that for the million or more ghosts who had just been created by law, life got harder. This was where Abraham Zogoiby and all those who had jumped on the great Reclamation bandwagon came in, generously hiring as many phantoms as they could to work on the huge construction sites springing up on every inch of the new land, and even going so far – O philanthropists! – as to pay them small amounts of cash for their work. 'Nobody ever heard of paying spooks until we began the practice,' said ancient Abraham, cackling wheezily. 'But naturally we accepted no responsibility in case of ill-health or injury. It would have been, if you follow my line, illogical. After all, these persons were not just invisible, but actually, according to official pronouncements, simply not at all there.'

We had been sitting in thickening gloom on the thirty-first floor of the jewel of the New Bombay, I. M. Pei's masterpiece, Cashondeliveri Tower. Through the window I could see the shining spear of K. K. Chambers lancing the night. Now Abraham rose and opened a door. Light poured in, and high arpeggios of music. He led me into a giant atrium stocked with trees and plants from more temperate climes than our own – there were orchards of apple-trees and *poiriers*, and heavy grapevines, too – all under glass, maintained at ideal conditions of temperature and humidity by a climate-control system whose cost would have been unimaginable if it had not been invisible; for, by some happy chance, no electricity bill had ever been presented to Abraham for payment. From this atrium comes my last memory of him – of my old, old father, whom I, with my thirty-six-going-on-seventy-two appearance, was beginning more and more to resemble; my unrepentant, serpentine father, who had taken over Eden in the absence of Aurora and God.

'Now, but, I'm done for,' he sighed. 'It's all coming apart in my hand. The magic stops working when people start seeing the strings. To hell! I had a damn fine run. Have a bloody apple.'

# 12

I GREW IN ALL directions, willy-nilly. My father was a big man but by the age of ten my shoulders had grown wider than his coats. I was a skyscraper freed of all legal restraints, a one-man population explosion, a megalopolis, a shirt-ripping, button-popping Hulk. 'Look at you,' my big sister Ina marvelled when I reached my full heft and height. 'You have become Mr Gulliver-Travel and we are your Lilliputs.' Which was true at least in this respect: that if our Bombay was my personal not-Raj-but-Lilli-putana, then my great size was indeed succeeding in tying me down.

The wider my physical bounds were set, the more limited my horizons seemed to become. Education was a problem. Many boys from 'good homes' on Malabar Hill, Scandal Point and Breach Candy began their education at Miss Gunnery's Walsingham House School, which was co-educational at kindergarten and junior level, before they went on to Campion or Cathedral or one of the city's other in-those-days-boys-only élite establishments. But the legendary 'Gunner' in her horn-rims with their Batmobile fins refused to accept the truth about my condition. 'Too old for KG,' she snorted, at the end of an interview in which she treated my three-and-a-half-year-old self at all times as if I were the seven-year-old she could not help seeing seated in my chair, 'and for the junior school, I am deploring to be informing, sub-normal.' My mother was incensed. 'Who-all have you got in class?' she demanded. 'Einsteins, is it? Little Alberts and Albertinas, must be? A whole schoolful of emcee-squares?'

But La Gunnery was not to be moved, and so it was home tuition for me. A string of male tutors followed, few of them lasting more than a few months. I bear them no grudge. Faced with, for example, an eight-year-old who had decided, in honour of his friendship with the painter V. Miranda, to sport a fully waxed pointy-tipped moustache, they understandably fled. In spite of all my efforts to create a neat, tidy, obedient, moderate, *unexceptional* persona, I was simply too weird for them; until that is, my first female tutor was hired. O Dilly Hormuz of sweet memory! Like Miss Gunnery, her thick glasses wore fins, or wings; but these were the wings of angels. Arriving in a white frock and ankle-socks early in 1967, her hair bunched in thin tails, books gathered to her bosom, myopically blinking and nervously chatterboxy, she looked at first glance more like a kid than yours truly. But Dilly was worth a second look, for she, too, was in disguise. She wore flat shoes and the practised stoop with which tall girls learn to hide their height; but she soon began, when we were alone, to uncoil – ah, the pale magnificent length of her, from her smallish head to her shapely but enormous feet! Also – and even after all these years the memory of it creates in me a blushy heat of nostalgic longing – she commenced to stretch. Stretching Dilly – pretending to reach for a book, a ruler, a pen – revealed to me, and me alone, the fullness of the body beneath the frock, and soon began to return, with her level unblinking gaze, my own crude bug-eyed gawps. Pretty Dilly – for when we were alone and she let down her hair, when she took off her glasses to blink at me blindly through those haunting, deep-set, absent eyes, then her true looks were unveiled – looked long and hard upon her new pupil, and sighed.

'Ten years old, men,' she said softly the first time we were alone. 'Man cub, you are the eighth wonder and no mistake.' And after that, remembering her didactic rôle, began her first lesson by making me learn by heart – to 'ruttofy', as we said – the world's seven ancient and seven modern wonders, mentioning, as she did so, the interesting proximity on Malabar Hill of myself ('young Master Colossus') and the Hanging Gardens – as if the Wonders were gathering here, and taking Indian form.

It seems to me now that in my younger self, in that appalling monster in whom a child's mind peered out in confusion through the portals of a young man's beautiful body (for, in spite of my hand, of all my sense of self-disgust and need for comfort, Dilly would have seen beauty in me; beauty, our family curse!), my teacher Miss Hormuz found a kind of personal liberation, understanding that I was hers to command as a child, and also – and here I venture into dangerous water – hers to touch, and be touched by, as a man.

I do not remember now how old I was (though I had certainly shaved off my Vascoid moustache) when Dilly ceased to simply marvel at my physique and began, timidly at first, and then with increasing freedom, to caress it. I was at an internal age at which such caresses were innocent gestures of the love for which I was so wolfishly hungry; externally, my body had become capable of wholly adult responses. Do not condemn her, for I cannot; I was a wonder of her world, and she was simply entranced.

For almost three years my lessons took place at *Elephanta,* and during these thousand days and a day, there were limits imposed by the location, and the fear of being caught in the act. Refrain, if you will, from asking me to say how far our caresses went; from obliging me, in my remembering, to stop, once again, at the frontiers for which we possessed no passport! The memory of that time remains a breathless ache, it makes my heart pound, it is a wound that does not heal; for my body knew what I did not, and though the child sat half-bewildered in the prison of his flesh, still my lips, my tongue, my limbs began to act, under her expert tutelage, quite independently of my mind; and on some blessed days, when we felt safe, or when what drove us on grew too maddening to care about the risk, her hands, her lips, her breasts moving at my groin brought me a measure of hot and desperate relief.

She took my ruined hand, some days, and placed it thus and so. She was the first human being to make me feel, for those stolen moments, whole . . . and most of the time, no matter what her body might be up to with mine, she kept up a constant stream of information. We had no lovers' chit-chat; the battle of Srirangapatnam and the principal exports of Japan were all our bill and coo. While her fluttering fingers raised my body temperature to unbearable heights, she kept things under control by obliging me to recite my thirteen times table or enumerate the valencies of each element in the periodic table. Dilly was a girl with a lot to say, and infected me with gabbiness, which to this day retains, for me, a powerful erotic charge. When I chatter on, or am assailed by the garrulity of others, I find it – how-to-say? – arousing. Often, in the heat of *bavardage*, I must place my hands upon my lap to conceal the movements there from the eyes of my companions, who would be puzzled by such arousal; or, more probably, amused. I have had, until now, no wish to become the source of such amusement. But now all must, and will, be told; now, my life's story, that tissue of erectile volubility, is drawing to a close.

Dilly Hormuz was a spinster of perhaps twenty-five when we met, and in her mid-thirties when I last saw her. She lived with her tiny, elderly and stone-blind mother, who sat on a balcony all day long, sewing quilts, her needlewoman's fingers having long ago ceased to need the assistance of her eyes. How could such a small, frail woman have produced so tall and voluptuous a daughter, I wondered, when at the age of thirteen it was agreed that I was old enough to be sent to Dilly's place for my lessons, because it would do me good to get out of the house. Some days I would forgo the car, waving away the driver, and walk – I would actually *skip* – down the hill to see her, passing the gracious old pharmacy at Kemp's Corner – this was long before it turned into the flyover-and-boutique spiritual wasteland it is today – and the Royal Barber Shop (where a master barber with a cleft palate offered a circumcision service as a sideline). Dilly lived in the dark, peeling depths of an old grey Parsi house, all balconies and curlicues, on Gowalia Tank Road, a few doors up from Vijay Stores, that numinous mixed business where you could buy both Time, with which you could polish your wooden furniture, and Hope, with which you could wipe your bum. We Zogoibys used to call it Jaya Stores, pretending it was named after our sourpuss ayah, Miss Jaya Hé, who went there to buy herself little packets of Life, inside which were eucalyptus cleaning-sticks for the teeth, and Love, with which she henna'ed her hair . . . With my heart singing, and with a feeling something very like ecstasy I would enter Dilly's home, that small apartment of impoverished, but still tasteful, gentility. The presence of a baby grand piano in the front room and of silver-framed photographs upon it, portraits of patriarchs in tasselled flowerpot hats and of a saucy young society belle who turned out to be old Mrs Hormuz herself, indicated that her family had once known better times; as did Dilly's skill in Latin and French. I have forgotten most of my Latin, but what I remember of French − language, literature, kisses, letters; the sweat-soaked afternoon pleasures of the *cinq à sept* − Dilly, I learned it all from you ... Now, however, the two women were doomed to a life of private tuition and quilts. This may explain why Dilly was so hungry for a man that she settled for an overgrown boy; why she would leap on to my lap, her legs straddling me, and whisper as she bit my lower lip: 'I took my specs off, men; now I see my lover only, nothing but.'

❧

She was indeed my first lover, but I think I did not love her. I know this because she made me glad of my condition, glad that my outward form was older than my years should have allowed. I was still a child; so I wanted for her sake to hurtle towards adulthood with all possible speed. I wanted to be a man for her, a real man and not manhood's simulacrum, and if that meant sacrificing even more of my already abbreviated span, then I would happily have made that devil-deal for her blessed sake. But when real love, the great grand thing itself, came along after Dilly had gone, how bitterly, then, I resented my lot! With what hunger and rage I yearned to slow down the too-fast ticking of my unheeding internal clock! Dilly Hormuz never shook in me the child's conviction of his own immortality, which was why I could wish so lightly to throw away my childhood years. But Uma, my Uma, when I loved her, made me hear Death's lightning footsteps as they ran towards me; then, O then, I heard each lethal scything of his blade.

❧

I grew towards manhood under Dilly Hormuz's soft, knowing hand. But − and here is a hard confession indeed, perhaps my hardest yet – she was not the first woman to touch me. Or so I have been told, though it should be said that the witness – our ayah, Miss Jaya Hé, peg-leg Lambajan's domineering wife – was a liar and a thief.

The children of the rich are raised by the poor, and since both my parents were dedicated to their work I was frequently left with only the chowkidar and the ayah for company. And even though Miss Jaya was as snappy as a claw, with lips as sharp as scratches and eyes as narrow as squeaks, even though she was as thin as ice and as bossy as boots, I was and am grateful to her, for in her time off she was a peripatetic sort of bird, she liked to wander the city in order to disapprove of it, clucking her tongue and pursing her lips and shaking her head at its various infelicities. So it was with Miss Jaya that I rode the B.E.S.T. trams and buses, and while she disapproved of their overcrowding I was secretly rejoicing in all that compacted humanity, in being pushed so tightly together that privacy ceased to exist and the boundaries of your self began to dissolve, that feeling which we only get when we are in crowds, or in love. And it was with Miss Jaya that I ventured into the fabulous turbulence of Crawford Market with its frieze by Kipling's dad, with its vendors of chickens both live and plastic, and it was with Miss Jaya that I penetrated the rum dens of Dhobi Talao and ventured into the chawls, the tenements, of Byculla (where she took me to visit her poor – I should say her *poorer* – relations, who with yet-more-impoverishing offers of cold drinks and cakes treated her arrival like the visit of a queen), and it was with her that I ate watermelon at Apollo Bunder and chaat on the seafront at Worli, and with all these places and their loud inhabitants, with all these commodities and comestibles and their insistent vendors, with my inexhaustible Bombay of excess, I fell deeply and for ever in love, even while Miss Jaya was enjoying herself by giving full vent to her outsized capacity for derision, even while she was firing out judgments from which she would permit no appeal: 'Too costly!' (Chickens.) 'Too disgusting!' (Dark rum.) 'Too slummy!' (Chawl.) 'Too dry!' (Watermelon.) 'Too hot!' (Chaat.) And always, on our return home, she turned to me with a glittering, resentful look and spat out, 'You, baba: too lucky! Thank your lucky stars.'

One day in my eighteenth year – it was in the early days of the Emergency, as I recall – I went with her to Zaveri Bazaar, where jewellers sat like wise monkeys in tiny shops that were all mirrors and glass, buying and selling antique silver by weight. When Miss Jaya produced a pair of heavy bracelets and handed them to the valuer, I recognised them at once as my mother's. Miss Jaya's stare pierced me like a spear; I felt my tongue dry and could not speak. The transaction was soon completed and we moved away from the jeweller's into the bustle of the street, avoiding the pushcarts laden with cotton bales wrapped in jute sacking and bound with metal bands, the street stalls selling plantains, mangoes, bush-shirts, filmi magazines and belts, the coolies with huge baskets on their heads, the scooters, the bikes, the truth. We made our way home to *Elephanta*, and it was not until we had descended from the bus that the ayah spoke. 'Too much,' she said. 'In the house. So-much too-much things.'

I didn't answer. 'People also,' Miss Jaya said. 'Coming. Going. Waking. Sleeping. Eating. Drinking. In drawing-rooms. In bedrooms. In all rooms. Too much people.' Meaning, I understood, that because Aurora would find it hard to place her circle of friends under suspicion, nobody would ever be able to identify the thief; unless I spoke up.

'You will not speak,' Miss Jaya said, playing her trump. 'For Lambajan. Because of him.'

⁓

She was right. I could not have betrayed Lambajan; he taught me how to box. He made my father's despairing prophecy come true. *You're going to knock the whole world flat with a fist on you like that.*

In the days when Lambajan had two legs and no parrot, in the days before he had become Long John Silverfellow, he had used his fists to supplement his meagre sailor's pay. In the city's gambling alleys, where fighting-cocks and baited bears provided the warm-up entertainment, he had earned something of a reputation and fair sums of money as a bare-knuckle boxer. He had originally wanted to be a wrestler, because in Bombay a wrestler could become a great star like the famous Dara Singh, but after a series of defeats he turned to the rawer, rougher world of the street fighters, and became known as a man who could take a punch. His win–loss record was creditable; he lost all his teeth, but he had never been knocked out.

Once a week, throughout my early life, he came into the gardens at *Elephanta* carrying long strips of rag, with which he would bandage my hands, before pointing to his hairy chin. 'Right there, baba,' he commanded. 'Land your super bomb.' This was how we discovered that my crippled right was a hand to be reckoned with, a torpedo, a fist of fists. Once a week I slugged Lamba as hard as I could, and at first his toothless smile never faltered. 'Bas?' he taunted me. 'That feather-tickle only? That I can get from my parrot buddy here.' After a time, however, he stopped grinning. He still presented his chin, but now I could see him bracing himself for the blow, calling up his old professional reserves ... on my ninth birthday I took my swing and Totah rose noisily into the air as the chowkidar fell to earth.

'Mashed White Elephants!' screeched the parrot. I ran for the garden hose. I had knocked poor Lamba cold.

When he revived he turned down the corners of his mouth in impressed respect, then sat up and prodded at his bleeding gums. 'Shot, baba,' he praised me. 'Now it is time to start learning.'

We hung a rice-filled bolster from the branch of a plane-tree and after Dilly Hormuz had finished her unforgettable lessons, Lambajan gave me his. For the next eight years, we sparred. He taught me strategy, what would have been called ringcraft if there had been a ring. He sharpened my positional sense and above all my defence. 'Don't expect you'll never get hit, baba, and even with that fist you can't punch if you're hearing tweet-tweets.' Lambajan was a coach of all-too-plainly reduced mobility; but with what herculean determination he strove to shrug off his handicap! When we worked out he would cast aside his crutch and bounce around like a human pogo-stick.

As I grew older, so my weapon increased in might. I found myself having to hold back, to pull my punches. I did not want to knock Lambajan out too often, or too violently. In my mind's eye I saw an image of a chowkidar grown punchy, slurring his words and forgetting my name, and it made me reduce the force of my blows.

By the time Miss Jaya and I went to Zaveri Bazaar I had become expert enough for Lambajan to whisper, 'Baba, if you want some action for real, just say one little word.' This was thrilling, terrifying. Was I up to this? My punchbag did not hit back, after all, and Lambajan was a sparring partner of long familiarity. What if a biped opponent, made of flesh-and-blood rather than rice-and-sackcloth, danced two-legged circles round me and beat me black-and-blue? 'Your fist is ready,' said Lambajan, shrugging. 'But about your heart, I cannot say.'

And so, out of bloody-mindedness, I had said the word, and we went for the first time, into those Bombay Central alleys that have no name. Lamba introduced me simply as 'The Moor', and because I came with him there was less contempt than I had expected. But when he told them I was a new fighter of seventeen-plus the guffaws began, because it was obvious to all the onlookers that I was a man in his thirties who was beginning to go grey, I must be guy on his last legs that one-legged Lamba was training as a favour. But as well as taunts there were raised voices in misplaced admiration. 'Maybe he is good,' these voices said, 'because he is still pretty after so many years.' Then they brought out my opponent, a loose-haired Sikh salah at least as big as me, and mentioned casually that even though this bucko had just turned twenty he had murdered two men in such bouts already and was on the run from the law. I felt my nerve going then, and looked towards Lambajan, but he just nodded quietly and spat on his right wrist. So I spat on mine and walked towards the murderer. He came straight at me, brimming with confidence, because he thought he held a fourteen-year advantage and would be able to put away this old-timer pronto. I thought about the rice bolster and let fly. The first time I touched him he went down and stayed there for a lot longer than the count of ten. As for me, even after that single blow I was visited by an asthmatic attack of gasps and tears so severe that in spite of my victory I began to doubt whether I had a future in this line of work. Lambajan pooh-poohed such uncertainties, 'Just a little virgin nerves,' he assured me on the way home. 'I have seen many boys have fits and fall down frothing after their first time, win or lose. You don't know what goods you got there, baba,' he added delightedly. 'Not only a pile driver but too much speed as well. Also, balls.' There wasn't a mark on my body, he pointed out, and what was more we had a goodly wad of pocket-money to divide.

So of course I could not accuse Lamba's wife of thievery, and see them both dismissed. I could not lose my manager, the man who had shown me my gift . . . once Miss Jaya was certain of her power over me, she began to flaunt it, stealing our possessions while I watched, making sure she didn't do it too often or steal too much – now a small jade box, now a tiny gold brooch. There were days when I saw Aurora and Abraham shaking their heads as they stared at an empty space, but Miss Jaya's calculations proved correct: they grilled the servants, but they never called the cops, not wanting to subject their household staff to the gentle ministrations of the Bombay police, nor to embarrass their friends. (And I wonder, too, if Aurora remembered her own purloinings and disposals of little Ganesha-ornaments on Cabral Island long ago. From *too-many-elephants* to *Elephanta* had been a long journey; did her younger self rebuke her then, and even make her feel some sympathy, some solidarity with the thief?)

It was during this period of thievery that Miss Jaya told me the dreadful secret of my earliest days. We were walking at Scandal Point, across the way from the big Chamchawala house, and I think I had made some remark – the Emergency remember, was still quite new – about the unhealthy relationship between Mrs Indira Gandhi and her son Sanjay. 'The whole nation is paying for that mother-son problem,' I said. Miss Jaya, who had been clucking her disapproval of the young lovers holding hands as they walked along the sea wall, snorted disgustedly. 'You can talk,' she said. 'Your family. Perverts. Your sisters and mother also. In your baby time. How they played with you. Too sick.'

I did not know, have never known, if she was telling the truth. Miss Jaya Hé was a mystery to me, a woman so deeply angry at her lot in life that she had become capable of the most bizarre revenges. So it was a lie, then; yes, it was probably a foul lie; but what is true – let me reveal this while I am in the mood for revelations – is that I have grown up with an unusually laissez-faire attitude towards my primary sexual organ. Permit me to inform you that people have grasped at it from time to time – yes! – or have in other ways, both gentle and peremptory, demanded its services, or instructed me how and where and with whom and for how much to use it, and on the whole I have been perfectly willing to comply. Is this quite usual? I think not, begums 'n' sahibs . . . More conventionally, on other occasions this same organ has issued instructions of its own, and these, too, I have tried – as men will – to follow if possible; with disastrous results. If Miss Jaya was not lying, the origins of this behaviour may lie in those early fondlings to which she so viciously alluded. And if I am honest I can picture such scenes, they seem completely credible to me: my mother fooling with my soo-soo while suckling me at her breast, or my three sisters crowding round my cot, pulling my little brown chain. *Perverts. Too sick.* Aurora, dancing above the Ganpati crowds, spoke of the limitlessness of human perversity. So it may have been true. It may. It may.

My god, what kind of family were we, diving together down Destruction Falls? I have said that I think of the *Elephanta* of those days as a Paradise, and so I do – but you may imagine to an outsider it could have looked a great deal more like Hell.

∽

I am not sure whether my great-uncle Aires da Gama can really be called an outsider, but when he showed up in Bombay for the first time in his life at the age of seventy-two he was so sadly reduced a human being that Aurora Zogoiby only recognised him by the bulldog Jawaharlal at his side. The only remaining trace of the preening Anglophile dandy he had once been was a certain eloquent indolence of speech and gesture which, in my continuing effort to fight my too-many-r.p.m. fate by cultivating the pleasures of slowness, I tried hard to emulate. He looked ill – hollow-eyed, unshaven, underfed – and it would not have been a surprise to learn that his old disease had returned. But he wasn't sick.

'Carmen is dead,' he said. (The dog was dead too, of course, had been for decades. Aires had had Jaw-jaw stuffed, and there were little furniture-wheels screwed into the undersides of his paws, so that his master could continue to pull him along on a lead.) Aurora took pity on him and set aside all the old family resentments, installing him in the most lavish of the guest rooms, the one with the softest mattress and quilt and the best view of the sea, and forbidding us all to titter at Aires's habit of talking to Jawaharlal as if he were still alive. For the first week Great-Uncle Aires was very quiet at table, as if he were reluctant to draw attention to himself in case it resulted in the resumption of ancient hostilities. He ate little, although he did show a great liking for the new Braganza Brand lime and mango pickles which had lately taken the city by storm; we tried not to stare, but out of the corners of our eyes we saw the old gentleman slowly turning his head from side to side, as if looking for something he had lost.

On his trips to Cochin, Abraham Zogoiby had occasionally paid brief, awkward courtesy calls at the house on Cabral Island, so we knew something of the astonishing developments in that almost-severed branch of our quarrelsome clan, and as time went by Great-Uncle Aires told us the whole sad, beautiful tale. The day Travancore-Cochin became the state of Kerala, Aires da Gama had given up his secret fantasy that the Europeans might one day return to the Malabar Coast, and entered a reclusive retirement during which he set aside his lifelong philistinism to begin a complete reading of the canon of English literature, consoling himself with the best of the old world for the distasteful mutabilities of history. The other members of that unusual domestic triangle, Great-Aunt Carmen and Prince Henry the Navigator, were increasingly thrown together, and became fast friends, playing cards late into the night for high, if notional, stakes. After some years Prince Henry picked up the notebook in which they kept their betting records and informed Carmen with only half a smile that she now owed him her entire fortune. At that moment the Communists came to power, fulfilling Camoens da Gama's dream, and Prince Henry's fortunes rose with those of the new government. With his good connections in the Cochin docks he had run for office and had been elected by a landslide to membership of the state legislature, without having needed to campaign. On the night he told her of his new career, Carmen, inspired by the news, won back every last rupee of her lost fortune in a marathon poker-game which culminated in a single gigantic pot. Prince Henry had always hinted to Carmen that she lost so heavily because of her reluctance to fold, but on this occasion it was he who was drawn into her web, seduced by the four queens in his hand into raising the bet to vertiginous heights. When she finally had a chance to show him her four kings, he understood that in all the years of her long losing streak she had been quietly learning how to deal a crooked hand, that he had been the victim of the longest hustle in the history of card-games. Impoverished once more, he applauded her under-hand skills.

'The poor will never be as sneaky as the rich, so they will always lose in the end,' she told him, fondly. Prince Henry got up from the card-table, kissed the top of her head, and dedicated the rest of his working life, in and out of power, to the Party's educational policies, because only education would give the poor the means to disprove Carmen da Gama's dictum. And indeed the literacy rate in the new State of Kerala rose to become the best in India – Prince Henry himself proved a quick learner – and then Carmen da Gama launched a daily newspaper aimed at the masses of readers in the seaside fishing-villages and also the rice-villages on the hyacinth-infested backwaters. She discovered that she had a real talent as a hands-on proprietor, and her journal became a great hit with the poor, much to Prince Henry's rage, because even though it pretended to be taking a good leftist line it somehow managed to turn the people's heads away from the Party, and when the anti-Communist coalition took power in the State it was card-sharp Carmen's sneaky, fork-tongued newspaper that Prince Henry blamed as much as the interference of the central government in Delhi.

In 1974 Aires da Gama's former lover (for their affair was long past) went on a trip into the Spice Mountains to visit the thriving elephant sanctuary of which he had been made patron, and disappeared. Carmen heard the news on her seventieth birthday, and became hysterical. Her newspaper's headlines grew inches high, making accusations of foul play. But nothing was ever proved; Prince Henry's body was never found, and after a decent interval the case was closed. The loss of the man who had become her closest friend and friendliest rival knocked the stuffing out of Carmen, and one night she dreamed that she was standing by a lake surrounded by forested hills, and Prince Henry was beckoning to her from the back of a wild elephant. 'Nobody killed me,' he told her. 'It was just time to fold my hand.' The next morning Aires and Carmen sat for the last time in their island garden and Carmen told her husband about the dream. Aires bowed his head, having perceived the meaning of the vision, and did not look up until he heard his wife's china teacup fall from her lifeless hands.

⸏

I try to imagine how *Elephanta* must have seemed to Great-Uncle Aires when he arrived with a stuffed dog and a broken heart, what bewilderment it must have created in his diluted spirit. What, after the near-isolation of Cabral Island, would he have made of the daily mayhem of *chez nous,* of Aurora's towering ego and the great working jags which would conceal her from us for days at a time, until she staggered out of her studio cross-eyed with starvation and fatigue; of my three crazy sisters and Vasco Miranda, of thieving Miss Jaya and one-legged Lambajan and Totah and Dilly Hormuz's myopic lust? What about *me*?

And then there was the constant come-and-go of painters and collectors and gallery-folk and gawpers and models and assistants and mistresses and nudes and photographers and packers and stone-merchants and brush-salesmen and Americans and layabouts and dope-fiends and professors and journalists and celebrities and critics and the endless talk about *the West as problematic* and *the myth of authenticity* and *the logic of dream* and the *languid contours* of Sher-Gil's figuration and the presence in the work of B. B. Mukherjee of both *exaltation* and *dissent* and the derivative *progressivism* of Souza and the *centrality of the magical image* and the *proverb* and the relationship between *gesture* and *revealed motifs,* to say nothing of rivalrous discussions of *how-much* and *to-whom* and *group-hang* and *one-man-show* and *New York* and *London,* and the arriving and departing processions of paintings, paintings, paintings. For it seemed that every painter in the country had developed the urge to make pilgrimages to Aurora's door to ask for her blessing on their work – which she gave to the ex-banker with his luminous Indianised *Last Supper,* and withheld with a harrumph from the talentless New Delhi self-publicist with the beautiful dancer wife, with whom Aurora went off to practise her Ganpati routine, leaving the painter alone with his awful canvases . . . was this glorious too-muchness simply too much for poor old Aires? – In which case, our earlier supposition, that one boy's Paradise could be another fellow's Hell, would be, perhaps, well proven.

Alas for such hypotheses! The truth was nothing of the sort. Let me say at once that Great-Uncle Aires found more than sanctuary at *Elephanta.* He found, to his amazement and everyone else's, a moment of late, sweet fellowship. Not love, perhaps. But 'something'. The 'something' that is far, far better than 'nothing', even near the end of all our half-satisfied days.

Many of the painters who came to sit at great Aurora's feet earned their livings in other professions and were known within our walls as – to name only a few – the Doctor, the Lady Doctor, the Radiologist, the Journalist, the Professor, the Sarangi Player, the Playwright, the Printer, the Curator, the Jazz Singer, the Lawyer, and the Accountant. It was the last of these – the artist who is without a doubt the present-day inheritor of Aurora's fallen mantle – who adopted Aires: a fortyish floppy-haired fellow he was then, wearing huge glasses with lenses the size and shape of portable TV's, and, behind them, an expression of such perfect innocence that it instantly made you suspicious of a prank. He had become my great-uncle's close friend within weeks. In that last year of his life, Great-Uncle Aires became the Accountant's regular model, and in my opinion his lover as well. The paintings are there for all to see, above all the extraordinary *You Can't Always Get Your Wish*, 114×114 cms., oil on canvas, in which a teeming Bombay street-scene – Muhammad Ali Road, perhaps – is surveyed from a first-floor balcony by the full-length nude figure of Aires da Gama, trim-and-slim as a young god, but with the unfulfilled, unfulfil-lable, unexpressed, inexpressible longings of old age in every brush-stroke of his painted form. There is an old bulldog sitting at his feet; and it may just be my imagination, but down below him in the crowd – yes, just there! – those two tiny figures on the back of the elephant with the Vimto advertisements painted on its flanks! – could they be – surely they are! – Prince Henry the Navigator and Carmen da Gama, beckoning Great-Uncle to join them on their trip?

(Once upon a time, there were two figures in a boat, one in a wedding-dress, one not, and a third figure left alone in her nuptial bed. Aurora immortalised that painful scene; and here in the Accountant's work, surely, were the same three figures. Only their disposition was different. The dance had moved on; had become a dance of death.)

Soon after the completion of *You Can't Always Get Your Wish*, Aires da Gama passed away. Aurora, as well as Abraham, made a trip south to bury him. Disregarding the custom of the tropics, where men go hastily to their sleep, lest by their tarrying they leave the world in bad odour, my mother called the undertakers, Mahalaxmi Deadbody Disposicians Pvt Ltd (motto: 'Corpse is here? Want it there? Okay, dear! It's your affair!'), and had Aires put on ice for the journey, so that he could be laid beside Carmen in the consecrated family plot on Cabral Island, where Prince Henry the Navigator could find him if he ever chose to ride down from the Spice Hills on his elephant. When Aires arrived at his last destination and they opened up his aluminium Dispotainer to transfer him to his coffin he looked – Aurora told us – like a 'big blue Popsicle'. There was a hoar-frost on his eyebrows and he was colder than the grave. 'Never mind, Uncle,' Aurora murmured during the funeral service at which she and Abraham were the only mourners. 'Where you're off to they'll soon warmofy you up.'

But her heart wasn't in it. The quarrels of the past were long forgotten. The house on Cabral Island felt like a leftover, an irrelevance. Even the room which Aurora, as a young prodigy, had covered with painting during the period of her 'house arrest' no longer concerned her, for she had returned to its themes many times, had gone back obsessively to the mythic-romantic mode in which history, family, politics and fantasy jostled each other like the great crowds at V.T. or Churchgate Stations; and had returned, too, to that exploration of an alternative vision of India-as-mother, not Nargis's sentimental village-mother but a mother of cities, as heartless and lovable, brilliant and dark, multiple and lonely, mesmeric and repugnant, pregnant and empty, truthful and deceitful as the beautiful, cruel, irresistible metropolis itself. 'My father thought I had made a masterpiece here,' she said to Abraham as they stood in the painted room. 'But as you see they are only a child's first steps.'

Aurora had the old house dust-sheeted and locked up. She never returned to Cochin, and even after she died Abraham spared her the humiliation of being flown south like a frozen fish. He sold the old place and it became a decaying, modestly priced hotel for young back-packers and old India hands returning, on inadequate pensions, for a last look at their lost world. Eventually, or so I heard, it fell down. I am sorry that it did; but then, I was, I think, the only member of our family to give a fig for the past.

When Great-Uncle Aires died, every one of us had the sense of arriving at a turning-point. Iced, blue, he marked the end of a generation. It was our turn now.

༄

I decided I would no longer accompany Miss Jaya on her sorties around town. Even that act of distancing proved insufficient; the events in Zaveri Bazaar continued to rankle. So, finally, I went to see Lambajan at the gates, and, blushing hotly with the knowledge that I was humiliating him, told him what I knew. When I had finished I watched him in trepidation. Never before, after all, had I told a man that his wife was a thief. Would he want to fight me for his family's honour, to kill me where I stood? Lambajan said nothing, and his silence spread outwards from him, muffling the hooting of taxis, the cigarette-vendor's cries, the shrieks of street-urchins as they played fighting-kite and hoop and dodge-the-traffic, and the loud playback music emerging from the 'Sorryno' Irani restaurant up the hill (so called because of the huge blackboard at the entrance reading *Sorry, No Liquor, No Answer*

*Given Regarding Addresses in Locality, No Combing of Hair, No Beef, No Haggle, No Water Unless Food Taken, No News or Movie Magazine, No Sharing of Liquid Sustenances, No Taking Smoke, No Match, No Feletone Calls, No Incoming with Own Comestible, No Speaking of Horses, No Sigret, No Taking of Long Time on Premises, No Raising of Voice, No Change,* and a crucial last pair, *No Turning Down of Volume — It Is How We Like,* and *No Musical Request — All Melodies Selected Are To Taste of Prop).* Even the blasted parrot seemed interested in the chowkidar's response.

'In my job, baba,' Lambajan said at length, 'one sees many things to guard against. A man comes with cheap gemstones, the ladies of the house must be protected. Another person comes with bad watches up his wrist, I must pack him off. Beggars, badmashes, lafangas, all. Better they go from here and so I do my job. I stand and face the street and what it asks I answer. But now I learn that I must have eyes also in the back of my head.'

'Okay, forget it,' I said clumsily. 'You're angry. Let's forget the whole thing.'

'You don't know, baba, but I am a god-fearing man,' Lamba went on, as if I had not spoken. 'I stand outside this godless house on guard and I do not say. But at Walkeshwar Tank and Mahalaxmi Temple they know my poor face. Now I must go and make offering to Lord Ram and ask for extra back-side eyes. Also for deaf ears, so that I cannot hear such so-bad too-bad things.'

After I accused Miss Jaya the thieving stopped. Nothing was said between us, but Lamba had done the needful and her pilfering days were over. And there was another ending, too: Lambajan no longer acted as my boxing coach, no longer pogo'ed around the garden shouting 'Come on, mister parrot; you want to feather-tickle me? Come with your best hit!', no longer wished to take me into the alley of the street fighters to try my hand against the biggest ruffians in town. The question of whether my breathing problems would cancel out my natural pugilistic talent would have to wait many years to be resolved. Our relations were badly strained, and did not really recover until my own great fall. And in the interim Miss Jaya Hé plotted, and successfully achieved, her revenge.

Such was my time in Paradise: a full life but a friendless one.

Kept out of school, I was starved for contemporaries; and in this world in which appearance becomes reality and we must be what we seem, I quickly became an honorary grown-up, spoken to and treated as such by one and all, excluded from the world of what I was. How I have dreamed of innocence! – of childhood days playing cricket on the Cross Maidan, of excursions to Juhu or Marvé beaches or the Aarey Milk Colony, of making fish-lips at the angel-fish in the Taraporevala Aquarium and musing sweetly with one's chums on how they might be to eat; of short trousers and snake-buckled belts and the ecstasy of pistachio kulfi and outings for Chinese food and the first incompetent kisses of the young; of being taught to swim on Sunday mornings at the Willingdon Club by that instructor who liked to terrify his pupils by lying flat on the floor of the pool and letting all the air out of his lungs. The larger-than-lifeness of a child's life, its roller-coaster highs and lows, its alliances and treacheries, its boy-stuff rollick 'n' scrape, were denied me by my size and appearance. Mine was a knowing Eden. Still I was happy there.

– *Why? – Why? – Why?* –

– *That's easy: because it was home.* –

So, yes, I was happy amid the wildnesses of its adult lives, amid the travails of my siblings and the parental bizarreries which came to feel like everyday occurrences, and in a way still do, they still persuade me that it is the idea of the norm that is bizarre, the notion that human beings have *normal, everyday* lives . . . go behind the door of any household, I want to argue, and you'll find a macabre wonderland as untamed as our own. And maybe I'm right; or maybe this attitude, too, is a part of my complaint, maybe this – what? – this fucked–up dissident mind-set, too, is all my mother's fault.

My sisters would probably say it was. O my Ina, Minnie, Mynah long ago! How hard for them to be their mother's girls. Though they were beautiful, she was lovelier. The magic mirror on her bedroom wall never preferred the younger women. And she was brainier, and more gifted, and with the knack of captivating any young beaux her daughters might dare to introduce to her, of intoxicating them so deeply as to ruin the girls' chances for good;

the youths, blinded by the mother, could no longer see poor Eeny-Meenie-Miney at all . . . and there was her sharp tongue, and her lack of a shoulder to cry on, and her willingness to leave them for long stretches of their childhood in Miss Jaya Hé's bony, joyless clutches . . . Aurora lost them all, you know, they all found ways of leaving her, though they loved her bitterly, loved her more passionately than she could love them back, loved her harder than, in the absence of her reciprocating love, they could ever feel allowed to love themselves.

Ina, the eldest, Ina of the halved name, was the greatest beauty of the trio and also, I'm afraid, what her sisters liked to call 'the Family Stupe'. Aurora, ever the kind and generous mama, would wave airily in Ina's direction at the most exalted of gatherings and tell her guests, 'She-tho is just to lookofy at, not to talk-o to. Poor girl is limitoed in brain.' At the age of eighteen Ina screwed up the courage to have her ears pierced at Jhaveri Bros, the jewellery store on Warden Road, and was unfortunately rewarded for her courage by an infection; the backs of her ears came up in suppurating lumps which were made worse by her decision, taken for reasons of vanity, to keep pricking them and mopping up the pus. In the end she had to be treated as a hospital out-patient and the whole sorry three-month episode gave her mother a new weapon to use against her. 'Maybe it would have been better to have them slice-o'd off,' Aurora scolded her. 'Maybe it would have fixofied the blockage. Because some blockage there is, isn't it? Some ear wax or plug. Outside shape is super, but nothing ever goes in.'

Certainly she blocked her ears against her mother, and competed with her in the only way she thought she could: by using her looks. One by one she offered herself as a model to the male artists in Aurora's circle – the Lawyer, the Sarangi Player, the Jazz Singer – and when she unveiled her extraordinary physique in their studios its gravitational force drew them into her at once; like satellites falling from their orbits they crash-landed on her soft hills. After every conquest she arranged for her mother to discover a lover's note or a pornographic sketch, as if she were an Apache brave displaying scalps to the big chief in his tent. She entered the field of commerce as well as art, becoming the first Indian catwalk model and cover girl – *Femina, Buzz, Celebrity, Patakha, Debonair, Bombay, Bombshell, Ciné Blitz, Lifestyle, Gentleman, Eleganza, Chic*-pronounced-chick – whose fame grew to rival those of the Bollywood movie stars. Ina became a silent goddess of sex, prepared to wear the most exhibitionist garments designed by the new breed of radical young designers emerging in the city, garments so revealing that many of the top girls felt embarrassed. Ina, unembarrassable, with her hip-swinging Super Sashay, stole every show. Her face on a magazine cover was estimated to increase sales by a third; but she gave no interviews, rebuffing all attempts to discover her most intimate secrets, such as the colour of her bedroom, or her favourite movie *heero,* or the song she liked to hum while taking a bath. No beauty tips were handed out, nor autographs given. She remained aloof: every inch the upper-crust femme from Malabar Hill, she allowed people to imagine she only modelled 'for a laugh'. Her silence increased her allure; it allowed men to dream their own versions of her and women to imagine themselves into her strappy sandals or crocodile shoes. At the height of the Emergency, when in Bombay it was almost business-as-usual except that everyone kept missing trains because they had started leaving on time, when the plague-spores of communal fanaticism were still spreading and the disease had not yet erupted in the metropolis – in that strange time my sister Ina was voted #1 Role Model by the city's young magazine-reading females, beating Mrs Indira Gandhi by a factor of two to one.

But Mrs Gandhi was not the rival she was trying to defeat, and her triumphs were rendered meaningless by Aurora's failure to rise to the bait, to condemn her licentiousness and exhibitionism; until at last Ina was able to send her great mother epistolary proof of a liaison – a stolen weekend, as it turned out, at the Lord's Central House at Matheran – with Vasco Miranda. That did it all right. Aurora summoned her eldest daughter, cursed her for a nympho-maniac whore and threatened to throw her into the street. 'You don't have to push,' Ina answered, proudly. 'Don't worry on; I-tho will jump.'

Within twenty-four hours she had eloped to Nashville, Tennessee with the young playboy who was the sole heir of what was left of the Cashondeliveri family fortune after Abraham's buy-out of his father and uncle. Jamshedjee Jamibhoy Cashondeliveri had become well known in Bombay's nightclubs as the purveyor, under the stage name of 'Jimmy Cash', of what he liked to call 'Country and Eastern' music, a set of twangy songs about ranches and trains and love and cows with an idiosyncratic Indian twist. Now he and Ina had lit out for the territory, they were taking their love to town. She took the stage name of Gooddy (that is, 'Dolly') Gama – the use of a shortened version of her mother's family name suggested Aurora's continued influence over her daughter's thoughts and deeds – and there was a further development. She, who had become a legend by remaining silent, now opened her mouth and sang. She led a group of three back-up singers, and the name of their act, to which she agreed in spite of its regrettable equine connotations, was Jimmy Cash and the G.G.s.

Ina came home in disgrace a year later. We were all shocked. She was greasy-haired and dishevelled and had put on over seventy pounds: not-so-Gooddy Gama now! Immigration officers had trouble believing she was the young woman in her passport photograph. Her marriage was over, and though she said Jimmy had turned out to be a monster and 'we didn't know' the things he had done, it also emerged, as time passed, that her omnivorous sexual appetite for yodelling rhinestone cowboys and her ever-increasing exhibitionism had not gone down well with the moralistic arbiters of singers' fates in Tennessee, or, indeed, with her husband Jamshed; and to top it off she sang with the untrainable terminal squawk of a strangled goose. She had spent money as freely as she had partaken of the joys of American cooking, and her tantrums had grown larger along with the rest of her. In the end Jimmy had run away from her, and had given up Country and Eastern music to become a law student in California. 'I have to get him back,' she begged us. 'You must help me with my plan.'

Home is the place to which you can always return, no matter how painful the circumstances of your leaving. Aurora made no mention of their year-old rift, and took the prodigal child into her arms. 'We will fix-o that rotter,' she comforted weeping Ina. 'Just tell us what you want.'

'I have to bring him here,' she wept. 'If he thinks I am dying then he will surely return. Send a cable saying there is suspicion of I don't know what. Something not infectious. Heart attack.'

Aurora fought back a grin. 'How about', she suggested, hugging her newly girthsome child, 'some type of *wasting sickness*?'

Ina missed the sardonic note. 'No, stupid,' she said into Aurora's shoulder. 'How to lose so much weight in time? Don't have any more bad ideas. Tell him,' and here she brightened hugely, '*cancer*.'

∽

And Minnie: in the year Ina was away she found her own escape route. I am sorry to inform you that our sweet Inamorata, most mild-natured of young women, became, that year, enamoured of no less a personage than Jesus of Nazareth himself; of the Son of Man, and his holy mother, too. Mousey Minnie, always the easily shocked one, always the sister for whom our household's beatnik licence had been a matter for tuttings and hand-over-mouth shocks, our wide-eyed, innocent mini-Minnie who had been studying nursing with the nuns of Altamount Road, announced her desire to swap Aurora, the mother of her flesh, for Maria Gratiaplena, the Mother of God, to give up her sisterhood in favour of Sisterhood, and to spend the rest of her days away from *Elephanta*, in the house of, and wrapped in the love of . . .

'Christ!' Aurora swore, angrier than I had ever seen her. 'This is how you payofy us back for everything we have done.'

Minnie coloured, and you could see her wanting to tell her mother not to take the name of the Lord in vain, but she bit her lip until it bled, and went on hunger strike. 'Let her die,' said Aurora obdurately. 'Better a corpse than a nun.' But for six days little Minnie neither ate nor drank, until she started fainting and becoming more and more resistant to being revived. Under pressure from Abraham, Aurora relented. I did not often see my mother weep, but on that seventh day she wept, the tears being wrenched from her and emerging in harsh, hacking sobs. Sister John from the Gratiaplena nunnery was summoned – Sister John who had assisted at all our births – and she arrived with the serene authority of a conquering queen, as if she were Queen Isabella of Spain entering Granada's Alhambra to accept the surrender of Boabdil the Moor. She was a large old boat of a woman with white sails around her head and soft billows of flesh under her chin. Everything about her took on symbolic resonances that day; she seemed to be the vessel in which our sister would sail away. There was a knotty tree-stump of a mole – signifying the recalcitrance of true faith – on her upper lip, and from it there protruded like arrows – hinting at the sufferings of a true believer – half a dozen needles of hair. 'Blessed is this house,' she said, 'for it gives a bride to Christ.' It took Aurora Zogoiby all her self-control not to kill her on the spot.

So Minnie had become a novice and when she visited us in her Audrey Hepburn *Nun's Story* outfit the servants called her – of all things – Minnie *mausi*. Little mother, they meant, but I couldn't help finding the sound of it a bit creepy, as if Vasco Miranda's Disney figures on our nursery wall were somehow responsible for my sister's metamorphosis. Also, this new Minnie, this composed, remote, certain Minnie with the Mona Lisa smile and the devotional sparkle in her eternity-fixated eye, this Minnie felt as alien to me as if she had become a member of a different species: an angel, or a Martian, or a two-dimensional mouse. Her elder sister, however, acted as if nothing had changed in their relationship, as if Minnie – in spite of having been drafted into a different army – were still obliged to obey her Big Sis's commands.

'Talk to your nuns,' Ina ordered her. 'Get me a bed in their nursing home.' (The Gratiaplena nuns of Altamount Road specialised in the two ends of life, in helping people in and out of this sinful world.) 'I must be in such a place when my Jimmy Cash returns.'

Why did we do it? – For we all collaborated in Ina's plot, you know; Aurora sent the cancergram and Minnie persuaded the Altamount sisters to make a bed available on compassionate grounds, arguing that anything that might save a marriage, that might protect that high sacrament, was pure in the eyes of God. And when the cable worked and Jamshed Cashondeliveri flew into town, the fiction was maintained. Even Mynah, third and toughest

211

of my sisters, who had recently been admitted to the Bombay Bar, and of whom we saw less and less in those days, rallied round.

We have been a cussed lot, we da Gama-Zogoibys, each of us needing to strike out in a direction unlike the others, to lay claim to a territory we could call our own. After Abraham's business and Aurora's art came Ina's professionalisation of her sexuality and Minnie's surrender to God. As for Philomina Zogoiby – she dropped the 'Mynah' as soon as she could, and the magic child who imitated bird-calls had vanished long ago, though with the obstinacy of family we continued to annoy her by using the loathed nickname whenever she visited us at home – she had chosen to make a career out of what every youngest-daughter must do to get attention; that is, protest. No sooner had she qualified as an advocate than she told Abraham that she had joined a radical all-woman group of activists, film-makers and lawyers whose purpose was to expose the double scandals of invisible people and invisible skyscrapers out of which he had done so well. She took Kéké Kolatkar and his cronies at the Municipal Corporation to court, in a landmark case that lasted many years and shook the old F. W. Stevens Corporation building – 'How old?' – 'Old. From Old Time' – to its foundations. Years later she would succeed in putting crooked old Kéké in jail; Abraham Zogoiby, however, escaped, having been offered a deal by the court after negotiations with the tax authorities, much to his daughter's fury. He paid a large fine cheerfully, testified for the prosecution against his old ally, was granted immunity from prosecution in return, and, some months later, bought the beautiful K. K. Chambers for a song from the jailed politico's crumbling property company. And there was one further defeat for Mynah; for although she had successfully proved the existence of the invisible buildings, she failed to establish the reality of the invisible people who built them. They continued to be classified as phantoms, to move through the city like wraiths, except that these were the wraiths that kept the city going, building its houses, hauling its goods, cleaning up its droppings, and then simply and terribly dying, each in their turn, unseen, as their spectral blood poured out of their ghostly mouths in the middle of the bitch-city's all-too-real, uncaring streets.

When Ina holed up at the Altamount sisters' nursing home to await Jimmy Cash's return, Philomina surprised us all by paying her sister a visit. There was a Dory Previn song that you heard a lot back then – we sometimes got to things a little late – in which she accused her lover of being prepared to die for total strangers, though he would not live with her . . . Well, we thought much the same of our Philomina. Which was why her concern for poor Ina was so unexpected.

Why did we do it? I think because we understood that something had broken, that this was Ina's last throw of the dice. I think because we had always known that although Minnie was smaller and Mynah was younger it was Ina who was the most fragile, that she had never really been all there ever since her parents chopped her name in half, and that what with her nymphomania and all she had been cracking up for years. So she was drowning, she was clutching at straws as she had always clutched at men, and cheesy Jimmy was the last straw on offer.

Mynah offered to collect Jamshed Cashondeliveri from the airport, reasoning that, what with his new life as a law student and all, he might find it easiest to open up to her. He arrived looking very scared and very young, and to put him at his ease she began prattling, as she drove into town, about her own work, her 'struggle against the phallocracy' – about the case of the invisible world, and also her women's group's efforts to fight the Emergency in the courts. She spoke of the climate of fear pervading much of the country and the importance of the struggle for democratic and human rights. 'Indira Gandhi', she said, 'has lost the right to call herself a woman. She has grown an invisible dick.' Because she was so absorbed in her own concerns and so convinced of their justness she failed to notice that Jimmy was becoming more tense by the minute. He was no intellectual – law school was proving a great struggle – and, even more importantly, he had not a single drop of political radicalism in his blood. So it was that Mynah was the first of us to put a spoke in Ina's wheel. When she told him that she and her colleagues expected to be arrested any day now he thought seriously about jumping from the car and heading straight back to the airport before he became guilty by association with so tainted an in-law.

'Ina is dying to see you,' Mynah said at the end of her monologue, and then reddened at her choice of metaphor. 'I mean, no, she's not,' she corrected herself, hotly, making matters worse. A silence opened. 'Oh, hell, here we are, anyway,' she added a while later. 'Now you can see for yourself.'

Minnie met them at the door of the Maria Gratiaplena nursing home, looking more like Audrey Hepburn than ever, and all the way to the room where Ina waited like a miserable balloon she spoke of hellfire and damnation and till-death-us-do-part in a seraphic voice as sharp as breaking glass. Jimmy tried to tell her that he and Ina had not signed the full, holy, brimstone-and-treacle type of contract, having opted instead for the fifty-dollar Midnight Special country-style civil nuptial 'n' hoedown in a Reno quickie 'Wed-Inn' parlour, that they had been married to the music of Hank Williams Sr rather than hymns ancient or modern, standing not before an altar but beside a 'Hitching Post'; that there had been no priest officiating, but a man in a ten-gallon hat with a pair of pearl-handled six-guns riding on his hips, and that at the moment they were pronounced man and wife, a rodeo cowboy in chaps, and with a polka-dotted bandanna round his neck, had stepped up behind them with a mighty yahoo and lassoed them tightly together, crushing Ina's bridal bouquet of yellow roses against her chest. Its thorns had pricked her bosom until it bled.

My sister was unmoved by such secularist excuses. 'That cowpoke', she pronounced, 'was – don't you *see*? – the Messenger of God.'

The encounter with Minnie intensified the flight-response which Mynah's monologue had already prompted; and next, I must admit, I also did my inadvertent bit. When Minnie and Jimmy arrived outside Ina's room I was leaning against a corridor wall, daydreaming. Absent-mindedly, as I saw in my mind's eye a huge young Sikh bearing down upon me in a crowded alley, I spat on my deformed right hand. Jamshed Cashondeliveri leapt backwards in fright, colliding with Mynah, and I realised that I must have looked like the avenging brother, a six-and-a-half-foot giant preparing to strike down the man who had caused his sister so much misery. I tried putting up my hands in peace but he mistook this for a boxer's challenge, and plunged into Ina's room with a look of pure terror on his face.

He skidded to a halt a few inches away from Aurora Zogoiby herself. Behind my mother, on the bed, Ina had gone into a routine of moans and groans; but Jimmy had eyes only for Aurora. The great lady was at that time a woman in her fifties, but time had only increased her allure; she froze Jimmy like a dumb animal caught in the headlamps of her power, she turned the great beam of her attention upon him, wordlessly, and made him her slave. Afterwards, when that tragic farce was over, she told me – she actually admitted – that she should not have done it, she should have stood aside and let the estranged couple make what they could of their wretched lives. 'What to do?' she told me (I was her model then, and she was chatting as she worked). 'I just wanted to see if an old hen like me could still stoppofy a young fellow in his tracks.'

*I couldn't help it*, my scorpion-mother meant. *It was in my nature*.

Ina, behind her, was quickly losing control. It had been her pathetic plan to win back Jimmy's love by telling him how slim her chances were, how the cancer was systemic, it was pernicious, it was invasive, the lymph nodes were diseased, and the odds were that it had been discovered too late. Once he had fallen to his feet and begged forgiveness, she would allow him to sweat for a few weeks while she pretended to undergo chemotherapy (she was prepared to starve, even to thin her hair in the pursuit of love). Finally she would announce a miracle cure and they would live happily ever after. All these schemes were undone by the look of mooncalf adoration with which her husband was regarding her mother.

At that moment Ina's panicky need for him spilled over into insanity. In her frenzy she made the irreversible mistake of accelerating her plan. 'Jimmy,' she shrieked, 'Jimmy, it's a miracle, men. Now that you are here I am fixed, I know it, I swear it, let them test me and you will see. Jimmy, you saved my life, Jimmy, only you could do it, it is the power of love.'

He looked carefully at her then, and we could all see the scales falling from his eyes. He turned to each of us in turn and saw the conspiracy standing naked in our faces, saw the truth we could no longer hide. Ina, defeated, unleashed a foaming cascade of grief. 'What a family,' said Jamshed Cashondeliveri. 'I swear. Absolutely *crack*.' He left the Gratiaplena nursing home and never saw Ina again.

↢

Jimmy's parting shot was a prophecy; Ina's humiliation was a cracking-point in our family history. After that day and for all the next year she was mad, entering a kind of second childhood. Aurora had her put back into Vasco's nursery where she – where all of us – began; when her madness increased she was placed in a straitjacket and padding was put up against the walls, but Aurora would not permit her to be committed to a mental home. Now that it was too late, now that Ina had snapped, Aurora became the most loving mother in the world, spoonfeeding her, washing her like a baby, hugging and kissing her as she had never been hugged or kissed when she was sane – giving her the love, that is to say, which, had it been offered earlier, might have built in her eldest daughter the fortitude to resist the catastrophe that had ruined her mind.

Soon after the end of the Emergency, Ina died of cancer. The lymphoma developed quite suddenly, and gobbled up her body like a beggar at a feast. Only Minnie, who had completed her novitiate and been reborn as Sister Floreas – 'sounds like the blooming Fountain,' Aurora snorted in frustrated scorn – had the nerve to say that Ina had called the illness down upon herself, that she had 'chosen her own gathering'. Aurora and Abraham never spoke of Ina's death, honouring it in silence, the silence which had once helped make Ina a celebrated beauty, and which was now the silence of the tomb.

So Ina was dead, and Minnie was gone, and Mynah was briefly in jail – for she was arrested at the very end of the Emergency, but quickly released, her reputation much enhanced, after Mrs

Gandhi's electoral defeat. Aurora wanted to tell her youngest daughter how proud she was of her, but somehow she never got round to it, somehow the coldness, the brusqueness of Philomina Zogoiby's manner whenever she had any contact with her folks succeeded in stopping her mother's loving tongue. Mynah did not often visit *Elephanta*; which left me.

⌣

One last person had fallen through the crack in the world. Dilly Hormuz had been dismissed. Miss Jaya Hé, whose job in the household had evolved from ayah into housekeeper, had taken advantage of her position to pull off one final heist. From Aurora's studio she stole three charcoal sketches of me as a young boy, sketches in which my ruined hand had been wondrously meta-morphosed, becoming, variously, a flower, a paintbrush and a sword. Miss Jaya took these sketches to my Dilly's flat and said they were a gift from the 'young Sahib'. Then she told Aurora that she had seen the teacher pinching them, *and, excuse me, Begum Sahib, but that woman's attitude to our boy is not a moral one*. Aurora visited Dilly the same day, and the pictures, which the sweet woman had placed in the silver frames on the piano, concealing her own family portraits, were all the proof my mother needed of the teacher's guilt. I tried to plead Dilly's case, but once my mother's mind was closed, no force on earth could open it. 'Anyhow,' she told me, 'you are too old for her now. There is nothing more you can learnofy from her.'

Dilly spurned all my overtures – my telephone calls, letters, flowers – after she was sacked. I walked one last time down the hill to the house by Vijay Stores and when I got there she would not let me in. She opened the door about three inches and refused to move out of the way. That long stripe of her, framed in teak, that mutinous jaw and short-sighted blink, was my sweaty journey's only reward. 'Go your ways, you poor boy,' she told me. 'I wish you well on your hard road.'

Such was Miss Jaya Hé's revenge.

# 13

THE SO-CALLED 'MOOR paintings' of Aurora Zogoiby can be divided into three distinct periods: the 'early' pictures, made between 1957 and 1977, that is to say between the year of my birth and that of the election that swept Mrs G. from power, and of Ina's death; the 'great' or 'high' years, 1977–81, during which she created the glowing, profound works with which her name is most often associated; and the so-called 'dark Moors', those pictures of exile and terror which she painted after my departure, and which include her last, unfinished, unsigned masterpiece, *The Moor's Last Sigh* (170 × 247 cms., oil on canvas, 1987), in which she turned, at last, to the one subject she had never directly addressed – facing up, in that stark depiction of the moment of Boabdil's expulsion from Granada, to her own treatment of her only son. It was a picture which, for all its great size, had been stripped to the harsh essentials, all its elements converging on the face at its heart, the Sultan's face, from which horror, weakness, loss and pain poured like darkness itself, a face in a condition of existential torment reminiscent of Edvard Munch. It was as different a picture from Vasco Miranda's sentimental treatment of the same theme as could possibly be imagined. But it was also a mystery picture, that 'lost painting' – and how striking that both Vasco's and Aurora's treatments of this theme should disappear within a few years of my mother's death, the one stolen from the private collection of C. J. Bhabha, the other from the Zogoiby Bequest itself! Gents, gentesses: permit me to titillate your interest by revealing that it was a picture within which Aurora Zogoiby, in her fretful last days, had concealed a prophecy of her death. (And Vasco's fate, too, was bound up with the story of these canvases.)

As I set down my memories of my part in those paintings, I am naturally conscious that those who submit themselves as the models upon whom a work of art is made can offer, at best, a subjective, often wounded, sometimes spiteful, wrong-side-of-the-canvas version of the finished work. What then can the humble clay usefully say about the hands that moulded it? Perhaps simply this: that *I was there*. And that during the years of sittings I made a kind of portrait of her, too. She was looking at me, and I was looking right back.

This is what I saw: a tall woman in a paint-spattered, mid-calf-length homespun kurta worn over dark blue sailcloth slacks, barefoot, her white hair piled up on her head with brushes sticking out of it, giving her an eccentric Madame Butterfly look, Butterfly as Katharine Hepburn or – yes! – Nargis in some zany Indian cover version, *Titli Begum*, might have played her: no longer young, no longer prinked and painted, and certainly no longer bothered about any pathetic Pinkerton's return. She stood before me in the least luxurious of studios, a room lacking so much as a comfortable chair, and 'non-A.C.' so that it was as hot and humid as a cheap taxi, with one slow ceiling fan moving lazily above. Aurora never showed any signs of giving a damn about the weather conditions; so neither, naturally, did I. I sat where and how she set me, and made a point of never complaining of the aches in my variously arranged limbs until she remembered to ask if I'd like a break. In this way a little of her legendary stubbornness, her determination, seeped through the canvas into me.

I was the only child she suckled at her breast. It made a difference: for although I received my share of the sharp end of her tongue, there was something in her attitude towards me that was less destructive than her treatment of my sisters. Perhaps it was my 'condition', which she refused to permit anyone to call an illness, that softened her heart. The doctors gave my misfortune first one name, then another, but when we sat in her studio as artist and model Aurora told me constantly that I must not think of myself as the victim of an incurable premature-ageing disorder, but a magic child, a time traveller. 'Only four and a half months in the womb,' she reminded me. 'Baby mine, you just startofied out going too fast. Maybe you'll just take off, and zoom-o right out of this life into another space and time. Maybe – who knows? – a better.' It was as close as she ever came to stating a belief in an after-life. It seemed that she had decided to fight fear – hers as well as my own – by espousing such strategies of conjecture, by making my lot a privileged one, and presenting me to myself as well as to the world as someone special, someone with a meaning, a supernatural Entity who did not truly belong to this place, this moment, but whose presence here defined the lives of those around him, and of the age in which they lived.

Well, I believed her. I needed consolations and was happy to take whatever was on offer. I believed her, and it helped. (When I learned about the missing post-Lotus night in Delhi four and a half months before my conception, I wondered if Aurora were covering up a different problem; but I don't think she was. I think she was trying to will my half-life into wholeness, by the power of mother-love.)

She suckled me, and the first 'Moor' pictures were done while I nestled at her breast: charcoal sketches, watercolours, pastels and finally a large work in oils. Aurora and I posed, somewhat blasphemously, as a godless madonna and child. My stunted hand had become a glowing light, the only light-source in the picture. The fabric of her amorphous robe fell in starkly shadowed folds. The sky was an electric cobalt blue. It was what Abraham Zogoiby might have been hoping for when he had commissioned Vasco to paint her picture almost a decade earlier; no, it was more than Abraham could ever have imagined. It showed the truth about Aurora, her capacity for profound and selfless passion as well as her habit of self-aggrandisement; it revealed the magnificence, the grandeur of her falling-out with the world, and her determination to transcend and redeem its imperfections through art. Tragedy disguised as fantasy and rendered in the most beautiful, most heightened colour and light she could create: it was a mythomaniac gem. She called it *A Light to Lighten the Darkness*. 'Why not?' she shrugged, when questioned, by Vasco Miranda among others. 'I am getting interested in making religious pictures for people who have no god.'

'Then keep a ticket to London in your pocket,' he advised her. 'Because in this god-rotten joint, you never know when you might have to run.'

(But Aurora laughed at such advice; and in the end it was Vasco who left.)

As I grew, she went on using me as a subject, and this continuity, too, was a sign of love. Unable to find a way of preventing me from 'going too fast', she painted me into immortality, giving me the gift of being a part of what would persist of her. So, like the hymn-writer, let me with a gladsome mind praise her, for she was kind. *For her mercy ay endures* . . . And in truth if I am asked to put my finger – my whole birth-maimed hand – on the source of my belief that in spite of speeding and crippled limb and friendlessness I had a happy childhood in Paradise, I would finally put it here, I would say that my joy in life was born in our collaboration, in the intimacy of those private hours, when she talked of everything under the sun, absently, as if I were her confessor, and I learned the secrets of her heart as well as her mind.

I learned, for example, about how she fell for my father: about the great sensuality that had burst out of my parents in an Ernakulam godown one day, forcing them together, making possible what was impossible, demanding to be allowed to come-to-be. What I loved most in my parents was this passion for each other, the simple fact of its having once been there (though as time passed it became harder and harder to see the young lovers they had been in the increasingly distant married couple they were becoming). Because they had loved so greatly I wanted such a love for myself, I thirsted for it, and even as I lost myself in the surprising tendernesses and athleticisms of Dilly Hormuz I knew she wasn't what I was looking for; O, I wanted, wanted that *asli mirch masala*, the thing that made you sweat beads of coriander juice and breathe hot-chilli flames through your stinging lips. I wanted their pepper love.

And when I found it, I thought my mother would understand. When I needed to move a mountain for love, I thought my mother would help.

Alas for us all: I was wrong.

~

She knew about Abraham's temple girls, of course, had known from the beginning. 'Man who wants to keep-o secrets should not babble in his sleep,' she muttered vaguely one day. 'I got so bored of your Daddy's night-lingo that I moved out of his bedroom. A lady needs her rest.' And as I look back upon that proud, busy woman I hear her telling me something else beneath those casual sentences – I hear her admitting that she, who refused all compromises and made no accommodations, had settled for Abraham in spite of the weaknesses of the flesh which made him incapable of resisting the temptation to sample the goods he was importing from down south. 'Old men,' she snorted another day, 'always droolo'ing after bachchis. And the ones with many daughters are the worst.' For a time I was young and innocent enough to think of these musings as part of the process by which she thought herself into the lives of the figures in her paintings; but by the time my own lust had been awakened by Dilly Hormuz's hand I had begun to get the point.

I had always wondered about the eight-year gap between Mynah and myself, and so, when understanding descended upon my young-old child-self like a tongue of flame, I – who had been denied the company of children, and so found myself at an early age using an adult vocabulary without an adult's delicacy or control – was unable to resist blurting out my discovery: 'You stopped making babies,' I cried, 'because he was fooling around.'

'I'll give you one chapat', she promised, 'that will breakofy the teeth in your cheeky face.' The slap that followed, however, created no long-lasting dental problems. Its gentleness was all the confirmation I required.

Why did she never confront Abraham about his infidelities? I ask you to consider that in spite of all her freethinking bohemian ways, Aurora Zogoiby was still, in some deep recess of her heart, a woman of her generation, a generation that would find such behaviour tolerable, even normal, in a man; whose womenfolk shrugged off their pain, burying it beneath banalities about the *nature of the beast* and its need, periodically, to *scratch an itch*. For the sake of family, that great absolute in whose name all things were possible, women averted their eyes and kept their grief knotted in a twist of fabric at the end of a dupatta, or buttoned up in a small silk purse, like small change and the household keys. And it may have been, too, because Aurora knew she needed Abraham, she needed him to take care of business and leave her free for art. It may have been as simple, complaisant and chickenshit as that.

(A parenthesis on complaisance: in my musings on Abraham's decision to journey south when Aurora headed north for her last meeting with Mr Nehru and the scandal of the Lotus, I suspected my father of playing the complaisant spouse. Was this reciprocity what lay beneath his choice, this hollow open marriage, this whited sepulchre, this sham? – O, Moor, be calm, be calm. They have both gone beyond your reproach; this anger can do nothing, though it shake the very earth.)

How she must have hated herself for making such a cowardly, financially motivated soft option of a devil's deal with fate! For – generation or no generation – the mother I knew, the mother I came to know during all those days in her spartan studio, was not one to take anything in life lying down. She was a confronter, a squarer-up, a haver-out. Yet, when faced with the ruin of her life's great love, and offered a choice between an honest war and an untruthful, self-serving peace, she buttoned her lip, and never offered her husband an angry word. Thus silence grew between them like an accusation; he talked in his sleep, she muttered in her studio, and they slept in separate rooms. For a moment, after his heart almost gave way on the steps to the Lonavla caves, they were able to remember what had once been. But after that the reality soon returned. Sometimes I am convinced that they both saw my crippled hand, my ageing, as a judgment upon them – a deformed child born of a stunted love, half a life born of a marriage that was no longer whole. If there had been any ghost of a chance of their becoming reconciled, my birth put that phantom to flight.

First I worshipped my mother, then I hated her. Now, at the end of all our stories, I look back and can feel – at least in bursts – a measure of compassion. Which is a kind of healing, for her son as well as for her own, restless shade.

Strong desire drew Abraham and Aurora together; weak lust pushed them apart. In these last days, as I have written down my accounts of Aurora's overweenings, of her sharpnesses and shrillnesses, I have heard beneath that raucous drama these sadder notes of loss. She forgave Abraham for disappointing her once, in Cochin, in the matter of Flory Zogoiby's Rumpelstiltskin attempt to take away an as-yet-unborn son. In Matheran she tried – and in trying, created me – to forgive him a second time. But he did not improve his ways, and there was no third forgiveness . . . yet she stayed. She, who had shaken her world for love, now stifled her revolt, and chained herself to an increasingly loveless marriage. No wonder her tongue grew sharp.

And Abraham: if he had turned back towards her, forsaking all others, might she have saved him from sinking into the Mogambo-underworld of Kéké and Scar and worse criminals yet to come? Might he, with the blessed ballast of their love, have failed to sink into that pit? . . . No point trying to rewrite one's parents' lives. It's hard enough to try and set them down; to say nothing of my own.

∽

In the 'early Moors' my hand was transformed into a series of miracles; often my body, too, was miraculously changed. In one picture – *Courtship* – I was Moor-as-peacock, spreading my many-eyed tail; she painted her own head on top of a dowdy pea-hen's body. In another (painted when I was twelve and looked twenty-four) Aurora reversed our relationship, painting herself as the young Eleanor Marx and me as her father Karl. *Moor and Tussy* was a rather shocking idea – my mother girlish, adoring, and I in patriarchal, lapel-gripping pose, frock-coated and bewhiskered, like a prophecy of the all-too-near future. 'If you were twice as old as you look, and I was half as old as I am, I could be your daughter,' my forty-plus mother explained, and at the time I was too young to hear anything except the lightness she used to disguise the stranger things in her voice. Nor was this our only double, or ambiguous, portrait; for there was also *To Die Upon a Kiss*, in which she portrayed herself as murdered Desdemona flung across her bed, while I was stabbed Othello, falling towards her in suicided remorse as I breathed my last. My mother described these canvases, self-deprecatingly, as 'panto-pictures', intended for the household's private entertainment: the artist's frivolous equivalent of fancy-dress parties. But – as in the episode of her notorious cricket-picture, which will be recounted presently – Aurora was often at her most iconoclastic, her most *épatante*, when she was most light-hearted; and the high-voltage eroticism of all these works, which she did not exhibit in her lifetime, created a posthumous shock-wave that only failed to grow into a full-scale tsunami because she, the brazen eroticist, was no longer around to provoke decent folks by refusing to apologize, or even to express the merest scrap of regret.

After the Othello picture, however, the series changed direction, and began to explore the idea of placing a re-imagining of the old Boabdil story – 'not Authorised Version but Aurorised Version', as she told me – in a local setting, with me playing a sort of Bombay remix of the last of the Nasrids. In January 1970, for the first time, Aurora Zogoiby placed the Alhambra on Malabar Hill.

I was thirteen years old, and in the first flush of my intoxication with Dilly Hormuz. While she painted the first of the 'true', the *echt* Moors, Aurora told me about a dream. She had been standing on the 'back verandah' of a rattletrap train in a Spanish night, holding my sleeping body in her arms. Suddenly she knew – knew in the way of dreams, without being told, but with absolute certainty – that if she were to toss me away, if she were to sacrifice me to the night, then she would be safe, invulnerable, for the rest of her life. 'I tell you, kiddo, I thought about it pretty hard.' Then she refused the dream's offer, and took me back to my bed. You didn't have to be a Bible expert to work out that she had cast herself in an Abrahamic rôle, and even at thirteen, in that house of artists, I was familiar with pictures of the Michelangelo Pietà, so I got the point, or most of it. 'Thanks a lot, ma,' I told her. 'Nothing to it,' she answered. 'Let them do their worst.'

This dream, like so many dreams, came true; but Aurora, when her Abrahamic moment really came, did not make the choice which she had dreamed.

Once the red fort of Granada arrived in Bombay, things moved swiftly on Aurora's easel. The Alhambra quickly became a not-quite-Alhambra; elements of India's own red forts, the Mughal palace-fortresses in Delhi and Agra, blended Mughal splendours with the Spanish building's Moorish grace. The hill became a not-Malabar looking down upon a not-quite-Chowpatty, and the creatures of Aurora's imagination began to populate it – monsters, elephant-deities, ghosts. The water's edge, the dividing line between two worlds, became in many of these pictures the main focus of her concern. She filled the sea with fish, drowned ships, mermaids, treasure, kings; and on the land, a cavalcade of local riff-raff – pickpockets, pimps, fat whores hitching their saris up against the waves – and other figures from history or fantasy or current affairs or nowhere, crowded towards the water like the real-life Bombayites on the beach, taking their evening strolls. At the water's edge strange composite creatures slithered to and fro across the frontier of the elements. Often she painted the water-line in such a way as to suggest that you were looking at an unfinished painting which had been abandoned, half-covering another. But was it a waterworld being painted over the world of air, or vice versa? Impossible to be sure.

'Call it Mooristan,' Aurora told me. 'This seaside, this hill, with the fort on top. Water-gardens and hanging gardens, watchtowers and towers of silence too. Place where worlds collide, flow in and out of one another, and washofy away. Place where an air-man can drowno in water, or else grow gills; where a water-creature can get drunk, but also chokeofy, on air. One universe, one dimension, one country, one dream, bumpo'ing into another, or being under, or on top of. Call it Palimpstine. And above it all, in the palace, you.'

(For the rest of his life Vasco Miranda would remain convinced that she had taken the idea from him; that his painting-over-a-painting was the source of her palimpsest-art, and that his lachrymose Moor was the inspiration for her dry-eyed pictures of me. She neither confirmed nor denied. 'Nothing new under the sun,' she would say. And in her vision of the opposition and intermingling of land and water there was something of the

Cochin of her youth, where the land pretended to be a part of England, but was washed by an Indian sea.

There was no stopping her. Around and about the figure of the Moor in his hybrid fortress she wove her vision, which in fact was a vision of *weaving*, or more accurately interweaving. In a way these were polemical pictures, in a way they were an attempt to create a romantic myth of the plural, hybrid nation; she was using Arab Spain to re-imagine India, and this land-sea-scape in which the land could be fluid and the sea stone-dry was her metaphor – idealised? sentimental? probably – of the present, and the future, that she hoped would evolve. So, yes, there was a didacticism here, but what with the vivid surrealism of her images and the kingfisher brilliance of her colouring and the dynamic acceleration of her brush, it was easy not to feel preached at, to revel in the carnival without listening to the barker, to dance to the music without caring for the message in the song.

Characters – so plentiful outside the palace – now began to appear within its walls. Boabdil's mother, the old battleaxe Ayxa, naturally turned up wearing Aurora's face; but in these early paintings the gloom of the future, the reconquering armies of Ferdinand and Isabella, were hardly to be glimpsed. In one or two canvases you saw, on the horizon, the protrusion of a flag-waving lance; but for the most part, during my childhood, Aurora Zogoiby was seeking to paint a golden age. Jews, Christians, Muslims, Parsis, Sikhs, Buddhists, Jains crowded into her paint-Boabdil's fancy-dress balls, and the Sultan himself was represented less and less naturalistically, appearing more and more often as a masked, particoloured harlequin, a patchwork quilt of a man; or, as his old skin dropped from him chrysalis-fashion, standing revealed as a glorious butterfly, whose wings were a miraculous composite of all the colours in the world.

As the Moor pictures moved further down this fabulist road, it became plain that I barely needed to pose for my mother any more; but she wanted me there, she said she needed me, she called me her *lucky talis-moor*. And I was happy to be there, because the story unfolding on her canvases seemed more like my autobiography than the real story of my life.

During the Emergency years, while her daughter Philomina went into battle against tyranny, Aurora stayed in her tent and worked: and maybe this, too, was a spur for the Moor paintings of the period, maybe Aurora saw the work as her own answer to the brutalities of the time. Ironically enough, however, an old picture by my mother, innocently included by Kekoo Mody in an otherwise banal exhibition of paintings on sporting themes, provoked a greater rumpus than anything Mynah was able to stir up. The painting, dating from 1960, was called *The Kissing of Abbas Ali Baig*, and was based on an actual incident that occurred during the third Test Match against Australia at Bombay's Brabourne Stadium. The series was level at 1–1, and the third game had not been going India's way. In the second innings, Baig's half-century – his second of the match – enabled the home side to force a draw. When he reached 50, a pretty young woman ran out from the usually rather staid and upper-crust North Stand and kissed the batsman on the cheek. Eight runs later, perhaps a little overcome, Baig was dismissed (c Mackay b Lindwall), but by that time the match was safe.

Aurora liked cricket – back then more and more women were being drawn to the game, and young stars like A. A. Baig were getting to be as popular as the demi-gods of the Bombay talkies – and by chance she was at the ground on the day of the gasp-provoking, scandalous kiss, a kiss between beautiful strangers, perpetrated in broad daylight and in a packed stadium, and at a time when no movie house in the city was permitted to offer its audiences so obscenely provocative an image. Well! My mother was inspired. She rushed home and in a single sustained burst completed the painting, in which the 'real' shy peck, done for a dare, was transformed into a full-scale Western-movie clinch. It was Aurora's version – quickly displayed by Kekoo Mody and much reproduced in the national press – that everyone remembered; even those who had been at the ground that day began to speak – with much disapproving shaking of heads – of the moist licentiousness, the uninhibited writhings of that interminable kiss, which, they swore, had gone on for *hours*, until the umpires prised the couple apart and reminded the batsman of his duty to his team. 'Only in Bombay,' people said, with that cocktail of arousal and disapproval that only a scandal can properly mix'n'shake. 'What a loose town, yaar, I swear.'

In Aurora's picture, the Brabourne stadium in its excitement had closed in around the two smoochers, the ogling stands had curved up and over them, almost blotting out the sky, and in the audience were pop-eyed movie stars – a few of whom really had been present – and slavering politicians and coolly observant scientists and industrialists slapping their thighs and making dirty jokes. Even the cartoonist R. K. Laxman's celebrated Common Man, , was perched in the East Stand bleachers, looking shocked in his goofy, unworldly way. So it had become a state-of-India painting, a snapshot of cricket's arrival at the heart of the national consciousness, and, more controversially, a generational cry of sexual revolt. The explicit hyperbole of the kiss – a tangle of womanly limbs and the cricketer's pads and whites that recalled the eroticism of the Tantric carvings at the Chandela temples of Khajuraho – was described by a liberal art critic as 'the call of Youth for Freedom, an act of defiance under the very noses of the Status Quo', and by a more conservative editorial commentator as 'an obscenity fit to be burned in the public square'. Abbas Ali Baig was forced to deny publicly that he had kissed the girl back; the popular cricket columnist 'A.F.S.T.' wrote a witty piece in his defence, suggesting that mere artists should henceforth cease to poke their long brushes into the really important things of life, such as cricket; and after a time the little scandal seemed to have fizzled out. But in the following series, against Pakistan, poor Baig scored only 1, 13, 19 and 1, was dropped from the team, and hardly ever played for India again. He became the target of a vicious young political cartoonist, Raman Fielding, who – in a parody of Aurora's old Chipkali pictures – signed his caricatures with a little frog, usually shown making a snide comment in the edges of the frame. Fielding – already better known, after the frog, as *Mainduck* – vilely and falsely accused the honourable and richly gifted Baig of having deliberately thrown away his wicket against Pakistan because he was a Muslim. 'And this is the fellow who has the nerve to kiss our patriotic Hindu girls,' muttered the spotted frog in the corner.

Aurora, shocked by the attack on Baig, wrapped the painting up and stored it away. If she allowed it to be exhibited again fifteen years later, it was because she had come to think of it as a quaint period piece. The batsman concerned had retired long ago, and kissing was no longer as outrageous an activity as it had been back in those bad old days. What she had not foreseen was that Mainduck – now a full-time communalist politician, one of the founders of 'Mumbai's Axis,' the party of Hindu nationalists named after the mother-goddess of Bombay, which was growing rapidly in popularity among the poor – would return to the attack.

He no longer drew cartoons, though in the strange dance of attraction and repulsion that he would afterwards dance with my mother – who, let it be remembered, invariably used the word 'cartoonist' as an insult – it was always possible to discern the heavy chip on his shoulder. He seemed undecided whether he wanted to fall on his knees before the great artist and Malabar Hill grandee, or drag her down into the dirt in which he lived; and no doubt this ambiguity is what drew grand Aurora towards him, too – towards that motu-kalu, that fatty-blacky fellow who represented most of what she most profoundly abhorred. Many of my family members have had a fondness for slumming.

Raman Fielding's name derived, according to legend, from a cricket-mad father, a street-wise Bombay ragamuffin who hung around the Bombay Gymkhana pleading to be given a chance: 'Please, babujis, you give this poor chokra one batting? One bowling only? Okay, okay – then *just one fielding*?' He turned out to be a lousy cricketer but when the Brabourne Stadium was opened in 1937 he gained employment as a security guard, and over the years his skill at nabbing and expelling gatecrashers came to the notice of the immortal C. K. Nayudu, who recognised him from the old days at the Gymkhana and joked, 'So, my little just-one-fielding – you sure grew up to take some expert catches.' After that the fellow was always known as J. O. Fielding, and proudly accepted the name as his own.

His son learned a different lesson from cricket (to the distress, it was said, of his father). Not for him the humble democratic pleasure of simply being a part, however menial, however marginal, of that cherished world. No: as a young man in the Bombay Central rum-dens he would harangue his friends about the Indian game's origins in inter-community rivalry. 'From the start the Parsis and Muslims tried to steal the game from us,' he would declaim. 'But when we Hindus got our teams together, naturally we proved too strong. By-the-same-token we must make changes beyond the boundary. For too long we have been lying back and allowing un-Indian types to steal a march. Let us only marshal our forces, and what can stand against us?' In his bizarre conception of cricket as a fundamentally communalist game, essentially Hindu but with its Hindu-ness constantly under threat from the country's other, treacherous communities, lay the origins of his political philosophy, and of 'Mumbai's Axis' itself. There was even a moment when Raman Fielding considered naming his new political movement after a great Hindu cricketer – Ranji's Army, Mankad's Martinets – but in the end he went for the goddess – a.k.a Mumba-Ai, Mumbadevi, Mumbabai – thus uniting regional and religious nationalism in his potent, explosive new group.

Cricket, most individualistic of all team sports, ironically enough became the basis of the rigidly hierarchic, neo-Stalinist inner structures of 'Mumbai's Axis', or the MA, as it quickly came to be known: for – as I afterwards discovered at first hand – Raman Fielding insisted on grouping his dedicated cadres into 'elevens', and each of these little platoons had a 'team captain' to whom absolute allegiance had to be sworn. The ruling council of the MA is known as the First XI to this day. And Fielding insisted on being addressed as 'Skipper' from the start.

His old nickname from the cartoonist days was never used in his presence, but throughout the city his famous frog-symbol – *Vote for Mainduck* – could be seen painted on walls and stuck on the sides of cars. Oddly for so successful a populist leader, he was a man who detested familiarity. So it was always Captain to his face and Mainduck behind his back. And in the fifteen years between his two attacks on *The Kissing of Abbas Ali Baig*, like a man who comes to resemble his pet, he had truly grown into a giant version of that long-abandoned cartoon frog. He held court beneath a gulmohr tree in the garden of his two-storey villa in the Lalgaum suburb of Bandra East, surrounded by aides and supplicants, beside a lily-padded pond, and amid literally dozens of statues of Mumbadevi, large and small; golden blossoms floated down to anoint the statues' heads as well as Fielding's. Mostly he was a brooding stillness; but every so often, goaded by some visitor's injudicious remark, speech would burst from him, foul-tongued, terrifying, lethal. And in his low cane chair with his great belly slung across his knees like a burglar's sack, with his frog's croak of a voice bursting through his fat frog's lips and his little dart of a tongue licking at the edges of his mouth, with his hooded froggy eyes gazing greedily down upon the little beedi-rolls of money with which his quaking petitioners sought to pacify him, and which he rolled lusciously between his plump little fingers until at length he broke slowly into a huge, red-gummed smile, he was indeed a Frog King, a Mainduck Raja whose commands could not be gainsaid.

By this time he had decided to rewrite his father's life-story, erasing the tale of just-one-fielding from his repertoire. He had started telling visiting foreign journalists that his father had been an educated, cultured, literary man, an internationalist, who had taken the name of 'Fielding' as a genuflection to the author of *Tom Jones*. 'You call me narrow and parochial,' he reproached the journalists. 'Bigot and prude, you have also called. But from my childhood time, intellectual horizons were broad and free. They were – let me so put it – *picaresque*.'

Aurora first heard that her work had re-ignited the wrath of this mighty amphibian when Kekoo Mody phoned in some agitation from his gallery on Cuffe Parade. The MA had announced its intention to march on Kekoo's little showroom, claiming it was flagrantly displaying a pornographic representation of a sexual assault by a Muslim 'sportsman' on an innocent Hindu maiden. Raman Fielding himself was expected to head the march, and to address the crowd. Police were present, but in insufficient numbers; the danger of violence, even of a fire-attack on the gallery, was very real. 'Wait on,' my mother told him. 'This little frog-face, I know how to fixofy. Give me thirty ticks.'

Within half an hour the march had been called off. In a prepared statement, a representative of the First XI of the MA told a hastily convened press conference that on account of the imminence of Gudhi Padwa, the Maharashtrian New Year, the pornography protest had been suspended, lest an outbreak of violence – God forbid! – should mar the happy day. Additionally, in deference to the outrage of the people, the Mody Gallery had agreed to withdraw the offending painting from view. Without leaving *Elephanta*, my mother had averted a crisis.

But mother: it was not a victory. It was a defeat.

The first-ever conversation between Aurora Zogoiby and Raman Fielding had been short and to the point. For once she had not asked Abraham to do her dirty work. She made her own telephone call. I know it: I was there. Years later I learned that the telephone on Raman Fielding's desk was a special instrument, an American import; the receiver looked like a bright green plastic frog, and croaked instead of ringing. Fielding must have put the frog against his face and heard my mother's voice issuing through its lips.

'How much?' she asked.

And Mainduck named his price.

~

I have chosen to set down the full saga of *The Kissing of Abbas Ali Baig* because the entry of Fielding into our lives was a moment of some significance; and because for a while this cricket-scene was the picture for which Aurora Zogoiby became, let us say, too well-known. The threat of violence receded a little, but the work was obliged to remain concealed – could only be rescued by joining the city's many invisibles. A principle had been eroded; a pebble bounced down a hill: plink, plonk, plank. There would be many further such erosions in the years that followed, and the bouncing pebble would be joined by many larger stones. But Aurora herself never made great claims – whether of principle or quality – for *The*

*Kissing*; to her it was a jeu d'esprit, quickly conceived, lightly executed. It became, however, an albatross, and I witnessed both her ennui at having endlessly to defend it, and her fury at the ease with which this 'teapot monsoon' had distracted attention from the body of her real work. She was required by the public prints to speak ponderously of 'underlying motives' when she had had only whims, to make moral statements where there had been only ('only'!) play, and feeling, and the unfolding inexorable logic of brush and light. She was obliged to counter accusations of social irresponsibility by divers 'experts', and took to muttering bad-temperedly that, throughout history, efforts to make artists socially accountable had resulted in nullity: tractor art, court art, choco-late-box junk. 'What I resent most, but, about these Ologistas springofying up like dragon's teeth,' she told me, painting furiously, 'is they force me to become too much an Olojee myself.'

Suddenly she found herself being described – by MA voices, but not only by them – as a 'Christian artist', even, on one occasion, as 'that Christian female married to a Jew'. At first such formulations made her laugh; but she soon saw that they weren't funny. How easily a self, a lifetime of work and action and affinity and opposition, could be washed away under such an attack! 'It's as if', she said to me, falling accidentally into a cricketing image, 'I don't have any runs on the bloody board.' Or, at another time: 'It's as if I don't have any money in the bloody bank.' Remembering Vasco's warnings, she responded in a characteristically unpredictable fashion. One day in those dark years of the mid-Seventies – years that somehow seem darker in the memory because so little of their tyranny could be seen, because on Malabar Hill the Emergency was as invisible as the illegal skyscrapers and disenfranchised poor – she presented me, at the end of a long studio day, with an envelope containing a one-way airline ticket to Spain, and my passport, stamped with a Spanish visa. 'Always keep it valid,' she told me. 'The ticket you can renew-o every year, and the visa too. I-tho will run nowhere. If that Indira who always hate-o'ed me to pieces wants to come and get, she will know where to find me. But maybe the day will come when you should takeofy Vasco's tip.

Only don't go to the English. We have had enough of them. Go find Palimpstine; go see Mooristan.'

And for Lambajan at the gates she also had a present: a black leather cartridge-belt, and hanging from it a police holster with a button-down flap, and inside the holster, loaded, a gun. She arranged for him to be given shooting lessons. As for me, I tucked her gift away; and thereafter, superstitiously, never failed to do as she had suggested. I kept my back door open, and made sure there was a plane standing on the runway. I had begun to come unstuck. We all had. After the Emergency people started seeing through different eyes. Before the Emergency we were Indians. After it we were Christian Jews.

Plank, plonk, plink.

∽

Nothing happened. No mob came to the gate, no arresting officers arrived to perform the rôle of Indira's avenging angels. Lamba's gun remained in its holster. It was Mynah who was detained, but only for a few weeks, and she was treated with great courtesy and allowed to receive visitors, books and food in her cell. The Emergency ended. Life went on.

Nothing happened, and everything. There was turmoil in Paradise. Ina died, and after her funeral Aurora came home and painted a Moor painting in which the line between land and sea had ceased to be a permeable frontier. Now she painted it as a harshly-delineated zig-zag crack, into which the land was pouring along with the ocean. The munchers of mango and singhani, the drinkers of electric-blue syrups so sugary that one endangered one's teeth just by looking at them, the office workers in their rolled trousers with their cheap shoes in their hands, and all the barefoot lovers walking along the version of Chowpatty Beach beneath the Moor's Palace were screaming as the sand beneath their feet sucked them down towards the fissure, along with the cutpurses, the neon-lit stalls of the snack vendors, and the trained monkeys in soldier's uniform who had been dying-for-their-country to entertain the promenading crowds. They all poured into the jagged darkness along with the pomfret and jellyfish and crabs. The evening arc of Marine Drive itself, Marine Drive with its banal, cultured-pearl necklace of lights, had grown distorted; the very esplanade was being pulled towards the void. And in his palace on the hill, the harlequin Moor looked down at the tragedy, impotent, sighing, and old before his time. Dead Ina stood translucent by his side, the pre-Nashville Ina, shown at the height of her voluptuous beauty. This painting, *Moor and Ina's Ghost Look into the Abyss*, was afterwards seen as the first in the 'high period' of the Moor series, those high-energy, apocalyptic canvases into which Aurora poured all her agony at the death of a daughter, all the maternal love that had remained unexpressed for too long; but also her larger, prophetic, even Cassandran fears for the nation, her fierce grief at the sourness of what had once, at least in an India of dreams, been sweet as sugar-cane juice. All that was in the pictures, yes, and her jealousy, too.

– Jealousy? – Of what, of whom, of which? –

Everything happened. The world changed. Uma Sarasvati arrived.

# 14

T HE WOMAN WHO TRANSFORMED, exalted and ruined my life entered it at Mahalaxmi racecourse forty-one days after Ina's death. It was a Sunday morning at the beginning of the late-year cool season, and according to ancient custom – 'How ancient?' you ask, and I reply Bombay-fashion, '*Ancient*, men. From *ancient* time' – the city's finest citizens had risen early and taken the place of the highly strung, pedigreed local steeds, both in the paddock and on the track. No races were scheduled; only the shades of departed jockeys in their bright-hooped shirts, the phantom echoes of once and future hooves and the fading notes of the chargers' steaming whinnies, only the tumbling rustle of old, discarded copies of Cole's race-day booklets – O invaluable guides to form! – might be discerned, by the eyes and ears of fancy, glimmering like the faint traces of an overpainted picture beneath this weekly *rus in urbe* scene, this parasolled procession of the leisured great. Swiftly in running-shoes and shorts with their babies strapped to their backs, or gently perambulating with walking-sticks and wearing straw panamas they came, the nobles of fish and steel, the counts of cloth and shipping, the lords of finance and property, the princes of land and sea and of the powers of the air, and their ladies too, dolled up to the nines in silks and gold, or track-suited and pony-tailed, with pink headbands stretched like royal circlets across athletic brows. Some there were who sped past furlong markers, stop-watches at the ready; others who sailed slowly past the old grandstand, like ocean liners coming in to dock. It was a time for encounters both licit and il-; for deals to be done and hands to be shaken on their doing; for the city's matriarchy to eye up its youth and plot its future nuptials, and for young men and women to exchange glances, and make choices of their own. It was a time for family members to come together, and a gathering of the metropolis's mightiest clans. Power, money, kinship and desire: these, concealed beneath the simpler benefits of an hour's health-giving stroll around the old course, were the driving forces behind the Mahalaxmi Weekend Constitutional, a horseless race with a class field, a derby without a starter's gun or photo-finish, but one in which there were many prizes to be won.

That Sunday six weeks after Ina died we were making an effort to close the family's sadly depleted ranks. Aurora in elegant slacks and open-necked white linen shirt made a point of displaying the family's solidarity by walking arm-in-arm with Abraham, who was white of mane and magnificently straight of back, at seventy-four every inch the suited-and-booted patriarch, no longer a country cousin among the grandees, but the very grandest of them all. The morning had not begun auspiciously, however. On our way to Mahalaxmi we had picked up Minnie – Sister Floreas – who had been excused, on compassionate grounds, from morning worship at the Maria Gratiaplena convent. She sat beside me on the back seat in her coiffed nun's get-up, fidgeting with her rosary and mumbling hailmarys under her breath, looking – I thought – like a version of the Duchess in *Alice*; much prettier, of course, but just as absolutist; or like a gamine court card – Funny Face meets the Queen of Spades. 'I saw Ina last night,' she pronounced without preamble. 'She says to tell you she is happy in Heaven and the music is very nice.' Aurora flushed purple, jammed her lips shut and set her jaw. Minnie had started seeing visions lately, although Aurora was not convinced. The Duchess's view of her baby boy could, if paraphrased, apply to my holy duchess of a sister, too: *She only does it to annoy, because she knows it teases.*

Abraham said, 'Don't upset your mother, Inamorata,' and now it was Minnie's turn to frown, because that name belonged to her past, it had no connection with the person she was becoming, the wonder of the Gratiaplena nuns, the most ascetic of all the faithful, the most uncomplaining of workers, the hardest-scrubbing of floor-scrubbers, the gentlest and most dedicated of nurses, and – as if seeking to atone for a lifetime of privilege – the wearer of the roughest and itchiest undergarments in the Order, which she had sewn for herself out of old jute sacks stinking of cardamoms and tea, and which brought her tender skin up in great weals, until the Mother Superior warned her that excessive mortification was itself a form of vanity. After that rebuke Sister Floreas stopped wearing sackcloth next to the skin, and the visions began.

Alone in her cell on her plank of wood (she had quickly dispensed with a bed) she was visited by a genderless elephant-headed angel who issued a strongly worded critique of the loose morals of the citizens of Bombay, whom it compared to Sodomites and Gomorrahis, and threatened with floods, droughts, explosions and fires, these punishments to be spread over a period of approximately sixteen years; and by a talking black rat who prophesied that the Plague itself would return as the last plague of all. The vision of Ina was something much more personal, and whereas the earlier manifestations had mostly made Aurora fear for her daughter's balance of mind this new apparition made her see red, perhaps not least beause of the recent appearance of Ina's ghost in her own work; but also because of a general feeling she had developed since her daughter's death – a feeling shared by many people in those paranoid, unstable times – that she was being followed. Wraiths were entering our family life, they were crossing the frontier between the metaphors of art and the observable facts of everyday life, and Aurora, unnerved, took refuge in her rage. But today had been designated as a day for family unity, and so, uncharacteristically, my mother bit her lip.

'She says the food is also good,' Minnie added, informatively. 'All the ambrosia, nectar and manna you can eat, and you never put on weight.' Fortunately the Mahalaxmi racecourse was only a few minutes' drive from Altamount Road.

And now Abraham and Aurora were arm-in-arm as they had not been for many long years, and Minnie, our very own cherub, was tripping along at their heels, while I lagged behind a little, lowering my head to avoid people's eyes, jamming my right hand deep into my trousers, and kicking at the turf for shame; because of course I could hear the whispers and giggles of the matriarchs and the young beauties of Bombay, I knew that if I walked too close to Aurora – who, for all her white hair, looked no more than forty-five at the age of fifty-three – then to the casual bystander, yours truly, at twenty-looking-forty, looked too old to be her child. *O catch him . . . misshapen . . . freaky . . . some peculiar disorder . . . I hear they keep him locked up . . . such a shame on the house . . . almost like an idiot, they say . . . and his poor father's only son.* Thus did the oily tongue of gossip lubricate the wheel of scandal. Our people do not react with grace to misfortunes of the body. Or, indeed, the mind.

Perhaps in a way they were right, those racecourse whisperers. In a way I was a sort of social idiot, severed by my nature from the everyday, made strange by fate. Certainly I have never considered myself to be a scholar of any sort. Thanks to my unusual, and (by conventional standards) hopelessly inadequate education I had become a kind of information magpie, gathering to myself all manner of shiny scraps of fact and hokum and books and art-history and politics and music and film, and developing, too, a certain skill in manipulating and arranging these pitiful shards so that they glittered, and caught the light. Fool's gold, or priceless nuggets mined from my singular childhood's rich bohemian seam? I leave it to others to decide.

It is true that I had managed to cling to Dilly, for extra-curricular reasons, much longer than I should. Nor was there any question of my going to college. I did some modelling for my mother, while my father accused me of wasting my life, and began to insist on introducing me to the family business. It was a long time since anyone – except Aurora – had dared to stand up to Abraham Zogoiby. In his middle seventies he was strong as a bullock, fit as a wrestler, and apart from his worsening asthma as healthy as any of the track-suited joggers at the racecourse. His relatively humble origins had been forgotten, and the old C-50 enterprise of Camoens da Gama had been assimilated into the huge corporate entity known acronymically in business parlance as 'Siodi Corp'. 'Siodi' was C.O.D. which was Cashondeliveri, and the use of this nickname was energetically encouraged by Abraham. It drove out the old – the memory of the decayed and assimilated empire of the Cashondeliveri grandees – and drove in the new. A financial-pages profile referred to him as '*Mr Siodi*' – *the brilliant new entrepreneur behind the House of Cashondeliveri*, and after that some of his business partners had mistakenly begun to call him 'Siodi Sahib'. Abraham did not always trouble to correct them. So he was beginning to paint a new layer over his own past . . . and as a father, too, age had painted a palimpsest-image over the memory of the man who had hugged my newborn form and wept comforting words. Now he had grown formidable, distant, dangerous, cold, and impossible to disobey. I bowed my head, and accepted his offer of an entry-level position in the marketing, sales and publicity department of the Baby Softo Talcum Powder Company (Private) Limited. After that I had to schedule my work with Aurora around my office commitments. But of modelling and babies, more anon.

As for the question of a bride, my ruined limb – a handicap in the zone of the handicap-free – was indeed a sort of spectre at the matrimonial feast, it made young ladies shudder fastidiously, reminding them of life's ugliness when in their high-born way they sought to concentrate on its beauty. Ugh! It was a fearsome fist. (As regards its long-term future: I'll say only that while Lambajan had shown me a little of my club-hard right mitt's true potential, I had not yet discovered my vocation. My sword still slept in my hand.)

No, I did not belong amongst these thoroughbreds. In spite of my discontinued peregrinations with our larcenous housekeeper Jaya Hé, I was an alien in their town – a Kaspar Hauser, a Mowgli. I knew little about their lives, and (what was worse) I did not care to know more. For while I might be a perpetual outsider among that racecourse breed, still in my twenty years I had gathered experience at such a rate that I had come to feel that time, in my vicinity, had begun to move at my own, doubled speed. I no longer felt like a young man trapped inside an old – or rather, to borrow the lingo of the city's textile industry, 'antiqued', even 'distressed' – covering of skin. My outer, apparent age had simply become my age.

Or so I thought: until Uma showed me the truth.

Jamshed Cashondeliveri, who had unexpectedly been plunged into a deep depression by his ex-wife's death and dropped out of law school soon after it, joined us at Mahalaxmi, as Aurora had arranged. Not far from the racecourse is the Great Breach, or Breach Candy, through which at certain seasons the ocean used to pour, flooding the low-lying Flats behind; just as Hornby Vellard was built to seal Breach Candy (completed, according to reliable sources, c. 1805), so the breach between Jimmy and Ina was to be posthumously healed, or so Aurora had decided, by the vellard of her indomitable will. 'Hi, Uncle, Auntie,' said Jimmy Cash, waiting awkwardly at the finishing-post, and essaying a crooked smile. Then his face changed. His eyes widened, the colour drained from his anyway-pretty-pale cheeks, his mouth dropped open. 'What's gottofied your goat?' asked Aurora, surprised. 'You look like you took a gander at a ghost.' But mesmerised Jimmy did not reply; and continued, wordlessly, to gape.

'Greetings, family members,' said Mynah's sardonic voice from behind our backs. 'I hope you guys don't mind, but I brought along a friend.'

∽

All of us who walked with Uma Sarasvati around Mahalaxmi racecourse that morning came away with a different view of her. A few facts were established: that she was twenty years old, and a star art student at the M.S. University in Baroda, where she had already won high praise from the so-called 'Baroda group' of artists, and where the noted critic Geeta Kapur had been moved to write a glowing appreciation of her gigantic stone-carving of Nandi, the great bull of Hindu mythology, which had been commissioned from her by the homonymous stockbroker and billionaire financier V. V. Nandy – 'Crocodile' Nandy himself. Kapur had compared the work to that of the anonymous masters of the eighth-century Parthenon-sized monolithic wonder, the Kailash Temple, greatest of all the Ellora caves; but Abraham Zogoiby, hearing about the statue as we strolled, unleashed a remarkably bull-like bellow of laughter. 'That young muggermutch V.V. never had any shame,' he roared. 'A Nandi bull, is it? Should have been one of those blind crocs from the rivers up north.'

Uma had presented herself, with an introduction from a friend in the Gujarati branch of the United Women's Anti-Price Rise Front, at the tiny, crowded office in a run-down three-storey block near Bombay Central station from which Mynah's group of women activists against corruption and for civil and women's rights – known as the WWSTP Committee after its best-known slogan, *We Will Smash This Prison (Is Jailko Todkar Rehengé)*, but also called, mockingly, by its detractors, 'Women Who Sleep Together Probably' – was doing battle against half-a-dozen Goliaths. She had spoken of her high regard for Aurora's painting, but also of the importance of the work being done by highly motivated groups such as Mynah's in exposing the evils of bride-burning, in setting up women's patrols against rape, and in a dozen other areas. Her passion and knowledge charmed my notably hard-nosed sister; hence her presence at our little family reunion on Mahalaxmi turf.

So much for what was beyond dispute. What was truly remarkable was that during that morning amble at Mahalaxmi the newcomer found a way to spend a few private minutes with each of us in turn, and after she departed, saying modestly that she had already intruded for too long on our family gathering, every one of us had a fiercely held opinion about her, and many of these opinions contradicted each other utterly and were incapable of being reconciled. To Sister Floreas, Uma was a woman from whom spirituality seemed to flow like a river; she was abstinent and disciplined, a great soul who saw through to the final unity of all religion, whose differences she was convinced would dissolve under the blessed brilliance of divine light; whereas in Mynah's opinion she was hard as nails – this, from our Philomina, was a high compliment – and a dedicated secularist marxian feminist whose inexhaustible commitment to the struggle had renewed Mynah's own appetite for the fray. Abraham Zogoiby dismissed both these views as 'so much foolishness' and praised Uma's razor-sharp financial brain, and her mastery of the very latest in modern deal-making and takeover theory. And Jamshed Cashondeliveri, he of the bulging eye and dropping jaw, confessed in hushed tones that she was the living reincarnation of gorgeous departed Ina, Ina as she had been before the burgers of Nashville ruined her, 'only she', he blurted out, like the fool he had always been, 'is like an Ina with a singing voice, and also brains.' He had just begun to explain that Uma and he had slipped away behind the grandstand for a few moments, and there the young girl had sung to him in the sweetest country voice he had ever heard; but Aurora Zogoiby had had enough. 'Everybody here has gone to pot today,' she thundered. 'But Jimmy boy, you just passofied the point of no return. Be off with you! Get going ek-dum and never darken our door.'

We left Jimmy standing in the paddock with a stunned-fish glaze in his eye.

Aurora resisted Uma from the start; she alone left the racecourse with a sceptical twist to her lip. Permit me to emphasise this point: she never gave the younger woman a chance, though Uma was unfailingly modest about her own artistic abilities, volubly worshipful of my mother's genius, and asked no favours. Indeed, after her triumph at the 1978 Documenta show in Kassel, when the most illustrious of London and New York dealers snapped her up, she telephoned Aurora long-distance from Germany and shouted through the international crackle, 'I made Kasmin and Mary Boone promise to show your work as well. Otherwise, I said, I could not permit them to show mine.'

Like a goddess from the machine she came among us, speaking to our inmost selves. Only godless Aurora failed to hear. Uma came diffidently to *Elephanta* two days later and Aurora locked her studio door. Which was – to put it mildly – neither adult nor polite. To make up for my mother's rudeness, I offered to show Uma around the old place, and said hotly, 'You are welcome in our home as often as you like.'

What Uma said to me at Mahalaxmi I repeated to no-one. For public consumption she had said laughingly, 'So if this is a racecourse then I want to race,' kicked off her chappals, picked them up in her left hand, and gone flying down the track, her long hair zooming out behind her like speed-lines in strip cartoons, marking the air through which she had passed as jet trails mark the sky. I had run after her, of course; it had not occurred to her that I would not. She was a speedy runner, faster than me, and finally I had to give up, because my chest commenced to heave and wheeze. I leaned gasping against the white rails, with both hands pressing against my lungs, trying to calm the spasm. She came back to me and placed her hands over mine. As my breathing settled down she caressed my mangled right hand lightly and said in a voice almost too quiet to be audible, 'This hand could smash down whatever stood in its way. I would feel very safe near a hand like this.' Then she looked into my eyes and added, 'There is a young guy in there. I can see him looking out at me. What a combination, yaar. Youthful-spirit, plus this older-man look that I must tell you I have gone for all my life. Too hot, men, I swear.'

So this is it, I told myself in wonderment. This prickle of tears, his throat-lump, this heat risen in the blood. My perspiration had acquired a peppery smell. I felt my self, my true self, the secret identity I had hidden so long that I feared it might no longer exist, come rising out of the corners of my being and filling my centre. Now I was nobody's man, and also wholly, immutably and for ever, hers.

She took away her hands; leaving behind a Moor in love.

&

On the morning of Uma's first visit my mother had decided she wanted to paint me in the nude. Nudity was nothing special in our circle; over the years many of the painters and their friends had posed for one another in the buff. Not so long ago, the guest toilet at *Elephanta* had been decorated by Vasco Miranda's mural of himself and Kekoo Mody in bowler hats and nothing else. Kekoo was as thin and elongated as ever, but success and years of debauchery and carousing had plumped out Vasco, who was also much the shorter man. The interest of the painting lay in the obvious fact that the two men seemed to have exchanged penises. The cock on Vasco was astoundingly long and thin, like a pale pepperoni sausage, whereas tall Kekoo sported a squat dark organ of impressive diameter and circumference. However, both men swore that there had been no switch. 'I have the paintbrush and he has the bankroll,' Vasco explained. 'What could be more appropriate?' It was Uma Sarasvati who gave the painting the name by which it was always subsequently known. 'Looks like Laurel and Hardon,' she giggled, and it stuck.

After our visit to Laurel and Hardon I found myself telling Uma about the history of the Moor pictures, and about the new project for a *Nude Moor*. She listened gravely as I proudly described my artistic collaboration with my mother, and then she blasted me with that huge smile, with the ray-gun beams she could unleash from her pale grey eyes. 'It isn't right you should stand naked in front of your Mummyji at your age,' she reproved. 'Let us only get to know each other better and I will be the one to sculpt your beauty in imported Carrara marble. Like the David with his too-big hand I will make your big old club the loveliest limb in the world. Until then, Mister Moor, please to save yourself for me.'

She left soon afterwards, not wishing to disturb the great painter at work. In spite of this proof of the refinement of her sensibilities, my egotistical mother was unable to find a good word for our new friend. When I told her I would be unable to pose for her new painting on account of the long hours I felt obliged to put in at my new job at the Baby Softo offices in Worli, she erupted. 'Don't you Softo me,' she yelled. 'That little fisherwoman has her hook in you and like a stupid fish you think she only wants to play. Soon you will be out of water and she will fryofy you in ghee with ginger-garlic, mirch-masala, cumin seed, and maybe some potato chips on the side.' She slammed her studio door, shutting me out for good; I was never asked to pose for her again.

The picture, *Mother-Naked Moor Watches Chimène's Arrival*, was as formal as Velázquez's *Las Meninas*, a picture to which, in its play with sight-lines, it was somewhat in debt. In a chamber of Aurora's fictional Malabar Alhambra, against a wall decorated with intricate geometric patterns, the Moor stood naked in the lozenge-patterned Technicolor of his skin. Behind him on the sill of a scalloped window stood a vulture from the Tower of Silence, and leaning on the wall next to this macabre casement was a sitar, with a mouse nibbling through its lacquered-melon drum. To the Moor's left was his fearsome mother, Queen Ayxa-Aurora in flowing dark robes, holding up a full-length mirror to his nakedness. The mirror-image was beautifully naturalistic – no harlequin there, no pretence at 'Boabdil'; just me. But the lozenged Moor was not looking at himself in the mirror, for in the doorway to his right

stood a beautiful young woman – Uma, naturally, Uma fictional-
ised, Hispanicised, as this 'Chimène', Uma incorporating aspects of
Sophia Loren in *El Cid*, pinched from the story of Rodrigo de
Vivar and introduced without explanation into the hybrid
universe of the Moor – and between her outspread, inviting hands
were many marvels – golden orbs, bejewelled birds, tiny homun-
culi – floating magically in the lucent air.

Aurora in her maternal jealousy of her son's first true love had
created this cry of pain, in which a mother's attempts to show her
son the simple truth about himself were doomed to failure by a
sorceress's head-turning tricks; in which mice gnawed away the
possibility of music and vultures waited patiently for lunch. Ever
since Isabella Ximena da Gama on her deathbed had united in her
own person the figures of the Cid Campeador and his Chimène,
her daughter Aurora who had picked up Belle's fallen torch had
seen herself, too, as hero and heroine combined. That she should
now make this separation – that the painted Moor should be given
the Charlton Heston rôle and a woman with Uma's face should be
baptised with a Frenchified version of my grandmother's middle
name – was almost an admission of defeat, an intimation of
mortality. Now Aurora, like the old dowager Ayxa, was not the
one looking into the mirror-mirror; now it was Boabdil-Moor
who was reflected there. But the real magic mirror was the one in
his (my) eyes; and in that occult glass, there could be no doubt that
the sorceress in the doorway was the fairest one of all.

The picture, painted like many of the mature Moors in the
layered manner of the old European masters, and important in art-
history for the entry into the Moor sequence of the 'Chimène'
character, seemed to me to demonstrate that art, ultimately, was
not life; that what might feel truthful to the artist – for example, this
tale of malevolent usurpation, of a pretty witch come to separate a
mother from her son – did not necessarily bear the slightest
connection to events and feelings and people in the real world.

Uma was a free spirit; she came and went as she pleased. Her
absences in Baroda tore at my heart, but she refused me permission
to visit her. 'You must not see my work until I am ready for you,'
she said. 'I want you to fall for me, not for what I do.' For against all

247

probability and with the royal whimsicality of beauty she, who could have had her pick, had set her heart on this damaged young-old fool, and whispering in my ear she promised me entry into the garden of earthly delights. 'Wait on,' she told me. 'Wait on, beloved innocent, for I am the goddess who knows your secret heart, and I will surely give you everything you want, and more.' *Wait just some while*, she pleaded without saying why, but my puzzlement was wiped away by the lyric excitement of her promises. *And then until death I will be your mirror, your self's other self, your equal, your empress and your slave.*

I must confess it surprised me to learn that she made a number of visits to Bombay without contacting me. Minnie telephoned from the Gratiaplena to tell me in a trembling voice that Uma had visited her to inquire how a non-Christian might embark on a life in Christ. 'I truly think she will come to Jesus,' said Sister Floreas, 'and to his Holy Mother too.' I think I may have snorted, whereupon Minnie's voice took on a strange note. 'Yes,' she said. 'Uma, blessed girl, told me how worried she is that the Devil has got a stranglehold on you.'

Mynah, too – Mynah, who never called! – rang to report exhilarating encounters with my beloved on the front-line of a political demonstration that had temporarily prevented the demolition of the invisible shacks of the invisible poor that were taking up valuable space within sight of the high-rises of Cuffe Parade. Apparently Uma had led the demonstrators and shack-dwellers in a rousing chorus of *We launched a movement, what's there to fear?* Abruptly Mynah confided – Mynah, who never confided! – that she had formed the opinion that Uma was definitely a lesbian. (Philomina Zogoiby had revealed to no-one the secrets of her own sexuality, but it was well known that she had never stepped out with any man; nearing thirty, she cheerfully admitted she was 'on the shelf – it's a spinster's life for me.' But now, perhaps, Uma Sarasvati had found out more.) 'We have become pretty close – you know?' Mynah startlingly confessed, with an odd combination of girlishness and defiance. 'Finally, somebody to curl up with, and gossip through the night with a bottle of rum and a couple of packs of ciggies. My bloody sisters were never any fucking use.'

What nights? When? And in Mynah's digs there wasn't enough room for a spare chair, let alone an extra mattress: so where had this 'curling up' occurred? 'I hear you've been hanging your tongue out, by the way,' my sister's voice said in my ear, and was it just the hyper-sensitivity of love or was I actually being warned off? 'Little bro, let me give you a tip: no chance. Go hunt a different chicky. This one prefers hens.'

I did not know what to make of these telephone calls, particularly as Uma's telephone in Baroda was never answered. At the shoot of a Baby Softo television commercial, amid the gurgles of seven well-talcumed babies, I was so distracted by my inner wranglings that I neglected the simple task I had been given – that is, to make sure, with the help of a stop-watch, that the powerful klieg-lights were never on the babies for more than one minute in five – and was jerked from my reverie only by the wrath of the camera crew, the shrieks of mothers, and the wails of the babies as they began, bubbling and blistering, to fry. I fled in shame and confusion from the studio and found Uma sitting on the doorstep, waiting for me. 'Let's go for dosa, yaar,' she said. 'I'm starving.'

And of course over lunch she showed me that everything had a perfectly reasonable explanation. 'I wanted to know you,' she said, her eyes brimming with tears, 'I wanted to amaze you with how hard I had tried to learn everything there is to know. Also I want to be close to your blood family, close as blood, or closer even. Now you must know that our poor Minnie is a little bothered-up by God; out of friendship I asked her questions and she, poor holy dear, got the wrong end of the stick. Me a nun! Don't kid me, mister. And that Devil line was just a joke. I meant, if Minnie is on the God squad then you and me and everybody normal is on the Devil's team, isn't it?' And all the while my face cradled in her hands, her hands caressing mine as they had at our first meeting; her face suffused with such love, such pain at having been doubted . . . and *Mynah?* – I persisted, though it felt like an act of appalling cruelty to continue to interrogate so loving, so devoted a creature. 'Of course I came to see her. For her sake I joined in her fight. And because I can sing, I sang. So what?' And *curling up*? 'O goodness. If you want to know who is the lady's lady, you complete ignoramus, look at your tough-guy sis, not me. Sharing a bed is nothing, in college we girls do it all the time. But curling up is your Philomina's wet dream, excuse me for being frank. Yes, frankly, I am pretty angry. I try to make friends and you all accuse me of being a holy roller and a liar and even fucking your sister. What are you people that you act so nasty? Why can't you see that I have done everything for love?' The big splashy tears were bouncing off her empty plate. Misery had not affected her healthy appetite.

'Stop, please stop,' I begged, apologising. 'I'll never – never again. . .'

Her smile burst through her tears, so bright that I almost expected a rainbow.

'Maybe it's time', she breathed, 'that I proved to you that I am hetero as hell.'

～

And she was seen with Abraham Zogoiby himself, wolfing club sandwiches by the poolside at the Willingdon Club before losing gracefully to the old man at golf. 'She was a wonder, that Uma of yours,' he told me years later, high in his I. M. Pei Eden. 'So knowledgeable, so original, and staring so intently with those swimming-pool eyes. Never seen anything like them since I first gazed upon your mother's own face. God knows how much I babbled on! My own children had no interest – you, for example, my only son! – and an old man must talk to someone. I would have employed her on the spot but she said she had to prioritise her art. And Jesus Christ, the tits on her. Tits the size of your head.' He cackled disgustingly and made a perfunctory apology without troubling to put the faintest trace of sincerity into his voice. 'What to tell you, boy, women have been my lifetime weakness.' Then suddenly a great cloud did pass across his face. 'We both lost your beloved mother because we looked at other girls,' he mumbled.

Corrupt global-scale banking schemes, stock market fixing at the super-epic Mogambo level, multi-billion-dollar arms deals, nuclear technology conspiracies involving stolen computers and Maldivian Mata Haris, export of antiquities including the symbol of the nation itself, the four-headed Lion of Sarnath . . . how much of his 'black' world, how many of his grand designs, did Abraham disclose to Uma Sarasvati? How much, for example, about certain special export consignments of Baby Softo powder? When I asked him he just shook his head. 'Not much, I suppose. I don't know. Everything. I am told I talk in my sleep.'

⌒

But I am getting ahead of myself. Uma told me about the game she played with my father, praising his golf swing – 'not a wobble – and at his age!' – and his generosity to a young girl new in town. We had taken to meeting in a series of modestly-priced rooms in Colaba or at Juhu (the city's five-star joints were too risky; too many telephoto eyes and long-distance tongues). But our favourites were the Railway Retiring Rooms at V.T. and Bombay Central: in those high-ceilinged, shuttered, cool, clean, anonymous chambers I began my journey to Heaven and Hell. 'Trains,' Uma Sarasvati said. 'All those pistons-shistons. Don't they just turn you on?'

It is hard for me to speak of our lovemaking. Even now, and in spite of everything, the memory of it makes me shiver with yearning for what is lost. I remember its ease and tenderness, its quality of revelation; as if a door were opened in the flesh and through it poured an unsuspected fifth-dimension universe: its ringed planets and comets' tails. Its whirling galaxies. Its bursting suns. But beyond expression, beyond language was the plain *bodyness* of it, the movement of hands, the tensing of buttocks, the arching of backs, the rise and fall of it, the thing with no meaning but itself, that meant everything; that brief animal doing, for the sake of which anything – anything – might be done. I cannot imagine – no, even now, my fancy will not stretch to it – that such passion, such essentiality, could have been faked. I do not believe she lied to me there, in that way, above the come and go of trains. I do not believe it; I believe it; I do not believe; I believe; I do not; I do not; I do.

There is one embarrassing detail. Uma, my Uma, murmured in my ear near the Everest of our ecstasy, on the South Col of desire, that there was a thing which made her sad. 'Your Mummyji I revere; she-tho doesn't like me, but.' And I, gasping, and otherwise engaged, consoled her. *Yes she does.* But Uma – sweating, panting, hurling her body upon mine – repeated her grief. 'No, my darling boy. She doesn't. *Bilkul* not.' I confess that at that high instant I had no stomach for this talk. An obscenity sprang unbidden to my lips. *Fuck her then.* – 'What was that you said?' – *I said fuck her. Fuck my mother. O.* – At which she dropped the subject and concentrated on matters in hand. Her lips at my ear spoke of other things. *You want this my darling and this, to do this, you can do this, if you want to, if you want. O God yes I want to let me yes yes O . . .*

Such chitter-chatter is better participated in than eavesdropped upon, so I will not set down any more. But I must admit – and it makes me blush to do so – that she, Uma, returned time and again to the topic of my mother's hostility, until it seemed to become a part of what excited her. – *She hates me hates me tell me what to do.* – And I was expected to reply, and, forgive me, in the grip of lust I answered as required. *Screw her* I said. *Screw her stupid the stupid bitch.* And Uma: *How? Darling, my darling, how?* – *Fuck her. Fuck her upside down and sideways too.* – *O, you can, my only sweet, if you want to, if you only say you want.* – *God yes. I want to. Yes. O God.*

Thus at the moment of my greatest joy I spilt the seeds of ruin: my ruin, and my mother's, and the ruin of our great house.

∽

We were, all but one of us, in love with Uma in those days, and even Aurora, who was not, relented; for Uma's presence in our house brought my sisters home, too, and in addition she could also see the delight on my face. No matter how occasional a mother she had been, a mother she remained, and accordingly softened her heart. Also, Aurora was serious about work, and after Kekoo Mody visited Baroda and came back raving about the young woman's pieces, great Aurora melted further. Uma was installed as guest of honour at one of my mother's now-infrequent *Elephanta* soirées. 'To genius,' she pronounced, 'everything must be forgiven.' Uma looked sweetly flattered and shy. 'And to the second-rate,' added Aurora, 'nothing must be given – not one paisa, not one kauri, not one dam. Ohé, Vasco – what do you say to that?' Vasco Miranda in his fifties no longer spent very much time in Bombay; when he did turn up, Aurora wasted no time on niceties, and laid into his 'airport art' with a venom that was unusual even for that most abrasive of women. Aurora's own work had never 'travelled'. A few important European galleries – the Stedelijk, the Tate – had bought pieces, but America remained impervious, with the exception of the Gobler family of Fort Lauderdale, Fla., without whose collecting zeal so many Indian artists would have been penniless; so it was possible that envy had honed my mother's tongue. 'How are your Transit Lounge Specials, eh, Vasco?' she wanted to know. 'Have you noticed how passengers on Travolators never pause to take a look at your stuff? And jet-lag! Is it good for the critical faculties?' Under these assaults, Vasco smiled weakly and bowed his head. He had amassed a huge foreign-currency fortune, and had recently given up his residences and studios in Lisbon and New York to construct a hilltop folly in Andalusia, on which, according to rumour, he was spending more than the combined lifetime income of the entire community of Indian artists. This story, which he did nothing to deny, served only to heighten his unpopularity in Bombay, and the intensity of Aurora Zogoiby's attacks.

His waistline had ballooned, his moustache was a Daliesque double exclamation mark, his greasy hair was parted just above his left ear and plastered across his bald, Brylcreem-shiny dome. 'No wonder you're still a bachelor boy,' Aurora taunted him. 'A spare tyre the ladies can tolerate, but boy, you bought the whole Goodyear factory.' For once, Aurora's gibes were in tune with majority opinion. Time, which had been kind to Vasco's bank balance, had dealt harshly with his Indian reputation as well as his body. In spite of his myriad commissions, his work's stock was presently in free fall, dismissed as thin and meretricious, and although the national collection had acquired a couple of his pieces in the early days it had not done so for years. Not one of its purchases was presently on show. Among the sharper critics and the younger generation of artists V. Miranda was a busted flush. As Uma Sarasvati's star rose, Vasco's plummeted; but when Aurora kicked out at him, he kept his answers to himself.

The Picasso-Braque collaboration between Vasco and Aurora had never materialised; recognising the inadequacy of his gift, she had gone her own way, allowing him to maintain his studio at *Elephanta* only for old times' sake, and perhaps because she enjoyed having him around to poke fun at. Abraham, who had always loathed Vasco, showed Aurora news clippings from abroad, proving that V. Miranda had more than once been charged with violent behaviour, and had only narrowly avoided deportation from both the United States and Portugal; and that he had been obliged to undergo extensive treatment in mental homes, drying-out centres for alcoholics, and drug rehabilitation clinics across Europe and North America. 'Get rid of this posturing old phoney,' he implored.

As for myself, I remembered Vasco's many kindnesses when I was a young and frightened child, and loved him for them still, but could see that his demons had won their battle against his lighter side. The Vasco who visited us on Uma's evening, that bloated comic-opera clown, was a sad sight indeed.

Towards the end of the night, when alcohol had lowered his defences, he cracked. 'To hell with the lot of you,' he cried. 'I'm off to my Benengeli soon, and if I've got any brains I will never return.' Then he burst into tuneless song. '*Good*bye, Flora *Fount*ain,' he began. '*Fare*well, Hutatma Chowk.' He stopped, blinking, and shook his head. 'No. Not right. Goodbye, Marine *Dri-ive*, Farewell, Netaji-Subhas-Chandra-Bose-Road!' (Many years later, when I, too, came to Spain, I would remember Vasco's uncompleted ditty, and even sing a version of it quietly to myself.)

Uma Sarasvati walked over to this sad, painful figure, put her hands on his shoulders, and kissed him on the mouth.

Which had an unexpected effect. Instead of being grateful – and there were many in that salon, myself included, who would very happily have received such a kiss – Vasco rounded on Uma. 'Judas,' he said to her. 'I know you. Devotee of Our Lord Judas Christ the Betrayer. I know you, missy. I've seen you in that church.' Uma coloured deeply, and retreated. I sprang to her defence. 'You're making a fool of yourself,' I told Vasco, who stalked out, nose-in-air; and a moment later, fell noisily into the pool.

'Good, that's that,' said Aurora briskly. 'Let's play *Three characters, seven sins.*'

It was her favourite parlour game. Random selection by coin-toss determined the sex and age of three imaginary 'characters', and papers picked from a hat were used to specify the deadly sin of which each was 'guilty'. The assembled company was then required to improvise a story involving the three sinners. On this occasion the characters came out as *Old Woman, Young Woman* and *Young Man*; and their sins were, respectively, *Wrath, Vainglory* and *Lust*. No sooner were the choices made than Aurora, sharp as ever and possibly more affected than she seemed by Vasco's latest little hurricane, cried: 'I've got one.'

Uma applauded, admiringly. 'Tell, na.'

'Okay, here goes,' said Aurora, looking straight at her young guest of honour. 'A wrathful old queen discovers that her lustful fool of a son has been seduced by her young and vainglorious deadly rival.'

'Great story,' Uma said, beaming serenely. 'Wah-wah! Plenty of meat on that bone. Yes, sir.'

'Your turn,' said Aurora, her smile as wide as Uma's. 'What happens next? What should the Wrathful Old Queen do? Should she maybe banish the lovers for good – should she just let rip and drive them out of her sight?'

Uma pondered. 'Not good enough,' she said. 'I think so some more permanent solution would be needed. Because such an opponent – e.g. this Vainglorious Young Pretender – if she was not finished off, and I mean completely funtooshed, would certainly set out to smash the Wrathful Old Queen. Sure! She would want the Lusty Young Prince all to herself, and the kingdom, too; and she would be too proud to share the throne with his Ma.'

'What do you suggest, then?' Aurora asked, glacial sweet in the suddenly hushed drawing-room.

'Murder,' said Uma, shrugging. 'Obviously it is a murder story. One way or the other, somebody-tho has to die. White Queen takes Black Pawn, or else Black Pawn, reaching the queening square, becomes a Black Queen and takes the White Queen instead. No other ending that I at least can see.'

Aurora looked impressed. 'Uma, daughter, you're a secretive one. Why didn't you tell me you'd played this game before?'

~

*You're a secretive one* . . . My mother could not let go of the idea that Uma had something to hide. 'She comes out of nowhere and chipkos to our family,' Aurora constantly worried – as, it must be said, she had never worried, in the old days, about Vasco Miranda's equally questionable past. 'But who are her people? Where are her friends? What is her past life?' I conveyed these doubts to Uma as the shadows of a Retiring Room ceiling fan stroked her naked body and the fan's breeze towelled her dry. 'Your family can't talk about secrets,' she said. 'Excuse *me*. I hate to speak badness about your loved ones but I am not the person with one crazy sister already dead, another seeing talking rats in a convent and the third trying to untie the cord of her lady-friends' pajamas. And please: whose father is up to here in dirty business and under-age tarts? And whose mother – forgive me, my love, but you must know it – is currently having not one, not two, but three different love affairs?'

I sat up in bed. 'Who have you been talking to?' I cried. 'Who has been pouring this snake poison for you to swallow down and then throw up?'

'The whole town is talking,' Uma said, embracing me. 'Poor softo. You think she is some sort of goddess or what. But it is common knowledge. Number one, that Parsi retard Kekoo Mody, number two Vasco Miranda the fat fraud, and the worst is number three: that MA bastard Mainduck. Raman Fielding! That bhaenchod! I am sorry but the lady has no class. People even whisper that she has seduced her own son – yes! my poor innocent boy, you don't know what people are like! – but I tell them there are limits, it is not so, I can vouch for it myself. So you see your good name is now in my hands.'

It was the occasion of our first real quarrel, but even as I defended Aurora I felt the truth of Uma's accusations in my heart. Kekoo's canine devotion had had its reward, and Aurora's prolonged tolerance, and simultaneous abuse, of Vasco finally made sense, if seen in the context of an 'involvement', however decayed. Now that she and Abraham no longer shared a bed, where could Aurora look for comfort? Her genius and grandeur had isolated her; powerful women scare men off, and there were few Bombay males who would have dared to woo her. That explained Mainduck. Coarse, physically strong, ruthless, he was one of the few men in the city for whom Aurora would hold no terrors. Their encounter in the matter of *The Kissing of Abbas Ali Baig* would have aroused him; he had taken her bribe and would have wanted – or so I speculated – to conquer her in return. And in my mind's eye I saw her both revolted and entranced by this gutter-creature of real potency, this savage, this walking slum. If her husband preferred Falkland Road cage-girls to her, then she, Aurora the great, would gain her revenge by surrendering her body to Fielding's pawings and thrustings; yes, I could see how that would arouse her, how it might unleash her own wildness. Maybe Uma was right: maybe my mother was Mainduck's whore.

No wonder she had started to be a little paranoid, to worry about being followed; such a complex secret life, and so much to lose if it came to light! Art-loving Kekoo, the ever more Westernised figure of V. Miranda, and the communalist toad; add to these Abraham Zogoiby's invisible world of money and black markets, and you have a portrait of the things my mother truly loved, the points of her inner compass, revealed by her choice of men. Seen through this lens, her work looked rather like a distraction from the harsh realities of her character; like a gallant coat laid over the filthy mud-puddle of her soul.

In my confusion I found myself simultaneously weeping and becoming erect. Uma laid me back on the bed and straddled me, kissing away the tears. 'Does everyone know but me?' I asked her. 'Mynah? Minnie? Who?'

'Don't think about your sisters,' she said, moving slowly, soothingly. 'Poor man, you love everyone, you want nothing but love. If only they cared for you as you care for them. But you should hear what they say about you to me. Such things! You don't know the fights I have had with them over you.'

I made her stop. 'What are you saying? What are you saying to me?'

'Poor baby,' she said, curling against me like a spoon. How I adored her; how grateful I was, in this treacherous world, to have her maturity, her serenity, her worldly wisdom, her strength, her love.

'Poor unlucky Moor. I will be your family now.'

# 15

*T*HE PAINTINGS GREW STEADILY *less colourful, until Aurora was working only in black, white and occasional shades of grey. The Moor was an abstract figure now, a pattern of black and white diamonds covering him from head to foot. The mother, Ayxa, was black; and the lover, Chimène, was brilliant white. Many of these pictures were love-scenes. The Moor and his lady made love in many settings. They left their palace to travel the city streets. They sought out cheap hotels, and lay naked in shuttered rooms above the come and go of trains. Ayxa the mother was always somewhere in these pictures, behind a curtain, stooped at a keyhole, flying up to the window of the lovers' eyries. The black-and-white Moor turned towards his white love and away from his black dam; yet both were a part of him. And now, on the paintings' far horizons, there were armies massing. Horses stamped, lances glittered. The armies drew nearer over the years.*

But the Alhambra is invincible, *the Moor told his beloved.* Our stronghold – like our love – will never fall.

*He was black and white. He was the living proof of the possibility of the union of opposites. But Ayxa the Black pulled one way, and Chimène the White, the other. They began to tear him in half. Black diamonds, white diamonds fell from the gash, like teardrops. He tore himself away from his mother, clung to Chimène. And when the armies came to the foot of the hill, when that great white force was gathered on Chowpatty beach, a figure in a hooded black cloak slipped out of the fortress and down the hill. In her traitorous hand was the key to the gates. The one-legged watchman saw her and saluted. It was his mistress's cloak. But at the foot of the hill the traitor let the cloak fall away. She stood in brilliant white with the key of Boabdil's defeat held in her faithless hand.*

*She gave it to the besieging armies, and her whiteness faded into theirs. The palace fell. Its image faded; into white.*

At the age of fifty-five Aurora Zogoiby allowed Kekoo Mody to curate a large retrospective of her work at the Prince of Wales Museum – the first time this institution had so honoured a living artist. Jade, china, sculpture, miniatures and antique textiles shuffled respectfully out of the way as Aurora's pictures took their places. It was a considerable event in the life of the city. Banners advertising the show were everywhere. (Apollo Bunder, Colaba Causeway, Flora Fountain, Churchgate, Nariman Point, Civil Lines, Malabar Hill, Kemp's Corner, Warden Road, Mahalaxmi, Hornby Vellard, Juhu, Sahar, Santa Cruz. O blessed mantra of my lost city! The places have slipped away from me for ever; all I possess of them is memory. Forgive, please, if I yield to the temptation to conjure them up, by the power of naming, before my absent eyes. Thacker's Bookstore, Bombelli's Cakes, Eros Cinema, Pedder Road. *Om mani padmé hum . . .*) The specially designed 'A.Z.' symbol was inescapable; it was on the ubiquitous fly-posted bills, and in all the papers and magazines. The opening, from which no figure of consequence in the city was absent, for to miss such an event would have been social death, felt more like a coronation than an art show. Aurora was garlanded, eulogised, and showered with flower-petals, flattery and gifts. The city bowed down before her and touched her feet.

Even Raman Fielding, the powerful MA boss, turned up, blinking his toady eyes, and made a respectful pranam. 'Let everyone see today what-what we do for minorities,' he said loudly. 'Is it a Hindu who is given this honour? Is it one of our great Hindu artists? No matter. In India every community must have its place, its leisure activity – art et cetera – all. Christians, Parsis, Jains, Sikhs, Buddhists, Jews, Mughals. We accept this. This too is part of ideology of Ram Rajya, rule of Lord Ram. Only when other communities are usurping our Hindu places, when minority seeks to dictate to majority, then we say that the small also must accept to bend and move before the big. In the case of art also this applies. I myself was an artist originally. Therefore I say with some authority that art and beauty must serve national interest also. Madame

Aurora, I congratulate you on your privileged exhibit. As to what art survives, rarefied-élite-intellectual or beloved-of-the-masses, noble or degenerate, self-aggrandising or demure, great-souled or gutter-sleeping, spiritual or pornographic, you will agree I am sure' – and here he laughed to indicate a joke – 'that-tho the *Times* alone will tell.'

The next morning the *Times of India* (Bombay edition), along with every other newspaper in the city, would carry prominent news reports of the gala opening, and jumbo-sized reviews of the work. In these reviews, the long and distinguished career of Aurora da Gama-Zogoiby would come close to being completely destroyed. Familiar as she had become, over the years, with high praise, but also with aesthetic, political and moral attacks, with charges ranging from arrogance, immodesty and obscenity to inauthenticity and even – in the Manto-inspired *Uper the gur gur the annexe the bay dhayana the mung the dal of the laltain* – covert pro-Pakistani sympathies, my mother was a thick-skinned old bird; nothing, however, had prepared her for the suggestion that she had become, quite simply, an irrelevance. Yet, in one of those disorientating but also radical shifts by which a changing society all at once reveals that it is of a new mind, the tigers of the critical fraternity, burning bright and with fearful symmetry, turned upon Aurora Zogoiby and savaged her as a 'society artist', out of tune with, and even 'deleterious' to, the temper of the age. On the same day the lead story on every front page was that of the dissolution of Parliament after the disintegration of the post-Emergency, anti-Indira coalition government; and several editorials made use of the contrast in the two old rivals' fortunes. *Aurora Plunged Into Darkness*, said the headline on the *Times*'s op-ed page, *but for Indira, Another New Dawn*.

Elsewhere in town, at the Gandhys' Chemould Gallery, the work of the young sculptor Uma Sarasvati was receiving its first Bombay showing. The centrepiece of the show was a group of seven roughly spherical, metre-high stone pieces with a small hollow scooped out at the top and filled with richly coloured powders – scarlet, ultramarine, saffron, emerald, purple, orange, gold. This work, entitled *Alterations in/Reclamations of the Essence of*

*Motherhood in the Post-Secularist Epoch*, had been the hit of the Documenta in Germany the year before, and had only now returned after showings in Milan, Paris, London and New York. Back home, the critics who had mauled Aurora Zogoiby hailed Uma as Indian art's new star – young, beautiful, and driven by her strong religious faith.

These were sensational events; but for me the shock of the two shows was of a more personal nature. My first exposure to Uma's work    for until this moment she had maintained her ban on my visiting her Baroda studio – was also my first intimation that she was in any sense religious. That she should now commence giving interviews declaring herself a devotee of Lord Ram was bewildering, to say the least. For days after her opening she professed herself to be 'busy', but at length she agreed to meet me at the Retiring Rooms above Victoria Terminus, and I asked her why she had concealed so great a part of her mind from me.

'You even called Mainduck a bastard,' I reminded her. 'And now the papers are full of you spouting out this stuff that will be music to his ears.'

'I did not tell you before, because religion is a private business,' she said. 'And, as you know, I am maybe too much a private person. Also, I do think Fielding is a goonda and a salah and a snake, because he is trying to make my love of Ram into his weapon to hit out at "Mughals", i.e. what-else-but Muslims. But my dear boy' – she persisted in using such youthy epithets even though, in 1979, I had been alive for twenty-two years, and my body had turned forty-four – 'you must see that just as you are from a tiny minority, so I am a child of the gigantic Hindu nation, and as an artist I must reckon with the same. I must make my own encounter with origins, my own accommodations with eternal verities. And it is just none of your business, mister; no, not at all. Plus, if I am such a fanatic, then, please, sir, what am I doing with you?' Which was a reasonable point.

Aurora, in deep retreat at *Elephanta*, had a different view. 'That girl of yours is the most ambitious person I ever met, excuse me,' she told me. 'Bar none. She sees how the breeze is changeofying and her public attitudes are blowing in that wind. Wait on; in two minutes she will be standing on MA platforms and shriekofying with hate.' Then her face grew dark. 'You think I don't know how hard she workoed to wreckofy my show?' she said softly. 'You think I haven't traced her links to those people who wrote that abuse?'

This was too much; it was unworthy. Aurora in her emptied studio – for all the Moors were down at the Prince of Wales Museum – faced me hollow-eyed across an untouched canvas with brushes falling from her piled-up hair, like arrows missing their mark. I stood in the doorway, fuming. I had come for a fight – because there had been a great shock for me in her show, too; until it opened I had not been shown those monochrome canvases in which her lozenged Moor and his snow-white Chimène made love while the black mother watched. Aurora's gibes about Uma – which were pretty rich, I raged inwardly, coming from Mainduck's secret mistress! – allowed me to start lashing out. 'I am sorry your show got panned,' I yelled. 'But even if Uma wanted to fix the notices, Mummyji, how could she do it? Don't you realise she was embarrassed that she was praised at your expense? Poor girl is so red-faced she doesn't dare to come over! From the beginning she worshipped you, and you rewarded her by throwing filth. Your persecution mania has gotten out of control! And as to tracing links, how do you think I felt to see those pictures of you peeping-tomming at us in our room? How long have you been prying and spying?'

'Save yourself from that woman,' said Aurora, quietly. 'She is a madwoman and a liar too. She is a bloodsucker lizard who loves your blood, not you. She will suck you like a mango and throw away the stone.'

I was horrified. 'You are sick,' I shouted at her. 'Sick, sick in the head.'

'Not I, my son,' she replied, yet more softly. 'A sick woman, however, there is – sick, or evil. Mad, or bad, or both. I can't decide. As to being a nosey parker, I plead guilty as charged. Since some time I have employoed Dom Minto to find out the truth about your mystery lady friend. May I tell you what he dug up?'

'Dom Minto?' The name stopped me in my tracks. She might as

well have said 'Hercule Poirot' or 'Maigret' or 'Sam Spade'. She might as well have said 'Inspector Ghote' or 'Inspector Dhar'. Everyone knew the name, everyone had seen *Minto's Mysteries*, the railway-station penny-dreadfuls chronicling the career of the great Bombay private eye. There had been a series of movies about him in the 1950s, the last one following his involvement in the celebrated murder case (for, yes, there had once been a 'real' Minto who had 'really' been a private detective) in which the Indian Navy's high-flying hero, Commander Sabarmati, had shot his wife and her lover, killing the man and seriously wounding the lady. It was Minto who had tracked the cheating couple to their love-nest and given the irate Commander the address. Profoundly distressed by the shootings, and by the unsympathetic portrayal of him in the film based upon the case, the old man – for he had been ancient and lame even then – had retired from his profession, and the fantasists had taken over, creating the heroic super-sleuth of the cheap paperbacks and radio serials (and lately the motion picture remakes, as big-budget superstar vehicles, of the old 50s B-features), transforming him from an old has-been into a myth. What was this masala-fiction of a fellow doing in the story of my life?

'Yes, the real guy,' said Aurora, not unkindly. 'Now he is eighty-plus. Kekoo found him.' *O, Kekoo. Another one of your fancyboys. O, darling Kekoo found him, and he's just too darling, the darling oldster, I set him straight to work.*

'He was in Canada,' Aurora said. 'Retired, living with grandkids, bored, making the youngsters' life miserable as hell. Then it turns out that Commander Sabarmati has come out of jail, and patchofied things up with his wife. What do you know? Right there in Toronto they were live-o'ing happily ever after. After that, according to Kekoo, Minto felt free of his old misdeed, came back to Bombay, and in spite of advanced years went right back to work, fut-a-fut. Kekoo is a big fan; me too. Dom Minto! Back then, you know, he really was the best.'

'Wonderful!' I said, as sarcastically as I could. But my heart, I must confess, my penny-dreadful heart was pounding. 'And what has this Bollywood Sherlock Holmes to tell me about the woman I love?'

'She's married,' said Aurora, flatly. 'And currently fooling around with not one, not two, but three lovers. You want photos? Your poor sister Ina's stupid Jimmy Cash; your stupid father; and, my stupid peacock, you.'

⤳

'Listen on, because I'll tell you once only,' she had said in response to my persistent inquisitiveness about her background. She came from a respectable – though not by any means wealthy – Gujarati Brahmin family, but had been orphaned young. Her mother, a depressive, had hanged herself when Uma was twelve and her schoolteacher father, driven mad by the tragedy, had set himself on fire. Uma had been rescued from penury by a kindly 'uncle' – actually, not an uncle, but a teaching colleague of her father's – who paid for her education in return for sexual favours (so not 'kindly', either). 'From the age of twelve,' she said. 'Until just now. If I followed my heart I would put a knife in his eye. Instead I have asked the god to curse him and simply turned my back. So maybe you understand why I do not choose to talk about my past. Never speak of it again.'

Dom Minto's version, as reported by my mother, was rather different. According to him Uma was not from Gujarat but Maharashtra – the other half of the divided self of the former Bombay State – and had been raised in Poona, where her father was a high-ranking officer in the police force. At a young age she had shown prodigious artistic gifts and been encouraged by her parents, without whose support it was improbable that she would have achieved the required standard for a scholarship at the M.S. University, where she was universally praised as a young woman of exceptional promise. Soon, however, she had started giving signs of an exceptionally disordered spirit. Now that she was becoming a celebrated figure, people were reluctant or afraid to speak against her, but after patient inquiries Dom Minto had discovered that she had on three occasions agreed to take heavy medication intended to control her repeated mental aberrations, but on all three she had abandoned the treatment almost as soon as it had begun. Her ability to take on radically different personae in the company of different people – to become what she guessed a given man or woman (but usually man) would find most appealing – was exceptional; but this was a talent for acting that had been pushed to the point of insanity, and beyond. In addition she would invent long, elaborate personal histories of great vividness, and would cling to them obstinately, even when confronted with internal contradictions in her rig-maroles, or with the truth. It was possible that she no longer had a clear sense of an 'authentic' identity that was independent of these performances, and this existential confusion had begun to spread beyond the borders of her own self and to infect, like a disease, all those with whom she came into contact. She was known in Baroda for telling malicious and manipulative lies, for instance about certain faculty members with whom she fantasised absurdly steamy love affairs, and eventually wrote to their wives with explicit details of sexual encounters that had, in more than one case, led to separations and divorces. 'The reason she did not let you go to her college', my mother said, 'is that up there everybody hateofies her guts.'

Her parents had reacted to the news of her mental illness by abandoning her to her fate; not an uncommon response, as I was well aware. They had neither hanged nor immolated themselves – these violent fictions were born out of their spurned daughter's (pretty legitimate) rage. As for the lecherous 'uncle': according to Aurora and Minto, Uma after her rejection by her family – not at the age of twelve, as she had said! – had quickly latched on to an old Baroda acquaintance of her father's, an elderly, retired deputy commissioner of police by the name of Suresh Sarasvati, a melancholy old widower whom the young beauty effortlessly seduced into a quick marriage at a time when, as a disowned woman, she had a desperate need for the respectability of marital status. Soon after their marriage the old fellow had been rendered helpless by a stroke ('And what brought *that* on?' demanded Aurora. 'Do I have to spellofy it out? Must I draw-o you a picture?'), and now lived a dreadful half-life, mute and paralysed, cared for only by a solicitous neighbour. His young wife had taken off with everything he owned and had never given him a second thought. And now, in Bombay, she had started playing the field. Her powers of attraction, and the persuasiveness of her performances, were at their peak. 'You must break her magic spell,' my mother said. 'Or you are done for. She is like a rakshasa from the Ramayana, and for sure she will cookofy your poor goose.'

Minto had been thorough; Aurora showed me documentation – birth and wedding certificates, confidential medical reports acquired by the usual greasing of already-slippery palms, and so on – which left little doubt that his account was accurate in all important particulars. Still my heart refused to believe. 'You don't understand her,' I protested to my mother. 'OK, she lied about her parents. I would also lie about parents of that type. And maybe this ex-cop Sarasvati is not such an angel as you make out. But evil? Mad? A demon in human form? Mummyji, I think some personal factors have intervened.'

That night I sat alone in my room, unable to eat. It was plain that I had a choice to make. If I chose Uma, I would have to break away from my mother, probably for good. But if I accepted Aurora's evidence – and in the privacy of my own four walls I had to concede its overwhelming force – then I was condemning myself, in all probability, to a life without a partner. How much longer did I have? Ten years? Fifteen? Twenty? Could I face my strange, dark fate alone, without a lover by my side? What mattered more: love or truth?

But if Aurora and Minto were to be believed, she did not love me, was simply a great actress, a predator of the passions, a fraud. All at once I realised that many of the judgments I had recently made about my family were based on things Uma had said. I felt my head spin. The floor fell away beneath my feet. Was it true about Aurora and Kekoo, about Aurora and Vasco, about Aurora and Raman Fielding? Was it true that my sisters spoke ill of me behind my back? And if not, then it must be true that Uma – O my best beloved! – had sought deliberately to damage my opinion of those to whom I was closest, so that she could insert herself between me and mine. To give up one's own picture of the world and become wholly dependent on someone else's – was not that as good a description as any of the process of, literally, *going out of* one's mind?

In which case – to use Aurora's contrast – I was the mad one. And lovely Uma: the bad.

Faced with the possibility that evil existed, that pure malevolence had walked into my life and convinced me it was love, faced with the loss of everything I wanted from my life, I fainted. And dreamed dark dreams of blood.

⤺

The next morning I sat on the terrace at *Elephanta* staring out at the glittering bay. Mynah came to see me. At Aurora's request she, too, had assisted Dom Minto in his inquiries. It turned out that nobody in the Baroda branch of the UWAPRF had ever met Uma Sarasvati or knew of her involvement in any kind of activist campaigning. 'So even her introduction was a phoney,' she said. 'I tell you, little bro, this time Mummyji is spot on.'

'But I love her,' I said helplessly. 'I can't stop. I just can't.'

Mynah sat beside me and took my left hand. She spoke in a voice so gentle, so un-Mynah-like, that it caught my attention. 'I also liked her too much,' she said. 'But then it went wrong. I didn't want to tell you. Not my place. Anyhow, you wouldn't have listened.'

'Listened to what?'

'One time she came to me after being with you,' Mynah said, squinting into the distance. 'She told me some things about how it was. About what you. Anyway. Doesn't matter. She said she didn't like it. She said more but to hell. It doesn't matter now. Then she said something to me about me. That is to say: wanting. I sent her packing. Since then we don't speak.'

'She said it was you,' I told her dully. 'I mean. Who was after her.'

'And you believed her,' Mynah snapped, then swiftly kissed my forehead. 'Of course you believed her. What do you know about me? Who I like, what I need? And you were crazy for love. Poor sap. Now, but, you better wise up quick.'

'I should dump her? Just like that?'

Mynah stood up, lit a cigarette, coughed: a deep, unhealthy, choking sound. Her hard, front-line voice was back, her anti-civic-corruption lawyer's cross-examination voice, her fighting-against-murder-of-girl-babies, no-more-sati no-more-rapes loud-hailer instrument. She was right. I knew nothing about what it might be like to be her, about the choices she had had to make, about whose arms she might turn to for comfort, or why men's arms might be places not of pleasure but of fear. She might be my sister, but so what? I didn't even call her by her proper name. 'What's the big prob?' she shrugged, waving an ashy cigarette as she left. 'Giving up this stuff is harder. Trust me on this. Just cold-turkey the bitch and be thankful you don't also smoke.'

⁓

'I knew they would try and break us up. From the beginning I knew.'

Uma had moved into an eighteenth-floor apartment with sea view on Cuffe Parade, in a high-rise next door to the President Hotel and not far from the Mody Gallery. She was standing, theatrically ravaged by grief, on a little balcony against a suitably operatic backdrop of wind-agitated coco-palms and sudden, voluminous rain; and now, sure enough, here came the quiver of the sensuously full lower lip, here came her very own waterworks. 'For your own mother to tell you – that with your *father*! – well, excuse me but I am disgusted. *Chhi!* And Jimmy Cashondeliveri! That dumbo guitar-wallah with a missing string! You know perfectly well that from the first day at the racecourse he thought I was some avatar of your sister. Since then he follows me like a dog with his tongue hanging. And I'm supposed to be *sleeping* with him? God, who else? V. Miranda, maybe? The one-legged chowkidar? Have I no bloody *shame*?'

'But what you said about your family. And the "uncle".'

'What gives you the right to know everything about me? You were pushy and I didn't want to tell you. Bas. That's all.'

'But it wasn't true, Uma. Your parents are alive and the uncle is a husband.'

'It was a metaphor. Yes! A metaphor of how wretched my life

was, of my pain. If you loved me you would understand that. If you loved me you would not give me the third degree. If you loved me you would stop shaking your poor fist, and put it here, and you would shut your sweet face, and bring it here, and you would do what lovers do.'

'It wasn't a metaphor, Uma,' I said, backing away. 'It was a lie. What's scary is, you don't know the difference.' I stepped backwards through her front door, and closed it, feeling as if I'd just leapt from her balcony towards the wild palms. That was how it felt: like a falling. Like a suicide. Like a death.

But that was an illusion, too. The real thing was still two years away.

~

I held out for months. I lived at home, went to work, became skilled in the art of marketing and promoting Baby Softo Talcum Powder and was even appointed marketing manager by a proud father. I got through the hollow calendar of days. There were changes at *Elephanta*. In the aftermath of the débâcle of the retrospective, Aurora had finally got round to throwing Vasco out. It was icily done. Aurora mentioned her increased need for solitude, and Vasco with a cold bow agreed to clear out his studio. If this was the end of an affair, I thought, then it was creditably dignified and discreet: though the Arctic coldness of it made me shiver, I confess. Vasco came to say goodbye to me, and we went together to the cartoon-nursery, long unoccupied, where everything had begun. '*That's all, folks*,' he said. 'Time for V. Miranda to go West. Got a castle to build in the air.' He was lost in the flood of his own flesh, he looked like a toady, fairground-mirror reflection of Raman Fielding, and his mouth was twisted in pain. His voice was controlled, but I did not miss the blaze of feeling in his eye.

'She was my obsession, you must have guessed that,' he said, caressing the exclamatory walls (*Pow! Zap! Splat!*). 'As she was and is and will be yours. Maybe one day you'll feel like facing up to that. Then come to me. Come before that needle hits my heart.' I had not thought for years about Vasco's lost point, his Snow Queen's splinter of ice; and reflected, now, that the heart of this altered, swollen Vasco had more conventional attacks to worry about than needles. He left India for Spain soon afterwards, never to return.

Aurora also fired her dealer. She informed Kekoo that she held him personally responsible for the 'public relations fiasco' of her show. Kekoo went noisily, arriving at the gates each day for a month to entreat Lambajan for admission (which was refused), sending flowers and gifts (which were returned), writing endless letters (which were thrown away unread). Aurora had told him that as she no longer intended to exhibit any work, her need for a gallery no longer existed. But Kekoo, pathetically, was sure she was deserting him for his great rivals at the Chemould. He begged and pleaded with her by telephone (to which Aurora would not come when he called), in telegrams (which she would contemptuously set on fire), even via Dom Minto (who turned out to be a purblind, blue-spectacled old gent with the huge horse-teeth of the French comedian Fernandel, and whom Aurora instructed to stop carrying his messages). I could not help but wonder about Uma's accusations. If these two alleged lovers had been disposed of, then what of Mainduck? Had Fielding, too, been dumped, or was he now the sole tenant of her heart?

Uma, Uma. I missed her so. There were withdrawal symptoms: at night I felt her phantom-body move under my broken hand. As I was falling asleep (my misery did not prevent me from sleeping soundly!) I saw before my mind's eye the scene in an old Fernandel movie in which, not knowing the English word for 'woman', he uses his hands to trace the outline of a curvaceous female form.

I was the other man in the dream. 'Ah,' I nodded. 'A bottle of Coke?'

Uma walked past us, swinging her hips. Fernandel leered and jabbed a thumb in the direction of her departing posterior.

'My bottle of Coke,' he said, with understandable pride.

~

Ordinary life. Aurora painted every day, but I no longer had access to her studio. Abraham worked long hours, and when I asked him why I was being permitted to languish in the world of baby's behinds – I, with my time shortage! – he answered, 'Too much in your life has gone too fast. Do you good to slow down for some period.' In an act of silent solidarity, he had stopped golfing with Uma Sarasvati. Perhaps he, too, was missing her versatile charms.

Silence in Paradise: silence, and an ache. Mrs Gandhi returned to power, with Sanjay at her right hand, so it turned out that there was no final morality in affairs of state, only Relativity. I remembered Vasco Miranda's 'Indian variation' upon the theme of Einstein's General Theory: *Everything is for relative. Not only light bends, but everything. For relative we can bend a point, bend the truth, bend employment criteria, bend the law. D equals mc squared, where D is for Dynasty, m is for mass of relatives, and c of course is for corruption, which is the only constant in the universe – because in India even speed of light is dependent on load shedding and vagaries of power supply.* Vasco's departure, too, made home a quieter place. The rambling old mansion was like a denuded stage across which, like rustling phantoms, wandered a depleted cast of actors who had run out of lines. Or perhaps they were acting on other stages now, and only this house was dark.

It did not fail to occur to me – indeed, for a time it occupied most of my waking thoughts – that what had happened was, in a way, a defeat for the pluralist philosophy on which we had all been raised. For in the matter of Uma Sarasvati it had been the pluralist Uma, with her multiple selves, her highly inventive commitment to the infinite malleability of the real, her modernistically provisional sense of truth, who had turned out to be the bad egg; and Aurora had fried her – Aurora, that lifelong advocate of the many against the one, had with Minto's help discovered some fundamental verities, and had therefore been in the right. The story of my love-life thus became a bitter parable, one whose ironies Raman Fielding would have relished, for in it the polarity between good and evil was reversed.

I was sustained in that null time at the beginning of the 1980s by Ezekiel, our ageless cook. As if sensing the establishment's need for cheering up, he embarked upon a gastronomic programme combining nostalgia with invention and stirring in a generous sprinkling of hope. Before setting off for Baby Softo-land, and after I came home, I found myself gravitating more and more to the kitchen, where he squatted, grizzle-chopped and grinning gummily, tossing parathas optimistically in the air. 'Joy!' he cackled, wisely. 'Baba sahib, sit only and we will cook up the happy future. We will mash its spices and peel its garlic cloves, we will count out its cardamoms and chop its ginger, we will heat up the ghee of the future and fry its masala to release its flavour. Joy! Success in his enterprises for the Sahib, genius in her pictures for the Madam, and a beautiful bride for you! We will cook the past and present also, and from it tomorrow will come.' So I learned to cook Meat Cutlass (spicy minced lamb inside a potato patty) and Chicken Country Captain; to me the secrets of prawn padda, ticklegummy, dhope and ding-ding were revealed. I became a master of balchow and learned to spin a mean kaju ball. I learned the art of Ezekiel's 'Cochin special', a mouth-wateringly piquant red banana jam. And as I journeyed through the cook's copybooks, deeper and deeper into that private cosmos of papaya and cinnamon and spice, my spirits did indeed pick up; not least because I felt that Ezekiel had succeeded in joining me, after a long interruption, to the story of my past. In his kitchen I was transported back to a long-departed Cochin in which the patriarch Francisco dreamed of Gama rays and Solomon Castile ran off to sea and reappeared in blue synagogue tiles. Between the lines of his emerald-jacketed copybooks I saw Belle's struggle with the books of the family business, and in the scents of his culinary magic I smelled a godown in Ernakulam where a young girl had fallen in love. And Ezekiel's prophecy began to feel true. With yesterday in my tummy, my prospects felt a lot better.

'Good food,' grinned Ezekiel, slurping his tongue. '*Fattening* food. Time to put a little pot on your front. A man without a belly has no appetite for life.'

On 23rd June 1980 Sanjay Gandhi tried to loop the loop over New Delhi and nose-dived to his death. At once, in the period of instability that followed, I, too, was plunged towards catastrophe. Within days of Sanjay's death I heard that Jamshed Cashondeliveri had died in a car accident on the road to Powai Lake. His passenger, who had miraculously been thrown clear and escaped with minor cuts and concussion, was the brilliant young sculptor Uma Sarasvati to whom, it was said, the dead man had been intending to propose at the well-known beauty spot. Forty-eight hours later it was reported that Miss Sarasvati had been discharged from hospital and had been driven to her residence by friends. She continued, understandably, to suffer greatly from grief and shock.

The news of Uma's injury unleashed all the feelings for her which I had spent so long trying to tie down. I spent two days fighting against myself, but once I heard she was back at Cuffe Parade, I left the house, telling Lambajan I was off to the Hanging Gardens for a stroll, and grabbed a cab the moment I was out of his sight. Uma answered the door in black tights and a loosely tied kimono-style Japanese shirt. She looked panicky, hunted. It was as if her internal gravitational force had diminished; she seemed like a shaky assemblage of particles that might fly apart at any moment.

'Are you badly hurt?' I asked her.

'Shut the door,' she replied. When I turned back towards her she had untied her shirt and let it fall. 'See for yourself,' she said.

After that there was no keeping us apart. The thing between us seemed to have grown more potent during our separation. 'Oh boy,' she murmured as I caressed her with my twisted right hand. 'Oh yes, this. Oh boyoboy.' And, later: 'I knew you didn't stop loving me. I didn't stop. I told myself, confusion to our enemies. Whoever stands in our way will fall.'

Her husband, she confessed, had died. 'If I'm such a mean woman,' she said, 'then answer me why he left me everything? After his illness he didn't know who anybody was, he thought I was the servant girl. So I arranged for his care and left. If that is a bad thing then I am bad.' I absolved her easily. No, not bad, my darling, my life, not you.

There was not a scratch on her body. 'Bloody newspapers,' she said. 'I wasn't even in the bloody car. I took my own vehicle because I had plans for later. So he was in his stupid Mercedes' – how charmingly she mispronounced the name: *Murs'deez*! – 'and I in my new Suzuki. And on that second-rate road the crazy playboy wants to race. On that road where trucks come and buses with doped-up drivers and donkey-carts and camel-carts and god knows what-all.' She wept; I dried her tears. 'What could I do? I just drove like a sensible woman and shouted at him, no, get back, no. But Jimmy always had something missing up top. What to tell you? He didn't look, he stayed on the wrong side of the road to overtake, a corner came, a cow was sitting, he tried to avoid, he could not pull across because my car was there, he went off the road on the right side, and there was a poplar tree. *Khalaas*.'

I tried to feel sorry for Jimmy and failed. 'The papers said you were going to be married.' She gave me a furious look. 'You never understood me,' she said. 'Jimmy was nothing. For me it was always you.'

We met as often as we could. I kept our assignations secret from my family, and apparently Aurora had dispensed with Dom Minto's services, because she found out nothing. A year passed; more than a year. The happiest fifteen months of my life. 'Confusion to our enemies!' Uma's defiant phrase became our greeting and farewell.

Then Mynah died.

My sister perished of – what else? – a shortage of breath. She had been visiting a chemical factory in the north of town to investigate its maltreatment of its large female workforce – mostly women from the slums of Dharavi and Parel – when there was a small explosion in her near vicinity. The 'integrity' of a sealed vat of dangerous chemicals was, to use the official report's anaesthetised language, 'compromised'. The practical consequence of this loss of chemical integrity was the release into the atmosphere of a substantial quantity of the gas methyl isocyanate. Mynah, who had been knocked unconscious by the explosion, inhaled a lethal dose of the gas. The official report failed to account for the delay in summoning medical assistance, though it did list forty-seven separate counts on which the factory had failed to observe prescribed safety norms. First-aid-qualified staff on site were also rapped for the slowness with which they reached Mynah and her party. In spite of being given a shot of sodium thiosulphate in the ambulance, Mynah died before they reached the hospital. She died in pop-eyed agony, retching and gasping for air, while poison ate her lungs. Two of her colleagues from the WWSTP also died; three more lived on with severe disabilities. No compensation was ever paid. The investigation concluded that the incident had been a deliberate attack on Mynah's organisation by 'unnamed outside agents' and the factory could therefore not be deemed culpable. Only a few months previously Mynah had finally succeeded in sending Kéké Kolatkar to jail for his property swindles, but no trail connecting the politico to the killing was ever established. And Abraham, as has been stated, got himself off with a fine . . . listen, Mynah was his *daughter*. His *daughter*. Okay?

Okay.

'Confusion to our . . .' Uma stopped in mid-phrase, seeing the look on my face, when I went to see her after Philomina Zogoiby's funeral. 'No more of that,' I said, sobbing. 'No more confusion. Please.'

I lay in bed with my head in her lap. She stroked my white hair. 'You're right,' she said. 'Time to simplify. Your mummy-daddy must accept us, they must bow down before our love. Then we can get married and hey presto. It's happy ever after for us, and another artist in the family, too.'

'She won't . . .' I began, but Uma laid a finger across my lips. 'She must.'

Uma in this mood was an irresistible force. Our love was simply an imperative, she insisted; it demanded, and had a right, to be. 'When I explain this to your mother and father they will come round. It is my bona-fides that they doubt? Very well then. For our love I will go to see them – tonight! – and show them that they are wrong.'

I protested, but weakly. It was too soon. Their hearts were full of Mynah, I demurred, and there was no room for us. She overrode all my arguments. There was no heart that had no room in it for declarations of love, she said; just as there was no shame that true love did not erase – and now that Mr Sarasvati was no more, what stain lay upon our love except that she had been married once before and was not a virgin bride? My parents' objections were not reasonable. How could they stand in the way of their one son's chance of happiness? A son who had had to bear such burdens from the day of his birth? 'Tonight,' she repeated, grimly. 'You just wait on here. I will go and convince.' She leapt to her feet and began to dress. As she left she clipped a Walkman to her belt and donned headphones. 'Whistle while you work,' she grinned, clicking a cassette into place. I was terrified. 'Good luck,' I said loudly. 'Can't hear a word,' she said, and left. Once she had gone I wondered idly why she had bothered with the Walkman when she had a perfectly good sound system in the car. Probably bust, I thought. Nothing in this goddamn country works for very long.

She came back after midnight, full of love. 'I really think it will be OK,' she whispered. I had been lying awake in bed; tension had turned my body into knotted steel. 'Are you sure?' I said, begging for more. 'They are not evil people,' she said softly, sliding in beside me. 'They listened to everything and I am sure they got the point.'

At that moment I felt my life coming together as never before, I felt as if the tangled mess of my right hand were unscrambling, rearranging itself into palm and knuckles and jointed fingers and thumb. In elation's grip, I may even have danced. Damn it, I did dance: and shrieked, and boozed, and made wild love for joy. Verily she was my miracle worker and had achieved the unachievable thing. We slipped towards sleep wrapped in each other's bodies. Near oblivion I mumbled, vaguely, 'Where's the Walkman?'

'Oh, that damn thing,' she whispered. 'Always mangling up my tapes. I stopped on the way and chucked it in a bin.'

~

When I got home the next morning Abraham and Aurora were waiting for me in the garden, standing shoulder to shoulder, with darkness on their faces.

'What?' I asked.

'From this moment on,' said Aurora Zogoiby, 'you are no longer our son. All steps to disinherit you have been put in place. You have one day in which to collectofy your effects and get out. Your father and I never wish to see you again.'

'I support your mother fully,' said Abraham Zogoiby. 'You disgust us. Now get out of our sight.'

(There were further harsh words; louder, many of them mine. I will not set them down.)

⤳

'Jaya? Ezekiel? Lambajan? Will somebody tell me what's happened? What is going on?' Nobody spoke. Aurora's door was locked, Abraham had left the premises, and his secretaries had instructions not to put through any of my calls. Finally Miss Jaya Hé allowed herself to utter three words.

'Better you pack.'

⤳

Nothing was explained – not the fact of my expulsion, nor the brutality of its manner. Such an extreme penalty for so minor a 'crime'! – The 'crime' of falling into delirious love with a woman of whom my mother disapproved! To be cut off the family tree, like a dead branch, for so trivial – no, so wonderful – a reason . . . it was not enough. It made no sense. I knew that other people – most people – were living in this country of parental absolutism; and in the world of the masala movie these never-darken-my-doorstep scenes were two-a-penny. But we were different; and surely this place of fierce hierarchies and ancient moral certitudes had not been my country, surely this kind of material had no part in the script of our lives! – Yet it was plain that I was wrong; for there was no further discussion. I called Uma to give her the news, and then, having no option, faced my fate. The gates of Paradise were opened, and Lambajan averted his eyes. I stumbled through them, giddy, disoriented, lost. I was nobody, nothing. Nothing I had ever known was of use, nor could I any longer say that I knew it. I had been emptied, invalidated; I was, to use a hoary but suddenly fitting epithet, *ruined*. I had fallen from grace, and the horror of it shattered the universe, like a mirror. I felt as though I, too, had shattered; as if I were falling to earth, not as myself, but as a thousand and one fragmented images of myself, trapped in shards of glass.

After the fall: I arrived at Uma Sarasvati's with a suitcase in my hand. When she answered the door her eyes were red, her hair was wild, her manner was deranged. Old-style Indian melodrama was exploding over the surface of our fraudulently sophisticated ways, like the truth bursting through a thinly painted veneer of sweet lies. Uma erupted into shrieky apologies. Her inner gravity had weakened dramatically; now she really was coming apart. 'O god – if I'd ever thought – but how could they, it's something from pre-history – from *ancient time* – I thought they were such civilised people – I thought it was us religious nuts who acted like this not you modern secular types – O god, I'll go see them again, just now I'll go, I'll swear never to see you . . .'

'No,' I said, still dulled by shock. 'Please don't go. Don't do another thing.'

'Then I will do the only thing you cannot forbid,' she howled. 'I will kill myself. I will do it now, tonight. I will do this for my love of you, to set you free. Then they must take you back.' She must have been working herself up ever since my telephone call. Now she was operatic, immense.

'Uma, don't be mad,' I said.

'*I am not mad,*' she shouted at me, madly. 'Don't call me mad. All of your family calls me mad. I am not mad. I am in love. A woman will do great things for love. A man in love would do no less for me, but this I do not ask. I do not expect great things from you, from any man. I am not mad, unless I am mad about you. Call me mad for love. And – for god's sake! – shut the goddamn door.'

⤵

Fervid, with blood standing in her eyes, she began to pray. At the little shrine to Lord Ram in the corner of her living-room she lit a dia–lamp and moved it in tense circles through the air. I stood there in the gathering darkness with a suitcase at my feet. She means it, I thought. This is not a game. This is happening. It is my life, our life, and this its shape. This its true shape, the shape behind all shapes, the shape that reveals itself only at the moment of truth. At that moment an utter despair came over me, crushing me beneath its weight. I understood that I had no life. It had been taken from me. The illusion of the future which Ezekiel the cook had restored to me in his kitchen stood revealed as a chimera. What was I to do? Was it to be the gutter for me, or a final, supreme moment of dignity? Did I have the courage to die for love, and by doing so to make our love immortal? Could I do that for Uma? Could I do it for myself?

'I'll do it,' I said aloud. She set down her lamp and turned to me.

'I knew it,' she said. 'The god told me you would. He said you were a brave man, and you loved me, and so of course you would accompany me on the journey. You would not be a coward who let me go alone.'

∽

She had always known that her attachment to life was not firm, that the time might come when she would be ready to give it up. So, since her childhood, like a warrior going into battle, she had brought her death with her. In case of capture. Death before dishonour. She came out of her boudoir with clenched fists. In each fist was a white tablet. 'Don't ask,' she said. 'Policemen's houses contain many secrets.' She requested me to kneel beside her in front of the portrait of the god. 'I know you don't believe,' she said. 'But for me, you will not refuse.' We knelt. 'To show you how truly I have always loved you,' she said, 'to prove to you at last that I have never lied, I will swallow first. If you too are true, then follow me at once, at once, for I will be waiting, O my only love.'

At that moment something in me changed. There was a refusal. 'No,' I cried, and snatched at the tablet in her hand. It fell to the floor. With a cry she dived down towards it, as did I. Our heads clashed. 'Ow,' we said together. 'Ohoho, ai-aiee. *Ow.*'

When my head cleared a little both our tablets were lying on the floor. I snatched at them; but in my dizzy pain succeeded in capturing only one. Uma seized the remaining tablet and stared at it with a new wideness of eye, in the grip of some new, private horror, as if she had unexpectedly been asked an appalling question, and did not know how to reply.

I said: 'Don't. Uma, don't. It's wrong. It's mad.'

The word stung her again. 'Don't say mad,' she shrieked. 'If you want to live, live. But it will prove you never loved me. It proves you have been the liar, the charlatan, the quick-change artist, the manipulator, the conspirator, the fake. Not me: you. You are the rotten egg, the evil one, the devil. See! My egg is good.'

She swallowed the pill.

There was a moment when an expression of immense and genuine surprise crossed her face, followed at once by resignation. Then she fell to the ground. I knelt beside her in terror and the bitter-almond smell filled my nostrils. Her face in death seemed to pass through a thousand changes, as if the pages of a book were turning, as if she were giving up, one by one, all her numberless selves. And then a blank page, and she was no longer anyone at all.

No, I would not die, I had already decided that. I put the remaining tablet in my trouser pocket. Whoever and whatever she had been, good or evil or neither or both, it is undeniable that I had loved her. To die would not immortalise that love, but devalue it. So I would live, to be the standard-bearer of our passion; would demonstrate, by my life, that love was worth more than blood, than shame – more, even, than death. *I will not die for you, my Uma, but I will live for you. However harsh that life may be.*

The doorbell rang. I sat with Uma's dead body in the dark. There was a hammering. Still I made no reply. A loud voice shouted out. *Open up. Polis.*

I rose and opened the door. The landing was thick with short-trousered blue uniforms, dark skinny legs wth knobbly knees, and hands clenched around waving lathis. A flat-hatted inspector was pointing a gun right at my face.

'You are Zogoiby, isn't it?' he asked at the top of his voice.

I said I was.

'*I.e.* Shri Moraes Zogoiby, marketing manager of Baby Softo Talcum Powder Private Limited?'

The same.

'Then on basis of information laid before me I arrest you on a charge of narcotics smuggling and in the name of Law I command you to accompany me peaceably to the vehicle below.'

'Narcotics?' I repeated helplessly.

'Bandying of words is forbidden,' blared the Inspector, pushing his pistol closer to my face. 'Detenu must unquestioning obey instructions of the in-charge. Forward march.'

I stepped meekly into the knobbly throng. At that moment the Inspector caught his first sight of the body of the dead woman lying on the apartment floor.

# III
# BOMBAY CENTRAL

# 16

I N A STREET I had never heard of I stood in manacles before a building I had never seen, a structure of such size that my entire field of vision was occupied by a single featureless wall, in which, a little way to my right, I perceived a tiny iron door – or, rather, a door that looked small, small as a metal mousehole, on account of being set in that ghastly grey immensity of stone. I was prodded forward by the arresting officer's stick, and walked obediently away from the windowless vehicle in which I had been transported from the macabre scene of my lover's demise. I crossed that empty and silent thoroughfare in astonishment, for streets in Bombay are never silent, and never, never empty – here there is no 'dead of night', or so, until now, I had always supposed. As I approached the door I saw that in reality it was extremely large, and towered above me like the entrance to a cathedral. How vast the wall must be, then! Close to, it spread over and about us and hid the dirty moon. I felt my heart sink. I found I could remember very little about the journey. Tied down in the dark, I had evidently lost all sense of direction and of the passage of time. What was this place? Who were these people? Were they truly police officers; was I really accused of drug trafficking and now also under suspicion of murder; or had I slipped accidentally from one page, one book of life on to another – in my wretched, disoriented state, had my reading finger perhaps slipped from the sentence of my own story on to this other, outlandish, incomprehensible text that had been lying, by chance, just beneath? Yes: some such slippage had plainly occurred. 'I am not a criminal,' I cried out. 'Nor do I belong here, in this Under World. There has been a mistake.'

'Give up such delusive esperance, you rotter,' replied the Inspector. 'Here many bhoots of the Under World, many fearful

285

blighters, are turning into lost shadows. No mistake, you bally chump! Enter! Within, the rotfulness is terrific.'

The great door opened with many clanks and groans. At once the air was full of hellish wails. 'Oooh! Hai-hai! Grooh! Oi-yoi-yoi! *Yarooh!*' Inspector Singh gave me an unceremonious shove. 'Left-right left-right one-two one-two!' he cried. 'Scurry along, Beelzebooby! Your After Life awaits.'

I was led down dim corridors stinking of excrement and torment, of desolations and violations, by whip-cracking men with, as it seemed to me, the heads of beasts and poisonous snakes for tongues. Either the Inspector had left or else he had metamorphosed into one of these hybrid monsters. I tried to ask the monsters questions but their communications did not extend beyond the physical. Blows, pushes, even the tip of a whip burning fiercely across my ankle: this was the sum total of what they had to say. I stopped talking and moved deeper into the jail.

After a long while I found my way blocked by a man with – I narrowed my eyes and peered – the head of a bearded elephant, who held in his hand an iron crescent dripping with keys. Rats scurried respectfully around his feet. 'To this place we are bringing godless men like you,' said the elephant man. 'Here you will suffer for your sins. We will humiliate you in fashions of which you have not even been able to dream.' I was ordered to remove my clothes. Naked, shivering in the hot night, I was manhandled into a cell. A door – a whole life, a whole way of understanding life – closed behind me. I stood in darkness, lost.

Solitary confinement. The heat intensified the stench of ordure. Mosquitoes, straw, pools of fluid, and, everywhere, in the dark, cockroaches. My bare feet crunched them as I walked. When I stood still they scrambled up my legs. Bending in panic to brush them off, I felt my hair brush against the walls of my black cage. Cockroaches swarmed over my head and down my back. I felt them on my stomach, dropping into my pubes. I began to jerk like a marionette, hitting at myself, screaming. Something – a defilement – had begun.

In the morning, some light did find its way into the cell and the roaches retreated to await the dark's return. I had not slept; my battle against those vile creatures had used up all my strength. I fell on to the straw pile that was my only bed, and rats flurried into holes in the wall. A little window opened in the cell door. 'Pretty soon you will be catching those crunchy cockies for food,' the Warder laughed. 'Even vegetarian jailbirds go for them in the end; and you–tho, I am thinking, are definitely non–veg from before.'

The illusion of an elephant's head, I now saw, had been created by the hood of a cloak (the flapping ears) and a hookah (for a nose). This fellow was no mythological Ganesha, but a coarse, sadistic brute. 'What is this place?' I asked him. 'I never came across it in my life.'

'You laad–sahibs,' he said, contemptuously sending a long jet of bright vermilion sputum towards my bare feet. 'You live in the city and know nothing of its secret, of its heart. To you it is invisible, but now you have been made to see. You are in Bombay Central lock–up. It is the stomach, the intestine of the city. So naturally there is much of shit.'

'I know the Bombay Central area,' I protested. 'Railway stations, dhabas, bazaars. I found no place resembling this.'

'A city does not show itself to every bastard, sister–fucker, mother–fucker,' the elephant man shouted before slamming the window shut. 'You were blind, but now wait and see.'

Shit–bucket, gruel–bucket, the rapid slide towards utter degradation: I will spare you the details. My forebears Aires and Camoens da Gama, and my mother too, had spent time in British–Indian jails; but this post–Independence made–in–India institution was far beyond their worst imaginings. This was not just a jail; it was an education. Hunger, exhaustion, cruelty and despair are good teachers. I learned their lessons quickly – my guilt, my worthlessness, my abandonment by everyone I might have called mine. I deserved no better than I had received. We all get what we deserve. I huddled against a wall with my forehead upon my knees and my arms clasped around my shins, and let the cockies come and go. 'This is nothing,' the Warder comforted me. 'Wait on till diseases start.'

How true, I thought. Soon there would be trachoma, inner–ear infection, rickets, dysentery, infection of the urinary tract. Malaria, cholera, TB, typhoid. And I had heard about a new killer, a thing without a name. Whores were dying of it – turning into living skeletons and then giving up the ghost, the rumour was – and the Kamathipura pimps were hushing it up. Not that there was much chance of my coming into contact with a whore.

As roaches crawled and mosquitoes stung, so I felt that my skin was indeed coming away from my body, as I had dreamed so long ago that it would. But in this version of the dream, my peeling skin took with it all elements of my personality. I was becoming nobody, nothing; or, rather, I was becoming what had been made of me. I was what the Warder saw, what my nose smelled on my body, what the rats were beginning, with growing enthusiasm, to approach. I was scum.

I tried to cling to the past. In my bitter turmoil I sought to apportion blame; and mostly I blamed my mother, to whom my father never could say no. – For what kind of mother would set out on such flimsy provocation to destroy her child, her only son? – Why, a monster! – O, an age of monsters is come upon us. Kalyug, when cross-eyed red-tongued Kali, our mad dam, moves among us wreaking havoc. – And remember, O Beowulf, that Grendel's mother was more fearsome than Grendel himself . . . Ah, Aurora, how easily you turned to infanticide – with what cold zeal you determined to choke the last breath from your own flesh and blood, to eject him from the atmosphere of your love into the airless deeps of space, there to gasp and perish horribly, with protruding eyes and swollen tongue! – I wish you had pulverised me as a baby, mother, before I grew so old-young with my club. You had the stomach for it – for punch and kick, for pinch and smack. See, beneath your blows the child's dark skin acquires the iridescence characteristic of bruises and oil-slicks. O, how he howls! The very moon is darkened by his cries. But you are relentless, inexhaustible. And when he is flayed, when he is a shape without frontiers, a self without walls, then your hands close about his neck, and squash, and squish; air rushes out from his body through all available orifices, he is farting out his life, just as once you, his mother, farted him into it . . . and now he has just one breath left in him, one last shuddering bubble of hope . . .

'Wah, wah!' the Warder cried, startling me out of my self-pitying reverie and into the knowledge that I had spoken aloud. 'Keep your big ears to yourself, elephant man,' I yelled. 'Call me what you want,' he replied, affably. 'Your fate is already written.' I subsided, squatting, and buried my head in my hands.

'Case for the prosecution you have given,' said the Warder. 'Very powerful, bhai. Damn strong. But for the defence? A mother must be defended, isn't it? Then who will speak for her?'

'This is not a court of law,' I answered, in the grip of the sick emptiness that remains when anger drains away. 'If she has another version, then let her tell it where she pleases.'

'Okay, okay,' said the Warder, in mock-appeasement. 'Keep up the good work. For me, your entertainment value is presently number one. Top-notch. Kudos, mister. Kudos to you.'

And I thought about mad love, about all the *amours fous* down the da Gama-Zogoiby generations. I remembered Camoens and Belle, and Aurora and Abraham, and poor Ina eloping with her Country and Eastern Cashondeliveri beau. I even included Minnie-Inamorata-Floreas finding ecstasy in Jesus Christ. And of course I thought – endlessly, like a child scratching at a wound – about Uma and myself. I tried to cling to our love, to the fact of it, even though there were voices within deriding me for the size of the mistake I had made with her. *Let her go*, the voices advised. *At least now, after all this, cut your losses.* But I still wanted to believe what lovers believe: that the thing itself is better than any alternative, be it unrequited, or defeated, or insane. I wanted to cling to the image of love as the blending of spirits, as mélange, as the triumph of the impure, mongrel, conjoining best of us over what there is in us of the solitary, the isolated, the austere, the dogmatic, the pure; of love as democracy, as the victory of the no-man-is-an-island, two's-company Many over the clean, mean, apartheiding Ones. I tried to see lovelessness as arrogance, for who but the loveless could believe themselves complete, all-seeing, all-wise? To love is to lose omnipotence and omniscience. Ignorantly is how we all fall in love; for it is a kind of fall. Closing our eyes, we leap from that cliff in hope of a soft landing. Nor is it always soft; but still, I told myself, still, without that leap nobody comes to life. The leap itself is a birth, even when it ends in death, in a scramble for white tablets, and the scent of bitter almonds on your beloved's breathless mouth.

*No*, said my voices. *Love, as well as your mother, has done you down.*

My own breath came with difficulty; the asthma tore and rasped. When I did manage to doze off I dreamed strangely of the sea. Never until now had I slept out of earshot of the waves, of the collision of the spheres of air and water, and my dreams yearned for that plashy sound. Sometimes in the dreams the sea was dry, or made of gold. Sometimes it was a canvas ocean, sewn tightly to the land along the edge of the beach. Sometimes the land was like a torn page and the sea a glimpse of the hidden page below. These dreams showed me what I was not pleased to be shown: that I was my mother's son. And one day I awoke from such a sea-dream in which, while attempting to escape from unknown pursuers, I came upon a lightless subterranean flow, and was instructed by a shrouded woman to *swim beyond the limit of my breath*, for only then would I discover the one and only shore upon which I might be safe for ever, *the shore of Fancy itself*; and I obeyed her with a will, I swam with all my might towards my lungs' collapse; and as they gave way at last, and the ocean rushed into me, I awoke with a gasp to find before me the impossible figure of a one-legged man with a parrot on his shoulder and a treasure-map in his hand. 'Come, baba,' said Lambajan Chandiwala. 'Time to seek your fortune, wheresoever it may be.'

⤳

It was not a treasure-map, but golden treasure itself: *viz.*, a document authorising my immediate release. Not a fortune-hunter's passport, but a stroke of unlooked-for fortune. It brought me clean water and clean clothing. The turning of keys in locks was heard, and the envious delirium of my fellow prisoners. The Warder, elephantine master of this rathouse, this overcrowded roach motel, was not to be seen; cowering, deferential flunkeys tended to my needs. On my way out no animal-headed demons poked their pitchforks at me, or ululated with snaky tongues. The door was open, and of conventional size; the wall in which it was set was just a wall. No magical machine awaited us outside – no, not even our old driver Hanuman and his winged Buick! – but an ordinary yellow-and-black taxi-cab with, painted in small white letters on its black dashboard, the legend *Hypothecated to Khazana Bank International Limited*. We entered familiar streets above which loomed familiar messages from the manufacturers of Metro shoes and Stayfree sanitary panties; on hoardings and in neon, Rothmans and Charminar cigarettes, Breeze and Rexona soaps, Time polish and Hope toilet tissue and Life neem-sticks and Love henna all welcomed me home. For there was no doubt in my mind that I was en route to Malabar Hill, and if there was a shadow on my otherwise sunny horizon it was because I felt obliged to rehearse the old arguments about repentance and forgiveness. My parents' forgiveness, plainly, was now mine; should my repentance be my homecoming gift to them? But the Prodigal Son got the fatted calf – was loved – without ever having to say he was sorry. And repentance's bitter pills stuck in my throat; as with all my kin, there was overmuch mulishness in my blood. Damn it, I frowned, what was there for me to repent? – It was at about this point in my cogitations that I registered the fact that we were driving north – not towards the parental bosom, but away from; so that this was not a return to Paradise, but a further stage in my fall.

I began, panickily, to jabber. *Lamba, Lamba, tell this fellow.* Lambajan was soothing. Just take out some time to rest baba. After your experience your nervous condition is natural. But to balance Lambajan there was psittacoid scorn. Totah the parrot on the ledge by the rear window screeched its painful contempt. I slid down in my seat and closed my eyes, remembering. The Inspector was examining Uma's body and I was being body-searched too. From my pocket emerged a white rectangle. 'Is what?' demanded the Inspector, coming up close (he was almost a head shorter than I), pushing his moustache up against my chin. 'Fresh-breath peppermint?' And at once I was blubbering helplessly about suicide pacts. 'Shut off your tap!' the Inspector commanded, snapping the tablet in half. 'Just suck this and we'll see.'

That sobered me up. I scarcely dared to part my lips; the

Inspector was jabbing the half-tablet towards my mouth. *But it will kill me, good sir, it will lay me cold beside my departed love.* 'In which case we found two persons dead,' said the Inspector, as if stating the obvious. 'Sad story of love gone wrong.'

Reader: I resisted his request. Hands grasped me by the arms the legs the hair. In a moment I was lying on the floor not far from dead Uma, whose corpse was being buffeted somewhat by the over-eager short-trousered crowd. I had heard about people dying in what were euphemistically called 'police encounters'. The Inspector's hand grasped my nose and squeezed . . . Airlessness demanded my full attention. And when I yielded to the inevitable, pop! In went the fatal pill.

But – as you will have divined – I did not die. The half-tablet was not almond-bitter, but sugar-sweet. I heard the Inspector say, 'The fiend gave the female the lethal dose while indulging self with a sweetie. So it is murder, then! The open-and-shutfulness is terrific.' And as the Inspector metamorphosed into Hurree Jamset Ram Singh, Bunter's dusky nabob of Bhanipur, so the men in shorts became a rabble of schoolboys, the terrors of the Remove. They removed me all right, by frog-march into the lift. And as the contents of that potent tablet took effect – at high speed, given my accelerated systems – everything began to change. 'Yarooh, you fellows,' I shouted, twitching convulsively in the hallucinogen's tightening grip. 'Ooh, I say – *leave off.*'

Chasing a white rabbit, tumbling towards Wonderland past rocking-horse flies, a young girl had to make eat-me drink-me choices; go ask Alice, as the old song goes. But my Alice, my Uma, had made her selection, which was not simply a question of size; and was dead, and could not answer. *Ask me no questions, I'll tell you no lies.* Put that on her tombstone. What was I to make of these two tablets, deadly and dreamy? Had it been my beloved's intention to die, and allow me, after a time of visions, to survive; or to watch my death through the drug's transcendent eyes? Was she a tragic heroine; or a murderess; or, in some way as yet unfathomable, both at once? There was a mystery in Uma Sarasvati which she had taken to her grave. I thought in that hypothecated taxi that I had never known her, and would never know. But she was dead, dead with shock on her face, and I was coming through, was being reborn into a new life. She deserved my kind remembrance, the benefit of the doubt, and all the generous good feelings I could find. I opened my eyes. Bandra. We were in Bandra. 'Who did this?' I said to Lambajan. 'Who worked this magic trick?'

'Shh, baba,' he soothed. 'Not long and you will see.'

Raman Fielding in the gulmohr-tree-shaded garden of his Lalgaum villa wore a straw hat, sunglasses and cricket whites. He perspired heavily and carried a heavy bat. 'First class,' he said in that guttural croak of his. 'Borkar, good work.' Who was this Borkar? I wondered, and then saw Lambajan saluting and realised that I had long forgotten that injured sailor's real name. So Lamba was a covert MA cadre. He had told me he was religious, and I half-remembered that he came from a village somewhere in Maharashtra, but it was being made shamefully plain that I had known nothing of importance about him, nor made it my business to know. Mainduck came across to us and patted Lambajan on the shoulder. 'A true Mahratta warrior,' he said, breathing betel-fumes into my face. '*Beautiful Mumbai, Marathi Mumbai*, isn't it, Borkar?' he grinned, and Lambajan, standing as close to attention as he could with a crutch, assented. 'Sir skipper sir.' Fielding was amused by the incredulity on my face. 'Whose town do you think this is?' he asked. 'On Malabar Hill you drink whisky-soda and talk democracy. But our people guard your gates. You think you know them but they have also their own lives and tell you nothing. Who cares about you godless Hill types? *Sukha lakad ola zelata*. You don't speak Marathi. "When the dry stick burns, everything goes up in flame." One day the city – my beautiful goddess-named Mumbai, not this dirty Anglo-style Bombay – will be on fire with our notions. Then Malabar Hill will burn and Ram Rajya will come.'

He turned to Lambajan. 'On your recommendation I have done much. Murder charge is quashed and suicide verdict has been agreed. As to narcotics question, authorities have been directed towards the big badmashes and not this small potato. Now you justify to me why I have done it.'

'Sir skipper sir.' And with that the old chowkidar turned to me. 'Hit me, baba,' he encouraged.

I was taken by surprise. 'Beg pardon?' Fielding clapped his hands, impatiently. 'Deaf or what?'

Lambajan's expression was almost beseeching. I understood then that he had put himself out, made himself vulnerable, to save me from prison; that he had gambled everything to persuade Mainduck to move a mountain on my behalf. Now, it seemed, I must return the compliment and rescue him, by living up to his praises. 'Baba, just like in the old days,' he coaxed. 'Hit me there, there.' That is, on the point of the chin. I took a breath, and nodded. 'OK.'

'Sir permission to set aside parrot sir.' Fielding waved an impatient hand and settled down like dough in an outsized – but still groaning – orange cane chair, set by the lily pond. Mumbadevi statues crowded around him to watch the demonstration. 'Mind your tongue, Lamba,' I said, and let fly. He fell hard, and lay unconscious at my feet.

'Pretty good,' croaked Mainduck, impressed. 'He said that crooked fist of yours was a hammer worth having. What do you know? Seems like it's true.' Lambajan came round, slowly, nursing his jaw. 'Not to worry, baba,' were his first words. Suddenly Mainduck went into one of his famous rants. 'You know why it's OK that you hit him?' he screamed. 'It is because I said so. And why is that OK? Because I own his body and also his soul. And how did I purchase? Because I have looked after his people. You-tho don't even know how many family members does he have in his village. But I have been getting kiddies educated and solving health and hygiene problems since many years. Abraham Zogoiby, old man Tata, C. P. Bhabha, Crocodile Nandy, Kéké Kolatkar, Birlas, Sassoons, even Mother Indira herself – they think they are the in-charges but they care nothing for Common Man. Soon that little fellow will show them they are wrong.' I was rapidly losing interest in this harangue when he switched to a more intimate note. 'And you, my friend Hammer,' he said. 'I have raised you from the dead. You are my zombie now.'

'What do you want from me?' I asked, but even as I spoke the words I knew not only the question but my answer. Something that had been captive all my life had been released when I k.o.'d

Lambajan, something whose captivity had meant that my entire existence up to this point all at once seemed unfulfilled, reactive, characterised by various kinds of drift; and whose release burst upon me like my own freedom. I knew in that instant that I need no longer live a provisional life, a life-in-waiting; I need no longer be what ancestry, breeding and misfortune had decreed, but could enter, at long last, into myself – my true self, whose secret was contained in that deformed limb which I had thrust for too long into the depths of my clothing. No more! Now I would brandish it with pride. Henceforth I would be my fist; would be a Hammer, not a Moor.

Fielding was talking, the words coming quick and hard. *Do you know who your Daddyji is, high in his Siodi Tower? This man who has cast his only male child from his bosom, can you imagine the depth of his evil-doing, the breadth of his heartlessness? How much do you know about the Musulman gang boss who goes under the name of Scar?*

I confessed my ignorance. Mainduck waved a dismissive hand. 'You will come to know. Drugs, terrorism, Musulmans-Mughals, weapons-systems-delivery computers, scandals of Khazana Bank, nuclear bombs. Hai Ram how you minorities stick together. How you gang together against Hindus, how good-natured we are that we do not see how dangerous is your threat. But now your father has sent you to me and you will know it all. About the robots even I will tell you, the manufacture of high-technology minority-rights cybermen to attack and murder Hindus. And about babies, the march of minority babies who will push our blessed infants from their cots and grab their sacred food. Such are their plans. But they shall not prevail. *Hindu-stan*: the country of Hindus! We shall defeat the Scar-Zogoiby axis, whatsoever the cost. We shall bow their mighty knees. My zombie, my hammer: are you for us or against us, will you be righteous or will you be lefteous? Say: are you with us or without?'

Unhesitating, I embraced my fate. Without pausing to ask what connection there might be between Fielding's anti-Abrahamic tirade and his alleged intimacy with Mrs Zogoiby; without let or hindrance; willingly, even joyfully, I leapt. *Where you have sent me, mother – into the darkness, out of your sight – there I elect to go. The names*

*you have given me – outcast, outlaw, untouchable, disgusting, vile – I clasp*
*to my bosom and make my own. The curse you have laid upon me will be*
*my blessing and the hatred you have splashed across my face I will drink*
*down like a potion of love. Disgraced, I will wear my shame and name it*
*pride – will wear it, great Aurora, like a scarlet letter blazoned on my breast.*
*Now I am plunging downwards from your hill, but I'm no angel, me. My*
*tumble is not Lucifer's but Adam's. I fall into my manhood. I am happy so*
*to fall.*

'Sir righteous skipper sir.'

Mainduck unleashed a mighty noise of joy and struggled to rise from his chair. Lambajan – Borkar – came forward and assisted. 'So, so,' said Fielding. 'Well, there is much use for that hammer of yours. By the way, any other gifts?'

'Sir cooking sir,' I said, remembering happy times in the kitchen with Ezekiel and his copybooks. 'Anglo-Indian mulligatawny, South Indian meat with coconut milk, Mughlai kormas, Kashmiri shirmal, reshmi kababs; Goan fish, Hyderabadi brinjal, dum rice, Bombay club-style, all. Even if it is to your taste then pink, salty numkeen chai.' Fielding's delight knew no bounds. It was plain he was a man who liked his food. 'Then you are a true all-rounder,' he said, thumping my back. 'Let's see if you are Test class, if you can take that all-important number six position and make it your own. R. J. Hadlee, K. D. Walters, Ravi Shastri, Kapil Dev.' (India's cricketers were on a tour of Australia and New Zealand at the time.) 'Always room for a fellow like that on my team.'

⌒

My time in Raman Fielding's service began with what he called a 'getting-to-know-you guest spot' in his domestic kitchen, much to the displeasure of his regular cook, Chhaggan Five-in-a-Bite, a snaggletoothed giant who looked as if he were carrying an overcrowded cemetery inside his enormous mouth. 'Chhagga-baba is a wild man,' said Fielding admiringly, explaining the cook's cognomen as he made the introductions. 'One time in a wrestle he bit off his adversary's toes, all in one go.' Chhaggan glowered at me – cutting an incongruously dishevelled and canteen-medalled scarecrow figure in that otherwise spotless kitchen – and began sharpening large knives and muttering direly. 'Now, but, he is just honey,' bellowed Fielding. 'Isn't it, Chhaggo? Stop sulking now. Guest chef should be greeted like a brother. Or maybe not,' he added, turning to me heavy-lidded. 'It was his brother who lost the wrestling match. Those toes, I swear! Looked like little kofta balls, except for the dirty nails.' I remembered Lambajan's old saga about having his leg bitten off by a fabulous elephant and wondered how many of these loss-of-limb tall tales were wandering around the city, attaching themselves to amputor or amputee. I congratulated Chhaggan on his kitchen's sparkle, and told the staff that I would expect no drop in standards. A love of neatness was one thing I had in common with old snagglepuss, I averred, making no reference to Five-in-a-Bite's somewhat haphazard personal style; also, I added quietly to myself, an instrument of war. His fangs and my hammer; even-steven, or so I reckoned. I gave him my sweetest smile. 'Sir no problem sir,' I said smartly to my new boss. 'We two are going to get along just fine.'

In those days of cooking for Mainduck I learned some of the intricacies of the man. Yes, I know there is a fashion nowadays for these Hitler's-valet type memoirs, and many people are against, they say we should not humanise the inhuman. But the point is they are not inhuman, these Mainduck-style little Hitlers, and it is in their humanity that we must locate our collective guilt, humanity's guilt for human beings' misdeeds; for if they are just monsters – if it is just a question of King Kong and Godzilla wreaking havoc until the aeroplanes bring them down – then the rest of us are excused.

I personally do not wish to be excused. I made my choice and lived my life. No more! Finish! I want to get on with the story.

Among his many non-Hindu tastes, Fielding loved meat. Lamb (which was mutton), mutton (which was goat), keema, chicken, kababs: couldn't get enough of it. Bombay's meat-eating Parsis, Christians and Muslims – for whom, in so many other ways, he had nothing but contempt – were often applauded by him for their non-veg cuisine. Nor was this the only contradiction in the make-up of that fierce, illogical man. He kept up, and carefully cultivated, a façade of philistinism, but all around his house were the antique Ganeshas, the Shiva Natarajas, the Chandela bronzes, the Rajput and Kashmiri miniatures that revealed a genuine interest in Indian high culture. The ex-cartoonist had been to art school once, and while he would never have said so in public an influence remained. (I never asked Mainduck about my mother, but if indeed she was drawn to him, the evidence of his walls gave me a new reason why. Although it was also evidence of another kind, a disproof of the alleged improving power of art. Mainduck had the statues and the pictures, but his moral fibre remained of low quality, a fact which, had it been drawn to his attention, would I suspect have given him cause for pride.)

As to the toffs on Malabar Hill, he cared about them, too; more deeply than he liked to admit. My own family background flattered him: to turn Moraes Zogoiby, great Abraham's only son, into his personal Hammer-man was *quite* a titillation, disinheritance or no disinheritance. I was allotted quarters in the Bandra house, and treated, always, with just a hint of a cosseting tenderness he extended to no other employee; letting slip, on occasion, the formal Hindi 'you', the *aap* of respect, rather than the *tu* of command. It is to the credit of my colleagues that they gave no sign of resenting this special treatment, and to my discredit, I suppose, that I took whatever was going – regular use of a hot-and-cold-running-water bathroom, gifts of lungis and kurta-pajamas, offers of beer. A soft upbringing leaves a residue of softness in the blood.

What was interesting was how much the city's blue-bloods cared for Fielding. There was a steady stream of visitors from Everest Vilas and Kanchenjunga Bhavan, from Dhaulagiri Nivas, Nanga Parbat House and Manaslu Mansion and all the other super-desirable super-high-rise Himalayas of the Hill. The youngest, sleekest, hippest young cats in the urban jungle came to prowl in his Lalgaum grounds, and all of them were hungry, but not for my banquets; they hung on Mainduck's words and lapped up every syllable. He was against unions, in favour of breaking strikes, against working women, in favour of sati, against poverty and in favour of wealth. He was against 'immigrants' to the city, by which he meant all non-Marathi speakers, including those who had been born there, and in favour of its 'natural residents', which included Marathi-medium types who had just stepped off the bus. He was against the corruption of the Congress (I) and for 'direct action', by which he meant paramilitary activity in support of his political aims, and the institution of a bribery-system of his own. He derided the Marxist analysis of society as class struggle and lauded the Hindu preference for the eternal stability of caste. In the national flag he was in favour of the colour saffron and against the colour green. He spoke of a golden age 'before the invasions' when good Hindu men and women could roam free. 'Now our freedom, our beloved nation, is buried beneath the things the invaders have built. This true nation is what we must reclaim from beneath the layers of alien empires.'

It was while serving up my own cooking at Mainduck's table that I first heard of the existence of a list of sacred sites at which the country's Muslim conquerors had deliberately built mosques on the birthplaces of various Hindu deities – and not only their birthplaces, but their country residences and love-nests, too, to say nothing of their favourite shops and preferred eateries. Where was a deity to go for a decent evening out? All the prime sites had been hogged by minarets and onion domes. It would not do! The gods had rights, too, and must be given back their ancient way of life. The invaders would have to be repulsed.

The eager young things from Malabar Hill agreed enthusiastically. Yes, indeed, a campaign for divine rights! What could be smarter, more *cutting edge*? – But when they began, in their guffawing way, to belittle the culture of Indian Islam that lay palimpsest-fashion over the face of Mother India, Mainduck rose to his feet and thundered at them until they shrank back in their seats. Then he would sing ghazals and recite Urdu poetry – Faiz, Josh, Iqbal – from memory and speak of the glories of Fatehpur Sikri and the moonlit splendour of the Taj. An intricate fellow, indeed.

There were women, but they were peripheral. They were imported at night and he would slobber over them, but he never seemed very interested. He had a power-drive rather than a sex-drive, and women bored him, no matter how assiduously they tried to hold his interest. I must record that I never saw any sign of my mother, and what I did see suggested to me that any liaison between her and my new employer would have been a very short-lived affair.

He preferred male company. There would be evenings when in the company of a group of saffron-headbanded MA Youth Wingers he would institute a sort of macho, impromptu mini-Olympiad. There would be arm-wrestling and mat-wrestling, push-up contests and living-room boxing bouts. Lubricated by beer and rum, the assembled company would arrive at a point of sweaty, brawling, raucous, and finally exhausted nakedness. At these moments Fielding seemed truly happy. Shedding his flower-patterned lungi he would loll among his cadres, itching, scratching, belching, farting, slapping buttocks and patting thighs. 'Now nobody can stand against us!' he would bellow as he passed out in a state of Dionysiac bliss. 'Bloody hell! Now we are one.'

I joined in when requested, and in those nocturnal boxing bouts the reputation of the Hammer grew and grew. The oiled perspiring bodies of naked Youth Wingers lay down and took the count. (The gathered Olympians, crowding around us in a rough square, chanted the numbers in unison: 'Nine! . . . Ten! . . . Kayo!!') And Five-in-a-Bite, likewise, was the champion wrestler of us all.

Listen: I do not deny that there was much about Mainduck that elicited in me profound reactions of nausea and disgust, but I schooled myself to overcome these. I had hitched my fortunes to his star. I had rejected the old, for it had rejected me, and there was no point bringing its attitudes into my new life. I too would be like this, I resolved; I would become this man. I studied Fielding closely. I must say as he said, do as he did. He was the new way, the future. I would learn him, like a road.

Weeks passed, then months. At length my probationary period came to an end; I had come through some invisible test. Mainduck summoned me into his office, the one with the green frog-phone. When I entered it I saw standing before me a figure so terrifying, so bizarre, that in a rush of dreadful enlightenment I understood that I had never really left the phantasmal city, that other Bombay-

Central or Central-Bombay into which I had been plunged after my arrest on Cuffe Parade and from which, in my naïvety, I believed that Lambajan had rescued me in the hypothecated taxi of my blessed freedom-ride.

It was the figure of a man, but a man with metal parts. A sizeable steel plate had somehow been bolted into the left side of his face, and one of his hands, too, was shiny and smooth. The iron breastplate, it gradually dawned on me, was not a part of his body, but an affectation, a defiant embellishment of the eerie cyborg-image created by the metal cheek and hand. It was *fashion*. 'Say namaskar to Sammy Hazaré, our famous Tin-man,' said Mainduck from his seat behind the desk. 'He is the Captain of your appointed XI. It is time for you to take off your cook's hat, put on your whites, and go out into the field.'

～

The 'Moor in exile' sequence – the controversial 'dark Moors', born of a passionate irony that had been ground down by pain, and later unjustly accused of 'negativity', 'cynicism', even 'nihilism' – constituted the most important work of Aurora Zogoiby's later years. In them she abandoned not only the hill-palace and sea-shore motifs of the earlier pictures, but also the notion of 'pure' painting itself. Almost every piece contained elements of collage, and over time these elements became the most dominant features of the series. The unifying narrator/narrated figure of the Moor was usually still present, but was increasingly characterised as jetsam, and located in an environment of broken and discarded objects, many of which were 'found' items, pieces of crates or vanaspati tins that were fixed to the surface of the work and painted over. Unusually, however, Aurora's re-imagined 'Sultan Boabdil' was absent from what became known as the 'transitional' painting of the long Moor series, a diptych entitled *The Death of Chimène*, whose central figure – a female corpse tied to a wooden broom – was borne aloft, in the left-hand panel, by a mighty, happy throng, like a statue of rat-riding Ganesha making its way to the water on the day of the Ganpati festival. In the second, right-hand panel the crowd had dispersed, and the composition concerned itself only with a section of beach and water, in which, among broken effigies and empty bottles and soggy newspapers, lay the dead woman, lashed to her broomstick, blue and bloated, denied beauty and dignity, reduced to the status of junk.

When the Moor did reappear it was in a highly fabulated milieu, a kind of human rag-and-bone yard that took its inspiration from the jopadpatti shacks and lean-to's of the pavement dwellers and the patched-together edifices of the great slums and chawls of Bombay. Here everything was a collage, the huts made of the city's unwanted detritus, rusting corrugated iron, bits of cardboard boxes, gnarled lengths of driftwood, the doors of crashed motor-cars, the windshield of a forgotten tempo; and the tenements built out of poisonous smoke, out of water-taps that had started lethal quarrels between queuing women (e.g. Hindus versus Bene-Issack Jews), out of kerosene suicides and the unpayable rents collected with extreme violence by gangland Bhaiyyas and Pathans; and the people's lives, under the pressure that is only felt at the bottom of a heap, had also become composite, as patched-up as their homes, made of pieces of petty thievery, shards of prostitution and fragments of beggary, or, in the case of the more self-respecting individuals, of boot-polish and paper garlands and earrings and cane baskets and one-paisa-per-seam shirts and coconut milk and car-minding and cakes of carbolic soap. But Aurora, for whom reportage had never been enough, had pushed her vision several stages further; in her pieces it was the people themselves who were made of rubbish, who were collages composed of what the metropolis did not value: lost buttons, broken windscreen wipers, torn cloth, burned books, exposed camera film. They even went scavenging for their own limbs: discovering great heaps of severed body parts, they pounced on what they lacked, and they weren't too particular, couldn't afford to be choosers, so that many of them ended up with two left feet or gave up the search for buttocks and fixed a pair of plump, amputated breasts where their missing behinds should be. The Moor had entered the invisible world, the world of ghosts, of people who did not exist, and Aurora followed him into it, forcing it into visibility by the strength of her artistic will.

And the Moor-figure: alone now, motherless, he sank into immorality, and was shown as a creature of shadows, degraded in tableaux of debauchery and crime. He appeared to lose, in these last pictures, his previous metaphorical rôle as a unifier of opposites, a standard-bearer of pluralism, ceasing to stand as a symbol – however approximate – of the new nation, and being transformed, instead, into a semi-allegorical figure of decay. Aurora had apparently decided that the ideas of impurity, cultural admixture and mélange which had been, for most of her creative life, the closest things she had found to a notion of the Good, were in fact capable of distortion, and contained a potential for darkness as well as for light. This 'black Moor' was a new imagining of the idea of the hybrid – a Baudelairean flower, it would not be too far-fetched to suggest, of evil:

> . . . Aux objets répugnants nous trouvons des appas;
> Chaque jour vers l'Enfer nous descendons d'un pas,
> Sans horreur, à travers des ténèbres qui puent.

And of weakness: for he became a haunted figure, fluttered about by phantoms of his past which tormented him though he cowered and bid them begone. Then slowly he grew phantom-like himself, became a Ghost That Walked, and sank into abstraction, was robbed of his lozenges and jewels and the last vestiges of his glory; obliged to become a soldier in some petty warlord's army (here Aurora – interestingly enough – for once stayed close to the historically established facts about Sultan Boabdil), reduced to mercenary status where once he had been a king, he rapidly became a composite being as pitiful and anonymous as those amongst whom he moved. Garbage piled up, and buried him.

Repeated use was made of the diptych format, and in the second panels of these works Aurora gave us that anguished, magisterial, appallingly unguarded series of late self-portraits in which there is something of Goya and something of Rembrandt, but much more of a wild erotic despair of which there are few examples in the whole history of art. Aurora/Ayxa sat alone in these panels, beside the infernal chronicle of the degradation of her son, and never shed a tear. Her face grew hard, even stony, but in her eyes there shone a horror that was never named – as if she were looking at a thing that struck at the very depths of her soul, a thing standing before her, where anyone looking at the pictures would naturally stand – as if the human race itself had shown her its most secret and terrorising face, and by doing so had petrified her, turning her old flesh to stone. These 'Portraits of Ayxa' are ominous, lowering works.

In the Ayxa panels, too, there recurred the twin themes of doubles, and of ghosts. A phantom-Ayxa haunted the garbaged Moor; and behind Ayxa/Aurora, at times, hovered the faint translucent images of a woman and a man. Their faces were left blank. Was the woman Uma (Chimène), or was it Aurora herself? And was I – or rather 'the Moor' – the phantom male? And if not I, then who? In these 'ghost' or 'double' portraits, the Ayxa/Aurora figure looks – or am I imagining this? – hunted, the way Uma looked when I went to see her after the news of Jimmy Cash's accident. I'm not imagining it. I know that look. She looks as if she might be coming to pieces. She looks pursued.

～

As, in those pictures, she pursued me. As if she were a witch upon a crag, watching me in her crystal ball with a winged monkey by her side. For it was true: I was moving through those dark places, across the moon, behind the sun, which she created in her work. I inhabited her fictions and the eye of her imagination saw me plain. Or almost: because there were things she could not imagine, things which even her piercing eye could not see.

What she missed in herself was the snobbery that her contemptuous rage revealed, her fear of the invisible city, the Malabar-ness of her. How radical Aurora, the nationalists' queen, would have hated that! To have it pointed out that in her later years she was just another *grande dame* on the Hill, sipping tea and looking with distaste upon the poor man at her gate . . . And what she missed in me was that in that surreal stratum, with a tin man, a toothsome scarecrow and a cowardly frog for company (for Mainduck was certainly a coward – he did none of his own rough stuff), I found, for the first time in my short-long life, the feeling of normality, of being *nothing special*, the sense of being among kindred spirits, among people-like-me, that is the defining quality of home.

There was a thing that Raman Fielding knew, which was his power's secret source: that it is not the civil social norm for which men yearn, but the outrageous, the outsize, the out-of-bounds – for that by which our wild potency may be unleashed. We crave permission openly to become our secret selves.

So, mother: in that dreadful company, doing those dreadful deeds, without need of magic slippers, I found my own way home.

◡

I admit it: I am a man who has delivered many beatings. I have brought violence to many doorsteps, the way a postman brings the mail. I have done the dirty as and when required – done it, and taken pleasure in the doing. Did I not tell you with what difficulty I had learned left-handedness, how unnaturally it came to me? Very well: but now I could be right-handed at last, in my new life of action I could remove my doughty hammer from my pocket and set it free to write the story of my life. It served me well, my club. In quick time I became one of the MA's élite enforcers, alongside Tin-man Hazaré and Chhaggan Five-in-a-Bite (who, it will come as no surprise to learn, was something of an all-rounder, too, with talents that no kitchen could contain). Hazaré's XI – whose eight other component hoodlums were every whit as deadly as we three – reigned unchallenged for a decade as the MA's Team of Teams. So as well as the pure magnificence of our unleashed force there were the rewards of high achievement, and the virile pleasures of comradeship and all-for-one.

Can you understand with what delight I wrapped myself in the simplicity of my new life? For I did; I revelled in it. At last, I told myself, a little straightforwardness; at last you are what you were born to be. With what relief I abandoned my lifelong quest for an unattainable normality, with what joy I revealed my super-nature to the world! Can you imagine how much anger had been banked in me by the circumscriptions and emotional complexities of my previous existence – how much resentment at the world's rejections, at the overheard giggles of women, at teachers' sneers, how much unexpressed wrath at the exigencies of my sheltered, necessarily withdrawn, friendless, and finally mother-murdered life? It was that lifetime of fury that had begun to explode from my fist. *Dhhaamm! Dhhoomm!* O, sure thing, misters 'n' begums: I knew how to give what-for, and I also had a good idea of why Keep your disapproval! Put it where the sun don't shine! Go sit in a movie theatre and take note that the guy getting the biggest cheers is no longer the loverboy or heero – it's the guy in the black hat, stabbing shooting kickboxing and generally pulverising his way through the film! O, *baby*. Violence today is *hot*. It is what people *want*.

My early years were spent breaking the great textile mill strike. My allotted task was to form part of Sammy Hazaré's unofficial flying wedge of masked avengers. After the authorities moved in to break up a demonstration with sticks and gas – and in those years there were agitations in every part of the city, organized by Dr Datta Samant, his Kamgar Aghadi political party and his Maharashtra Girni Kamgar union of textile workers – the MA's crack teams would select and pursue individual, randomly selected demonstrators, not giving up until we had cornered them and given them the beating of their lives. We had given much deep thought to the matter of our masks, finally rejecting the idea of using the faces of the Bollywood stars of the time in favour of the more historic Indian folk-tradition of bahurupi travelling players, in mimicry of whom we gave ourselves the heads of lions and tigers and bears. It proved a good decision, enabling us to enter the strikers' consciousness as mythological avengers. We had only to appear on the scene for the workers to flee screaming into the dark gullies where we ran them to ground to face the consequences of their deeds. As an interesting side-effect of this work I got to know large new sections of the city: in '82 and '83 I must have gone down every back-alley in Worli, Parel and Bhiwandi in pursuit of union-wallah dross, activist scruff and Communist scum. I use these terms not pejoratively but, if I may so put it, technically. For all industrial processes produce waste matter that must be scraped away, discarded, purged, so that excellence may emerge. The strikers were instances of such waste matter. We removed them. At the end of the strike there were sixty thousand fewer jobs in the mills than there had been at the beginning, and industrialists were at last able to modernise their plant. We skimmed off the filth, and left a sparkling, up-to-date powerloom industry behind. This was how Mainduck explained it, personally, to me.

I punched, while others preferred to kick. With my bare hand I clubbed my victims viciously, metronomically – like carpets, like mules. Like time. I did not speak. The beating was its own language and would make its own meaning plain. I beat people by night and by day, sometimes briefly, rendering them unconscious with a single hammer-blow, and on other occasions more lingeringly, applying my right hand to their softer zones and grimacing inwardly at their screams. It was a point of pride to keep one's outward expression neutral, impassive, void. Those whom we beat did not look us in the eye. After we had worked them over for a while their noises stopped; they seemed at peace with our fists boots clubs. They, too, became impassive, empty-eyed.

A man who is beaten seriously (as dreaming Oliver D'Aeth had intuited long ago) will be irreversibly changed. His relationship to his own body, to his mind, to the world beyond himself alters in ways both subtle and overt. A certain confidence, a certain idea of liberty is beaten out for good; always provided the beater knows his job. Often, what is beaten in is detachment. The victim – how often I saw this! – detaches himself from the event, and sends his consciousness to float in the air above. He seems to look down upon himself, on his own body as it convulses and perhaps breaks. Afterwards he will never fully re-enter himself, and invitations to join any larger, collective entity – a union, for example – are instantly rebuffed.

Beatings in different zones of the body affect different parts of the soul. To be beaten for a long time upon the soles of the feet, for example, affects laughter. Those who are so beaten never laugh again.

Only those who embrace their fate, who accept their thrashing, taking it like men – only those who put their hands up, acknowledge their guilt, say their *mea culpas* – can find something of value in the experience, something positive. Only they can say: 'At least we learned our lesson.'

As for the beater: he, too, is changed. To beat a man is a kind of exaltation, a revelatory act, opening strange gates in the universe. Time and space come away from their moorings, their hinges. Chasms yawn. There are glimpses of amazing things. I saw, at times, the past and the future too. It was hard to cling to these memories. At the end of the work, they faded. But I remembered that something had happened. That there were visions. This was enriching news.

We broke the strike in the end. I will allow that I was surprised at how long it took, at the workers' loyalty to scum and dross and scruff. But – as Raman Fielding told us – the mill strike was the MA's proving ground, it honed us, it made us ready. In the next municipal elections Dr Samant's party got a handful of seats and the MA won more than seventy. The bandwagon had begun to roll.

And shall I tell you how – at the local feudal landowner's invitation – we visited a village near the Gujarat border, where the freshly gathered red chillies stood around the houses in low hills of colour and spice, and put down a revolt of female workers? But no, perhaps not; your fastidious stomach would be upset by such hot stuff. Shall I speak of our campaign against those out-caste unfortunates, untouchables or Harijans or Dalits, call them what you please, who had in their vanity thought to escape the caste system by converting to Islam? Shall I describe the steps by which we returned them to their place beyond the social pale? – Or shall I speak of the time Hazaré's XI was called upon to enforce the ancient custom of sati, and elaborate on how, in a certain village, we persuaded a young widow to mount her husband's funeral pyre?

No, no. You've heard enough. After six years' hard work in the field we had reaped a rich harvest. The MA had taken political control of the city; it was Mayor Mainduck now. Even in the most remote rural areas, where ideas such as Fielding's had never before taken root, people had begun to speak of the coming kingdom of Lord Ram, and to say that the country's 'Mughals' must be taught the same lesson that the millworkers had so painfully learned. And events on a greater stage also played their part in the bloody game of consequences that our history has a way of becoming. A golden temple harboured armed men, and was attacked, and the armed men were slain; and the consequence was, armed men murdered the Prime Minister; and the consequence was, mobs, armed and unarmed, roamed the capital and murdered innocent persons who had nothing in common with any of the armed men except a turban; and the consequence was, that men like Fielding who spoke of the need to tame the country's minorities, to subject one and all to the tough-loving rule of Ram, gained a certain momentum, a certain extra strength.

. . . And I am told that on the day of Mrs Gandhi's death – the same Mrs Gandhi whom she had loathed and who had enthusiastically returned the compliment – my mother Aurora Zogoiby burst into torrential tears . . .

Victory is victory: in the election that brought Fielding to power, the millworkers' organisations backed the MA candidates. Nothing like showing people who is boss . . .

. . . And if at times I found myself vomiting without apparent cause, if all my dreams were infernos, what of it? If I had a constant and growing sense of being followed, yes, perhaps by vengeance, then I set such thoughts aside. They belonged to my old life, that amputated limb; I wanted nothing to do with such qualms, such foibles now. I awoke sweating with terror from a nightmare, mopped my brow, and went back to sleep.

It was Uma who pursued me through my dreams, dead Uma, made frightful by death, Uma wild-haired, white-eyed, fork-tongued, Uma metamorphosed into an angel of revenge, playing a hellbat Dis-demona to my Moor. Fleeing from her, I would run into a mighty fortress, slam its doors shut, turn – and find myself outside once again, and she floating in air, above me and behind, Uma with vampire's fangs the size of elephant's tusks. And again in front of me was a fortress, its doors standing open, offering me sanctuary; and again I ran, and slammed the door, and found myself still in the open air, defenceless, at her mercy. 'You know how the Moors built,' she whispered to me. 'Theirs was a mosaic architecture of interlinked insides and outsides – gardens framed by palaces framed by gardens and so on. But you – I condemn you to exteriors from now on. For you there are no safe palaces any more; and in these gardens I will wait for you. Across these infinite outsides I will hunt you down.' Then she came down to me, and opened her awful mouth.

To the devil with such fear-of-the-dark childishness! – Or so, waking from these horrors, I reproved myself. I was a man; would act as a man acts, making my way and bearing any consequential burdens. – And if, at times in those years, both Aurora Zogoiby and I had a feeling of being pursued, then it was because – O most prosaic of explanations! – it was true. As I would learn after my mother's death, Abraham Zogoiby had had us both followed for years. He was a man who liked to be in possession of information. And while he had been prepared to tell Aurora most of what he knew about my activities – thus becoming the source from which she created the 'exile' paintings; so much for crystal balls! – he did not feel it necessary to mention that he had also been checking up on her. In their old age they had drifted so far apart as to be almost out of each other's earshot, and exchanged few unnecessary words. At any rate, Dom Minto, almost ninety years old now but once again the head of the city's leading private investigation agency, had kept us under surveillance at Abraham's behest. But Minto must take a back seat for a while. Miss Nadia Wadia is waiting in the wings.

~

Yes, there were women, I won't attempt to deny it. Crumbs from Fielding's table. I recall a Smita, a Shobha, a Rekha, an Urvashi, an Anju and a Manju, among others. Also a striking number of non-Hindu ladies: slightly soiled Dollies, Marias and Gurinders, none of whom lasted long. Sometimes, too, at the Skipper's request I 'undertook commissions': that is, I was sent out like a party girl to pleasure some rich bored matron in her tower, offering personal favours in return for gifts to party coffers. I also accepted payment if it was offered. It made no difference to me. I was congratulated by Fielding on 'showing a genuine aptitude' for such work.

But I never touched Nadia Wadia. Nadia Wadia was different. She was a beauty queen – Miss Bombay and Miss India 1987, and, later the same year, Miss World. In more than one magazine, comparisons were made between this newly arrived just-seventeen-year-old and the lost, lamented Ina Zogoiby, my sister, to whom she was alleged to bear a strong resemblance. (I couldn't see it; but then, in the matter of resemblances, I was always a little slow. When Abraham Zogoiby suggested that Uma Sarasvati had something in her of the young Aurora, that imposing fifteen-yearold with whom he had fallen so fatefully in love, it came as news to me.) Fielding wanted Nadia – tall, Valkyrean Nadia, who had a walk like a warrior and a voice like a dirty phone call, serious Nadia who donated a percentage of her prize-money to hospitals for children and who wanted to be a doctor when she had grown tired of making the planet's males ill with desire – wanted her more than anyone on earth. She had what he lacked, and what, in Bombay, he knew he needed before his package was complete. She had glamour. And she called him a toad to his face at a civic reception; so she had guts, and needed to be tamed.

Mainduck wanted to possess Nadia, to hang her like a trophy on his arm; but Sammy Hazaré, his most loyal lieutenant – hideous Sammy, half-man, half-can – made a bad mistake, and fell in love.

Me, I had grown uninterested in the love of women. Truthfully. After Uma, something had been switched off in me, some fuse had been blown. My employer's not infrequent magisterial leavings, and the 'commissions', were enough to satisfy me, easy-come-easy-go as they were. There was also the question of my age. When I turned thirty, my body turned sixty, and not a particularly youthful sixty, at that. Age flooded over my crumbling vellards and took possession of the lowlands of my being. My breathing difficulties had now increased to the point at which I had to retire from flying-wedge activities. No more chases down slum alleys and up the staircases of tawdry tenements for me. Long sensual nights were likewise no longer an option; these days, at best, I was strictly a one-trick pony. Fielding, lovingly, offered me work in his personal secretariat, and the least athletically inclined of his courtesans ... But Sammy, a decade older than me in years but twenty years younger in body, Sammy the Tin-man still dreamed. No breathing problems there; in Mainduck's nocturnal Olympics, either he or Chhaggan Five-in-a-Bite won the impromptu lung-power contests (holding of breath, blowing of a tiny dart through a long metal blowpipe, extinguishing of candles) every time.

Hazaré was a Christian Maharashtrian, and had joined up with Fielding's crew for regionalist, rather than religious reasons. O, we all had reasons, personal or ideological. There are always reasons. You can get reasons in any chor bazaar, any thieves' market, reasons by the bunch, ten chips the dozen. Reasons are cheap, cheap as politicians' answers, they come tripping off the tongue: *I did it for the money, the uniform, the togetherness, the family, the race, the nation, the god*. But what truly drives us – what makes us hit, and kick, and kill, what makes us conquer our enemies and our fears – is not to be found in any such bazaar-bought words. Our engines are stranger, and use darker fuel. Sammy Hazaré, for instance, was driven by bombs. Explosives, which had already claimed a hand and half his jaw, were his first love, and the speeches in which he sought – unsuccessfully, thus far – to persuade Fielding of the political value of an Irish-style bombing campaign were delivered with all the passion of Cyrano wooing his Roxane. But if bombs were the Tin-man's first love, Nadia Wadia was his second.

Fielding's Bombay Municipal Corporation had arranged to give their girl a big send-off to the beauty finals in Granada, Spain. At the party, Nadia, free-spirited Parsi lovely that she was, spurned the reactionary, hard-line Mainduck in full view of the cameras ('Shri Raman, in my personal opinion you are not so much frog as toad, and I do not think so that if I kissed you you would turn into a prince,' she replied loudly to his clumsily murmured invitation to a private tête-à-tête) and – to underline her point – deliberately turned her charms upon his rather metallic personal bodyguard. (I was the other one; but was spared.) 'Tell me,' she purred at paralysed, sweating Sammy, 'do you think so I can win?'

Sammy couldn't speak. He turned puce, and made a distant

gargling noise. Nadia Wadia nodded gravely, as if she had been the beneficiary of true wisdom.

'When I entered Miss Bombay competition,' she growled, as Sammy quaked, 'my boyfriend said to me, O, Nadia Wadia, look at those so-so beautiful ladies, I don't think so you can win. But anyway, you see, I won!' Sammy reeled beneath the violence of her smile.

'Then when I entered Miss India competition,' breathed Nadia, 'my boyfriend said to me, O, Nadia Wadia, look at those so-so beautiful ladies, I don't think so you can win. But again, you see, I won!' Most of us in that room were wondering at the lèse-majesté of this unseen boyfriend, and finding it unsurprising that he had not been asked to accompany Nadia Wadia to this reception. Mainduck was trying to look graceful about having recently been called a toad; and Sammy – well, Sammy was just trying not to faint.

'But now it is Miss World competition,' pouted Nadia. 'And I look in the magazine at the colour photos of all those so-so beautiful ladies, and I say to myself, Nadia Wadia, I don't think so you can win.' She looked yearningly at Sammy, craving the Tin-man's reassurance, while Raman Fielding stood ignored and desperate at her elbow.

Sammy burst into speech. 'But, Madam, never mind!' he blurted. 'You will get club-class round trip to Europe, and see such great things, and meet the great persons of the world. You will acquit yourself excellently and carry our national flag with honour. Yes! I am certain-sure. So, Madam, forget this winning. Who are those judges-shudges? For us – for people of India – you are already and always the winner.' It was the most eloquent speech of his life.

Nadia Wadia feigned dismay. 'Oh,' she moaned, breaking his inexpert heart as she moved away. 'Then you also don't think so I can win.'

There was a song about Nadia Wadia after she conquered the world:

> *Nadia Wadia you've gone fardia*
> *Whole of India has admiredia*

*Whole of world you put in whirlia*
*Beat their girls for you were girlia*

*I will buy you a brand new cardia*
*Let me be your bodyguardia*

*I love Nadia Wadia hardia.*
*Hardia, Nadia Wadia, hardia.*

Nobody could stop singing it, certainly not the Tin-man. *Let me be your bodyguardia . . .* the line seemed to him like a message from the gods, an intimation of destiny. I also heard a tuneless version of the song being hummed behind Mainduck's office doors; for Nadia Wadia after her victory became an emblem of the nation, like Lady Liberty or the Marianne, she became the repository of our pride and self-belief. I could see how this affected Fielding, whose aspirations were beginning to burst the bounds of the city of Bombay and the state of Maharashtra; he gave up the mayor's office to a fellow-MA politico and began to dream of bestriding the national stage, preferably with Nadia Wadia standing at his side. *Hardia, Nadia Wadia . . .* Raman Fielding, that hideously driven man, had set himself a new goal.

The Ganpati festival came round. It was the fortieth anniversary of Independence, and the MA-controlled Municipal Corporation tried to make this the most impressive Ganesha Chaturthi on record. Worshippers and their effigies were trucked in from outlying areas in their thousands. MA slogans on their saffron banners were all over the town. A special VIP stand was built just off Chowpatty, next to the footbridge; and Raman Fielding invited the new Miss World as guest of honour, and, out of respect for the festive day, she accepted. So the first part of his fantasy had come true, and he was standing beside her as the hooligan cadres came past in their MA trucks, waving clenched fists and hurling colour and flower petals into the air. Fielding made a stiff-armed, open-palmed reply; and Nadia Wadia, seeing the Nazi salute, turned away her face. But Fielding was in a kind of ecstasy that day; and as the noise of Ganpati mounted to almost unbearable heights, he turned to me – I was standing right behind him with Sammy the Tin-man, jammed against the back of the crowded little stand – and bellowed with all his might: 'Now it is time to take on your father. Now we are strong enough for Zogoiby, for Scar, for anyone. *Ganpati Bappa morya!* Who will stand against us now?' And in his voluptuous pleasure he seized the horrified Nadia Wadia's long, slender hand, and kissed it on the palm. 'Lo, I kiss Mumbai, I kiss India!' he screamed. 'Behold, I kiss the world!'

Nadia Wadia's reply was inaudible, drowned by the cheering of the crowds.

～

That night, on the news, I heard that my mother had fallen to her death while dancing her annual dance against the gods. It was like a validation of Fielding's confidence; for her death made Abraham weaker, and Mainduck had grown strong. In the radio and TV reports I thought I could detect a rueful apologetic note, as though the reporters and obituarists and critics were conscious of how grievously that great, proud woman had been wronged – of their responsibility for the grim retreat of her last years. And indeed in the days and months that followed her death her star rose higher than it had ever been, people rushed to re-evaluate and praise her work with an ambulance-chasing haste that made me very angry. If she merited these words now, then she had merited them before. I never knew a stronger woman, nor one with a clearer sense of who and what she was, but she had been wounded, and these words – which might have healed her if spoken while she could still hear – came too late. Aurora da Gama Zogoiby, 1924–87. The numbers had closed over her like the sea.

And the painting they found on her easel was about me. In that last work, *The Moor's Last Sigh*, she gave the Moor back his humanity. This was no abstract harlequin, no junkyard collage. It was a portrait of her son, lost in limbo like a wandering shade: a portrait of a soul in Hell. And behind him, his mother, no longer in a separate panel, but re-united with the tormented Sultan. Not berating him – *well may you weep like a woman* – but looking

315

frightened and stretching out her hand. This, too, was an apology that came too late, an act of forgiveness from which I could no longer profit. I had lost her, and the picture only intensified the pain of the loss.

O mother, mother. I know why you banished me now. O my great dead mother, my duped progenitrix, my fool.

# 17

ECALCITRANT, UNREGENERATE, PARAMOUNT: THE *Over World's* cackling overlord in his hanging garden in the sky, rich beyond rich men's richest dreams, Abraham Zogoiby at eighty-four reached for immortality, long-fingered as the dawn. Though he always feared an early death, he had made old bones; Aurora died instead. His own health had improved with age. He still limped, there were still breathing difficulties, but his heart was stronger than at any time since Lonavla, his sight sharper, his hearing more acute. He tasted food as if eating it for the first time, and in his business dealings could always smell a rat. Fit, mentally agile, sexually active, he already contained elements of the divine – had already risen far above the herd, and of course above the Law as well. Not for him those sinuous wordshackles, those due processes, those paper bounds. Now, after Aurora's fall, he decided to refuse death altogether. Sometimes, sitting astride the highest needle in the giant bright pincushion at the city's southern tip, he marvelled at his destiny, he filled with feeling, he looked down on moon-glistened nightwater and seemed to see, beneath its mask, his wife lying broken amid the crabs' dogged scuttles, the clinging of shells, and the bright knives of fish, whole regimented canteens of them, filleting her fatal sea. Not for me, he demurred. I have just begun to live.

Once by a southern shore he had seen himself as a part of Beauty, as one half of a magic ring, completed by that wilful brilliant girl. He had feared the defeat of loveliness by what was ugly in the earth, sea and ourselves. How long ago that was! Two daughters and a wife dead, a third girl gone to Jesus and the young-old boy to Hell. How long since he was beautiful, since beauty made him a conspirator in love! How long since unsanctified vows acquired legitimacy through the force of their desire, like coal crushed by heavy aeons into a faceted jewel. But she turned away from him, his beloved, she did not keep her part of the bargain, and he lost himself in his.

*In what was worldly, what was of the earth and in the nature of things, he found comfort for the loss of what he had touched, through her love, of the transcendent, the transformational, the immense. Now that she had gone, leaving him with the world in his hand, he would wrap himself in his might, like a golden cloak. Wars were brewing; he would win them. New shores were visible; he would take them by storm. He would not emulate her fall.*

*She received a state funeral. He stood by her open casket in the cathedral and let his thoughts run on new strategies of gain. Of the three pillars of life, God, family and money, he had only one, and needed a minimum of two. Minnie came to say her farewells to her mother but seemed somehow too glad.* The devout rejoice in death, *Abraham thought*, they think it's the door to God's chamber of glory. But that's an empty room. Eternity is here on earth and money won't buy it. Immortality is dynasty. I need my outcast son.

ᔕ

When I found a message from Abraham Zogoiby tucked neatly under the pillow of my bed in Raman Fielding's house, I understood for the first time how great his power had grown. 'Do you know who your Daddyji is, high in his tower?' Mainduck had asked me, before unleashing a mad tirade about anti-Hindu robots and what-not. The note under my pillow made me wonder what else might or might not be true, for there in the sanctums of the Under World I had been shown, by this casual demonstration of the length of my father's arm, that Abraham would be a formidable antagonist in the coming war of the worlds, Under versus Over, sacred versus profane, god versus mammon, past versus future, gutter versus sky: that struggle between two layers of power in which I, and Nadia Wadia, and Bombay, and even India itself would find ourselves trapped, like dust between coats of paint.

*Racecourse*, read the note, written in his own hand. *Paddock. Before the third race.* Forty days had passed since my mother was laid to rest in my absence, with cannons firing a salute. Forty days and now this magically delivered but utterly banal communication, this withered olive branch. Of course I would not go, I first thought in

318

predictable, wounded pride. But just as predictably, and without informing Mainduck, off I went.

Children at Mahalaxmi played ankh micholi, hide-and-go-seek, in and out of the crowds of adult legs. This is how we are to one another, I thought, divided by generations. Do jungle animals understand the true nature of the trees among which they have their daily being? In the parent-forest, amid those mighty trunks, we shelter and play; but whether the trees are healthy or corroded, whether they harbour demons or good sprites, we cannot say. Nor do we know the greatest secret of all: that one day we, too, will become as arboreal as they. And the trees, whose leaves we eat, whose bark we gnaw, remember sadly that they were animals once, they climbed like squirrels and bounded like deer, until one day they paused, and their legs grew down into the earth and stuck there, spreading, and vegetation sprouted from their swaying heads. They remember this as a fact; but the lived reality of their fauna-years, the how-it-felt of that chaotic freedom, is beyond recapture. They remember it as a rustle in their leaves. *I don't know my father*, I thought at the paddock before the third race. *We are strangers. He will not know me when he sees me, and will pass blindly by.*

Something – a small parcel – was being pushed into my hand. Somebody whispered, quickly: 'I need an answer before we can proceed.' A man in a white suit, wearing a white panama, pushed into the human forest, and was gone. Children screamed and fought at my feet. *Here I come ready or not.*

I tore open the packet in my hand. I had seen this thing before, clipped to Uma's belt. These headphones once adorned her lovely head. *Always mangling my tapes. I chucked it in a bin.* Another lie; another game of hide-and-seek. I saw her running away from me, dodging into the human thickets with an unnerving rabbit-like scream. What would I find when I found her? I put the headphones on, lengthening them until the earpieces fitted. There was the *play* button. I don't want to play, I thought. I don't like this game.

I pushed the button. My own voice, dripping poison, filled my ears.

You know those people who claim to have been captured by

aliens and subjected to unspeakable experiments and tortures – sleep deprivation, dissection without anaesthesia, prolonged tickling of the armpits, hot chillis inserted into the rectum, overexposure to marathon performances of Chinese opera? I must tell you that after I stopped listening to the tape in Uma's Walkman I felt I had been in the clutches of just such an unearthly fiend. I imagined a chameleon-like creature, a cold-blooded lizard from across the cosmos, who could take human form, male or female as required, for the express purpose of making as much trouble as possible, because trouble was its staple diet – its rice, its lentils, its bread. Turbulence, disruption, misery, catastrophe, grief: all these were on the menu of its preferred foods. It came among us – *she* (on this occasion) came among us – as a farmer of discontents, a fomentor of war, seeing in me (O fool! O thrice-assed dolt!) a fertile field for her pestilential seeds. Peace, serenity, joy were deserts to her – for if her noisome crops failed, she would starve. She ate our divisions, and grew strong upon our rows.

Even Aurora – Aurora, who saw the truth of her from the start – had succumbed in the end. No doubt it had been a point of pride for Uma; like the great predator she was, she had been most eager to devour the most elusive prey. Nothing she could have said would have taken my mother in. Knowing this, she used my words – my angry, awful, lust-provoked obscenities – instead. Yes, she had recorded it all, had gone that far; and with what seduction she led me down that road, eliciting the fatal phrases by making me think they were what she needed to hear! I do not excuse myself. The words were mine, I said them. A lesser fool would have said less. But loving her and knowing my mother's opposition I spoke at first in rage, then in confirmation of the primacy of romantic love over the mother-son variety; coming from a house where easy obscenities had always peppered and spiced our conversational dishes, I did not flinch from fuck and cunt and screw. And then continued these dark murmurs, because in our lovemaking she, my lover, asked – how often she asked! – that I tell her those things, to heal – O most false! O foully false and falsely foul! – her wounded confidence and pride. Your lover asks, in loving's midst, for your endorsement of her need; she needs you, so she says, to need it too: do you refuse? Well, if so, so. I do not know your secrets, nor desire to know more. But perhaps you do not refuse. Yes, you say, O my love, yes, I also need, I do.

I spoke in the privacy and complicity of the act of love. Which, too, was a part of Uma's deception, a necessary means to her end.

Forty-five minutes a side of our lovemaking's edited highlights were on that sad cassette, and running through the bump and grind, the loathsome leitmotif. *Fuck her. Yes I want to. God I do. Fuck my mother. Screw her. Screw the fucking bitch.* And each coarse syllable drove a skewer into my mother's broken heart.

When Aurora was already deep in shock, with Mynah newly dead, the creature seized its moment, disguising her errand of hate as a pilgrimage of love. She gave my parents the tape that night, she went there for that purpose and no other, and I can only guess at their terror and hurt, can only create my own image of the scene – Aurora slumped all night on the piano-stool in her orange and gold saloon, old Abraham hand-wringing helplessly against a wall, and through a shadowed doorway a glimpse of frightened servants, fluttering like trembling hands at the edges of the frame.

And the next morning, when I left her bed, Uma must have known what awaited me at home – the grimly ashen faces in the garden, the hand pointing at the gates: *go, get thee from hence and never return any more.* And when in my bewilderment I came back to her flat, how she surpassed herself! What a performance she gave that day! – But now I knew everything. No more benefits of doubts. Uma, my beloved traitor, you were ready to play the game to the end; to murder me and watch my death while hallucinogens blew your mind. Later, no doubt, you would have announced my tragic suicide: 'Such a sad family quarrel, poor tender-hearted man, he could not bear. And the death of a sister too.' But farce intervened, a lunge, a slapstick clash of heads, and then, like the great actress and gambler you were, you played the scene out to the end; and came out on the wrong side of a fifty-fifty bet. Even absolute evil has its impressive side. Lady, I doff my hat; and so goodnight.

That rabbity scream again; it hangs on the air, and fades. As if some ancient malignity, unable to bear truth's light, were dissolving into dust . . . but no, I will permit myself no such fancies.

She was a woman, of woman born. Let her be seen as such . . . *Mad or bad?* I no longer have a problem with that question. Just as I have rejected all supernatural theories (alien invaders, rabbit-screechy vampires), so also I will not allow her to be mad. Space-lizards, undead bloodsuckers and insane persons are excused from moral judgment, and Uma deserves to be judged. *Insaan*, a human being. I insist on Uma's insaanity.

This, too, is what we are like. We, too, are planters of winds, and harvesters of hurricanes. There are those among us – not alien but insaan – who eat devastation; who, without a regular supply of mayhem, cannot thrive. My Uma was one of those.

Six years! Six years of Aurora, twelve of Moor, lost. My mother was sixty-three when she died; I looked sixty myself. We might have been brother and sister. We might have been friends. 'I need an answer,' my father had said at the races. Yes, he must have one. It must be the plain truth; everything about Uma and Aurora, Aurora and me, me and Uma Sarasvati, my witch. I would set it all down, and surrender myself to his sentence. As Yul Brynner, in Pharaonic mode (that is, a rather fetching short skirt), was so fond of saying in *The Ten Commandments*: 'So let it be written. So let it be done.'

⌒

There had been a second note, placed beneath my pillow by an unseen hand. There had been instructions, and a master key, which had unlocked a certain unguarded service entrance at the rear of Cashondeliveri Tower, and also the door to a private elevator leading directly to the thirty-first floor penthouse. There had been a reconciliation, an explanation accepted, a son gathered to his father's bosom, a broken bond renewed.

'O my boy your age, your age.'

'O my father and also yours.'

There was a clear night, a high garden, a talk such as we had not had before.

'My boy, hide nothing from me. I know everything already. I

have eyes that see and ears that hear and I know your deeds and misdeeds.'

And before I could make any attempt at justification, there was a raised hand, a grin, a cackle. 'I am pleased,' he said. 'You left me as a boy and you have come back as a man. Now we can talk as men of manly things. Once you loved your mother more. I do not blame you. I was the same. But now it is your father's turn; a turn, I should more rightly say, for us. Now I can ask if you will join your force to mine, and hope to speak freely of many hidden things. There is at my age a question of trust. There is a need to speak my heart, to unlock my locks, to unveil my mysteries. Great things are afoot. That Fielding, who is he? A bug. At best a Pluto of the Under World and we know from Miranda's nursery what is Pluto. A stupid collared dog. Or now, one can maybe say, a frog.'

There was a dog. In a special corner of the soaring atrium, a stuffed bull terrier on wheels. 'You kept him,' I wondered. 'Aires's old Jawaharlal.'

'For old times' sake. Sometimes on this leash, in this little garden, I take Jaw-jaw for a walk.'

Now came danger.

Having agreed with my father to be his man, to know what he knew and assist him in his enterprises, I agreed, also, to remain for a time in Fielding's employ. So to betray my master to my father I returned into my master's house. And told Mainduck – for he was no fool – something of the truth. 'It is good to heal a family quarrel but it does not affect my choices.' Which Fielding, being kindly disposed towards me by reason of my six years of service, accepted; and suspected.

He would watch me always from now on, I knew. My first mistake would be my last. I am a part of the battlefield, I thought, and they are the bloody war.

When my team-mates – my old comrades in battle – heard my happy news:

Chhaggan shrugged. As though to say: 'You never were one of us, rich boy. Neither Hindu nor Mahratta. Just a cook with an upper-class blood-line and a fist. You came here to gratify that hammer. Pervert! Just another psycho in search of a rumble – you cared nothing for our cause. And now your class, your heredity, has come to fetch you back. You won't be here much longer. Why would you stay? You've grown too old to fight.'

But Sammy Hazaré the Tin-man gave me looks. So many that I knew at once whose hand had slipped papers under my pillow, who was my father's man. Sammy the Christian, seduced by Abraham the Jew.

O, Moor, beware, I murmured to myself. The conflict approaches, and the future itself is the prize. Beware, lest in that battle you lose your silly head.

~

Later, in his high-rise garden, Abraham told me how often, in those long years, Aurora had yearned to extend forgiveness's hand, and – undoing her gesture of banishment – beckon me home. But then she would remember my voice, my unspeakable words that could not be rendered unspoken, and harden her maternal heart. When I heard this, the lost years began to prey upon me, to obsess me day and night. In my sleep I invented time machines that would permit me to travel back beyond the frontier of her death; and I would be furious, when I woke, that the journey was just a dream.

After some months of such frustrations I remembered Vasco Miranda's portrait of my mother, and realised that in this small way, at least, I might be able to have her back again: in long art, if not short life. Of course her own work was full of self-portraits, but the lost Miranda picture, overpainted and sold off, somehow came to represent my lost mother, Abraham's lost wife. If we could but rediscover it! It would be like her younger self reborn; it would be a victory over death. Excitedly I told my father my idea. He frowned. 'That picture.' But his objections had faded with the years. I could see desire dawning on his face. 'But it was destroyed long ago.'

'Not destroyed,' I corrected him. 'Painted over. *The Artist as Boabdil, the Unlucky (el-Zogoybi), Last Sultan of Granada, Seen Departing from the Alhambra. Or, The Moor's Last Sigh.* That tearful equestrian chocolate-box picture which Mummyji said was worse than even a bazaar painter's scrawl. To remove it would be no loss. And then we would have her back.'

'Remove it, you say.' I could tell that the idea of vandalising a Miranda, in particular the Miranda in which Vasco had purloined our own family legends, found favour with old Abraham in his lair. 'This is possible?'

'It must be,' I said. 'There must be experts. If you wish I can inquire.'

'But the picture is Bhabha's,' he said. 'Will that old bastard sell?'

'If the price is right,' I replied. And, to clinch it, added, 'Doesn't matter how big a bastard he is, he isn't as big as you.'

Abraham cackled and picked up the telephone. 'Zogoiby,' he told the flunkey at the other end. 'C.P. is?' And a moment later, 'Arré, C.P. Why are you hiding out from your pals?' Then some phrases – almost barked – of negotiations, in which the staccato toughness of his delivery was strikingly at odds with the words he employed, soft, curlicued words of flattery and deference. Then a sudden cessation, as of a car engine that unexpectedly stalls; and Abraham replaced the handset with a puzzle on his brow. 'Stolen,' he said. 'Within last weeks. Stolen from his private home.'

⌒

News came from Spain that the veteran (and increasingly eccentric) Indian-born painter V. Miranda, presently a resident of the Andalusian village of Benengeli, had injured himself while attempting the enigmatic feat of painting a full-grown elephant from underneath. The elephant, an ill-fed circus performer hired for the day at excessive expense, had been intended to climb a concrete ramp, specially constructed for the purpose by the celebrated (but temperamentally erratic) Señor Miranda himself, and then to stand upon a sheet of improbably reinforced glass, beneath which old Vasco had set up his easel. Journalists and television crews massed in Benengeli to record this curious stunt. However, Isabella the elephant, in spite of being accustomed to all manner of three-ring tomfoolery, had the delicacy of sensibility to refuse to co-operate in what some local commentators had dubbed a 'degraded act' of 'underbelly voyeurism', in which the wastrel wantonness, self-indulgent amorality and ultimate inutility of all art seemed to be encapsulated. The artist emerged from his palazzo with his moustachio-tips standing at attention. He had dressed, with an absurdity that might have been a deliberate use of incongruity – or else simply deranged – in Tyrolean short trousers and embroidered shirt, and there was a stick of celery rising from his hat. Isabella had stopped halfway up the ramp and all her attendants' efforts could not budge her. The artist clapped his hands. 'Elephant! Obey!' At which command, backing contemptuously off the ramp, Isabella stepped on Vasco Miranda's left foot. The more conservative locals among the crowd that had gathered to witness the spectacle had the bad manners to applaud.

After that Vasco had a limp to match Abraham's, but in all other ways their paths remained divergent, or so, to outsiders, it would surely have appeared. The failure of his elephant venture did not in the least diminish the madcap enthusiasms of his old age, and soon, thanks to the payment of a substantial charitable donation to the municipality's schools, he was permitted to erect, in Isabella's honour, an enormous and hideous fountain in which cubist elephants spouted water from their trunks while posing, like ballerinas, on their left hind legs. The fountain was placed in the centre of the square outside Vasco's so-called 'Little Alhambra', and the square was renamed the 'Place of the Elephants', to the fury of the older residents. Assembling in a nearby bar, called La Carmencita in tribute to the late dictator's daughter, the old-timers recalled, in liquid bursts of nostalgic outrage, that the vandalised square had until then been the Plaza de Carmen Polo, named after the Caudillo's wife herself – named in her honour and honoured by her name, which was now besmirched by this pachydermous connection; or so these disapproving dotards unanimously averred. In the old days, they reminded one another, Benengeli had been the generalissimo's favourite Andalusian village, but the old days had been swept away by this amnesiac, democratic present, which thought of all yesterdays as garbage, to be disposed of as soon as possible. And that such a monstrosity as the elephant fountain should be visited upon them by a non-Spaniard, an

Indian, who should in any case have gone to make his mischief in Portugal, not Spain, on account of the traditional Lusophilia of persons of Goan extraction – well! – it was downright intolerable. But what was one to do about artists, who brought shame on the good name of Benengeli by importing their women and licentious ways and foreign gods – for although this Miranda claimed to be a Catholic, was it not well known that all Orientals were pagans under the skin?

Vasco Miranda was blamed by the old guard for most of the changes in Benengeli, and if you had asked these locals to pinpoint the moment of their ruination they would have chosen the ludicrous day of the elephant on the ramp, because that inelegant but widely reported burlesque episode brought Benengeli to the attention of the whole world's human detritus, and within a few years that once-quiet village which had been the fallen Leader's preferred Southern retreat became a nesting-place for itinerant layabouts, expatriate vermin, and all the flotsam-jetsam scum of the earth. Benengeli's Guardia Civil chief, Sargento Salvador Medina, a vociferous opponent of the new residents, would give his opinion to anyone who wanted it and many who did not. 'The Mediterranean, the ancients' Mare Nostrum, is dying of filth,' he opined. 'And now the land – Terra Nostra – is perishing too.'

Vasco Miranda, in an attempt to win over the Guardia chief, sent him twice the expected Christmas gift of money and alcohol, but Medina was not appeased. He personally brought the excess cash and booze back to Vasco's door and told him to his face: 'Men and women who leave their natural places are less than human. Either something is lacking in their souls or else something surplus has gotten inside – some manner of devil seed.' After that insult Vasco Miranda retired behind the high walls of his fortress-folly and lived the life of a recluse. He was never seen in the streets of Benengeli again. The servants he employed (in those days many young men and women were descending on southern Spain – already plagued by unemployment problems – from the jobless zones of La Mancha and Extremadura, eager for work in restaurants, hotels or domestic service; so household servants were as readily available in Benengeli as in Bombay) spoke of the frightening patterns of his behaviour, in which periods of utterly withdrawn stillness would characteristically be punctuated by gabbled harangues on abstruse, even incomprehensible themes, and embarrassing revelations of the most intimate details of his past, and chequered, career. There were colossal drinking jags, and descents into wild depressions during which he railed manically against the savage mischances of his life, notably his love of one 'Aurora Zogoiby' and his fear of a 'lost needle' that he believed to be making its inexorable way towards his heart. But he paid well, and punctually, and so he kept his staff.

Perhaps Vasco's life and Abraham's were not so different after all. In the aftermath of Aurora Zogoiby's death they both became recluses, Abraham in his high tower and Vasco in his; they both sought to bury the pain of her loss beneath new activity, new enterprises, no matter how ill-conceived. And they both, as I would learn, claimed to have seen her ghost.

～

'She walks around here. I've seen her.' Abraham in sky-orchard with stuffed dog confessed to a vision – driven, for the first time in his life, and after a lifetime of utter scepticism on the subject, to allow the possibility of life after death to stumble off his irreligious tongue. 'She won't wait for me; eludes me in the trees.' Ghosts like children like to play hide-and-seek. 'She is not at rest. I know she is not at rest. What can I do to give her peace?' To my eye it was Abraham who seemed agitated, unable to accustom himself to her loss. 'Maybe if her work finds its resting-place,' he hypothesised, and there followed the huge Zogoiby Bequest, under the terms of which all of Aurora's own collection of her work – many hundreds of pieces! – was donated to the nation on condition that a gallery was built in Bombay to store and display it properly. But in the aftermath of the Meerut massacres, the Hindu-Muslim riots in Old Delhi and elsewhere, art was not a government priority, and the collection – apart from a few masterpieces which were put on show at the National Gallery in Delhi – languished. Bombay's civic authorities, being Mainduck-controlled, were not prepared to make good the funding which the central government's exchequer had denied. 'Then damn and blast all politicos,' cried Abraham. 'Self-help is best policy of all.' He found other backers to join him in the project; there was money from the rapidly expanding Khazana Bank and also from the super-stockbroker V. V. Nandy, whose George Soros-sized raids on the world's currency markets were acquiring legendary status, the more so because they came from a Third World source. 'The Crocodile is becoming a post-colonial hero to our young,' Abraham told me, hee-hee'ing at the vagaries of fate. 'He fits their empire-strikes-back plus get-rich-quick double bill.' A prime site was found – one of the few surviving old-time Parsi mansions on Cumballa Hill ('How old?' – 'Old, men. From *old* time') – and a brilliant young art theorist and devotee of Aurora's oeuvre, Zeenat Vakil, already the author of an influential study of the Mughal *Hamza-nama* cloths, was appointed curator. Dr Vakil at once set about compiling an exhaustive catalogue, and began work, too, on an accompanying critical appreciation, *Imperso-Nation and Dis/Semi/Nation: Dialogics of Eclecticism and Interrogations of Authenticity in A.Z.*, which gave the Moor sequence – including the previously unseen late pictures – its rightful, central place in the corpus, and would do much to fix Aurora's place in the ranks of the immortals. The Zogoiby Bequest opened to the public just three years after Aurora's sad demise; there followed a certain amount of inevitable if short-lived controversy, for example over the early, and to some eyes incestuous, Moor pictures – those 'panto-paintings' that she had made so lightly long ago. But high in Cashondeliveri Tower her ghost still walked.

Now Abraham began to express the conviction that her death had not been the straightforward accident that everyone had supposed. Dabbing at a rheumy eye he said in an unsteady voice that those who perish by foul play require a settlement before they find repose. He seemed to be falling further and further into the traps of superstition, apparently unable to accept the fact of Aurora's death. In ordinary circumstances this slippage into what he had always called mumbo-jumbo would have shocked me deeply; but I, too, was caught in obsession's strengthening grip. My mother was dead and yet I needed to repair a rift. If she was dead beyond recall then there could never be a reconciliation, only this gnawing, imperative need, this wound-that-could-not-heal. So I did not contradict Abraham when he spoke of phantoms in his hanging gardens. I may even have hoped – yes! – for a sudden tinkle of jhunjhunna ankle-bracelets, a flurry of fabric behind a bush. Or, better still, for the return of the mother of my favourite times, paint-spattered, and with brushes sticking out of her high-piled, chaotic hair.

Even when Abraham announced that he had asked Dom Minto to re-open, on a private basis, the inquiry into her fall – Minto of all people, blind, toothless, wheelchair-ridden, deaf, and kept alive, as he approached his century, by dialysis machines, regular blood transfusions, and that insatiable and undiminished inquisitiveness which had taken him to the top of his professional tree! – I made no demurral. Let the old man have what he needed to soothe his troubled spirit, I thought. Also, I must say, it was not easy to contradict Abraham Zogoiby, that ruthless skeleton. The more he took me into his confidence, opening his bank-books, his secret ledgers and his heart, the more profoundly I began to feel afraid.

'*Fielding, must be,*' he shouted his suspicion at Minto in the Pei orchard. '*As to Mody, fellow doesn't have what it takes. Investigate Fielding. Moor here will lend any assistance you may require.*'

My fear increased. If Raman Fielding – guilty or innocent – ever suspected I was spying on him with a view to incriminating him in a putative murder, it would not go well with me. Yet I could not refuse Abraham, my newly reacquired father. Nervously, however, I did at last bring myself to ask indelicate questions: why would Mainduck – what motive, what provocation did he have . . . ?

'*Boy wants to know why I suspect that froggy bastard,*' Abraham Zogoiby yelled between terrifying cackles, and ruined old Minto likewise slapped a mirthful thigh. '*Maybe he thinks his Mummy was a saint, and only his bad Daddy strayed from the fold. But she tried out most things in trousers, isn't it? Short attention span, only. Hell hath no fury like a froggy spurned. QE bleddy D.*'

Two macabrely laughing old men, accusations of marital

infidelities and murder, a walking ghost, and me. I was out of my depth. But there was nowhere to run, nowhere to hide. There was only what had to be done.

'Big Daddy, worry not,' whispered Minto, peering through blue glass, as softly spoken as Abraham had been stentorian. 'This Fielding, consider him quartered, drawn and hung.'

～

Children make fictions of their fathers, re-inventing them according to their childish needs. The reality of a father is a weight few sons can bear.

It was the conventional wisdom of the period that the (mainly Muslim) gangs controlling the city's organised crime, each with their ruling boss or *dada*, had been weakened by their traditional difficulties in forming any kind of lasting syndicate or united front. My own experience with the MA, working in the poorest quarters of the city to win friends and build support, suggested something different. I had begun to see hints and glimpses of something shadowy, so frightening that nobody would talk about it – some hidden layer under the surface of what-seemed-to-be. I had suggested to Mainduck that the gangs might have finally achieved unity, that there might even be a single Mafia-style *capo di tutti capi* in place, running all the rackets in town, but he laughed me to scorn. 'Stick to punching heads, Hammer,' he sneered. 'Leave the deep stuff to deeper minds. Unity takes discipline, and we have the monopoly of that commodity. Those sister-fuckers will be squabbling until the heavens fall.'

But now, with my own ears, I had heard Dom Minto name *my father* as the biggest dada of them all. Mogambo! The moment I heard it, I knew it was true. Abraham was a natural commander, a born negotiator, the deal-maker of deal-makers. He gambled for the highest stakes; had even been willing, as a young man, to wager his unborn son. Yes, the High Command did exist, and the Muslim gangs had been united by a Cochin Jew. The truth is almost always exceptional, freakish, improbable, and almost never normative, almost never what cold calculations would suggest. In the end, people make the alliances they need. They follow the men who can lead them in the directions they prefer. It occurred to me that my father's pre-eminence over Scar and his colleagues was a dark, ironic victory for India's deep-rooted secularism. The very nature of this inter-community league of cynical self-interest gave the lie to Mainduck's vision of a theocracy in which one particular variant of Hinduism would rule, while all India's other peoples bowed their beaten heads.

Vasco had said it years ago: corruption was the only force we had that could defeat fanaticism. What had been, on his lips, no more than a drunkard's gibe, had been turned by Abraham Zogoiby into living reality, into a union of hovel and high-rise, a godless crooked army that could take on and vanquish anything that the god-squad sent its way.

Maybe.

Raman Fielding had already made the grave error of underestimating his opponent. Would Abraham Zogoiby be any wiser? Early indications were not good. 'A bug,' he'd called Mainduck. 'A stupid collared dog.'

And if both sides went to war because they believed the enemy was easy to vanquish? And if both sides were wrong? What then?

Armageddon?

$\backsim$

In the matter of the Baby Softo narcotics scandal, Abraham Zogoiby – as he confirmed during our 'briefing sessions', with a wide, shameless grin – had received a complete exoneration by the investigating authorities. 'Clean bill of health,' he crowed. 'Pair of hands, likewise clean. Enemies may try to drag me down, but they must try harder than that.' There was no question that the Softo company's talcum powder exports had been used as cover for the dispatch overseas of rather more lucrative white powders, but in spite of herculean efforts by narcotics squad officers it had been impossible to prove that Abraham had been aware of any illegal activity. Certain minor functionaries of the company – in the canning and dispatch departments – had indeed been shown to be in the pay of a drugs syndicate, but thereafter all investigations simply hit a wall. Abraham was generous in caring for the families of the jailed men – 'Why should women-children suffer for activities of fathers?' he liked to say – and in the end the case was closed without any of the charges against high personages that had originally been trumpeted, not least by Raman Fielding's MA-controlled city corporation. It remained a matter of embarrassment that the drug overlord known as 'Scar' remained at liberty. The supposition was that he had taken refuge somewhere in the Persian Gulf. But Abraham Zogoiby had different news for me. 'How foolish we would be if immigration-emigration matters were not also capable of being arranged,' he cried. 'Of course our people can slip out and in whenever they may so choose. And drugs squad officers also are only human. On their low pay it is hard to make ends meet. What to tell you? It is the duty of the well-off to be generous. Philanthropy is our necessary rôle. *Noblesse oblige*.'

Abraham's victory in the Baby Softo affair had been a blow for Fielding, who urged me constantly to pump my father for information about drug-related activities. But I did not need to pump. Abraham was intent on opening his heart to me, and told me plainly that the Softo win had not been without long-term costs. With the talcum powder route closed, a more perilous operation had had to be constructed at some speed and in the teeth of the intensive police investigation. 'Start-up costs were ridiculous,' he confided. 'But what to do? In business a man's word is his bond, and there were contracts to fulfil.' Scar and his men had been working full-time to set up the new route, which culminated in the dusty wastes of the Rann of Kutch (thus necessitating the bribery of officials in Gujarat as well as Maharashtra). Small boats would ferry the 'talcum' out to waiting cargo ships. The new route was slower, riskier. 'Only a stop-gap,' said Abraham. 'In time we will find new friends at the air cargo terminal.'

I would go to his high-rise glass Eden at night and he would tell me his serpentine tales. And they were like fairy tales, in a way: goblin-sagas of the present day, tales of the utterly abnormal recounted in a matter-of-fact, banal, duty manager's normalising tones. (So this was what my feral father meant by burying himself in his work to help him bear his loss! This was what he did to assuage his pain!) . . . Armaments featured strongly, though the publicly listed activities of his great corporation included no such trade. A famous Nordic armaments house was negotiating to supply India with a range of essentially decent, elegantly designed and naturally lethal products. The sums of money involved were too large to have meaning, and as is the way with such Karakorams of capital, certain peripheral boulders of money came loose from the main bulk and began to roll down the mountain. What was needed was a discreet means of tidying away these tumbling boulders in a manner properly beneficial to those involved in the negotiations. The participants in the negotiations were of a great refinement, possessed of a delicacy that would have made it quite impossible for them to tidy away this rubble of lucre, even into their own bank accounts. Not a whisper of impropriety could ever attach itself to their high names! 'So,' said Abraham with a happy shrug, 'we do the dirty work, and plenty of pebbles end up in our pockets, too.'

It turned out that Abraham's 'Siodicorp' — as it was now universally known — was a major player in the Khazana Bank International, which by the end of the 1980s had become the first financial institution from the Third World to rival the great Western banks in terms of assets and transactions. The more or less moribund banking operation he had taken over from the Cashondeliveri brothers had been brilliantly refurbished, and its links with the KBI enterprise had made it the wonder of the city. 'The old days of setting up a dollar-bypass system for basket-case economies are gone,' declaimed my father. 'No more of that namby-pamby South-South co-operation bakvaas. Bring on the big boys! Dollar, DM, Swiss franc, yen – let them come! Now we will beat them at their own game.' In spite of his new frankness with me, however, it was several years before Abraham Zogoiby admitted that beneath this glittering monetarist vision there lurked a hidden layer of activity: the inevitable secret world that has existed, awaiting revelation, beneath everything I have ever known. – And if the reality of our being is that so many covert truths exist behind Maya-veils of unknowing and illusion, then why not Heaven and Hell, too? Why not God and the Devil and the whole blest-damned thing? If so much revelation, why not Revelation? – *Please.* This is no time to discuss theology. The subject on the table is terrorism, and a secret nuclear device.

Among KBI's largest clients were a number of gentlemen and organisations whose names featured on the most-wanted and most-dangerous lists of every country in the free world – but who, mysteriously, themselves seemed free to come and go, to board commercial airplanes and visit bank branches and receive medical treatment in the countries of their choice, without fear of arrest or harassment. These shadow-accounts were maintained in special files, shielded by an impressive battery of passwords, software 'bombs' and other defence mechanisms, and in theory at least could not be accessed through the main computer. But these precautions were as nothing, and this unsavoury clientèle looked positively angelic, when set beside the precautions taken to protect, and the personnel involved in, KBI's greatest enterprise: namely, the financing and secret manufacture 'for certain oil-rich countries and their ideological allies' of large-scale nuclear weaponry. Abraham's arm had grown long indeed. If there was a stockpile of suitably enriched uranium or plutonium to be had, the Khazana Bank would have a finger in that hot pie; if by some chance a long-range delivery system unexpectedly came on to the market in the fringe states of the recently collapsed Soviet Union, KBI money would move sinuously, invisibly, beneath carpets, through walls, towards that vendor's stall. So at last Abraham's invisible city, built by invisible people to do invisible deeds, was nearing its apotheosis. It was building an invisible bomb.

In May 1991 an all-too-visible explosion in Tamil Nadu added Mr Rajiv Gandhi to the list of his family's murdered dead, and Abraham Zogoiby – whose decisions could at times be so incomprehensibly dark as to suggest that he actually believed he was being funny – chose that awful day to 'brief' me on the existence of the secret H-bomb project. At that moment something changed within me. It was an involuntary alteration, born not of will or choice but of some deeper, unconscious function of my self. I listened carefully as he went into the specifics (the overarching problem the project faced at present, he noted, was the need for an ultra-fast supercomputer capable of running the complex weapons delivery programmes without which the missiles would never hit anything they were supposed to; in the whole world there existed less than two dozen such FPS or 'Floating Point System' computers with VAX accessing equipment that enabled them to make around seventy-six million calculations per second, and twenty of these were in the United States, which meant one of the remaining three or four – and such a machine had been located in Japan – must either be acquired by a front organisation so impenetrable as to deceive the enormously sophisticated security systems surrounding such a sale, or else it would have to be stolen, and then *made invisible*, smuggled to the end-user by means of an improbably complex chain of corrupt excise officials, falsified bills of lading and duped inspectorates) but, as I listened, I heard a voice within me making an absolute, non-negotiable refusal. Just as I had refused the death which Uma Sarasvati had planned for me, so I now believed I had passed the bounds of what was required of me by family loyalty. To my surprise, another loyalty had taken precedence. Surprise, because after all I had been raised in *Elephanta*, where all communal ties had been deliberately disrupted; in a country where all citizens owe an instinctive dual allegiance to a place and a faith, I had been made into a nowhere-and-no-community man – and proud of it, may I say. So it was with a keen sense of the unexpected that I found myself standing up to my formidable, deadly father.

'. . . And if we are found to be smuggling it,' he was saying, 'all aid agreements, favoured-nation privileges and other government-to-government economic protocols would be terminated on the spot.'

I took a breath, and plunged: 'I guess you must know who-all this bomb is meant to blow into more bits than poor Rajiv, and where?'

Abraham became stone. He was ice, and flame. He was God in Paradise and I, his greatest creation, had just put on the forbidden fig-leaf of shame. 'I am a business person,' he said. 'What there is to do, I do.' *YHWH. I am that I am.*

'To my astonishment,' I told this shadow-Jehovah, this anti-

Almighty, this black hole in the sky, my Daddyji, 'excuse me, but I find that I'm a Jew.'

⁓

By this time I was no longer working for Mainduck; so Chhaggan had been right, I suppose – the blood in my veins had proved thicker than the blood we had spilled together. It was not I, but Fielding who had suggested, not without a modicum of grace, that we had reached the parting of the ways. He probably knew that I was not prepared to spy on my father for him, and he may very well have intuited that information about his activities might be flowing in the opposite direction. It must be added that my appetite for office work was not great; for while my youthful habit of neatness, my urge-to-unexceptionality was well suited to the humble, mechanical tasks I was given to perform, my 'secret identity' – that is, my true, untamed, amoral self – rebelled violently against the tedium of the days. Nothing to be done with an old hoodlum, a superannuated goonda, except retire him. 'Go and rest,' Fielding told me, putting his hand on my head. 'You have earned it.' I wondered if I was being told he had decided not to have me killed. Or the opposite: that in the near future the Tin-man's knife, or Five-in-a-Bite's teeth, might be caressing my throat. I made my farewells and left. No assassins came after me. Not then. But the feeling of being pursued, that did persist.

The truth is that by 1991 Mainduck's stratagems had far more to do with the religious-nationalist agenda than the original, localised Bombay-for-the-Mahrattas platform on which he had come to power. Fielding, too, was making allies, with like-minded national parties and paramilitary organisations, that alphabet soup of authoritarians, BJP, RSS, VHP. In this new phase of MA activity I had no place. Zeenat Vakil at the Zogoiby Bequest – where I had started spending a large proportion of my time, wandering in my mother's dream-worlds, following Aurora's re-dreaming of myself through the adventures she had designed for me – clever leftish Zeeny, whom I didn't tell about my Mainduck affiliations, had nothing but contempt for Ram-Rajya rhetoric. 'What bunkum, I swear,' she expostulated. 'Point one: in a religion with a thousand and one gods they suddenly decide only one chap matters. Then what about Calcutta, for example, where they don't go for Ram? And Shiva-temples are no longer suitable places of worship? Too stupid. Point two: Hinduism has many holy books, not one, but suddenly it is all Ramayan, Ramayan. Then where is the Gita? Where are all the Puranas? How dare they twist everything in this way? Bloody joke. And point three: for Hindus there is no requirement for a collective act of worship, but without that how are these types going to collect their beloved mobs? So suddenly there is this invention of mass puja, and that is declared the only way to show true, class-A devotion. A single, martial deity, a single book, and mob rule: that is what they have made of Hindu culture, its many-headed beauty, its peace.'

'Zeeny, you're a Marxist,' I pointed out. 'This speech about a True Faith ruined by Actually Existing bastardisations used to be you guys' standard song. You think Hindus Sikhs Muslims never killed each other before?'

'Post-Marxian,' she corrected me. 'And whatever was true or not true in the question of socialism, this fundo stuff is really something new.'

Raman Fielding found many unexpected allies. As well as the alphabet-soupists there were the Malabar Hill fast-laners, joking at their dinner-parties about 'teaching minority groups a lesson' and 'putting people in their place'. But these were people he had wooed, after all; what must have come as something of a bonus was that, on the single issue of contraception, at least, he managed to acquire support from the Muslims, and even more surprisingly, the Maria Gratiaplena nuns as well. Hindus, Muslims and Catholics, on the verge of violent communal conflict, were momentarily united by their common hatred of sheath, diaphragm and pill. My sister Minnie – Sister Floreas – was, needless to say, energetic in the fray.

Ever since the failure of the attempt to introduce a birth-control campaign by force in the mid-1970s, family planning had been a difficult topic in India. Lately, however, a new drive for smaller families had been initiated, under the slogan *Hum do hamaré do* ('we two and our two'). Fielding used this to launch a scare campaign of his own. MA workers went into the tenements and slums to tell Hindus that Muslims were refusing to co-operate with the new policy. 'If we are two and we have two, but they are two and they have twenty-two, then soon they will outnumber us and drive us into the sea!' The idea that three-quarters-of-a-billion Hindus could be swamped by the children of one hundred million Muslims was curiously legitimised by many Muslim imams and political leaders, who deliberately exaggerated the numbers of Indian Muslims in an attempt to increase their own importance and the community's sense of self-confidence; and who were also fond of pointing out that Muslims were much better fighters than Hindus. 'Give us six Hindus to one of us!' they screamed at their rallies. 'Then we will be level pegging, at least. Then there may be a little bit of a fair fight before the cowards run.' Now, this surrealist numbers game was given a new twist. Catholic nuns began tramping up and down the Bombay Central chawls and the filthy lanes of the Dharavi slum, protesting vociferously against birth control. None worked longer hours, or argued more passionately, than our own Sister Floreas; but after a time she was withdrawn from the front line, because another nun overheard her explaining to terrified slum-dwellers that God had his own ways of controlling His people's numbers, and her visions had confirmed that in the very near future many of them would die anyway, because of the coming violence and plagues. 'I myself will be carried away to Heaven,' she was explaining sweetly. 'O, how dearly I look forward to the day.'

༄

I turned seventy on New Year's Day 1992, at the age of thirty-five. Always an ominous landmark, the passing of the Biblical span, all the more so in a country where life-expectancy is markedly lower than the Old Testament allows; and in the case of yrs. truly, to whom six months consistently did a full year's damage, the moment had a special, extra piquancy. How easily the human

339

mind 'normalises' the abnormal, with what rapidity the unthinkable becomes not only thinkable but humdrum, not worth thinking about! – Thus my 'condition', once it had been diagnosed as 'incurable', 'inevitable', and many other 'in's' that I can no longer call to mind, speedily became so dull a thing that not even I could bring myself to give it very much thought. The nightmare of my halved life was simply a Fact, and there is nothing to be said of a Fact except that it is so. – For may one negotiate with a Fact, sir? – In no wise! – May one stretch it, shrink it, condemn it, beg its pardon? No; or, it would be folly indeed to seek to do so. – How then are we to approach so intransigent, so absolute an Entity? – Sir, it cares not if you approach it or leave it alone; best, then, to accept it and go your ways. – And do Facts never change? Are old Facts never to be replaced by new ones, like lamps; like shoes and ships and every other blessed thing? – So: if they are, then it shows us only this – that they never were Facts to begin with, but mere Poses, Attitudes, and Shams. The true Fact is not your burning Candle, to subside limply in a stiff pool of wax; nor yet your Electric Bulb, so tender of filament, and short-lived as the Moth that seeks it out. Neither is it made of your common shoe-leather, nor should it spring any leaks. It shines! It walks! It floats! – Yes! – *For ever and a day*.

After my thirty-fifth or seventieth birthday, however, the truth of my life's great Fact became impossible for me to shrug off with a few nostrums about kismet, karma, or fate. It was borne in upon me by a series of indispositions and hospitalisations with which I will not trouble the squeamish, impatient reader; except to say that they impressed upon me the reality from which I had averted my gaze for so long. *I did not have very long to live*. That plain truth hung behind my eyelids in letters of fire whenever I went to sleep; it was the first thing I thought of when I awoke. *So you made it to today. Will you still be here tomorrow?* It's true, my squeamish, impatient friend: ignominious and unheroic as it may be to say so, I had commenced living with the minute-by-minute fear of death. It was a toothache for which no soothing oil of cloves could be prescribed.

One of the effects of my adventures in medicine was to render me physically incapable of that which I had long given up hope of doing; that is, to become a father myself, and so alleviate – if not escape – the burdens of being a son. This latest failure so angered Abraham Zogoiby, who was in his ninetieth year and healthier than ever, that he was unable to conceal his irritation beneath the flimsiest show of sympathy or concern. 'The one thing I wanted from you,' he spat at my bedside at the Breach Candy Hospital. 'Even that you can't give me now.' A degree of coolness had re-entered our relationship ever since I refused to be involved with the covert operations of the Khazana Bank, in particular the manufacture of the so-called Islamic bomb. 'You'll be wanting a yarmulke now,' my father sneered. 'And phylacteries. Lessons in Hebrew, a one-way trip to Jerusalem? Just, please, to let me know. Many of our Cochin Jews, by the way, complain of the racism with which they are treated in your precious homeland across the sea.' Abraham, the race traitor, who was repeating on an appalling, gigantic scale the crime of turning his back on mother and tribe, and walking out of Jewtown towards Aurora's Roman arms. Abraham, the black hole of Bombay. I saw him wrapped in darkness, a collapsing star sucking darkness around itself as its mass increased. No light escaped from the event-horizon of his presence. He had begun to scare me long ago; now he engendered in me a terror, and at the same time a pity, that my words are too impoverished to describe.

I say again: I'm no angel. I kept away from the KBI's business, but Abraham's empire was large, and nine-tenths of it was submerged below the surface of things. There was plenty for me to do. I, too, became an inhabitant of the upper reaches of Cashondeliveri Tower, and took no little satisfaction from the piratical pleasures of being my father's son. But after my medical reverses it became clear that Abraham had begun to look to others for some support; and, in particular, to Adam Braganza, a precocious eighteen-year-old with ears the size of Baby Dumbo's or of Star TV satellite dishes, who was rising through the ranks of Siodicorp so fast he ought to have died from the bends.

'Mr Adam', I gradually discovered in the course of my late-night chats with my father – who continued to use me as a kind of confessor for the many sins of his long life – was a youth with a spectacularly chequered past. It seems he was originally the illegitimate child of a Bombay hooligan and an itinerant magician from Shadipur, U.P., and had been unofficially adopted, for a time, by a Bombay man who was missing-believed-dead, having mysteriously disappeared fourteen years ago, not long after his allegedly brutal treatment by government agents during the 1974–1977 Emergency. Since then the boy had been raised in a pink skyscraper at Breach Candy by two elderly Goan Christian ladies who had grown wealthy on the success of their popular range of condiments, Braganza Pickles. He had taken the name of Braganza in the old ladies' honour, and, after they passed away, had taken over the factory itself. Soon afterwards, as smartly turned out and slick-styled at seventeen as many executives twice his age, he had come to Siodicorp in search of expansion capital, hoping to put the old ladies' legendary pickles and chutneys into the world market under the snappier brand name of *Brag's*. On the modernised packaging which he brought in to show Abraham's people was the slogan, *Plenty to Brag about*.

Which could, it seemed, be said of the boy wonder himself. In what seemed like the blink of an eye he had sold the business to Abraham, who had been quick to see the huge export potential of the brand, especially in countries with substantial NRI (Non-Resident Indian) populations. Now the young Turk was independently wealthy; but in the course of his first meeting with grand old Mr Zogoiby himself, he had so impressed my father with his knowledge both of the latest business and management theories, and of the new communications and information technologies that were just starting to explode into the Indian sector, that Abraham at once invited him to 'join the Siodi family' at vice-presidential level, with special responsibility for technical innovation and corporate behaviour. Cashondeliveri Tower started buzzing with the boy's new notions, developed, apparently, from his study of business practices in Japan, Singapore and around the Pacific Rim, 'the global capital of Millennium Three,' as he called it. His memos quickly became legendary. 'To optimise manpower utilisation, engendering of we-feeling is key,' they typically said. Executives were therefore 'encouraged', that is, instructed, to spend at least twenty minutes a week in small groups of ten or twelve, embracing one another. Further 'encouragement' was given to the idea that each employee should offer monthly 'evaluations' of his fellows' strengths and weaknesses – thus turning the building into a tower of hypocritical (overtly huggy-wuggy, secretly stabby-wabby) sneaks. 'We will be a listening corporation,' Adam informed us all. 'What you say, we will carefully note.' O, those ears were listening, all right. Any poison, any nastiness that was going fell into their capacious depths. 'All large organisations are a heterogenous mix of trouble-makers, trouble-shooters and healthy people,' said an Adam memo. 'Our management expectation is that the trouble-makers will, with your help, be *developed*.' (Emphasis added.) Old Abraham loved this stuff. 'Modern era,' he told me. 'Therefore, modern lingo. I just love it! This wet-eared punk with the tough-guy stance. He's making the joint jump.'

My own tough-guy stances had been of a different sort; possibly, in Abraham's view, an outmoded sort – and at any rate all that was over for me now. This was not the time to lay into young Adam Braganza. I kept mum; and smiled. There was a new Adam in Eden. My father invited the youth into the rooftop atrium and within months – weeks! Days! – Siodicorp was moving into computers; to say nothing of cable, fibre-optics, dishes, satellites, telecommunications of every sort; and guess who was running the new show? 'We're going to put our *footprint* on the world,' beamed Abraham, proud of knowing the word's new connotation. 'What villagers these locals are with their talk of the rule of Ram! Not Ram Rajya but RAM Rajya – that is our ace in the hole.'

*Not Ram but RAM*: I recognised at once the young fellow's sloganising touch. Abraham was right. The future had arrived. There was a generation waiting to inherit the earth, caring nothing for old-timers' concerns: dedicated to the pursuit of the new, speaking the future's strange, binary, affectless speech – quite a change from our melodramatic garam-masala exclamations. No wonder Abraham, inexhaustible Abraham, turned to Adam. It was the birth of a new age in India, when money, as well as religion, was breaking all the shackles on its desires; a time for the lusty, the hungry, the greedy-for-life, not the spent and empty lost.

I felt like a back number; born too fast, born wrong, damaged, and growing old too quickly, turning brutal along the route. Now my face was turned towards the past, towards the loss of love. When I looked forward, I saw Death waiting there. Death, whom Abraham continued effortlessly to cheat, might harvest the son in the immortal father's place.

'Don't look so bleddy miserable,' said Abraham Zogoiby. 'What you need is a wife. A good woman to wipe the worry off your brow. Now then: Miss Nadia Wadia. What do you say to her?'

~

Nadia Wadia!

Throughout the year of her Miss World incumbency, Raman Fielding had pursued her. He wooed her with flowers, cordless telephones, video cameras and microwave ovens. She sent them back. He invited her to every civic reception, but after his performance on the day of Ganpati she invariably turned him down. Fielding's desire for Nadia Wadia was leaked to the nation by *Mid-day*'s celebrated gossip columnist 'Waspyjee', a descendant of an earlier writer who, under the same pen-name, had written about 'Gama radiation' in the *Bombay Chronicle* and, in so doing, terminated my great-grandfather Francisco da Gama's brilliant career. After that Nadia Wadia's refusal to be possessed by Mainduck became, for a certain kind of Bombayite, a symbol of a greater resistance – it became heroic, political. There were cartoons. In that city which Fielding claimed to 'run like his private motor car', Nadia Wadia's hold-out was proof of the survival of another, freer Bombay. She gave great interviews, too. *I wouldn't kiss him if he was the last frog in town, vows Nadia . . . Duck, Mainduck! Nadia's taking boxing lessons!* . . . the entertainment went on and on.

Two things happened.

One: Fielding, his patience snapping, considered putting the frighteners on the stubborn beauty queen; and so, for the first time in his long unquestioned leadership of the MA, faced a revolt, led by Sammy Hazaré and supported unanimously by all the 'team captains' of the MA's 'special operations'. The Tin-man led a group that visited Fielding in his frog-phoned office. 'Sir not cricket sir,' was their terse critique. Mainduck backed down, but after that he watched Sammy with the same look in his eye that I had seen when I told him about my family reconciliation. And he was right to do so, for Sammy had changed. And in a not-too-distant time would be pushed out of his lifelong supporting-player's niche, forced by events and by the torments in his heart to play, in the great drama that was presently in rehearsal, an unforgettable leading rôle.

Two: Nadia Wadia ceased to be the reigning Miss World. There was a new Miss India, a new Miss Bombay. Nadia Wadia became an old story. Her song was no longer played on the radio or on the new, Indian version of MTV: *Masala Television* ignored the fallen queen. Nadia Wadia never made it to medical college, the boyfriend of whom she had once spoken vanished into the blue, an acting career was stillborn. Money goes quickly in Bombay. Nadia Wadia at eighteen was a has-been, broke, rudderless, adrift. At this point Abraham Zogoiby made his move. He offered her, and her widowed mother, a luxury apartment at the southern end of Colaba Causeway, and a generous stipend to go with it. Nadia Wadia was no longer in a strong negotiating position, but she had not lost her pride. When she visited Abraham at *Elephanta* to discuss his offer – and how quickly that news reached Mainduck's ears, via Lambajan Chandiwala, the double agent at our gates! How it enraged that wicked boss! – she spoke with dignity. 'I am thinking to myself, Nadia Wadia, what is the generous sir re-quiring in return for such a favour? Maybe it is something that Nadia Wadia cannot give, even to the great Abraham Zogoiby himself.'

Abraham was impressed. He told her that an enterprise like Siodicorp needed a friendly public face. 'Look at me,' he cackled. 'Am I not a horrible old man? Just now when people think of our company, they think of this mad old fool. From now on, if you agree, they will think of you.' So it was that Nadia Wadia became the face of Siodicorp: in commercials, on posters, and in person, hostessing the corporation's many prestige sponsored events – fashion galas, one-day cricket internationals, Guinness Book of Records winners' conventions, the Millennium Three Expo, the world wrestling championships. So it was that she was saved from the gutter and restored to the public celebrity her beauty deserved. So it was that Abraham Zogoiby scored another victory over Raman Fielding, and the Nadia Wadia song returned, re-released in a pounding dance remix, to the 'Hot-hot' playlist of *Masala Television*, and to the top of the hit parade.

Nadia Wadia and her mother, Fadia Wadia, moved into the Colaba Causeway apartment, and on their living-room wall Abraham hung the one picture by Aurora Zogoiby that Zeenat Vakil was still unable to show at the gallery on Cumballa Hill, a picture in which a beautiful young girl kissed a handsome young cricketer with a (pictorial) passion that had caused such trouble; once upon a time. 'Oh, how wonderful,' said Nadia Wadia, clapping her hands as Abraham personally unveiled *The Kissing of Abbas Ali Baig*. 'Nadia Wadia and Fadia Wadia *love* cricket, don't we, Fadia Wadia?'

'Very true, Nadia Wadia,' said Fadia Wadia. 'Cricket is sport of kings.'

'Oh, *silly* Fadia Wadia,' reproved Nadia Wadia. 'Sport of kings is *horsies*. Fadia Wadia should know *that*. *Nadia* Wadia knows.'

'Enjoy, daughter,' said Abraham Zogoiby, kissing Nadia on the top of the head as he left. 'But please: for your mother, a little more respect.'

He never laid a finger on her, was never anything but the perfect gent. And then, out of the blue, he offered her to me, as if she were his to hand out, in his gift, a trinket wife.

I told Abraham I would visit the Wadias and discuss his proposition. The two women awaited me in their Colaba high-rise, looking terrified. Nadia Wadia had been dressed up like a Christmas present for the occasion, nose-jewellery and all.

'Your father has been so good to us,' blurted Fadia Wadia, maternal feelings overcoming the exigencies of her situation. 'But surely, respected goodsir, my Nadia Wadia deserves kiddies . . . a younger man . . . '

Nadia Wadia was looking at me oddly. 'Has Nadia Wadia maybe met you someplace before?' she asked, half-remembering Ganpati. I ignored this question and addressed myself to the matter in hand. The problem was, I explained, that they were living on the patronage of one of the most powerful men in India. Should they refuse the offer of his only son's hand in marriage, it was entirely likely that the old man's protection would be withdrawn. Few hands would extend towards them after that, for fear of offending the great Zogoiby. Possibly the only interested party would be a certain gentleman who once, as a cartoonist, used to sign his efforts with the picture of a frog . . .

'Never!' cried Nadia Wadia. 'Mrs Mainduck? This, Nadia Wadia will never be. First I will ask Fadia Wadia to hold my hand, and together we will jump from this verandah, just here, see.'

'No need, no need,' I soothed her. 'My idea is a little better, I think.' What I proposed was an engagement in name only. Abraham would be humoured, it would be excellent public relations, and the period of the engagement could be infinitely prolonged. I told them the secret of my accelerated existence. It was plain, I said, that I did not have long to live. Once I died they would reap the considerable benefits of being attached to the Zogoiby family, to whose great fortune I was the only heir. Even should I live long enough for the marriage to become necessary, I vowed, our platonic arrangement would remain in place. I asked only for Nadia Wadia's agreement that she would keep up the appearance of a genuine match. 'The rest will be our secret.'

'Oh, Nadia Wadia,' moaned Fadia Wadia. 'See how rude we are! Your handsome fiancé is come a-calling and we have not even offered him one little piece of cake.'

⌒

Why did I do it? Because I knew what I said to be true; Abraham would have taken refusal as a personal insult, and hurled them into the street. Because I admired Nadia Wadia's stand against Fielding, and also the way in which she had dealt with my notoriously lecherous father. Oh, because she was so beautiful and young, and I was such a ruin. Perhaps because, after my years of violence and corruption, I was looking for redemption, I wanted to be shriven of my sins.

Redemption from what? Shriven by whom? Don't ask me difficult questions. I did it, that's all. The engagement of Moraes Zogoiby, only son of Mr Abraham Zogoiby and the late Aurora Zogoiby (née da Gama), and Miss Nadia Wadia, only daughter of Mr Kapadia Wadia, deceased, and Mrs Fadia Wadia, all of Bombay, was announced. And somewhere in the city, a Tin-man heard the news, and evil festered in his broken, heartless heart.

The engagement party was at the Taj, of course, and a lavish Bombay affair it surely was. In the spiteful presence of more than a thousand beautiful, razor-tongued and sceptically amused strangers, including my last sister, Sister Floreas, who was becoming more of a stranger by the day, I slipped a 'fabulous diamond', as the papers described it, on to that lovely girl's lovely finger, and so completed what 'Waspyjee' would call 'an amazing, almost sacrificial betrothal of the Sunset to the Dawn'. But Abraham Zogoiby – most malicious, coldest-hearted of old men – had, with his customary black humour, prepared a little sting in the evening's tail. After the ritual of the public engagement was complete, and the photographers had feasted on Nadia's never-more-radiant beauty, and were at last replete, Abraham stepped up on to the dais and asked for silence, because he had an announcement to make.

'Moraes, only son of my body, and Nadia, loveliest of daughters-in-law to be,' he cawed. 'Let me venture the hope that you will soon give this sadly depleted family some new members' – O empty-hearted father! – 'for an old man to enjoy. In the meantime, however, I myself have a new member to introduce.'

Much puzzlement, much anticipation. Abraham cackled and nodded. 'Yes, my Moor. At last, my boy, you will have a younger brother to call your own.'

Red curtains parted, theatrically on cue, behind the little dais. Adam Braganza – Little Big Ears himself! – stepped forward.

Among the many loud gasps were Fadia Wadia's, Nadia Wadia's, and mine.

Abraham kissed him on both cheeks, and on the lips. 'From this time forward,' he told the boy before the city's assembled élite, 'call yourself Adam Zogoiby – my beloved son.'

# 18

BOMBAY WAS CENTRAL, HAD been so from the moment of its creation: the bastard child of a Portuguese-English wedding, and yet the most Indian of Indian cities. In Bombay all Indias met and merged. In Bombay, too, all-India met what-was-not-India, what came across the black water to flow into our veins. Everything north of Bombay was North India, everything south of it was the South. To the east lay India's East and to the west, the world's West. Bombay was central; all rivers flowed into its human sea. It was an ocean of stories; we were all its narrators, and everybody talked at once.

What magic was stirred into that insaan-soup, what harmony emerged from that cacophony! In Punjab, Assam, Kashmir, Meerut – in Delhi, in Calcutta – from time to time they slit their neighbours' throats and took warm showers, or red bubble-baths, in all that spuming blood. They killed you for being circumcised and they killed you because your foreskins had been left on. Long hair got you murdered and haircuts too; light skin flayed dark skin and if you spoke the wrong language you could lose your twisted tongue. In Bombay, such things never happened. – Never, you say? – OK: never is too absolute a word. Bombay was not inoculated against the rest of the country, and what happened elsewhere, the language business for example, also spread into its streets. But on the way to Bombay the rivers of blood were usually diluted, other rivers poured into them, so that by the time they reached the city's streets the disfigurations were relatively slight. – Am I sentimentalising? Now that I have left it all behind, have I, among my many losses, also lost clear sight? – It may be said I have; but still I stand by my words. O Beautifiers of the City, did you not see that what was beautiful in Bombay was that it belonged to nobody, and to all? Did you not see the everyday live-and-let-live miracles thronging its overcrowded streets?

Bombay was central. In Bombay, as the old, founding myth of the nation faded, the new god-and-mammon India was being born. The wealth of the country flowed through its exchanges, its ports. Those who hated India, those who sought to ruin it, would need to ruin Bombay: that was one explanation for what happened. Well, well, that may have been so. And it may have been that what was unleashed in the north (in, to name it, because I must name it, Ayodhya) – that corrosive acid of the spirit, that adversarial intensity which poured into the nation's bloodstream when the Babri Masjid fell and plans for a mighty Ram temple on the god's alleged birthplace were, as they used to say in the Bombay cinema-houses, *filling up fast* – was on this occasion too concentrated, and even the great city's powers of dilution could not weaken it enough. So, so; those who argue thus have a point, too, it cannot be denied. At the Zogoiby Bequest, Zeenat Vakil offered me her usual sardonic take on the troubles. 'I blame fiction,' she said. 'The followers of one fiction knock down another popular piece of make-believe, and bingo! It's war. Next they will find Vyasa's cradle under Iqbal's house, and Valmiki's baby-rattle under Mirza Ghalib's hang-out. So, OK. I'd rather die fighting over great poets than over gods.'

I had been dreaming about Uma – O disloyal subconscious! – Uma sculpting her early work, the large Nandi bull. Like the bull, I thought when I awoke, and like blue Krishna of flute-and-milkmaid fame, Lord Ram was an avatar of Vishnu; Vishnu, most metamorphic of the gods. The true 'rule of Ram' should therefore, surely, be premised on the mutating, inconstant, shape-shifting realities of human nature – and not only human nature, but divine as well. This thing being advocated in the great god's name flew in the face of his essence as well as ours. – But when the boulder of history begins to roll, nobody is interested in discussing such fragile points. The *juggernaut* is loose.

. . . And if Bombay was central, it may have been that what transpired was rooted in Bombay quarrels. Mogambo versus Mainduck: the long-awaited duel, the heavyweight unification bout to establish, once and for all, which gang (criminal-entrepreneurial or political-criminal) would run the town. I saw something like this happen, and can only set down what I saw. Hidden factors? The meddling of secret/foreign hands? These I leave for wiser analysts to reveal.

I'll tell you what I think – what, in spite of a lifetime's conditioning against the supernatural, I cannot stop believing: something started when Aurora Zogoiby fell – not just a feud, but a lengthening, widening tear in the fabric of all our lives. She would not rest, she haunted us tirelessly. Abraham Zogoiby saw her more and more, floating in his Pei garden, demanding to be avenged. That's what I really think. What followed was her revenge. Disembodied, she hung above us in the sky, Aurora Bombayalis in her glory, and what rained down upon us was her wrath. Find the femme, say I. See: Aurora's phantom flying through the fiery air. And behold Nadia, too – Nadia Wadia, like the city whose true creature she was – Nadia Wadia, my fiancée, was also central to the tale.

So was this a Mahabharat-style conflict, then, a Trojan war, in which the gods took sides and played their part? No, sir. No, sirree. No old-time deities here, but johnny-come-latelies, the lot of us, Abraham-Mogambo and his Scars, Mainduck and his Five-in-a-Bites; all of us. Aurora, Minto, Sammy, Nadia, me. We were not, did not deserve to be thought of as being, of tragic status. If Carmen Lobo da Gama, my unhappy Great-Aunt Sahara, once gambled for her fortune with Prince Henry the Navigator, there's no need to hear echoes of Yudhisthira's loss of his kingdom on a fatal throw of the dice. And though men fought over Nadia Wadia, she was neither Helen nor Sita. Just a pretty girl in a hot spot, is all. Tragedy was not in our natures. A tragedy was taking place all right, a national tragedy on a grand scale, but those of us who played our parts were – let me put it bluntly – clowns. Clowns! Burlesque buffoons, drafted into history's theatre on account of the lack of greater men. Once, indeed, there were giants on our stage; but at the fag-end of an age, Madam History must make do with what she can get. Jawaharlal, in these latter days, was just the name of a stuffed dog.

Out of the goodness of my heart I approached my new 'brother' and proposed a getting-to-know-you lunch. Well, my dears, you should have heard the to-do. 'Adam Zogoiby' – I never could think of that name without putting it in quotes – went into a positive tizzy of social-climbing panic. Should we go Polynesian at the Oberoi Outrigger? No, no, it was only a buffet luncheon, and one did so appreciate a little fawning. Maybe just a bite at the Taj Sea Lounge? But, on second thoughts, too many old buffers reliving fading glories. How about the Sorryno? Close to home, and nice view, but darling, how to tolerate that old *groucho* of a proprietor? A quick businesslike in-and-out at an Irani joint – Bombay AI or Pyrke's at Flora Fountain? No, we needed less noise, and to talk properly one must be able to *linger*. Chinese, then? – Yes, but *impossible* to choose between the Nanking and Kamling. The Village? All that fake-rustic themeing, baby: *so* passé. After a long, agitated soliloquy (I have given only edited highlights) he settled – or rather, 'plumped' – for the celebrated Continental cuisine at the Society. And, once there, toyed fashionably with a leaf.

'Dimple! Simple! Pimple! So great to see you girls on speakers again. – Ah, bon-jaw, Kalidasa, my usual claret, silver-plate. – Now, then, Moor dear – it's OK-fine with you if I call you "Moor"? OK-fine. *Lovely.* – Harish, howdy! Buying OTCEI, a little birdie told. Good move! Damn high quality equity paper, even if just now little-bit underdeveloped. – Moor, sorry, sorry. You have my absolute *undivided*, I swear. – Mon-sooar Frah-swah! Kissy-*kissy*! – O, just send us whatever you think, we place ourselves in your hands totally. Only no butter, no fried element, no fatty meat, no carbo-fest, and hold the aubergines. One has the figure to preserve, isn't it? – *Finally*. Brother! What times we'll have! What super *maza*, eh? P-H-U-N fun. Are you into nitespots? Forget Midnite-Confidential, Nineteen Hundred, Studio 29, Cavern. All over for them, baby. I just happen to be a founder investor in the new happening joint. We're calling it W-3 for World Wide Web. Or maybe just The Web. Virtual-reality-meets-wet-sari DJs! Cyberpunk meets bhangra-muffin décor! And talent, yaar, on line, get me? The word is state-of-the-*art*. P-H-A-T fat.'

And if I was a little stony of face, a little curmudgeonly, what of it? I felt entitled. I watched the non-stop cabaret, the seven-veils floor-show that was 'Adam Zogoiby', and watched him watching me. He understood soon enough that the Mr Cool act wasn't playing, and switched into lower-voiced, conspiratorial mode. 'Hey, brother, you have a pretty damn hot fighting history, or so I hear. Damn unusual for you Jew boys. I thought you were all book-nosed, four-eyed members of the international world-domination conspiracy.'

That didn't go down well either. I muttered something about the mercenary warrior-Jews who had done so much to establish the community's presence on the Malabar coast, and he heard the icy note in my voice. 'Hey, come on, bro, can't you hear when you're being kidded? Hey, this is *me*. – Madhu, Mehr, Ruchi, *hi*. Gee, too much to see you girls. Meet my big bhai. Listen, this is one crazy guy, one of you should snap him up. – Moor, men, what do you think? Just the absolute top runway and cover girls just now, bigger than our sadly deceased sister Ina, even. You know what? I think they went for you. Classy, classy dames.'

On the subject of 'Adam Zogoiby', my mind was closing fast. Now he changed again, becoming businesslike, professional. 'You should fix up your own financial position, you know. Our father, sad to say, is not a young man. I am presently finalising my personal needs in detailed discussions with his guys.'

That did it. Something about Adam had been striking me as *déjà vu*, and now I saw what it was. His refusal to talk about his past, the fluidity of his changes of stride as he tried to bewitch and woo, the cold calculation of his moves: I had fallen for such an act once, though she had been a far greater practitioner of the chameleon arts than he, and made far less mistakes. I recalled, with a shudder, my old fantasy of the trouble-eating alien who could take human form. Last time a lady, this time a man. The Thing had returned.

'I used to know a woman like you,' I told Adam. 'And, brother, you've still got a lot to learn.'

'Well, *humph*,' flounced Adam. 'When *one* of us is making such an *effort*, I don't see why *one* of us is being so darn *offensive*. That's some attitude problem you've got there, Moor bhai. Bad show. Bad career move, also. I hear you came over all hoity with darling Daddyji as well. At his age! Luckily for him one of his sons at least is willing to do the needfuls without giving backchat or lip.'

∽

Sammy Hazaré lived in the suburb of Andheri, surrounded by a random tangle of light industries – Nazareth Leathercloths, Vajjo's Ayurvedic Laboratory (specialising in vajradanti gel for the gums), Thums Up Cola Bottle Caps, Clenola Brand Cooking Oil, and even a small film studio, mostly used for advertising commercials, which boasted – on a board beside its gate – an 'On-Site Stunter and Stuntess' and 'Manuel Function (6-Man Team) Crane Faslity'. His house, a rutputty single-storey wooden bungalow, long threatened with demolition but still standing, after the happenstance fashion of Bombay life, skulked between the stinking factory backs and a squat yellow group of lower-income housing units, as though it were doing its best to escape the demolition teams' attention. Limes and green chillies hung over the screendoor, to ward off evil spirits. Outdated calendars featuring brightly coloured representations of Lord Ram and elephant-headed Ganesh had for many years been the only other decorations; now, however, pictures of Nadia Wadia, torn from magazines, were Scotch-taped all over the blue-green walls. And there were also society-page photographs of the betrothal of Miss Wadia and Mr M. Zogoiby at the Taj Hotel, and in these pictures my face had been violently crossed out with a pen, or scratched off with the tip of a knife. In one or two I had been completely beheaded. Obscene words had been scrawled across my chest.

Sammy had never married. He shared these quarters with a bald, big-nosed dwarf named Dhirendra, a bit-part movie actor who claimed to have featured in over three hundred feature films and whose life's ambition it was to become the Guinness record-holder for most movie appearances. Dhiren the dwarf cooked and cleaned for fierce Sammy, and even oiled his tin hand when required. And at night, by the light of a paraffin lantern, he helped the Tin-man with his little hobby. Fire-bombs, time-bombs, rocker-triggers and tilt-bombs: the whole house – its cupboards, its nooks and crannies, and even several special holes which the two men had dug beneath the floor of their residence's single room and then boarded over for secrecy – had become a private arsenal. 'If they come to knock us down,' Sammy would tell his little sidekick with a ferocious, fatalistic satisfaction, 'boy, sir, we sure will go out with a bang.'

Once upon a time Sammy and I had been pals; with our non-matching hands we had thought of each other as blood brothers, and for a few years back then we were the terrors of the town, and pint-sized Dhirendra, like a jealous wife, would stay home, cooking meals which Sammy, returning exhausted from our labours, would wolf down without a word of thanks before falling asleep to fill the room with mighty eructations and farts. But now there was Nadia Wadia, and stupid Sammy, in the grip of his pathetic infatuation with that unattainable lady, my fiancée, was ready – or so his walls suggested – to blow off my hated head.

Once upon a time the Tin-man had been Raman Fielding's Cadre Number One, his super-skipper, his man of men. But then Mainduck, himself obsessed with Nadia, had ordered Sammy to rough the bint up a bit, and Hazaré had led a revolution. For a few months Mainduck had kept Sammy where he could see him, watching him with those cold dead eyes, like the eyes with which frogs target their buzzing prey. Then he summoned the Tin-man into his frog-phoned inner sanctum, and gave him the sack.

'Got to let you go, sport,' he said. 'No man is bigger than the game, isn't it, and you started to write your own rules.'

'Sir no skipper sir. Sir ladies and bachcha-log are not combatants sir.'

'Cricket has changed, Tin-man,' said Mainduck softly. 'I see you are of the gentleman era. But, Sammy boy, now it is total war.'

*Andhera* is darkness, and in Andheri, Sammy 'Tin-man' Hazaré sat silently for long hours, wrapped in gloom. In the early days of his Nadia Wadia intoxication, he would sometimes dance around the house, holding up, like a mask, a full-page colour photo of Nadia Wadia into which he had cut peep-holes, so that he could see the world through her eyes; and he would sing the latest movie hits in a girly falsetto voice. '*What is under my choli?*' he sang, jerking his torso suggestively. '*What is under my blouse?*' One day, Dhirendra, driven mad by the interminability of his companion's fixation and also by the appalling quality of his voice, had yelled back, '*Tits! She's got tits under her fucking choli, what do you think? Bleddy party balloons!*' But Sammy, unshaken, had gone on singing. '*Love*,' he warbled. '*Love is what's under my blouse.*'

Now, however, his singing days seemed to be over. Little Dhiren ricocheted around the room, cooking and joking, doing his party tricks – handstands, backflips, contortions – trying to cheer Sammy up, even going so far as to sing the naughty blouse-song, setting aside his own resentments of Nadia Wadia, this pin-up fiction who had materialised from nowhere and, in short order, ruined their lives. Little Dhiren was careful not to share the thought with Sammy, but Nadia Wadia was a female to whom he personally would willingly cause harm.

Finally, Dhirendra found the word of power, the open-sesame, that restored animation to morose Sammy Hazaré. He leapt up on to a table, posed like a little garden statue and spoke the occult syllables. 'RDX,' he announced.

Divided loyalties had never been a problem for Sammy; had he not taken my father's money and spied on Mainduck for years? A poor man must make his way, and backing both sides is never a bad idea. No, divided loyalties were OK: but no loyalties at all? That was confusing. And this Nadia Wadia business had somehow broken all the Tin-man's bonds – to Fielding, to 'Hazaré's XI' and the MA as a whole, to Abraham, and to me. Now he was playing for himself. And if he could not have her, why should anyone? And if his house was not to be permitted to stand, why should not other mansions and towers also crumble and fall? Yes, that was it. He knew secrets, and he could make bombs. These were his aptitudes, his remaining possibilities. 'I will do it,' he said aloud. Those who had hurt him would feel the weight of the Tin-man's hand.

'Stunter-Stuntess can guarantee,' Dhiren was saying. 'Grade A, and to old customers, discount price.' The husband-and-wife team of action-sequence specialists at the nearby film studio – purveyors of harmless flashes and bangs – were also, more privately, involved in enabling the real thing. Small fry they undoubtedly were, but for many years they had been the Tin-man's most reliable suppliers of gelignite, TNT, timers, detonators, fuses. But RDX explosive! Stunter-Stuntess must be going up in the world. For RDX, a person's pockets had to be deep, a person's contacts had to reach pretty high. The action-sequence couple must have been recruited by a bunch of heavy hitters. If RDX was being brought into Bombay, in sufficient quantities for the stuntists to be able to sell off a little on the side, there was serious trouble in the air.

'How much?' Sammy asked.

'Who knows?' cried Dhiren, capering. 'Enough horses for our hobby, that is certain.'

'I have gold saved,' said Sammy Hazaré. 'Also, there is cash. You also are having a nest-egg.'

'An actor's life is short,' protested the dwarf. 'Will you let me starve in twilight years?'

'No twilight for us,' the Tin-man replied. 'Soon we will be fire, like the sun.'

⁓

My 'brother' and I enjoyed no more lunches together. And for 'our' father, too, the years of feeding off the lifeblood of the country were almost over. My mother had already come a cropper. It was time for the paternal plunge.

The story of the headlong fall of Abraham Zogoiby from the very pinnacle of Bombay life has become all too well-known; the speed and size of the crash ensured its notoriety. And from this sorry tale one name is entirely absent, while another name recurs in its chapters, time and time again.

Absent: my name. The name of my father's only biological male child.

Recurring: 'Adam Zogoiby'. Known before that as: 'Adam Braganza'. And before that: 'Aadam Sinai'. And before that? If, as the admirable sleuths of the press discovered and afterwards informed us, his biological parents were named 'Shiva' and 'Parvati', and considering his – forgive me for harping on them – really very large ears indeed, may I suggest 'Ganesh'? Though 'Dumbo' – or 'Goofo', 'Mutto', 'Crooko' – or let's settle for 'Sabu' – might be more appropriate in the case of the detestable Elephant Boy.

So, that twenty-first century kid, that fast-track Infobahni, that *arriviste* crooning I-did-it-I-way, proved to be not only a scheming usurper, but a moron – who thought himself uncatchable, and therefore got caught with laughable ease. And a Jonah, too; dragged the whole shooting-match down with him. Yes, Adam's arrival in our family unleashed the chain-reaction that knocked the great magnate of Siodicorp off his high perch. Permit me, if you will, to recount, while keeping all traces of *schadenfreude* out of my voice, the principal highlights of the gigantic débâcle of the family business.

When the super-financier V. V. 'Crocodile' Nandy was arrested and arraigned on the extraordinary charge of bribing central government ministers to provide him with crore upon crore of public-exchequer funds, with which he actually intended to 'fix' the Bombay Stock Exchange itself, a simultaneous arrestee was the above-named – the so-called – 'Shri Adam Zogoiby', who had allegedly been the 'bagman' in the affair, carrying suitcases containing huge sums of used, out-of-sequence banknotes to the private residences of several of the nation's most prominent men, and then, as he subtly put it in his evidence for the defence, 'accidentally forgetting' them there.

Investigations into the wider activities of 'Shri Adam Zogoiby' – carried out with great zeal by the police force, fraud squad and other appropriate agencies, under intense pressure from, among others, the highly embarrassed central government, and also the MA-controlled Bombay Municipal Corporation, which, in the words of the MA President, Mr Raman Fielding, demanded that 'the nest of vipers must be cleaned with Flit and Vim' – soon revealed his involvement with an even more colossal scandal. The news of the vast global fraud perpetrated by the chiefs of the

Khazana Bank International, of the disappearance of its assets into so-called 'black holes', and of its alleged involvement with terrorist organisations and the large-scale misappropriation of fissile materials, delivery mechanisms and high-technology hard- and software was just beginning to reach the public's incredulous ears; and the name of Abraham Zogoiby's adopted son cropped up on a series of forged bills of lading that had been issued in connection with the ticklish affair of the smuggling of a stolen supercomputer from Japan to an unstated Middle Eastern location. As the Khazana Bank collapsed, and tens of thousands of ordinary citizens from the drivers of hypothecated taxi-cabs to the owners of newsagents and corner shops all over the NRI world found themselves bankrupted, details continued to emerge of the close involvement of Siodicorp's banking arm, the House of Cashondeliveri, with the crashed bank's corrupt principals, many of whom were languishing in British or American jails. Siodicorp stock went into free fall. Abraham – even Abraham – was all but wiped out. By the time the cash-for-armaments scandal broke, and the strong allegations regarding his personal involvement in organised crime brought him to court to face criminal charges including gangsterism, drug-smuggling, giant-scale 'black money' dealings and procuring, the empire he had built from the da Gama family's wealth had been smashed. Bombayites pointed at Cashondeliveri Tower in a sort of revolted awe and wondered when it would crack, like the House of Usher, and come toppling down to earth.

In a panelled courtroom, my ninety-year-old father denied all charges. 'I am not here to participate in some masala-movie remake of *The Godfather*, like some made-in-India Bollywood Mogambo,' he said, standing defiantly erect, and smiling disarmingly, the same smile that his mother Flory had recognised years ago as the rictus of a desperate man. 'Ask anyone from Cochin to Bombay who is Abraham Zogoiby. They will tell you he is a respectable gentleman in the pepper-and-spices business. I say here from the depths of my soul: that is all I am at heart, all I have ever been. My whole life has been spent in the spice trade.'

Bail was set at one crore of rupees, in spite of the prosecution's strenuous protests. 'One does not send one of our city's highest persons to the common lock-up until guilt is proved,' said Mr Justice Kachrawala, and Abraham bowed to the bench. There were still a few places into which his arm could reach. To make bail, the title deeds to the original spice-fields of the da Gama family had to be given in surety. But Abraham walked free, back to *Elephanta*, back to his dying Shangri-La. And sitting alone in a darkened office next to his garden in the sky, he came to the same decision that Sammy Hazaré had made in his condemned Andheri shack: if he was to go down, he would do it with all guns blazing. On the radio and TV, Raman Fielding was crowing about the old man's fall. 'A pretty girl's face on TV will not save Zogoiby now,' he said, and then, astonishingly, burst into song. '*When they come big, then they fall hardia,*' he croaked. '*Hardia, Nadia Wadia, hardia.*' Whereupon Abraham made an unpleasant, conclusive noise and reached for the phone.

Abraham made two telephone calls that night, and received just one. The phone company's records afterwards showed that the first call went to a number at one of the Falkland Road whorehouses controlled by the gang-boss known as 'Scar'. But there is no evidence that any women were sent to Abraham's office, or to his Malabar Hill residence. It seems his message was of another sort.

Later that night – well after midnight – Dom Minto, now over a hundred years old, was Abraham's lone caller. There is no verbatim transcript of their conversation, but I have my father's account of it. Abraham said that Minto had not sounded his usual cantankerous, ebullient self. He was depressed, despondent, and spoke openly about death. 'Let it come! For me, all of existence has been a blue movie,' Minto reportedly stated. 'I have seen enough of what in human life is most filthy and obscene.' The next morning, the old detective was found dead at his desk. 'Foul play', said the investigating officer, Inspector Singh, 'is not suspected.'

Abraham's second call was to me. At his request I arrived at the deserted Cashondeliveri Tower in the deep of the night and used my pass-key to enter and operate his private elevator. What he told me in his darkened room made me less certain than the Inspector about the nature of Dom Minto's demise. He confided that

Sammy Hazaré – apparently unwilling to be seen in the vicinity of Abraham's usual haunts – had visited Minto and sworn an oath on his mother's head that the death of Aurora Zogoiby had been a contract killing carried out by one Chhaggan Five-in-a-Bite at the behest of Raman Fielding.

'But why?' I cried. Abraham's eyes glittered. 'I told you about your Mummyji, boy. Have a taste and then discard unfinished, was her policy in men as well as food. But with Mainduck she bit the wrong fruit. Motive was sexual. Sexual. Sexual . . . revenge.' I had never heard him sound so cruel. Obviously, the pain of Aurora's infidelity still twisted in his gut. The barbarising pain of having to talk about it to their son.

'Then how?' I needed to know. The answer, he told me, was a small hypodermic dart in the neck, of the size used to anaesthetise smaller animals – not elephants, but wild cats, perhaps. Fired from Chowpatty Beach during the madness of Ganpati, it made her head spin, and she fell. On to the tide-washed rocks. The waves must have swept the dart away; and in all that damage, nobody noticed – nobody was looking for – a tiny hole in the side of her neck.

I had been in the VIP stand with Sammy and Fielding that day, I remembered; but Chhaggan could have been anywhere. Chhaggan, who, with Sammy, was the joint blow-pipe champion of Mainduck's indoor Olympiads. 'But this can't have been a blow-pipe,' I thought aloud. 'Much too far. And shooting up as well.'

Abraham shrugged. 'Then a dart-gun,' he said. 'Details are all in Sammy's deposition. Minto will bring it in the morning. You know,' he added, 'that it will not stand up in court.'

'It won't have to,' I answered him. 'This matter will not be decided by any jury or judge.'

Minto died before he could bring Sammy's testimony to Abraham. The document was not found among his papers. Inspector Singh did not suspect foul play; but that was a matter for him. Me, I had work to do. Ancient, irrefutable imperatives had claimed me. Against all expectation, my mother's perturbed shade was hovering at my shoulder, crying havoc. *Blood will have blood. Wash my body in my murderers' red fountains and let me R.I.P.*

Mother, I will.

The mosque at Ayodhya was destroyed. Alphabet-soupists, 'fanatics', or, alternatively, 'devout liberators of the sacred site' (delete according to taste) swarmed over the seventeenth-century Babri Masjid and tore it apart with their bare hands, with their teeth, with the elemental power of what Sir V. Naipaul has approvingly called their 'awakening to history'. The police, as the press photographs showed, stood by and watched the forces of history do their history-obliterating work. Saffron flags were raised. There was much chanting of *dhuns*: 'Raghupati Raghava Raja Ram' &c. It was one of those moments best described as irreconcilable: both joyful and tragic, both authentic and spurious, both natural and manipulated. It opened doors and shut them. It was an end and a beginning. It was what Camoens da Gama had prophesied long ago: the coming of the Battering Ram.

Nobody could even be sure, some commentators dared to point out, that the present-day town of Ayodhya in U.P. stood on the same site as the mythical Ayodhya, home of Lord Ram in the Ramayan. Nor was the notion of the existence there of Ram's birthplace, the Ramjanmabhoomi, an ancient tradition – it wasn't a hundred years old. It had actually been a Muslim worshipper at the old Babri mosque who had first claimed to see a vision of Lord Ram there, and so started the ball rolling; what could be a finer image of religious tolerance and plurality than that? After the vision, Muslims and Hindus had, for a time, shared the contested site without fuss . . . but to the devil with such old news! Who cared about those unhealthy, split hairs? The building had fallen. It was a time for consequences, not backward glances: for what-happened-next, not what might or might not have gone before.

What happened next: in Bombay, there was a nocturnal burglary at the Zogoiby Bequest. The thieves were swift and professional; the gallery's alarm system was revealed as hopelessly inadequate, and, in more than one zone, totally dysfunctional. Four paintings were taken, all belonging to the Moor cycle, and plainly pre-selected – one from each of the three major periods, and also the last, unfinished, but nevertheless supreme canvas, *The*

*Moor's Last Sigh*. The curator, Dr Zeenat Vakil, tried in vain to persuade radio and TV stations to carry the story. Events at Ayodhya, and their bloody after-effects, swamped the airwaves. Had it not been for Raman Fielding, the loss of these national treasures would not have made the news at all. The MA boss, commenting on Doordarshan, linked the mosque's fall and the pictures' disappearance. 'When such alien artefacts disappear from India's holy soil, let no man mourn,' he said. 'If the new nation is to be born, there is much invader history that may have to be erased.'

So we were invaders now, were we? After two thousand years, we still did not belong, and indeed, were soon to be 'erased' – which 'cancellation' need not be followed by any expressions of regret, or grief. Mainduck's insult to Aurora's memory made it easier for me to carry out the deed upon which I was resolved.

My assassin mood cannot properly be ascribed to atavism; though inspired by my mother's death, this was scarcely a recurrence of characteristics that had skipped a few generations! It might more accurately be termed a sort of *in-law inheritance*; for had not match after match imported violence into the da Gama household? Epifania brought her murderous Menezes clan, and Carmen her lethal Lobos. And Abraham had had the killer instinct from the start, though he preferred to employ others to carry out his commands. Only my true-loving maternal grandparents, Camoens and Belle, were innocent of such a charge.

My own amorous liaisons had scarcely been an improvement. I cast no slur upon sweet Dilly; but what of Uma, who deprived me of my mother's love by persuading her that I harboured indecent passions? What of Uma the would-be murderess, who only failed to kill me because of the head-banging intervention of slapstick comedy in a scene of *grand guignol*?

But, after all, there is no need to lay the blame on forebears or lovers. My own career as a beater of men – my pulverising Hammer period – had its origins in a sport of nature, which had packed so much punching power into my otherwise powerless right hand. It is true that I had, thus far, never killed a man; but given the weight and extended length of some of the poundings I administered, that can only be put down to luck. If, in the matter of

Raman Fielding, I took it upon myself to be judge, jury and executioner, it is because it was in my nature so to do.

Civilisation is the sleight of hand that conceals our natures from ourselves. My hand, gentle reader, lacked sleight; but it knew what manner of thing it was.

So, blood-lust was in my history, and it was in my bones. I did not waver in my decision for an instant; I would have vengeance – or die in the attempt. My thoughts had run constantly on dying of late. Here, at last, was a way of giving meaning to my otherwise feeble end. I realised with a kind of abstract surprise that I was ready to die, as long as Raman Fielding's corpse lay close at hand. So I had become a murdering fanatic, too. (Or a righteous avenger; take your pick.)

Violence was violence, murder was murder, two wrongs did not make a right: these are truths of which I was fully cognisant. Also: by sinking to your adversary's level you lose the high ground. In the days after the destruction of the Babri Masjid, 'justly enraged Muslims'/'fanatical killers' (once again, use your blue pencil as your heart dictates) smashed up Hindu temples, and killed Hindus, across India and in Pakistan as well. There comes a point in the unfurling of communal violence in which it becomes irrelevant to ask, 'Who started it?' The lethal conjugations of death part company with any possibility of justification, let alone justice. They surge among us, left and right, Hindu and Muslim, knife and pistol, killing, burning, looting, and raising into the smoky air their clenched and bloody fists. Both their houses are damned by their deeds; both sides sacrifice the right to any shred of virtue; they are each other's plagues.

I do not exempt myself. I have been a man of violence for too long, and on the night after Raman Fielding insulted my mother on TV, I brutally put an end to his accursed life. And in so doing called a curse down upon my own.

～

At night, the walls around Fielding's property were patrolled by eight paired teams of crack cadres working three-hour shifts; I knew most of their inner-circle nicknames. The gardens were protected by four throat-ripping Alsatians (Gavaskar, Vengsarkar, Mankad and – as evidence of their owner's lack of prejudice – Azharuddin); these metamorphosed cricket stars came up to me to be caressed, and wagged happy tails. At the door to the house proper were further guards. I knew these thugs, too – a couple of young giants going by the names of Badmood and Sneezo – but they searched me from head to foot anyway. I was carrying no weapon; or, at any rate, no weapon that they could remove from my person. 'Id's lige old tibes today,' Sneezo, the younger, permanently bung-nosed and – perhaps in compensation – less tight-lipped of these friskers told me. 'The Tid-bad stobbed by earlier to bay his resbegds. I thig he was hobig to be tagen bag on, but the sgibber is a tough-binded guy.' I said I was sorry to have missed Sammy; and how was old Five-in-a-Bite? 'He feld sorry for Hazaré,' the young guard mumbled. 'They wend off dogether to ged drung.' His colleague smacked the back of his head and he fell silent. 'It's odly Habber,' he complained, squeezing his nose between thumb and forefinger, and blowing hard. Mucus sprayed in all directions. I backed hastily away.

It was a stroke of luck, I knew, that Chhaggan was not on the premises. He had a sixth, even a seventh sense for trouble, and my chances of overcoming him as well as Fielding, and escaping without raising a general alarm, would have been nil. I had come expecting no better; this fortuitous absence gave me a chance, at least, of getting off the premises alive.

The taciturn one, the head-smacker, Badmood, asked me my business. I repeated what I had said at the gates. 'For skipper's ears only.' Badmood looked displeased: 'No chance.' I made a face. 'Then it's on your head, when he finds out.' He gave in. 'Fortunate for you, skipper is working late on account of national happenings,' he said furiously. 'Wait on and I will inquire.' And after some moments he returned and jerked an enraged thumb towards the inner lair.

Mainduck was working by the yellow light of a single Anglepoise lamp. His large bespectacled head was half-illuminated, half in darkness; the great bulk of his body merged with the night. Was he alone? Hard to be sure. 'Hammer, Hammer,' he croaked. 'And how have you come tonight? As your father's emissary, or a traitor to his fucked-up cause?'

'Messenger,' I said. He nodded. 'Then, deliver.'

'For your ears only,' I told him. 'Not for microphones.' Many years ago Fielding had spoken admiringly of the American President Nixon's decision to bug his own office. 'Guy had a sense of history,' he'd said. 'Guts, too. Everything on the record.' I'd pointed out that these tapes had helped to terminate his presidency. Fielding pooh-poohed the objection. 'What I say cannot undo me,' he proclaimed. 'My ideology is my fortune! And one day the kiddiwinks will study my statements at school.'

Therefore: *not for microphones*. He grinned from ear to ear, looking, in his pool of light, more Cheshire Cat than frog. 'You remember too damn much, Hammer,' he chided me fondly. 'So come, come, my dearie. Whisper sweet nothings in my ear.'

I had grown old, I worried as I walked over to him. Maybe the old KO punch had gone. *Give me the strength*, I prayed to nothing in particular: to Aurora's ghost, perhaps. *One last time. Let me still have my hammer-blow.* The green frog-phone stared up at me from his desk. God, I hated that phone. I bent towards Mainduck; who flung out his left hand, at high speed, caught me by the hair at the nape of my neck, and jammed my mouth into the left side of his head. Off-balance for a moment, I realised with some horror that my right hand, my only weapon, could no longer reach the target. But as I fell against the edge of the desk, my left hand – that same left hand which I had had to force myself, all my life, and against my nature, to learn how to use – collided, by chance, with the telephone.

'The message is from my mother,' I whispered, and smashed the green frog into his face. He made no sound. His fingers released my hair, but the frog-phone kept wanting to kiss him, so I kissed him with it, as hard as I could, then harder, and harder still, until the plastic splintered and the instrument began to come apart in my hand. 'Cheap fucking gimmick item,' I thought, and put it down.

❦

How Lord Ram slew the fair Sita's abductor, Ravan, King of
Lanka:

*Still the dubious battle lasted, until Rama in his ire*
*Wielded Brahma's deathful weapon flaming with celestial fire!*
*Weapon which the Saint Agastya had unto the hero given,*
*Winged as lightning dart of Indra, fatal as the bolt of heaven,*
*Wrapped in smoke and flaming flashes, speeding from the circled bow,*
*Pierced the iron heart of Ravan, laid the lifeless hero low . . .*
*Voice of blessing from the bright sky fell on Raghu's valiant son,*
*'Champion of the true and righteous! now thy noble task is done!'*

How Achilles slew Hector, Patroclus' killer:

*Then answered Hector of the flashing helm,*
*His strength all gone: 'I beg thee by thy life,*
*Thy knees, thy parents, leave me not for dogs*
*Of the Achaeans by the ships to eat . . . '*
*But scowling at him swift Achilles said:*
*'Do not entreat me, dog, by knees or parents.*
*I only wish I had the heart and will*
*To hack the flesh off thee and eat it raw,*
*For all that thou hast done to me! there lives*
*None who shall keep the dogs away from thee . . .*
*. . . but dogs and birds shall eat thee utterly.'*

You see the difference. Where Ram had the use of a heavenly
doomsday-machine, I had to make do with a telecommunicative
frog. And, afterwards, received no heavenly words of congratula-
tion for my deed. As for Achilles: I had neither his innard-
munching savagery (so reminiscent, if I may say so, of Hind of
Mecca, who gobbled the dead hero Hamza's heart) nor his poetic
turn of phrase. The Achaeans' dogs, however, did have their local
counterparts . . .

. . . After Ram killed Ravan he chivalrously arranged a lavish
funeral for his fallen foe. Achilles, much the less gallant of these
high heroes, tied Hector's corpse to his 'chariot-tail' and dragged
him thrice round dead Patroclus's grave. As for me: not living in
heroic times, I neither honoured nor desecrated my victim's body;

my thoughts were for myself, my chances of survival and escape. After I had murdered Fielding I turned him in his chair, so that he faced away from the door (though he no longer had a face). I set his feet up on a bookshelf and folded his arms across his pulpy wounds, so that he seemed to have fallen asleep, exhausted by his labours. Then quickly, quietly, I searched for the recording machines – there would be two, to back each other up.

They were easy enough to find. Fielding had never made a secret of his recording zeal, and his office cupboards – which were unlocked – revealed to me the spools whirling slowly, like dervishes, in the dark. I ripped out lengths of tape and stuffed them in my pockets.

It was time to go. I left the room and closed the door with exaggerated care. 'Do not disturb,' I whispered to Badmood and Sneezo. 'Skipper's catching forty winks.' That held them for the moment, but would I have time to leave the property? I had visions of yells, whistles, shots, and four transmogrified cricketers, snarling loudly as they leapt for my throat. My feet began to hurry; I slowed them down, and then came to a halt. Gavaskar, Vengsarkar, Mankad and Azharuddin came up and licked my good hand. I knelt and hugged them. Then I rose, left dogs and Mumbadevi statues behind me, went out through the gates, and got into the Mercedes-Benz I had taken from the Cashondeliveri Tower carpool. As I drove away I wondered who would get to me first: the police, or Chhaggan Five-in-a-Bite. On the whole, I would prefer the police. *A second dead body, Mr Zogoiby. Careless. The slackfulness is terrific.*

There was an animal noise behind me, except that no animal ever roared so loud, and a giant's hand spun my car around, twice, and blew out my rear windows. The Murs'deez stalled, facing the wrong way.

The sun had come out. The first thing I thought of was *The Walrus and the Carpenter*. 'The moon was shining sulkily,/Because she thought the sun/Had got no business to be there/After the day was done./"It's very rude of him," she said,/"To come and spoil the fun!" ' My second thought was that an aeroplane had crashed on the city. There were high flames now, and screams, and for the first time I realised that something had happened at the Fielding residence. I heard Sneezo's voice again: 'The Tid–bad stobbed by earlier to bay his resbegds.'

His last respects. His sacked old warrior's respects. How had Sammy the bomber smuggled this device past the searching guards? I could come up with just one answer. *Inside his metal limb.* Which meant it had to be pretty small. No room for dynamite sticks in there. What then? Plastique, RDX, Semtex? 'Bravo, Sammy,' I thought. 'Miniaturisation, eh? Wah-wah. Only the best, latest stuff for Mainduck.' Who would not be giving anyone else the sack in a hurry. It occurred to me that I had murdered a dead man. Even though he had still been alive when I got to him, Sammy had beaten me to the knockout punch.

It took me a few more moments to work out that there wouldn't be much left of Mainduck. Sammy was good enough to have made sure of that. It was quite possible, therefore, that I would not come under suspicion of having committed any crime at all. Though, as the last man to have seen Raman Fielding alive, I would no doubt have questions to answer. The car obediently started first time. The air was horrid with smoke and all-too-identifiable stenches. Many people were running. It was time to leave. As I reversed down the street I imagined I heard the barking of hungry dogs who had unexpectedly been thrown large chunks of meat, mostly still on the bone. That, and the flapping of vultures.

∽

'Get out,' said Abraham Zogoiby. 'Do it pronto. And stay out.'

It was my last walk with him in his aerial orchard. I had made my report about the fatal events in Bandra. 'So Hazaré is a loose cannon,' my father said. 'Doesn't matter. Side-issue. Some supplier is dealing on the side, that will have to be taken up. But, none of your business. Just now you are under no restraint. Therefore, goodbye. Take your leave. While you can do it, go.'

'What will happen here?'

'Your brother will rot in jail. Everything will end. I also am finished. But my finish: that has not yet begun.'

I took a ripe apple from a basket, and asked him my last question. 'Once,' I said, 'Vasco Miranda told you that this was no country for us. At that time he said to you what you are now saying to me. "Macaulay's Minutemen, get out." So, then: was he right? Vamoose, go West? That's it?'

'Your documents are in order?' Abraham, his power ended, seemed to be ageing before my eyes, like an immortal forced, at last, to step outside the magic portals of Shangri-La. But yes, I nodded, my documents were in order. That much-renewed passage to Spain which was my mother's legacy to me. That window to another world.

'Then go ask him yourself,' said Abraham, smiling his despairing smile as he walked away from me into the trees. I let the apple fall and turned to go.

'Ohé, Moraes,' he called after me. Shameless, grinning, defeated. 'Bleddy stupid fool. Who do you think had those pictures stolen if not your loony Miranda? Go find them, boy. Go find your precious Palimpstine. Go see Mooristan.' And his last command, the closest he came to a declaration of affection: 'Take the bleddy pooch.' I left that celestial garden with Jawaharlal under my arm. It was almost dawn. There was a red rim edging the planet, dividing us from the sky. It looked as if someone, or something, had been crying.

⌢

Bombay blew apart. Here's what I've been told: three hundred kilograms of RDX explosive were used. Two and a half thousand kilos more were captured later, some in Bombay, others in a lorry near Bhopal. Also timers, detonators, the works. There had been nothing like it in the history of the city. Nothing so cold-blooded, so calculated, so cruel. *Dhhaaiiiyn!* A busload of schoolkids. *Dhhaaiiiyn!* The Air-India building. *Dhhaaiiiyn!* Trains, residences, chawls, docks, movie-studios, mills, restaurants. *Dhhaaiiiyn! Dhhaaiiiyn! Dhhaaiiiyn!* Commodity exchanges, office buildings, hospitals, the busiest shopping streets in the heart of town. Bits of bodies were lying everywhere; human and animal blood, guts, and bones. Vultures so drunk on flesh that they sat lop-sidedly on rooftops, waiting for appetite to return.

Who did it? Many of Abraham's enemies were hit – policemen, MA cadres, criminal rivals. *Dhhaaiiiyn!* My father in the hour of his annihilation made a phone call, and the metropolis began to explode. But could even Abraham, with his immense resources, have stockpiled such an arsenal? How could gang warfare explain the legion of innocent dead? Hindu and Muslim areas were both attacked; men, women, children perished, and there was nobody to give the dignity of meaning to their deaths. What avenging demon bestrode the horizon, raining fire upon our heads? Was the city simply murdering itself?

Abraham went to war, and let his curse fall wheresoever it could. That was some of it. It wasn't enough; it wasn't everything. I don't know everything. I'm telling you what I know.

Here's what *I* want to know: who killed *Elephanta*, who murdered my home? Who blew it to bits, and 'Lambajan Chandiwala' Borkar, Miss Jaya Hé and Ezekiel of the magic copybooks along with the bricks and mortar? Was it dead Fielding's revenge, or freelance Hazaré's, or was there some more profound movement in history, deeper down, where not even those of us who had spent so long in the Under World could see it?

Bombay was central; had always been. Just as the fanatical 'Catholic Kings' had besieged Granada and awaited the Alhambra's fall, so now barbarism was standing at our gates. O Bombay! *Prima in Indis! Gateway to India! Star of the East with her face to the West!* Like Granada – al-Gharnatah of the Arabs – you were the glory of your time. But a darker time came upon you, and just as Boabdil, the last Nasrid Sultan, was too weak to defend his great treasure, so we, too, were proved wanting. For the barbarians were not only at our gates but within our skins. We were our own wooden horses, each one of us full of our doom. Maybe Abraham Zogoiby lit the fuse, or Scar: these fanatics or those, our crazies or yours; but the explosions burst out of our very own bodies. We were both the bombers and the bombs. The explosions were our own evil – no need to look for foreign explanations, though there was and is evil beyond our frontiers as well as within. We have chopped away our own legs, we engineered our own fall. And now can only weep, at the last, for what we were too enfeebled, too corrupt, too little, too contemptible to defend.

– Excuse, please, the outburst. Got carried away. Old Moor will sigh no more. –

⁓

Dr Zeenat Vakil was killed in the fireball that ripped through the Zogoiby Bequest gallery on Cumballa Hill. Nor was a single picture spared; thus consigning my mother Aurora to a region close to the realm of irretrievable antiquity – to the outskirts of that hellish garden filled with the helpless shades of those – now as headless and armless as their statues – whose life-work vanished away. (I think of Cimabue, known to us by a mere handful of pieces.) *The Scandal* was spared. It had been on permanent loan from the Bequest to the National Museum in Delhi, and it's still there, facing Amrita Sher-Gil with confidence. A few other canvases remain. Four early Chipkali drawings; *Uper the gur gur* . . . ; and the sharp, painful *Mother-Naked Moor*: which had all, by chance, been on loan, in India or abroad. Also, ironically, the troublesome cricket fantasy hanging on the Wadia ladies' sitting-room wall, *The Kissing of Abbas Ali Baig*. Eight. Plus the Stedelijk picture, the Tate picture, the Gobler collection. A few 'Red Period' pictures in private ownership. (How ironic that she had destroyed most of these herself!)

More surviving work than Cimabue, then; but a mere shred of the total output of that prolific woman.

And the four stolen Auroras now represented a crucial segment of her surviving body of work.

⁓

On the morning of the explosions, Miss Nadia Wadia personally answered her doorbell, because the servant had gone out at dawn to do the marketing and had failed to return. Standing before her were a couple of cartoons: a dwarf in khaki and a man with a metal face and hand. A scream and a giggle collided in her throat; but

373

before she could make any kind of sound Sammy Hazaré had raised a cutlass and slashed her twice across the face, in parallel lines running from top right to bottom left, expertly missing her eyes. She passed out on the doormat, and when she regained consciousness, her head was in her distraught mother's lap, her own blood was on her lips, and her unknown assailants had vanished, never to return.

~

The mahaguru Khusro perished in the bombings; the pink skyscraper at Breach Candy, where 'Adam Zogoiby' had been raised, was also destroyed. The body of Chhaggan 'Five-in-a-Bite' was found in a Bandra gutter; huge cutlass gouges had opened up its neck. Dhabas in Dhobi Talao, cinemas showing the wide-screen remake of the old classic *Gai-Wallah*, the Sorryno and Pioneer cafés: all these were no more. And Sister Floreas, my one true remaining sibling, turned out to have been wrong about the future; bombs claimed the Gratiaplena nursing home and nunnery, and Minnie was among the dead.

*Dhhaaiiiyn! Dhhaaiiiyn!* Not only sister, friends, paintings, and favourite haunts, but also feeling itself was blown apart. When life became so cheap, when heads were bouncing across the maidans and headless bodies were dancing in the street, how to care about any single early exit? How to care about the imminent probability of one's own? After each monstrosity came a greater; like true addicts, we seemed to need each increased dose. Catastrophe had become the city's habit, and we were all its users, its zombies, its undead. Disaffected and – to use the over-used word properly for once – shocked, I entered a remote and godlike state. The city I knew was dying. The body I inhabited, ditto. So what? *Que sera sera* . . .

And lo, what was to be, came to pass. Sammy 'the Tin-man' Hazaré, with little Dhirendra trotting determinedly by his side, marched into the lobby of Cashondeliveri Tower. Explosives were tied to their torsos, legs and backs. Dhirendra carried two detonators; Sammy was brandishing his sword. The building's guards saw that the heroin the bombers had taken to give them courage was weighing heavily on their eyes and making their bodies itch, and they backed away in terror. Sammy and Dhiren took the non-stop elevator to the thirty-first floor. The Chief of Security rang Abraham Zogoiby to screech warnings and make self-exculpatory remarks. Abraham interrupted curtly. 'Evacuate the building.' These are his last known words.

Tower workers started spilling madly into the street. Sixty seconds later, however, the great atrium at the top of Cashondeli-veri Tower burst like a firework in the sky and a rain of glass knives began to fall, stabbing the running workers through the neck the back the thigh, spearing their dreams, their loves, their hope. And after the glass knives, further monsoon rains. Many workers had been trapped in the tower by the blast. Lifts were inoperative, stairwells had collapsed, there were fires and clouds of ravenous black smoke. There were those who despaired, who exploded from the windows and tumbled to their deaths.

Finally, Abraham's garden rained down like a benediction. Imported soil, English lawn-grass and foreign flowers – crocuses, daffodils, roses, hollyhocks, forget-me-nots – fell towards the Backbay Reclamation; also alien fruits. Whole trees rose gracefully into the heavens before floating down to earth, like giant spores. The feathers of un-Indian birds went on drifting through the air for days.

Peppercorns, whole cumin, cinnamon sticks, cardamoms mingled with the imported flora and birdlife, dancing rat-a-tat on the roads and sidewalks like perfumed hail. Abraham had always kept sacks of Cochin spices close at hand. Sometimes, when he was alone, he would open their necks, and plunge his nostalgic arms into their odorous depths. Fenugreek and nigella, coriander seeds and asafoetida fell upon Bombay; but black pepper most of all, the Black Gold of Malabar, upon which, an eternity and a day ago, a young duty manager and a fifteen-year-old girl had fallen in pepper love.

~

*To form a class*, Macaulay wrote in the 1835 Minute on Education, ... *of persons, Indian in blood and colour, but English in opinions, in morals, and in intellect.* And why, pray? O, to be *interpreters between us and the millions whom we govern.* How grateful such a class of persons should, and must, be! For in India the dialects were *poor and rude*, and *a single shelf of a good European library was worth the whole native literature.* History, science, medicine, astronomy, geography, religion were likewise derided. *Would disgrace an English farrier . . . would move laughter in girls at an English boarding-school.*

Thus, a class of 'Macaulay's Minutemen' would hate the best of India. Vasco was wrong. We were not, had never been, that class. The best, and worst, were in us, and fought in us, as they fought in the land at large. In some of us, the worst triumphed; but still we could say – and say truthfully – that we had loved the best.

As my aeroplane banked over the city I could see columns of smoke rising. There was nothing holding me to Bombay any more. It was no longer my Bombay, no longer special, no longer the city of mixed-up, mongrel joy. Something had ended (the world?) and what remained, I didn't know. I found myself looking forward to Spain – to Elsewhere. I was going to the place whence we had been cast out, centuries ago. Might it not turn out to be my lost home, my resting-place, my promised land? Might it not be my Jerusalem?

'Eh, Jawaharlal?' But the stuffed mutt on my lap had nothing to say.

I was wrong about one thing, however: the end of a world is not the end of the world. My ex-fiancée, Nadia Wadia, appeared on television a few days after the attacks, when the scars across her face were still livid, the permanence of the disfiguration all too evident. And yet her beauty was so touching, her courage so evident, that in a way she looked even lovelier than before. A news interviewer was trying to ask her about her ordeal; but, in an extraordinary moment, she turned away from him, and spoke directly into the camera, and every viewer's heart. 'So I asked myself, Nadia Wadia, is it the end for you? Is it curtains? And for some time I thought, achha, yes, it's all over, khalaas. But then I was asking myself, Nadia Wadia, what you talking, men? At twenty-three to say that whole of life is funtoosh? What pagalpan, what nonsense, Nadia Wadia! Girl, get a grip, OK? The city will survive. New towers will rise. Better days will come. Now I am saying it every day. Nadia Wadia, the future beckons. Hearken to its call.'

# IV
# 'THE MOOR'S LAST SIGH'

# 19

I WENT TO BENENGELI because I had been told by my father that Vasco Miranda, a man I had not seen for fourteen years – or twenty-eight, according to my personal, quick-time calendar – was holding my dead mother prisoner there; or if not my mother, then the best part of what remained of her. I suppose I was hoping to reclaim these stolen goods, and, by so doing, to heal something in myself before I reached my own conclusion.

I had never been up in a plane before, and the experience of passing through clouds – I had left Bombay on a rare cloudy day – was so spookily like the images of the After Life in movies, paintings and story-books that I got the shivers. Was I travelling to the country of the dead? I half-expected to see a pair of pearly gates standing on the fluffy fields of cumulus outside my window, and a man holding a double-entry account-book of rights and wrongs. Sleep rolled over me, and in my first-ever high-altitude dreams I learned that I had indeed already left the land of the living. Perhaps I had died in the bombings like so many of the people and places I cared about. When I awoke, this sensation of having passed through a veil lingered on. A friendly young woman was offering me food and drink. I accepted both. The little bottle of red Rioja wine was delicious, but too small. I asked for more.

'I feel as if I have slipped in time,' I told the friendly stewardess some while later. 'But whether into the future or the past, I cannot say.'

'Many passengers feel that way,' she reassured me. 'I tell them, it is neither. The past and future are where we spend most of our lives. In fact, what you are going through in this small micro-cosmos of ours is the disorienting feeling of having slipped for a few hours into the present.' Her name was Eduvigis Refugio and she was a psychology major from the Complutense University of Madrid. A certain footloose quality of soul had led her to set aside her education and take up this peripatetic life, she confided freely, sitting down for a few minutes in the empty seat beside me, and taking Jawaharlal on to her own lap. 'Shanghai! Montevideo! Alice Springs! Do you know that places only yield up their secrets, their most profound mysteries, to those who are just passing through? Just as it is possible to confide in a total stranger encountered in a bus station – or aboard an aeroplane – such intimacies as would make you blush if you even hinted at them to those you live amongst. What a sweet stuffed dog, by the way! I myself have a collection of small stuffed birds; and, from the South Seas, a genuine shrunken head. But the real reason why I travel,' and here she leaned in close, 'is the pleasure I take from promiscuity, and in a Catholic country like Spain it isn't easy to have my fill.' Even then – such was my internal, in-flight turbulence – I did not understand that she was offering me her body. She had to spell it out. 'On this flight we help each other,' she said. 'My colleagues will keep watch and make sure we are not disturbed.' She led me to a small toilet cubicle and we had sex very briefly: she reached her orgasm with a few swift movements while I was unable to do so at all, especially as she appeared to lose all interest in me the instant her own needs had been satisfied. I accepted the situation passively – for passivity had me in its grip – and we both rearranged our clothing and briskly went our separate ways. Some time later I felt a great urge to talk to her some more, if only to fix her face and voice in my memory, from which they were already fading, but a different woman appeared in response to the little light I illuminated by pushing a button bearing a schematic representation of a human being. 'I wanted Eduvigis,' I explained, and the new young woman frowned. 'I beg your pardon? Did you say "Rioja"?' Sound is altered in an aeroplane, and perhaps I had slurred my words, so I repeated quite distinctly, 'Eduvigis Refugio, the psychologist.'

'You must have been dreaming, sir,' said the young woman with a peculiar smile. 'There is no stewardess by that name aboard this flight.' When I insisted that there was, and possibly raised my voice, a man with gold hoops round the cuffs of his blazer came up quickly. 'Be quiet and sit still,' he ordered me roughly, pushing at my shoulder. 'At your age, grand-dad, and with your deformity! You should be ashamed to make such propositions to decent girls. You Indian men all think our European women are whores.' I was aghast; but now that I looked at the second young woman, I saw that she was dabbing at the corners of her eyes with a handkerchief. 'I am sorry to have caused such distress,' I apologised. 'Let me state here and now that I unequivocally withdraw all my requests.'

'That's better,' nodded the man in the hooped blazer. 'Since you have seen the error of your ways, we'll say no more about it.' And he went off with the second woman, who had begun to look quite cheerful; indeed, as they disappeared down the aisle, they seemed to be having quite a giggle together, and I had the impression that they must be having a laugh at my expense. I could find no explanation for what had happened, and so fell back into a deep and, this time, dreamless sleep. I never saw Eduvigis Refugio again. I allowed myself to imagine that she was a sort of phantom of the air, called forth by my own desires. No doubt such houris did float up here, above the clouds. They could pass through the aircraft's walls whenever they chose.

You will see that I had entered an unfamiliar state of mind. The place, language, people and customs I knew had all been removed from me by the simple act of boarding this flying vehicle; and these, for most of us, are the four anchors of the soul. If one adds on the effects, some of them delayed, of the horrors of the last days, then perhaps it is possible to see why I felt as if all the roots of my self had been torn up like those of the flying trees from Abraham's atrium. The new world I was entering had given me an enigmatic warning, a shot across my bows. I must remember that I knew nothing, understood nothing. I was alone in a mystery. But at least there was a quest; I must cling to that. That was my direction, and by pursuing it as energetically as I could, I might come in time to comprehend this surreal foreignness whose meanings I could not begin, as yet, to decode.

I changed planes at Madrid, and was relieved to have left that strange crew behind. On the much smaller plane south I kept myself very much to myself, hugging Jawaharlal and answering all offers of food and wine with a curt, negative shake of the head. By the time I arrived in Andalusia the memory of my transcontinental flight was fading. I could no longer call to mind the faces or voices of the three attendants who had, I was now convinced, conspired to play a practical joke on me, no doubt selecting me because it was my maiden flight, a fact I may have revealed to Eduvigis Refugio – yes, indeed, now that I thought about it, I was sure I had. Apparently air travel was not nearly as enlivening as Eduvigis had suggested; those who were condemned to interminable, altered hours in the sky had to lend a little cheer to their lives, a little erotic thrill, by playing games with virgins such as I. Well, good luck to them! They had taught me a lesson about keeping my feet on the ground, and, after all, given my decrepit condition, any offer of sex rated as a positively charitable act.

I emerged from the second plane into brilliant sunlight and intense heat – not the 'rotten heat', heavy and humid, of my home town, but a bracing, dry heat that was much easier on my ruined, rackety lungs. I saw mimosa trees in bloom, and hills dotted with olive groves. The feeling of strangeness had not left me, however. It was as if I hadn't quite arrived, or not all of me, or perhaps the place I'd landed in wasn't exactly the right place – almost, but not quite. I felt dizzy, deaf, old. Dogs barked in the distance. My head ached. I was wearing a big leather coat and sweating hard. I should have drunk some water on the flight.

'A vacation?' a man in uniform asked me when it was my turn.

'Yes.'

'What will you see? While you are here you must see our great sights.'

'I hope to see some pictures by my mother.'

'That is a surprising hope. Do you not have many pictures of your mother in your own country?'

'Not "of". "By".'

'I do not understand. Where is your mother? Is she here? In this place, or in another place? Are you visiting relatives?'

'She is dead. We were estranged and now she is dead.'

'The death of a mother is a terrible thing. Terrible. And now you hope to find her in a foreign land. It is unusual. Maybe you will not have time for tourism.'

'No, maybe not.'

'You must make time. You must see our great sights. Definitely! It is necessary. You comprehend?'

'Yes. I comprehend.'

'What is the dog? Why is the dog?'

'It is the former Prime Minister of India, metamorphosed into canine form.'

'Never mind.'

I spoke no Spanish, so I was unable to haggle with the taxi-drivers. 'Benengeli,' I said, and the first cabbie shook his head and walked away, spitting copiously. The second named a number that had no meaning for me. I had come to a place where I did not know the names of things or the motives for men's deeds. The universe was absurd. I could not say 'dog', or 'where?', or 'I am a man'. Besides, my head was thick, like a soup.

'Benengeli,' I repeated, throwing my bag into the back of the third cab, and followed it in with Jawaharlal under my arm. The driver grinned a great golden-toothed smile. Those of his teeth that were not made of gold had been filed into menacing triangular shapes. But he seemed a pleasant enough sort. He pointed at himself. 'Vivar.' He pointed towards the mountains. 'Benengeli.' He pointed at his car. 'Okay, pardner. Less mak' track.' We were both citizens of the world, I realised. Our common language was the broken argot of dreadful American films.

The village of Benengeli lies in the Alpujarras, a spur of the Sierra Morena which separates Andalusia from La Mancha. As we climbed up into those hills I saw many dogs criss-crossing the road. Afterwards I learned that foreigners would settle here for a while, with their families and pets, and then, in their fickle, rootless fashion, depart, abandoning their dogs to their fates. The region was full of starving, disappointed Andalusian dogs. When I heard this I started pointing them out to Jawaharlal. 'Think yourself lucky,' I would say. 'There, but for the grace.'

We entered the small town of Avellaneda, famous for its three-hundred-year-old bull-ring, and Vivar the driver accelerated.

'Town of thieves,' he explained. 'Bad medicine.' The next settlement was Erasmo, a village smaller than Avellaneda, but substantial enough to boast a sizeable school building over whose doorway were inscribed the words *Lectura − locura*. I asked the driver if he could translate, and after some hesitations he found the words. 'Reading, *lectura*. *Lectura*, reading,' he said proudly.

'And *locura*?'

'Is madness, pardner.'

A woman in black, swathed in a rebozo, peered at us suspiciously as we bumped along Erasmo's cobbled streets. Some sort of passionate meeting was taking place under a spreading tree in a square. Slogans and banners were everywhere. I copied several of them down. I had supposed them to be political utterances, but they turned out to be far more unusual. 'Men are so necessarily mad that it would be crazy, through a further twist of madness, not to be mad oneself,' said one banner. Another pronounced: 'Everything in life is so diverse, so opposed, so obscure, that we cannot be certain of any truth.' And a third, more pithily: 'All is possible.' It seemed that a philosophy class from a nearby university had conceived the notion of meeting in this village, because of its name, to discuss the radical, sceptical notions of Blaise Pascal, the old folly-praiser Erasmus himself, and Marsilio Ficino, among others. The frenzy and ardour of the philosophers was so great that it gathered crowds. The villagers of Erasmo enjoyed taking sides in the great debates. − Yes, the world was what the case was! − No, it wasn't! − Yes, the cow was in the field when one did not regard it! − No, somebody could easily have left open the gate! − Item, personality was homogeneous and men were to be held responsible for their acts! − Quite the reverse: we were such contradictory entities that the concept of personality itself ceased, under close scrutiny, to have meaning! − God existed! − God was dead! − One might, indeed one was obliged to, speak confidently of the eternalness of eternal verities: of the absolute-ness of absolutes! − Good grief, but that was the purest drivel; relatively speaking, of course! − And in the matter of how a gentleman should arrange himself within his undergarments, all leading authorities have concluded that he must dress to the left. − Ridiculous! It is well known that, for the true philosopher, only the right will do. – The big end of the egg is best! – Absurd, sirrah! The little end, always! – 'Up!' I say. – But it is clear, my dear sir, that the only accurate statement is 'Down.' – Well, then, 'In.' – 'Out!' – 'Out!' – 'In!' . . .

'Some kinda funny folks in thees ol' burg,' opined Vivar, as we left town.

According to my map Benengeli was the next village; but when we left Erasmo the road started heading down the hill instead of up and along. I gathered from Vivar that ever since the Franco period, when Erasmo had been for the republic and Benengeli for the Falange, an undimmed hatred had stood between the inhabitants of Erasmo and those of Benengeli, a hatred so deep that they had refused to permit a road to be built between the two villages. (When Franco died the people of Erasmo had held a party, but Benengeli's folk had been plunged into deep mourning, except for the large community of 'parasites' or expatriates, who didn't even know what had happened until they started receiving worried phone calls from friends abroad.)

So we had to drive a long way down Erasmo's hill and a long way up the next one. At the place where the road from Erasmo met the much grander, four-lane highway to Benengeli there stood a large, gracious property ringed by pomegranate trees and jasmine in bloom. Hummingbirds hung in the gateway. In the distance you could hear the pleasing thwock of tennis balls. The sign over the arched gateway read *Pancho Vialactada Campo de Tenis*.

'That Pancho, huh,' said Vivar, jerking his thumb. 'One major hombre.'

Vialactada, a Mexican by birth, was one of the greats from the pre-open era, playing with Hoad and Rosewall and Gonzalez on the pro circuit, and barred, therefore, from the Grand Slam events which he would surely have dominated. He had been a sort of glorious phantom, hovering at the edges of the limelight while lesser men held the great trophies aloft. He had died of stomach cancer several years ago.

So this is where he wound up, teaching serve-and-volley to rich matrons, I thought: another limbo. This was the end of his trans-global pilgrimage; what would be the end of mine?

Though I could hear the tennis balls, there was not a player to be seen on the red clay courts. There must be more courts out of our field of vision, I decided. 'Who runs the club now?' I asked Vivar, and he nodded fervently, smiling his monstrous smile.

'Yes, Vialactada, of course,' he insisted. 'Ees Pancho's spread. The same.'

꙰

I tried to imagine this landscape as it might have been when our remote ancestors had been here. There was not so much to subtract from the scenery – the road, the black silhouette of an Osborne bull watching me from a height, some electricity pylons and telephone poles, a few Seat cars and Renault vans. Benengeli, a ribbon of white walls and red roofs, lay above us on its hillside, looking much as it would have looked all those centuries ago. *I am a Jew from Spain, like the philosopher Maimonides*, I told myself, to see if the words rang true. They sounded hollow. Maimonides's ghost laughed at me. *I am like the Catholicised Córdoba mosque*, I experimented. *A piece of Eastern architecture with a Baroque cathedral stuck in the middle of it*. That sounded wrong, too. I was a nobody from nowhere, like no-one, belonging to nothing. That sounded better. That felt true. All my ties had loosened. I had reached an anti-Jerusalem: not a home, but an away. A place that did not bind, but dissolved.

I saw Vasco's folly, its red walls dominating the crest of the hill above the town. I was particularly struck by its high, high tower, which looked like something out of a fairy story. It was crowned by a gigantic heron's nest, though I could not see any of those haughty, majestic birds. No doubt Vasco had bribed the local planning officers to allow him to build something so out of keeping with the low whitewashed coolness of the other houses in the area. The edifice was as high as the twin towers adorning the Benengeli church; Vasco had set himself up as God's rival, and this, too, I learned, had made him many enemies in the town. I instructed Vivar the cabbie to take me to the 'Little Alhambra' and he made his way through the village's winding streets, which were deserted, probably because it was the time of the siesta. However, the air was full of the noise of traffic and pedestrians – shouts, klaxons, the squeal of brakes. Round each corner I expected to find a bustle of people, or a traffic jam, or both. But we seemed by some chance to be avoiding that area of the village. Indeed, we were lost. When we had gone past a certain bar, La Gobernadora, for the third time, I decided to pay off the taxicab and make my way on foot, in spite of my weariness and the buzzing, achy 'jet-lag' disturbance in my head. The cabbie was annoyed to be dismissed so brusquely, and it is possible that in my ignorance of the local currency and customs I may have under-tipped.

'May you never find what you seek,' he shouted after me, in perfect English, making the sign of horns with his left hand. 'May you stay lost in this infernal maze, in this village of the damned, for a thousand nights and a night.'

I went into La Gobernadora to ask directions. My eyes, which had been squinting against the razor-sharp brilliance of the light bouncing off Benengeli's white walls, took a moment to adjust to the darkness inside the bar. A barman with a white apron was polishing a glass. There were a few shapes of old men near the back of the narrow, deep room. 'Does anyone speak English?' I asked. It was as if I had not spoken. 'Excuse me,' I said, going up to the bartender. He looked right through me and turned away. Had I become invisible? But no, obviously not, I had been visible enough to bad-tempered Vivar, and so had my money. I became irritable, and reached across the bar to tap the barman on the back. 'House of Señor Miranda,' I enunciated carefully. 'What road?'

The man, a thick-waisted fellow sporting a white shirt, green waistcoat and slicked-back black hair, gave a sort of groan – contempt? laziness? disgust? – and came out from behind his bar. He stood in the doorway and pointed. Now I could see, opposite the bar's entrance, a narrow lane passing between two houses, and, at the far end of the lane, many people moving quickly to and fro. That must be the throng I had been hearing; but how had I failed to notice this lane before? I was evidently in even worse shape than I had thought.

With my suitcase increasing in weight all the time, and pulling

Jawaharlal along by his lead (his wheels clattering and bouncing over the uneven cobbles) I made my way down the little lane and found myself in a most un-Spanish thoroughfare, a 'pedestrianised' street full of non-Spaniards – the majority being somewhat elderly, though immaculately turned-out, and the minority young and calculatedly scruffy in the manner of the fashion-conscious classes – who plainly had no interest in the siesta or any other local customs. This thoroughfare, which, as I would discover, was known by the locals as the Street of Parasites, was flanked by a large number of expensive boutiques – Gucci, Hermès, Aquascutum, Cardin, Paloma Picasso – and also by eating-places ranging from Scandinavian meatball-vendors to a Stars-and-Stripes-liveried Chicago Rib Shack. I stood in the midst of a crowd that pushed past me in both directions, ignoring my presence completely in the manner of city-dwellers rather than village folk. I heard people speaking English, American, French, German, Swedish, Danish, Norwegian, and what might have been either Dutch or Afrikaans. But these were not visitors; they carried no cameras, and behaved as people do on their own territory. This denatured part of Benengeli had become theirs. There was not a single Spaniard to be seen. 'Perhaps these expatriates are the new Moors,' I thought. 'And I am one of them, after all, arriving here in search of something that matters to nobody but myself, and staying, perhaps, to die. Perhaps, in another street, the locals are planning a reconquest, and it will all finish when, like our precursors, we are driven into ships at the port of Cádiz.'

'Notice that, although the street is crowded, the eyes of those crowding it are empty,' said a voice at my shoulder. 'It may be hard for you to pity these lost souls in alligator shoes and sports-shirts with crocodiles over their nipples, but compassion is what is required here. Forgive them their sins, for these blood-suckers are already in Hell.'

The speaker was a tall, elegant, silver-haired gentleman wearing a cream linen suit and a permanently sardonic expression. The first thing I noticed about him was his enormous tongue, which his mouth seemed unable to contain. It was forever licking at his lips in a suspiciously satirical way. He had beautiful twinkling blue eyes that were certainly not empty; indeed, they seemed replete with all manner of knowledge and mischief. 'You seem tired, sir,' he said, formally. 'Allow me to buy you a coffee and act, should you desire it, as your interlocutor and guide.' His name was Gottfried Helsing, he spoke twelve languages – 'oh, the usual dozen,' he said airily, as if they were oysters – and though he had the manners of a German grandee I noted that he lacked the resources to have the stains cleaned off his suit. Wearily, I accepted his invitation.

'It is hard to forgive life for the force with which the great machines of what-is bear down upon the souls of those-who-are,' he said carelessly when we were seated at a parasol-shaded café table with strong black coffees and glasses of Fundador. 'How to forgive the world for its beauty, which merely disguises its ugliness; for its gentleness, which merely cloaks its cruelty; for its illusion of continuing, seamlessly, as the night follows the day, so to speak – whereas in reality life is a series of brutal ruptures, falling upon our defenceless heads like the blows of a woodsman's axe?'

'I beg your pardon, sir,' I said, choosing my words so as not to give offence. 'I see that you are a man given to the contemplative life. But I have made a long journey, and it is not yet complete; my present needs do not permit me the luxury of chewing the fat . . .'

Once again I had the sensation of non-existence. Helsing simply continued to speak, without giving the impression of having heard a word I had said. 'Do you see that man?' he said, pointing to an old and unexpectedly Spanish-looking fellow drinking beer at a bar across the street. 'He used to be the mayor of Benengeli. During the Civil War, however, he took up the republican cause, alongside the men of Erasmo – do you know Erasmo?' He did not wait for my reply. 'After the war men like him, prominent citizens who had opposed Franco, were rounded up in the school at Erasmo, or in the bull-ring at Avellaneda, and shot. He decided to go into hiding. In his house there was a small alcove behind a wardrobe, and there he spent his days. At night his wife would shut the shutters and he would emerge. The only people who knew the secret were his wife, daughter and brother. His wife would walk all the way down the hill to buy food so that the locals did not see her buying enough for two. They were unable to make love because, being devout Catholics, they could not use contraceptives, and the consequences of her becoming pregnant would have been fatal for them both. This went on for thirty years, until the general amnesty.'

'Thirty years in hiding!' I burst out, gripped by the tale in spite of my fatigue. 'What a torment that must have been!'

'It was as nothing compared to what happened after he emerged,' said Helsing. 'For then his beloved Benengeli became the preserve of this international riff-raff; and, in addition, those of his generation who were still alive had all been Falangists, and refused to speak a single word to their old opponent. His wife died of influenza, his brother of a tumour, and his daughter married and moved away to Seville. In the end he was reduced to sitting here, among the Parasites, because there was no longer a place for him amongst his own people. So, you see, he has become a rootless foreigner, too. This is how his principles have been rewarded.'

There was a brief lull in Helsing's soliloquy while he contempted the mayor's tale, and I took advantage of it to ask him the way to Vasco Miranda's home. He looked at me with a faint puzzlement in his eyes, as if he had not quite understood what I was saying, and then, with a light, dismissive shrug, picked up his own thread.

'I, too, have had a similar reward,' he mused. 'I fled my country when the Nazis came to power and spent a number of years travelling in South America. I am a photographer by trade. In Bolivia I made a book showing the horrors of the tin mines. In Argentina, I photographed Eva Perón once in her lifetime and again after her death. I never returned to Germany because I felt too deeply the pollution of its culture by what had happened there. I felt the absence of the Jews like a great chasm; even though I am not a Jew.'

'I am half a Jew,' I said foolishly. Helsing paid me no heed.

'Eventually, in reduced financial circumstances, I came to Benengeli, because here I could afford to live simply on my small pension. When the Parasites heard that I was a German who had been in South America they began to call me "the Nazi". That is their name for me now. So my reward for a life in opposition to certain evil ideas is to have them hung round my neck in my old age. I no longer talk to the Parasites. I no longer talk to anyone. What a rare treat it is for me to have you, sir, to converse with! The old men here were once the middle-ranking evildoers of the earth: second-rate Mafia bosses, third-rate union-busters, fourth-rate racists. The women are of the type that is excited by jackboots and disappointed by the advent of democracy. The young people are trash: addicts, layabouts, plagiarists, whores. They are all dead, the old and the young, but because their pensions and allowances are still paying up they refuse to lie down in their graves. So they walk up and down this street and eat, and drink, and gossip about the hideous minutiae of their lives. Notice, please, that there are no mirrors to be seen here. If there were, none of these trapped shades would be reflected in them. When I understood that this was their Hell, as they are mine, I learned to feel sorry for them.

'Such is Benengeli, my home.'

'And Miranda . . .' I repeated, faintly, thinking that it would be best if I did not tell Helsing too much about my own morally compromised life.

'There is not the slightest chance that you will ever meet Señor Vasco Miranda, our greatest and most dreadful inhabitant,' said Helsing, smiling softly. 'I hoped you would take the hint I have been dropping by my refusal to answer your persistent questions, but since you have not I must tell you straight that you're here on a wild-goose chase. As Don Quixote would say, you're looking for this year's birds in last year's nests. Nobody sees Miranda from month to month, not even his servants. There was a woman asking for him recently – pretty little thing! – but she got nowhere and buggered off to God knows where. They say . . . '

'What woman?' I interrupted. 'How long ago? How do you know she didn't get in?'

'Just a woman,' he answered, licking his lips. 'How long ago? – *Not* long. Just a *while*. – And she didn't get in because nobody gets in. Aren't you listening? They say that everything inside that house has grown stagnant; everything. They wind up the clocks but time doesn't move. The great tower has been locked up for years. Nobody goes up there except, probably, the old madman himself.

They say the dust in the tower rooms comes up to your knees because he won't let the servants in to clean up. They say a whole wing of that huge palace has been invaded by the creosote bush, *la gobernadora*. They say . . . '

'I don't care what they say,' I cried, seeing that it was time for a firmer attitude. 'It is imperative that I see him. I will use the telephone in the café.'

'Don't be stupid,' said Helsing. 'He had the phone cut off years ago.'

⌒

Two handsome, fortyish Spanish women wearing white aprons over black dresses had somehow appeared at my elbow. 'We couldn't help overhearing your conversation,' said the first waitress, in excellent English. 'And, if you will excuse the interruption, I am obliged to point out that this Nazi is quite incorrect. Vasco maintains both a phone line, with an answering machine attached, and a fax line as well, though he answers none of his messages. However, the proprietor here, a mean-spirited Dane called Olé, does not permit the café's guests to use the telephone for any reason.'

'Hellcats! Vampires!' shouted Helsing, in sudden fury. 'Stakes should be driven through both your hearts!'

'You really should not spend any more time with this old confidence man and cretin,' said the second waitress, whose English was, if anything, even purer than her companion's, and whose features, too, were a little more refined. 'He is well known to us all as a bitter, twisted fantasist, a lifelong fascist who now pretends to have been an opponent of fascism, and an importuner of women, who invariably reject him, and on whom he heaps insults at every opportunity thereafter. He will no doubt have spun you all sorts of yarns, both about himself and our beautiful village. If you wish, you can come with us; we're just going off duty and can correct the false impression you will have gained from him. Alas, many fantasists have settled in Benengeli, wrapping themselves in lies as if they were winter shawls.'

'My name is Felicitas Larios, and she is my half-sister Renegada,' said the first waitress. 'If it is Vasco Miranda you're after, you should know that we have been his housekeepers ever since he first came to town. We do not really wait table at Olé's bar; today, we were just doing him a favour, because his regular girls were sick. Nobody can tell you more about Vasco Miranda than we.'

'Sows! Vixens!' cried Helsing. 'They're taking you for quite a ride, you know. They have worked here for pittances these many years, bowing and scraping, washing and sweeping, and the owner, by the way, is not a Dane called Olé, but a retired bargee from the Danube, named Uli.'

I had had enough of Helsing. Vasco's women had removed their aprons and put them into the large straw baskets they carried; they were plainly eager to be off. I rose and made my excuses. 'And has all my work on your behalf been worth so little to you?' said the wretched fellow. 'I have been your mentor, and this is how you repay me.'

'Give him nothing,' advised Renegada Larios. 'He is always trying to wheedle money out of strangers, like a common beggar.'

'I will pay for our drinks, at least,' I said, and set down a note.

'They will chew up your heart and imprison your soul in a glass bottle,' warned Helsing, wildly. 'Never say you were not warned. Vasco Miranda is an evil spirit, and these are his familiars. Beware! I have seen them metamorphose into bats . . . '

Although he was speaking loudly, nobody in that crowded street was paying the slightest attention to Gottfried Helsing. 'We are used to him here,' said Felicitas. 'We let him rant, and pass by on the other side. Every so often the Sargento of the Guardia Civil, Salvador Medina, locks him up for a night, and that cools him off.'

⌒

I must admit that Jawaharlal the stuffed dog had seen better times. Since I began carting him around he had lost most of one ear and there were a couple of missing teeth. Nevertheless, Renegada, the finer-boned of my two new acquaintances, was effusive in her praise for him, and found ways of touching me often, on the arm or shoulder, to underline her sentiments. Felicitas Larios held her peace, but I had the impression that she disapproved of these moments of physical contact.

We entered a small two-storey row house on a sharply sloping street which bore the name of Calle de Miradores even though the buildings on it were far too humble to boast the glassed-in balconies from which it took its unlikely name. However, the street-sign (white letters on a royal blue ground) remained unrepentant. It was further evidence that Benengeli was a place of dreamers as well as secrets. In the distance, at the very top of the road, I could make out the outlines of a large and hideous fountain. 'That is the Place of the Elephants,' said Renegada, affectionately. 'The main gate to the Miranda residence is up there.'

'But there is no point in knocking or ringing, for no-one will answer,' broke in Felicitas, with a worried frown. 'It will be better if you come in and rest. You have the look of a tired and, excuse me, also an unwell man.'

'Please,' said Renegada, 'take off your shoes.' I did not understand this rather religious request, but complied, and she showed me into a tiny room whose floor, ceilings and walls were covered in ceramic tiles, on which, in Delft blue, a host of tiny scenes were depicted. 'No two are identical,' said Renegada proudly. 'It is said that they are all that remains of the ancient Jewish synagogue of Benengeli, which was demolished after the final expulsions. It is said that they have the power to show you the future, if you have the eyes to see it.'

'Stuff and nonsense,' laughed Felicitas, who as well as being the more heavily built and coarser-looking of the two, with a large, unfortunate mole on her chin, was also the less romantic. 'The tiles are two-a-penny, not old at all; this same Dutchy blue has been in use locally for a long time. And as for fortune-telling, that's a lot of hogwash. So stop your hocus-pocus, dear Renegada, and let the tired gentleman get some sleep.'

I needed no further invitation to rest – insomnia, even at the worst of times, had never been my problem! – and threw myself down, fully clothed, upon the tiled room's narrow cot. In the few instants before I fell asleep my eyes chanced to fall on a certain tile near my head, and there was my mother's portrait staring back at me, giving a saucy smile. Dizziness claimed me, and I lost consciousness.

When I awoke I had been undressed, and a long nightshirt had been slipped over my head. Beneath this nightshirt I was completely naked. The two housekeepers were a bold pair, I thought; and how deeply I must have been sleeping! – A moment later I remembered the miracle of the tile, but try as I might I could find nothing that even remotely resembled the picture I was sure I had seen before nodding off. 'The mind plays strange tricks when sinking towards sleep,' I reminded myself, and got out of bed. It was daylight, and from the main room of the small house there came a strong, irresistible aroma of lentil soup. Felicitas and Renegada were at table, and there was a third place, at which a large steaming bowl had already been placed. They watched approvingly as I gulped down spoonful after spoonful.

'How long have I been asleep?' I asked them, and they gave each other a little look.

'A whole day,' said Renegada. 'Now it's tomorrow.'

'Nonsense,' Felicitas disagreed. 'You were just snoozing for a few hours. It's still today.'

'My half-sister is teasing,' said Renegada. 'Actually, I didn't want to shock you, and that is why I understated the case. The truth is that you have slept for forty-eight hours at least.'

'Forty-eight winks, more like,' said Felicitas. 'Renegada, don't confuse the poor man.'

'We have cleaned and pressed your clothes,' her half-sister said, changing the subject. 'I hope you don't mind.'

The effects of the journey had not worn off, even after my rest. If I really had snored my way into the day after tomorrow, though, a certain disorientation was to be expected. I turned my thoughts to business.

'Ladies, I am most grateful to you,' I said politely. 'But now I must ask you for some urgent advice. Vasco Miranda is an old friend of the family, and I need to see him on important family business. Permit me to introduce myself. Moraes Zogoiby, of Bombay, India, at your service.'

They gasped.

'Zogoiby!' muttered Felicitas, shaking her head in disbelief.

'I never thought to hear from another's lips that hated, hated name,' said Renegada Larios, colouring brightly as she spoke.

This was the story I managed to coax out of them.

When Vasco Miranda first came to Benengeli, as a painter with a world-wide reputation, the half-sisters (at that time young women in their mid-twenties) had offered him their services, and been employed at once. 'He said he was pleased by our command of English, our domestic skills, but most of all by our family tree,' said Renegada, surprisingly. 'Our father Juan Larios was a sailor, and Felicitas's mother was Moroccan, while mine hailed from Palestine. So Felicitas is half-Arab, and I am Jewish on my mother's side.'

'Then you and I have something in common,' I told her. 'For I, too, am fifty per cent in that direction.' Renegada looked inordinately pleased.

Vasco had told them they would renew, in his 'Little Alhambra', the fabulous multiple culture of ancient al-Andalus. They would be more like a family than master and servants. 'We thought he was a little crazy, of course,' said Felicitas, 'but all artists are, isn't that so, and the money he offered was well above the rate.' Renegada nodded. 'And anyhow it was just a pipe-dream. Just words. It was always boss and workers between us. And then he got more and more insane, dressing up like an old-time Sultan, and behaving even worse than one of those absolutist, infidel despots of Moors.' Now they went in every morning and cleaned the place as best they could. The gardeners had been dismissed and the water-garden, once a jewel-like miniature Generalife, was almost dead. The kitchen staff were long departed and Vasco would leave the Larios women shopping lists and money. 'Cheeses, sausages, wines, cakes,' said Felicitas. 'I do not think so much as an egg has been cooked in that house this year.'

Ever since the day of Salvador Medina's insult over five years ago, Vasco had been retreating. He spent his days locked in his high tower apartment into which they were not permitted to venture, on pain of instant dismissal. Renegada said she had seen a couple of canvases in his studio, blasphemous works in which Judas took the place of Christ upon the cross; but these 'Judas Christ' paintings had been there for months, half-finished, apparently abandoned. He did not seem to be working on anything else. Nor did he travel any more, as he once had, to execute murals to commission for the airport departure halls and hotel lobbies of the earth. 'He has bought a lot of high-technology equipment,' she confided. 'Recording machines, and even one of those X-ray gadgets. With the recording machines he makes strange tapes, all screeches and bangs, shouts and thumps. Avant-garde rubbish. He plays it at top volume in his tower and it has scared the herons away from their nest.' And the X-ray machine? 'That I don't know. Maybe he will make art from those see-through photos.'

'It isn't healthy,' said Felicitas. 'He sees nobody, nobody.'

Neither Felicitas nor Renegada had seen their employer for more than a year. But sometimes, on a moonlit night, his cloaked figure could be seen from the village, walking the high battlements of his folly, like a slow, fat ghost.

'And what's this about my "hated name"?' I asked.

'There was a woman,' said Renegada finally. 'Excuse me. Maybe your aunt?'

'My mother,' I said. 'A painter. Now deceased.'

'May she rest,' Felicitas interjected.

'Vasco Miranda is very bitter about this woman,' Renegada said in a rush, as if that were the only way she could bring herself to speak of it. 'I think he has loved her very much, no?'

I said nothing.

'I am sorry. I see it is hard for you. It is a hard thing. A son, a mother. You cannot betray her. But I think he has been, has been her, her, her.'

'Her lover,' said Felicitas, harshly. Renegada blushed.

'I am sorry if you don't know it,' she said, putting her hand on my left arm.

'Please go on,' I answered.

'Then she was brutal with him, and flung him away. Since then a kind of resentment has grown in him. I have seen it more and more. It is a possession.'

'It isn't healthy,' said Felicitas, again. 'Hatred burns up the soul.'

'And now you,' said Renegada. 'I think he will never agree to meet your mother's son. I believe the name you carry will be too much for him to bear.'

'He painted cartoon animals and super-heroes on my nursery wall,' I said. 'He must see me. And he will.'

Felicitas and Renegada looked at each other again; a knowing, I-give-up look.

'Ladies,' I said. 'I also have a story to tell.'

⟞

'There was a package some time ago,' said Renegada when I had finished. 'Maybe it was one painting. I don't know. Maybe it was the picture with your mother's picture underneath. He must have taken it up into the tower. But four big pictures? No, nothing of that sort has come.'

'It is too soon, perhaps,' I said. 'The burglary was very recent. You must watch for me. And as things stand, I now perceive, I should not present myself at his door in a hurry. It would scare him into keeping the pictures away from here. So you must watch, please, and I must wait.'

'If you wish to lodge in this house,' conceded Felicitas, 'we can come to an arrangement. If you wish.' At which Renegada turned her face away.

'You have come on a great pilgrimage,' she said, without turning back. 'A son in search of his lost mother's treasures, in search of healing and peace. It is our duty as women to help such a man find what he seeks.'

I remained under their roof for over a month. During this time I was well cared for, and enjoyed their company; but I learned very little more about their lives. Their parents were apparently dead, but they were disinclined to discuss the matter, so naturally I let it lie. They appeared to have neither siblings nor friends. There were no lovers. Yet they seemed perfectly, inseparably happy. They left for work in the mornings holding hands, and returned together, too. There were days when in my loneliness I entertained a half-formed lust for Renegada Larios, but there was no single occasion on which I was alone in her company, so I was unable to take matters any further. Each night, after supper, the half-sisters would retire upstairs to the bed they shared, and I would hear their murmurings, and the shiftings of their bodies, continuing late into the night; yet they would always be up before I stirred.

Finally curiosity got the better of me, and I asked them at supper why they had never married. 'Because all the men in these parts are dead from the neck up,' Renegada shot back, giving her sister a fierce look. 'And from the neck down, as well.'

'My half-sister is too fanciful, as usual,' said Felicitas. 'But it is true that we are not like the people round here. None of us was, in our family. The others are dead now, and we do not wish to lose each other to mere husbands. Ours is a closer bond. You see, our attitudes are not easily understood by most folk in Benengeli. For example, we are glad about the end of the Franco régime and the return of democracy. Also, to speak more personally, we do not like tobacco or babies, and around here everyone is crazy about both. Smokers are always going on about the social joys to be had from their packets of Fortuna or Ducados, about the intimate sensuality of lighting a friend's cigarette; but we detest waking up with that cloying smell on our clothes, or going to sleep with stale smoke clouding our hair. As to children, you're supposed to think you can never have too many of them, but we have no desire to be trapped by a brood of bouncing, squealing little jailers. And, if I may say so, we like your pet precisely because he is stuffed and therefore needs no attention from us.'

'Yet you have looked after me royally,' I argued.

'That is business,' Felicitas rejoined. 'You are a paying guest.'

'Surely there must be men who would love you for yourselves, without wanting to raise families,' I persevered. 'And if the men in Benengeli have the wrong politics, why not go across to Erasmo, for example? I hear they are different there.'

'Since you are so forward as to demand an answer,' replied Felicitas, 'I have never met a man who could see a woman as herself. And as to Erasmo: there is no road to Erasmo from here.'

I caught an odd expression in Renegada's eye. Perhaps she did not agree with everything her sister had said. After that conversation I would allow myself to imagine, during my solitary nights, that at any moment the door might open and Renegada Larios might slip in beside me in my cot, naked below her long white nightdress . . . but it never happened. I lay by myself, listening to the shifts and murmurs just above my unsleeping head.

During my month of waiting I wandered the streets of Benengeli – sometimes trundling Jawaharlal behind me, but more often by myself – in the grip of a numbing tedium that somehow made it impossible for me to dwell on the past. I wondered if I had acquired the same empty-eyed look that characterised so many of the so-called Parasites, who seemed to spend all their days crowding and jostling up and down 'their' Street, buying clothes, eating in restaurants and drinking in bars, talking furiously all the time, with a curious absentness of manner that suggested their utter indifference to the topics of their conversations. However, Benengeli was apparently capable of weaving its spell even on those who were not dull of eye, because whenever I chanced to pass that old slobberer Gottfried Helsing he twinkled at me brightly, gave me a cheery wave and cried, with a knowing wink, 'We really must have another of our excellent conversations some time soon!' as if we were the best of friends. I surmised that I had arrived at a place to which people came to forget themselves – or, more accurately, to lose themselves in themselves, to live in a kind of dream of what they might have been, or preferred to be – or, having mislaid what once they were, to absent themselves quietly from what they had become. Thus they could either be liars, like Helsing, or near-catatonics, like the 'honorary Parasite', the ex-mayor, who sat motionless on an outdoor bar stool from morning to night, and never spoke a word; as if he were still lingering in the shaded solitude of an alcove concealed behind a large wooden almirah in the house of his dead wife. And the air of mystery surrounding the place was in fact an atmosphere of unknowing; what seemed like an enigma was in fact a void. These uprooted drifters had become, by their own choice, human automata. They could simulate human life, but were no longer able to live it.

The locals – or so I guessed – were less befuddled by the town's narcotic quality than the Parasites; but the prevalent mood of vacuous alienation and apathy did affect them to some degree. Felicitas and Renegada needed to be asked three times about the visit to Benengeli of the young woman, mentioned by Gottfried Helsing, who had been asking after Vasco Miranda not long ago. On the first two occasions they shrugged and reminded me that Helsing was not to be trusted; but when I returned to the subject one evening, Renegada looked up from her sewing and burst out, 'Oh, yes, my goodness, now that I think of it, a woman did come – a bohemian type, some sort of art specialist from Barcelona, a picture restorer, or something similar. She got nowhere with her coquettish ways; and by now she must be safely back in Catalonia where she belongs.' Once again I had the strong feeling that Felicitas disapproved of her half-sister's indiscretion. She scratched at her mole and pursed her lips, but said nothing. 'So this Catalan woman got to see Vasco, after all?' I said, excited by the realisation. 'We didn't say that,' snapped Felicitas. 'There's no point in discussing this any further.' Renegada bowed her head in submission and returned to her needlework.

On my wanderings I occasionally encountered the heavily perspiring figure of the Guardia chief, Salvador Medina, who invariably frowned at me, and removed his cap to scratch his sweat-soaked locks, as if trying to remember who the dickens I might be. We never spoke, partly because my Spanish was still poor, although it was slowly improving, both through the nocturnal study of books and thanks to the daily lessons I was being given, in return for a supplementary charge added to my weekly bill for board and lodging, by the Larios sisters; and partly because the English language had vanquished all Salvador Medina's attempts to get hold of it, like a master criminal who remains always two steps ahead of the law.

I was happy that Medina was so unconcerned about me as to forget me so readily, because it suggested that the Indian authorities had expressed no interest in my whereabouts. I reminded myself that I had recently committed the crime of murder; and reflected that the explosion at my victim's home had evidently succeeded in obliterating my deed. The greater violence of the bomb had been painted over the scene in which I had participated, and hidden it for ever from the investigators' eyes. Further confirmation that I was not under suspicion came from my bank accounts. During my years in my father's Tower I had managed to stash away sizeable sums in overseas banks, including numbered accounts in Switzerland (so you see that I was not the mere thug and 'stupe' that 'Adam Zogoiby' had taken me for!). As far as I knew there had been no recent attempt to interfere with my arrangements, even though so many aspects of the crashed Siodicorp were under investigation, and so many bank accounts had been placed under the official receiver's administration, or blocked.

It was strange, however, that my crime – murder, after all; murder most foul, and the one and only murder for which I was ever responsible – had slipped so quickly to the back of my brain. Perhaps my unconscious mind had also accepted the greater authority, the successfully overwhelming reality of the bombs, and wiped my moral slate clean. Or perhaps this absence of guilt – this suspended moral animation – was Benengeli's gift to me.

Physically, too, I felt as if I were in some sort of interregnum, in some timeless zone under the sign of an hourglass in which the sand stood motionless, or a clepsydra whose quicksilver had ceased to flow. Even my asthma had improved; how lucky for my chest, I thought, to have fallen in with the only two non-smokers in town – for it was true that everywhere I went people were puffing away like mad. To avoid the stench of cigarettes I wandered down sausage-festooned streets of bakeries and cinnamon shops, smelling, instead, the sweet scents of meat and pastries and fresh-baked bread, and surrendered myself to the cryptic laws of the town. The village blacksmith, whose speciality was the manufacture of chains and manacles for the Avellaneda jail, nodded to me as he nodded to all passers-by and called out, in the heavily accented Spanish of the region, 'Sti' walki' free, huh? Som' day soo', soo',' upon which he would rattle his heavy chains and roar with laughter. As my Spanish improved, I strayed ever further from the Street of Parasites and thus gained a few glimpses into Benengeli's other self, that village defeated by history in which jealous men in stiff suits stalked their fiancées, sure of those chaste maidens' infidelity, and where the hoofs of the horses of long-dead philanderers were heard galloping down the cobbled streets at night. I began to understand why Felicitas and Renegada Larios spent their evenings at home, with the shutters closed, talking to each other in low voices while I studied Spanish in the comfort of my tiny room.

&#x223D;

On the Wednesday of my fifth week in Benengeli, I returned to my lodgings after a walk during which an uncouth young one-legged woman thrust into my unwilling hand a cheaply produced pamphlet enumerating the anti-abortionist demands of 'Suffer Ye Little Children, the revolutionary crusade for unborn Christians', and invited me to a meeting. I turned her down flat, but was at once beset by memories of Sister Floreas, who took the pro-life war into the most overpopulated regions of Bombay, and who had gone to a place in which unwanted pregnancies were presumably no longer a problem; sweet, fanatical Minnie, I thought, I hope you're happy now . . . and I thought, too, about my erstwhile boxing coach, the similarly peg-legged Lambajan Chandiwala Borkar, and of Totah – that parrot which I had always loathed, and which had disappeared after the Bombay bombings, never to be seen again. As I contemplated the vanished bird I was overcome by nostalgia and grief, and began to weep in the street, to the consternation and embarrassment of the young militant, who quickly hurried away to join her SYLC colleagues in their den.

The Moor who returned to the Larios women's little house on the Calle de Miradores was therefore a changed man, one restored by coincidence to the world of feelings and pain. Emotions, so long anaesthetised, were flowing around me like flood-waters. Before I could explain this development to my landladies, however, they launched into eager speech, interrupting each other in their haste to inform me that the stolen paintings had indeed arrived, as expected, at the 'Little Alhambra'.

'There was a van . . . ' began Renegada.

' – in the dead of night; it went right past our door – ' added Felicitas.

' – so I wrapped myself in my rebozo and ran out – '

' – and I ran out, too – '

' – and we saw the gate to the big house open, and the van – '

' – passed through – '

' – and today in the fireplaces there was lots of cheap wood – '

' – like packing-case wood – you know – '

' – he must have been up all night chopping it up! – '

' – and in the garbage there were piles of that plastic stuff – '

' – that children like to make go pop – '

' – bubble-wrap, that's it – '

' – yes, bubble-wrap, and corrugated cardboard, and metal hoops, too – '

' – so there were big parcels in that van, and what else could they be?'

It was not proof, but I knew it was the closest I would get, in this village of uncertainty, to a sure thing. I began for the first time to imagine my meeting with Vasco Miranda. Once I had been a child who loved to sit at his feet; now we were both old men, fighting over the same woman, you could say, and the fight would be no less strenuous because the lady in question was dead.

It was time for the next step to be planned. 'If he will not see me, you will have to smuggle me in,' I said to the Larios sisters. 'I can see no other way.'

Very early next morning, while the sun was still a rumour running along the crests of distant mountains, I accompanied Renegada Larios to work. Felicitas, the larger-boned and bulkier of the two women, had given me her loosest black skirt and blouse. On my feet I wore anonymous rubber sandals bought in the Spanish part of town. In the crook of my right arm I carried a basket containing my own clothes, concealed beneath an array of dusters, sponges and sprays; my right hand, like my head, was concealed under a rebozo, which my left hand clutched tightly to keep it in place. 'You make a poor counterfeit of a woman,' Felicitas Larios said, surveying me with her ever-critical eye. 'But luckily it's still dark and there's not so far to go. Stoop a little and take short steps. Be off with you! We are endangering our livelihoods for your sake, I hope you know that.'

'For the sake of a dead mother,' Renegada corrected her half-sister. 'We have a dead mother also. That is why we understand.'

'I leave my dog in your care,' I told Felicitas. 'He won't be any trouble.'

'You're quite right he won't,' she said, grumpily. 'He's going straight in that cupboard the moment you're out of the door, and you needn't imagine he'll be coming out before you return. We've got better sense in this house than to take a stuffed dog for a walk.'

I said my farewells to Jawaharlal. His had been a long journey, too, and it deserved a better end than a broom-cupboard in a foreign land. But a broom-cupboard it had to be. I was off for my showdown with Vasco Miranda, and Jawaharlal had, after all, become just another abandoned Andalusian dog.

∽

My first experience of being in women's clothing reminded me of the story of Aires de Gama climbing into his wife's wedding-dress and setting off for a wild night in the company of Prince Henry the Navigator; but what a falling-off was here, how much lowlier these dark threads were than Aires's fabulous frock, and how much less suited I was to such attire! As we set off, Renegada Larios told me that the ex-mayor of the village – that same fellow who now sat, nameless and friendless, sipping coffee in the Street of Parasites – had once been obliged to walk these streets dressed as his own grandmother, because near the end of his captivity his house had been scheduled for demolition and the family had had to move. So I had local as well as familial precedents for my disguise.

It was the first time Renegada and I had been by ourselves without Felicitas to chaperone us, but although she flashed me a series of explicitly meaningful looks I was too inhibited (both by my female dress and on account of the nervousness engendered by the unpredictability of what lay ahead) to respond. We reached the servants' entrance to the Little Alhambra unobserved, as far as I could tell, though it was impossible to be sure if there were curious eyes watching from the darkened windows of Miradores Street as we ascended it towards Vasco's detestable and incongruous elephant fountain. I caught a glimpse of a bright scrap of green flying over the folly's walls. 'Are there parrots in Spain?' I whispered to Renegada, but obtained no reply. Perhaps she was sulking at my refusal to take this rare opportunity for flirtation.

There was a small electronic key-pad next to the door, set into the terracotta-red wall, and Renegada quickly punched in a series of four numbers. The door clicked open, and we entered Miranda's lair.

At once I had a powerful feeling of *déjà vu*, and my head whirled. When I had recovered myself a little I marvelled at the skill with which Vasco Miranda had modelled the interior of his folly upon Aurora Zogoiby's Moor paintings. I was standing in an open courtyard with a chequerboard-tiled central piazza and arched cloisters round the sides, and through the windows on the far side I could see a spreading plain, shimmering in dawn light, like an ocean. A palace set by a mirage of the sea; part-Arab, part-Mughal, owing something to Chirico, it was that very place which Aurora once described to me as one 'where worlds collide, flow in and out of one another, and washofy away. Place where an air-man can drown in water, or else grow gills; where a water-creature can get drunk, but also chokeofy, on air.' Even in its present state of slight dilapidation and horticultural decay, I had truly found Mooristan.

In room after empty room I found the settings of Aurora's pictures brought to life, and I half-expected her characters to walk in and enact their sad narratives before my disbelieving eyes, half-expected my own body to grow into that lozenged, particoloured Moor whose tragedy – the tragedy of multiplicity destroyed by singularity, the defeat of Many by One – had been the sequence's uniting principle. And perhaps my crumpled hand might burst, at any moment, into flower, or light, or flame! Vasco, who had always believed that Aurora had pinched the idea for the Moor pictures from his kitsch portrayal of a lachrymose rider, had spent fortunes, and the kind of energy born of the most profound obsession, to appropriate her vision for himself. Was this a house built of love or hate? If the stories I'd heard were to be believed, it was a true Palimpstine, in which his present bitter wrath lay curdling over the memory of an old, lost sweetness and romance. For there was something sour here, some envy in the brilliance of the emulation; and as the first shock of recognition wore off, and the day rose up, I began to see the flaws in the grand design. Vasco Miranda was still the same vulgarian he had always been, and what Aurora had imagined so vividly and finely had been rendered by Vasco in colours that could be seen, as the daylight brightened, to have missed rightness by the small but vital distance that distinguishes the pleasingly apt from the crudely inappropriate. The building's sense of proportion was also poor, and its lines were misconceived. No, it was not a miracle, after all; my first impressions had been illusory, and the illusion had already faded. The 'Little Alhambra', for all its size and flamboyance, was no New Moorusalem, but an ugly, pretentious house.

I had seen no sign of the purloined paintings, nor of the machinery of which Renegada and Felicitas had spoken. The door leading to the high tower was firmly locked. Vasco must be up there, with his contraptions and stolen secrets.

'I want to change my clothes,' I said to Renegada. 'I can't confront the old bastard looking like this.'

'Go ahead and change,' she answered, bold as brass. 'There's nothing you've got I haven't seen already.' In fact it was Renegada who had changed; ever since we entered the 'Little Alhambra' her manner had become proprietorial, assertive. No doubt she had detected the growing distaste with which – after a few initial exclamations of delight – I had been inspecting the property for which, after all, she had cared over many years. It would not be unnatural for her to be annoyed by my lack of enthusiasm for the place. Nevertheless, this was a flagrant, shameless remark, and I would not stand for it.

'Be careful what you say,' I warned her, and went into an adjoining chamber to have some privacy, ignoring her angry glare. While I was changing I became aware of a noise, coming from some distance away. It was the vilest of dins – a mixture of female shrieks and feedback screeches, ululations of indeterminate gender, computer-generated whines and bangs, and a background clattering and clanking that put me in mind of a kitchen in an earthquake. This must be the 'avant-garde music' that had been mentioned. Vasco Miranda was awake.

Renegada and Felicitas had told me quite clearly that they had not seen their reclusive boss for over a year, so I was extremely surprised, on emerging from my changing-room, to find the voluminous figure of old Vasco himself awaiting me in the chequerboard piazza, with his housekeeper by his side; and not only by his side, but tickling him playfully with a feather duster while he giggled and squealed with delight. He was indeed wearing Moorish fancy dress, as the half-sisters had said he was prone to do, and in his baggy pantaloons and embroidered waistcoat, worn open over a ballooning collarless shirt, he looked like a wobbling mound of Turkish *rahat lacoum*. His moustache had dwindled – its stalagmites of wax-stiffened hair had vanished completely – and his head was as bald and pocked as the surface of the Moon.

'Hee, hee,' he chortled, slapping Renegada's duster away. 'Hola, namaskar, salaam, Moor, my boy. You look awful: ready to drop down dying-shying at a moment's notice. Haven't my two ladies been feeding you properly? Hasn't this little holiday been to your liking? How long has it been now? My, my – fourteen years. Well! They haven't been kind to *you*.'

'If I had known you were so . . . approachable,' I said, looking crossly at the housekeeper, 'I would have dispensed with this stupid charade. But it seems that these reports about your reclusiveness have been much exaggerated.'

'Whese reports?' he demanded, disingenuously. Then, 'Well, perhaps, but only as regards a few small details,' he said in a placatory voice, waving Renegada away. She put the duster down without a word and backed away to a corner of the courtyard. 'It is true that we in Benengeli value our privacy – as do you, by the way, considering what a fuss you've just made about changing your clothes in private! Renegada there was highly amused. – But what was my point? Ah, yes. Have you not noticed that Benengeli is defined by what it lacks – that unlike much of the region, certainly unlike the whole Costa, it is devoid of such excrescences as Coco-Loco nightclubs, coach parties on guided tours, burro-taxis, currency cambios, and vendors of straw sombreros. Our excellent Sargento, Salvador Medina, drives all such horrors away by administering nocturnal beatings, in the village's many dark alleys, to any entrepreneur who seeks to introduce them. Salvador Medina dislikes me intensely, by the way, as he dislikes all the town's newcomers, but like all well-settled immigrants – like the great majority of the Parasites – I applaud his policy of repulsing the new wave of invaders. Now that we're in, it's only right that somebody should slam the door shut behind us.

'Don't you find it admirable, my Benengeli?' he went on, sweeping an arm vaguely in the direction of the mirage-ocean visible through his windows. 'Goodbye to dirt, disease, corruption, fanaticism, caste politics, cartoonists, lizards, crocodiles, playback music and, best of all, the Zogoiby family! Goodbye, Aurora the great and cruel – farewell, crooked, scornful Abe!'

'Not exactly,' I dissented. 'For I see that you've tried – with, may I say, limited success – to build my mother's imaginative world around you, to use it like a fig-leaf to hide your own inadequacies; and then, too, there is this remaining Zogoiby to face, and a little matter of some stolen pictures to resolve.'

'They're upstairs,' said Vasco with a shrug. 'You should be pleased I had them pinched. What a hit-fortune for them! You should go down on your knees and thank me. If not for my gang of professionals, they would be burnt toasts.'

'I demand to see them at once,' I said firmly. 'And after that, perhaps Salvador Medina can do me a service. Perhaps we could send your housekeeper, Renegada, to call him, or even use the phone.'

'By all means let us go upstairs and take a peek,' said Vasco, looking unconcerned. 'Do me the courtesy, however, of walking slowly, for I am fat. As to the rest, I am sure you really have no desire to go gilloping-galloping to the law. In your circs, which is better: incognito or outcognito? In-, I am sure. Besides, my beloved Renegada will never betray me. And – didn't anybody tell you? – the telephone line has been cut off for years.'

' "My beloved Renegada", did you say?'

'And my beloved Felicitas, too. They would not hurt me for the world.'

'Then these half-sisters have played a cruel game with me.'

'They are not half-sisters, poor Moor. They are lovers.'

'Each other's lovers?'

'For fifteen years. And, for fourteen, mine. How many years I had to hear you people spouting-shouting rubbish about unity in diversity and I don't know what rot. But now I, Vasco, with my girls, have created that new society.'

'I don't care about your bedtime business. Let them bounce on you like a squashy mattress! What is it to me? It is your trickery that makes me mad.'

'But we had to wait for the paintings, isn't it? That was no trick. And then we had to get you in here without anybody knowing.'

'For what purpose?'

'Why, what do you suppose? To get rid of all the Zogoibys I can lay my hands on, four pictures and one person – the last of the whole accursed line, as it happens – with a boom-boom-badoom; or, to put it another way, five in a bite.'

'A gun? Vasco, are you serious? A gun you're pointing at me?'

'Just a small fellow. But it is in my hand. Which is my great hit-fortune; and your mis-.'

⤳

I had been warned. *Vasco Miranda is an evil spirit, and these are his familiars. I have seen them metamorphose into bats.*

But I had been caught in his web from the start. How much of the village was in league with him, I wondered. Not Salvador Medina, that seemed clear. Gottfried Helsing? Right about the telephones, but otherwise obfuscatory. And the rest? Had they all conspired against me in this pantomime, doing Vasco's imperious bidding? How much money changed hands? Were they all members of some occult, Masonic society – Opus Dei or the like?

– And how far back did the conspiracy stretch? – To the taxi-driver Vivar, to the immigration officer, to the strange cabin-crew on the flight from Bombay? – *Five in a bite*, Vasco said. He said that. So did the tentacles of this event really reach as far back as a bombed villa in Bandra, and was this the victims' revenge? I felt my reason slipping its moorings, and restrained my speculations, baseless and valueless as they were. The world was a mystery, unknowable. The present was a riddle to be solved.

∽

'So, the Lone Ranger and Tonto are in a dead-end valley encircled by hostile Indians,' said Vasco Miranda, puffing his way up the stairs behind me. 'And the Lone Ranger says, "It's no use, Tonto. We're surrounded." And Tonto answers, "What do you mean *we*, white man?" '

High above us was the source of the screeching feedback-music I'd been hearing. It was an unearthly, tortured – or rather torturing – noise, sadistic, dispassionate, aloof. I had complained about it at the beginning of our climb and Vasco had brushed my objections aside. 'In some parts of the Far East,' he informed me, 'such music is considered highly erotic.' As we climbed, Vasco had to speak louder to make himself heard. My head was beginning to throb.

'So, the Lone Ranger and Tonto are making camp for the night,' he shouted. ' "Make the fire, Tonto," says the Lone Ranger. "Yes, kemo sabay." "Fetch water from the stream, Tonto." "Yes, kemo sabay." "Make the coffee, Tonto." So on so forth. But suddenly Tonto exclaims in disgust. The Lone Ranger asks, "What's the matter?" "Yecch," answers Tonto, looking at the soles of his moccasins. "I think I just stepped in a big pile of kemo sabay." '

I half-remembered the taxi-driver Vivar, the Western-movie buff who bore the name of a mediaeval, armour-plated cowboy, Spain's second-greatest knight-errant – El Cíd, I mean, Rodrigo de Vivar, not Don Quixote – warning me about Benengeli in a drawl that was half John Wayne in anything, half Eli Wallach in *The Magnificent Seven*. 'Go careful, pardner – up there ees Indian contry.'

But had he really said that? Was it a false memory, or a half-forgotten dream? I was no longer sure of anything. Except, perhaps, that this was indeed Indian country, I was surrounded, and the kemo sabay was getting pretty deep.

In a way I had been in Indian country all my life, learning to read its signs, to follow its trails, rejoicing in its immensity, in its inexhaustible beauty, struggling for territory, sending up smoke-signals, beating its drums, pushing out its frontiers, making my way through its dangers, hoping to find friends, fearing its cruelty, longing for its love. Not even an Indian was safe in Indian country; not if he was the wrong sort of Indian, anyway – wearing the wrong sort of head-dress, speaking the wrong language, dancing the wrong dances, worshipping the wrong gods, travelling in the wrong company. I wondered how considerate those warriors encircling the masked man with the silver bullets would have been towards his feather-headed pal. In Indian country, there was no room for a man who didn't want to belong to a tribe, who dreamed of moving beyond; of peeling off his skin and revealing his secret identity – the secret, that is, of the identity of all men – of standing before the war-painted braves to unveil the flayed and naked unity of the flesh.

⌐

Renegada had not accompanied us into the tower. The little traitress had probably scampered back to the arms of her mole-faced lover to gloat over my entrapment. A ghostly light filtered into the spiral stairwell through narrow, slit-like windows. The walls were at least a metre thick, ensuring that the temperature in the tower was cool, even chilly. Perspiration was drying on my spine and I gave a little shiver. Vasco floated up behind me, puffing and blowing, a bulbous spectre with a gun. Here in Castle Miranda these two displaced spirits, the last of the Zogoibys and his maddened foe, would enact the final steps of their ghost-dance. Everyone was dead, everything was lost, and in the twilight there was time for no more than this last phantom tale. Were there silver bullets in Vasco Miranda's gun? They say that silver bullets are what you need to kill a supernatural being. So if I, too, had become spectral, then they would do for me.

We passed what must have been Vasco's studio, and I caught a glimpse of an unfinished work: a crucified man had been taken down from the cross and was lying across a weeping woman's lap, with pieces of silver – no doubt there were thirty of them – spilling from his stigmatised hands. This anti-*pietà* must be one of the 'Judas Christ' pictures I'd been told about. I had had only the briefest of looks, but the lurid, imitation-El-Greco feeling of the painting inspired queasiness, and made me hope that Vasco's abandonment of the project was final.

On the next floor he motioned me into a room in which I saw, with a leap of the heart, an unfinished picture of quite a different calibre: Aurora Zogoiby's last piece, her anguished declaration of a mother-love that could transcend and forgive the supposed crimes of her beloved child, *The Moor's Last Sigh*. Also in the room was a large piece of what I understood to be X-ray equipment; and, clipped to a great bank of light-boxes on one wall, a number of X-ray photographs. Apparently Vasco was examining the stolen picture segment by segment, as if by looking beneath its surface he might belatedly discover, and steal for himself, the secret of Aurora's genius. As if he were looking for a magic lamp.

Vasco shut the door, and I could no longer hear the ear-splitting music. Plainly, the room had been expensively soundproofed. However, the light in that chamber – the slit-windows had been covered over with black cloth, so that there was only the blinding white blare of light emanating from the wall of boxes – was almost as oppressive as the music had been. 'What are you doing here?' I asked Vasco, deliberately sounding as impolite as I could. 'Learning to paint?'

'I see you have developed the sharp tongue of the Zogoibys,' he answered. 'But it is careless to mock a man with a loaded gun; a man, what's more, who has done you the service of solving the puzzle of your mother's death.'

'I know the answer to that riddle,' I said. 'And this painting has nothing to do with it.'

'You are an arrogant bunch, you Zogoibys,' Vasco Miranda

went on, ignoring my remarks. 'No matter how badly you treat a man, you are sure he will go on caring for you. Your mother thought that about me. She wrote to me, you know? Not long before she died. After fourteen years of silence, a cry for help.'

'You're lying,' I told him. 'You could never have helped her with anything.'

'She was scared,' he said, ignoring me again. 'Someone was trying to kill her, she said. Someone was angry, and jealous, and ruthless enough to have her assassinated. She was expecting to be murdered at any time.'

I was trying to keep up a façade of contempt, but how could I fail to be moved by the image of my mother in a state of such terror – and such isolation – that she had turned to this played-out figure, this long-alienated madman for assistance? How could I not see her face before my mind's eye, contorted by fear? She was pacing up and down her studio, wringing her hands, and every noise startled her, as if it were a harbinger of doom.

'I know what happened to my mother,' I said quietly. Vasco exploded.

'Zogoibys always say they know everything! But you know nothing! Nothing at all! It is I – I, Vasco – Vasco whom you all derided, that airport-artist who was not fit to kiss the hem of your great mother's garment, Vasco the potboiler painter, Vasco the bleddy joke – this time it is I who know.'

He stood silhouetted before the bank of light-boxes, X-ray images to his right and left. 'If she was killed, she said, she wanted the murderer brought to book. So she had concealed his portrait under her work in progress. Get the picture X-rayed, she said to me, and you will see my killer's face.' He was holding the letter in his hand. So here, at last, in this time of mirages, this place of sleights, was a simple fact. I took the letter and my mother spoke to me from beyond the grave.

'Take a look.' Vasco waved the pistol at the X-ray images. Silenced, abashed, I did as I was told. There was no doubt that the canvas was a palimpsest; a full-length portrait could be made out in negative-image segments beneath the surface work. But Raman

Fielding had been a figure of Vasco-like corpulence, and the man in the ghost-image was slender, and tall.

'That's not Mainduck,' I said, the words emerging of their own volition.

'Correct! Absolute hit-take,' said Vasco. 'A frog is a harmless fellow. But this guy? Don't you know him? Follow your instincts and outstincts! Here he may be undercover but you have seen him overcover! Look, look – the boss baddie himself. Blofeld, Mogambo, Don Vito Corleone: don't you recognise the gent?'

'It's my father,' I said, and it was. I sat down heavily on the cold stone floor.

∽

In cold blood: the phrase never fitted anyone so well as Abraham Zogoiby. – From humble beginnings (persuading a reluctant sea-captain to set sail) he rose to Edenic heights; from which, like an icy deity, he wrought havoc upon the mere mortals below; but also, and in this he differed from most deities, among his own kith and kin. – Disjointed observations were presenting themselves to me for approval; or perusal; or what you will. – Like Superman, I had been given the gift of X-ray vision; unlike Superman, it had shown me that my father was the most evil man that ever lived. – By the way, if Renegada and Felicitas were not half-sisters, what were their last names? Lorenço, del Toboso, de Malindrania, Carcu-liambro? – But my father, I was speaking of my father Abraham, who had been the one to start the investigation into the mystery of Aurora's death; who could not leave her be, and saw her ghost walking in his garden in the sky – and was that his guilt at work, or a part of his grand, cold-blooded design? Abraham, who told me that Sammy Hazaré had sworn a deposition to Dom Minto, said deposition never in fact materialising, but on the evidence of which I went forth to bludgeon a man to death. – And Gottfried Helsing? Could it be that he did not know the truth about the self-styled 'Larios sisters' – or was his indifference so great that he felt no need to volunteer information to me; had the sense of human community so decayed among the Parasites of Benengeli that a man no longer felt a scrap of responsibility for his fellows' fate? – Yes, bludgeon, I say, bludgeon. Pounding his face until there was no face there. And Chhaggan, too, was found in a gutter; Sammy Hazaré was suspected of the crime, but maybe there had been an unseen hand at work. – Now, what the devil were the names of the actors who played the masked man and the Indian? A–B–C–D–E–F–Jay, that's it, Jay, and not Silverbullets but Silverheels. Chief Jay Silverheels and Clayton Moore. – O Abraham! How readily you sacrificed your son on the altar of your wrath! Whom did you hire to blow the poisoned dart? *Was* there such a dart, or were slipperier means employed – a little patch of Vaseline would have turned your murderous trick, just a drop in the right place, so easily spilled, so easily removed; why should I believe a word of that Minto story, after all? O, I was lost in fictions, and murder was all around. – My world was mad, and I was mad in it; how to accuse Vasco when Zogoibys perpetrated such lunacy upon one another, and upon their wretched times? – And Mynah, my sister Mynah, killed in an earlier blast; Mynah, who sent a crooked politico to jail and obliged her father to incur some considerable expense! Could the daughter, too, have died by the father's hand – might that have been our Daddyji's rehearsal for the subsequent termination of his wife? – And Aurora: was she innocent or guilty? She believed me guilty, and I was not; should I not avoid the selfsame trap? Did she, having been unfaithful, truly give Abraham cause for jealous rage – so that, after a lifetime of standing in her shadow, deferring to her whim (while in the rest of his life he grew monstrous, omnipotent, diabolical), he slew her, and then used her death's mystery to twist my mind, so that I'd slay his enemy, too? – Or was she chaste, was she pure and whole as Indian mothers should be, and did he, mistaking virtue for vice, play the unreasoning jealous loon? – How, when the past is gone, when all's exploded and in rags, may one apportion blame? How to find meanings in the ruins of a life? – One thing was certain; I was fortune's, and my parents', fool. – This floor's a cold floor. I should get up off this floor. There's still a fat fellow over there, and he's pointing a pistol at my heart.

# 20

I HAVE LOST COUNT of the days that have passed since I began my prison sentence in the topmost tower-room of Vasco Miranda's mad fortress in the Andalusian mountain-village of Benengeli, but now that it is over I must record my memories of that awful incarceration, if only to honour the heroic rôle played by my fellow-captive, without whose courage, inventiveness and serenity I am sure I would not have lived to tell my tale. For, as I discovered on that day when I discovered so many things, I was not the only victim of Vasco Miranda's deranged obsession with my late mother. There was a second hostage.

Still shaken to the foundations of my being by the revelations in the X-ray chamber, I was ordered by Vasco to resume my climb. Thus I came to the circular cell in which I would be left to rot for so long, deafened by the vile noises emanating from high wall-mounted speakers, certain of my own death's imminence, and consoled only by that amazing woman who glowed through my time of darkness like a beacon. I clung to her, and therefore did not sink.

There was a painting on an easel in the centre of this room, too: Vasco's own Boabdil, the weepy horseman, had galloped tearfully to Spain as well, leaving its purchaser C. P. Bhabha's home and returning to its maker. What had been made in *Elephanta* was coming to roost in Benengeli – murder, vengefulness, and art. Vasco's first work on canvas and Aurora's last, his new beginning and her sad conclusion: two stolen paintings, both treatments of the same theme, and each with one of my parents hidden underneath. (I never saw the other stolen 'Moors'. Vasco claimed to have chopped them up and burned them along with their crates:

he had only had them stolen, he said, to disguise the fact that *The Moor's Last Sigh* was the one he'd wanted.)

X-rays accused Abraham Zogoiby in a lower circle of this ascending hell, but for concealed Aurora photographs were not enough. Vasco's Moor was being destroyed, was being picked away flake by flake; the image of my mother when young, that bare-breasted Madonna-without-child which had so incensed Abraham once-upon-a-time, was emerging from her long imprisonment. But her freedom was being gained at her liberator's expense. It did not take me long to notice that the woman who stood at the easel, picking paint-flecks off the canvas and placing them on a dish, was chained – by the ankle! – to the red stone wall.

She was of Japanese origin, but had spent much of her professional life working as a restorer of paintings in the great museums of Europe. Then she married a Spanish diplomat, a certain Benet, and moved with him around the world until the marriage failed. Out of the blue, Vasco Miranda had called her at the Fundació Joan Miró in Barcelona – saying only that she 'came highly recommended' – and invited her to visit him in Benengeli to examine, and advise on, certain palimpsest-paintings he had recently acquired. Although she was not an admirer of his work, she had found it impossible to refuse without insulting him; and was curious, too, to peep behind the high walls of his legendary folly, and perhaps to discover what lay beneath the mask of the notorious recluse. When she arrived at the Little Alhambra, bringing with her the tools of her trade, as he had expressly requested she should, he showed her his own *Moor* and the X-rays of the portrait below; and asked her if it would be possible to exhume the buried painting by removing the top layer.

'It would be dangerous, but perhaps possible, yes,' she said, after making an initial study. 'But surely you would not choose to destroy your own work.'

'This is what I have asked you here to do,' he said.

She had refused. In spite of her distaste for Vasco's *Moor*, a picture she considered to have few merits, the prospect of spending laborious weeks, perhaps months, engaged on the destruction, rather than the preservation, of a work of art had little appeal. Her refusal was polite and delicate, but it threw Miranda into a rage. 'You want big money, is that it?' he asked, and offered her a sum so absurd as to confirm her worries about his state of mind. At her second refusal he had produced a pistol and her incarceration had commenced. She would not be freed, he told her, until she had completed her duties; if she declined to carry them out he would shoot her down 'like a dog'. So her labours had begun.

Arriving in her cell, I wondered at her chains. What a compliant fellow that blacksmith must be, I thought, so incuriously to install such devices in a private home. Then I recalled his cry – *Sti' walki' free, huh? Som' day soo', soo'* – and the notion of a grand conspiracy returned, and gnawed.

'Company for you,' Vasco informed the woman, and then, turning to me, announced that on account of our old acquaintance and his own kindly, whimsical nature he would postpone my execution for a time. 'Let's re-live the old times together,' he proposed, gaily. 'If Zogoibys are to be wiped off the face of the earth – if the wrong-doings of the father, yes, and the mother, too, are to be visited upon the son – then let the last Zogoiby recount their sinful saga.' Every day, after that, he brought me pencil and paper. He had made a Scheherazade of me. As long as my tale held his interest he would let me live.

My fellow-prisoner gave me good advice. 'Spin it out,' she said. 'That's what I am doing. Every day we stay alive, we improve our chances of rescue.' She had a life – work, friends, a home – and her disappearance would be bound to arouse suspicions. Vasco knew this, and forced her to write letters and postcards, taking leave of absence from her work, and explaining to her social circle that the 'fascination' of being inside the secret world of the famous V. Miranda had her in thrall. These would delay inquiries, but not for ever, for she had inserted deliberate mistakes into the letters, for example referring to a friend's lover, or pet, by the wrong name; and sooner or later someone might smell a rat. When I heard this I became inordinately excited, for the despondency that had settled over me in the aftermath of Vasco's X-ray revelations had caused me to despair of rescue. Now hope was reborn, and I became delirious with anticipation. At once she dragged me down to earth.

'It is only a long-shot,' she said. 'People are inattentive, by and large. They do not read closely, but skim. They are not expecting to be sent messages in code, and so they may not see any.' To illustrate her point she told me a story. In 1968, during the 'Prague Spring', an American colleague of hers had taken a group of art students to visit Czechoslovakia. They had been in Wenceslas Square when the first Russian tanks rolled into town. In the ensuing disturbances the American teacher had been one of those randomly arrested by the unleashed riot squads, and had spent two days in jail before the American consul had secured his release. During these days he had noticed a tapping code scratched into the wall of his cell, and had begun, eagerly, to send messages to whoever might be on the other side of the wall. After an hour or so of tapping, however, the door to his cell burst open, and an amused guard sauntered in to tell him, in filthy, broken English, that his neighbour wanted him to 'shot the fock op,' because, alas, 'nobody give to him the focking code.'

'Also,' she continued coolly, 'even if help arrives – even if policemen begin to batter down the gates of this terrible place – who knows if Miranda will permit us to be taken alive? Right now he is living wholly in the present moment – he has slipped the chains of the future. But if that tomorrow comes, and he is forced to face it, he may choose to die, like one of those cultist leaders one hears about more and more these days, and in all probability he will want to take us all along with him – Miss Renegada, Miss Felicitas, and me, and you as well.'

We met so near the end of our stories that I cannot do her justice. There is neither time nor space for me to pay her the compliment of setting her down, so to speak, in full; though she, too, had her history, she loved and was loved, she was a human being, not just a captive in that hateful space whose thick-walled cold made us shiver through the nights, even though we huddled together for warmth, wrapped up in my leather greatcoat. I cannot embark on her story – can only pay tribute to the generous strength with which she held me close through those interminable nights, while I felt Death approach, and quailed. I can only record her murmurs in my ears, how she sang to me, and joked. She had known other, kinder walls, had gazed through other windows than these mere razor-slashes in red stone, through which prison bars of light fell daily across our cage, and out of which no cry for help could make its way into a friendly ear. She must have called out, from those happier windows, to family or friends; she could not do so here.

This is what I can say. Her name was a miracle of vowels. Aoi Uë: the five enabling sounds of language, thus grouped ('ow-ee oo-ay'), constructed her. She was tiny, slender, pale. Her face was a smooth, unlined oval, on which two smudge-like eyebrows, positioned unusually high, gave her a permanent expression of faint surprise. It was an ageless face. She could have been anything from thirty to sixty. Gottfried Helsing had spoken of a 'pretty little thing' and Renegada Larios – or whatever her name really was – of a 'bohemian type'. Both descriptions were feebly off the mark. She was no chit of a girl but a formidably contained woman – indeed her self-possession might, in the outside world, have been a little alarming, but in the confines of our fatal circle it became my mainstay, my nourishment by day and my pillow at night. Nor was she the wanton drop-out type, but, rather, the most orderly of spirits. Her formality, her precision, awakened an old self in me, reminding me of my own adherence to ideas of neatness and tidiness in the childhood days before I surrendered to the imperatives awakening in my brutal, twisted fist. In the hideous circumstances of our chained existence she provided our necessary disciplines, and I unquestioningly followed her lead.

She shaped our days, creating a timetable to which we rigorously adhered. We were awakened early each morning by an hour of that 'music' which Miranda insisted on calling 'Oriental', even 'Japanese', but if the Japanese woman he had imprisoned found such epithets insulting, she never gave Vasco the satisfaction of expressing her annoyance. The noise appalled and bruised, but while it lasted we performed, at Aoi's suggestion, our daily private functions. Each of us in turn would avert our gaze, lying down to face the wall, while the other did what had to be done in one of the two latrine-buckets that Vasco, most nightmarish of jailers, had provided; and the din needling our ears spared us each other's sounds. (Each of us was, from time to time, given a few squares of coarse brown paper with which to clean ourselves, and these we treasured and defended as dragons defend their hoards.) After this we washed, using the aluminium bowls and jugs of water that one of the 'Larios sisters' brought up once a day. Felicitas and Renegada were stony-faced on these visits, refusing all entreaties, ignoring all expostulation and contumely. 'How far will you go?' I shouted at them. 'How far, for that fat madman? As far as murder? The end of the line? Or will you get off at an earlier station?' Under such questioning they were implacable, unconcerned, deaf. Aoi Uë taught me that only by remaining silent, in such a situation, could one maintain one's necessary self-respect. After that I let Miranda's women come and go without a word.

Once the music had ended we applied ourselves to our work: she to her paint-flakes, I to these pages. But as well as our allotted tasks we made time for conversation-hours during which, by agreement, we would speak of anything except our situation; and brief daily 'business talks' during which we considered our options and spoke tentatively of escape; and exercise periods; and times of solitude, too, when we did not speak, but sat alone and husbanded our private, eroding selves. Thus we clung to humanity, and refused to allow our captivity to define us. 'We are greater than this prison,' Aoi said. 'We must not shrink to fit its little walls. We must not become the ghosts haunting this stupid castle.' We played games – word-games, memory-games, pat-a-cake. And, often, without any sexual motive, we would hold each other. Sometimes she would let herself shake, and weep, and I would let her, let her. More often she performed this service for me. For I felt old, and spent. My breathing difficulties had returned, worse than ever; I had no medication, nor was any provided for me. Giddy, aching, I understood that my body was sending me a simple, absolute message: the jig was nearly up.

One part of the day could not be time-tabled. This was Miranda's visit, when he inspected Aoi's progress, removed my daily pages and provided me with new sheets and pencils if required; and in various ways amused himself at our expense. He had his pet-names for us, he announced, for were we not his pets, kept leashed and kennelled, transformed into dog and bitch? 'Well, Moor is Moor, of course,' he said. 'But you, my dear, must henceforth be his Chimène.'

I told Aoi Uë about my mother, whom she was bringing back from the dead – and about the sequence of works in which another Chimène had met, and loved, and betrayed another Moor. She said: 'I loved a man, you know; my husband, Benet. But he betrayed me, often, in many countries, he could not help himself. He loved me, and betrayed me while continuing to love. In the end it was I who stopped loving him and left: stopped loving him not because he betrayed me – I had gotten used to that – but because certain habits of his, which had always irritated me, just wore away my love. Very little habits. The relish with which he picked his nose. The length of time he took in the bathroom while I was waiting for him in bed. His reluctance to meet my eye with an affectionate smile when we were in company. Trivial things; or perhaps not? What do you think – perhaps my betrayal was greater than his, or as great? Never mind. Just let me say that our love is still the most important event in my life. Defeated love is still a treasure, and those who choose lovelessness have won no victory at all.'

*Defeated love* . . . O heartbreaking echoes of the past! On my little table in that death-cell young Abraham Zogoiby wooed his spice-heiress and aligned himself with love and beauty against the forces of ugliness and hate; and was that true, or was I putting Aoi's words into my father's thought-bubble? – Just as, at night, I still dreamed of being skinned; so when I set down Oliver D'Aeth's similar visions, or the masturbatory thoughts of Carmen da Gama long ago, when at my bidding and in the privacy of her own imagination she longed for flaying and annihilation, what was she but a creature of my mind? – As are all these; as they must be, having no means of being other than through my words. And I, too, knew about defeated love. Once I had loved Vasco Miranda. Yes, that was true. The man who wanted to murder me was a person I had loved . . . but I had suffered an even greater defeat than that.

Uma, Uma. 'What if the person you love did not really exist at all,' I asked Aoi. 'What if she created herself, out of her perception

425

of your need – what if she falsely enacted the part of the person you could not resist, could never resist, your dream-lover; what if she made you love her *so that she could betray you* – if betrayal were not the failure of love, but the purpose of the whole exercise from the start?'

'Still, you did love her,' said Aoi. 'You were not playing a part.'

'Yes, but – '

'So, even then,' she said with finality. 'Even then, you see.'

∽

Vasco said: 'Hey, Moor. I read in the paper that some guys in France have developed a wonder drug. It slows down the ageing process, men, what a thing! Skin stays springier, bones stay bonier, organs pull out the stops for longer, and general well-being and mental alertness are promoted in the old. Clinical trials with volunteers beginning shortly. Too bad; too late for you.'

'Sure, sure,' I said. 'Thanks for the sympathy.'

'Read for yourself,' he said, and handed me the clipping. 'Sounds like the elixir of life. *Boy*, how frustrated you must feel.'

∽

And at night there were cockroaches. Our sleeping-place was a straw palliasse covered with sackcloth, and in the darkness the creatures came out of it, they wriggled through hairline cracks in the universe, as cockroaches will, and we felt them moving on our bodies like dirty fingers. At first I would shudder and leap to my feet, I would stamp and flail about blindly, I would weep hot phobic tears. My breaths hee-hawed donkey-fashion as I wept. 'No, no,' Aoi comforted me as I shook in her arms. 'No, no. You must learn to let this go. Let go the fear, the shame.' She, most fastidious of women, led by example, neither twitching nor complaining, displaying an iron discipline, even when the roaches tried to burrow into her hair. And slowly I learned from her.

When she was my teacher she reminded me of Dilly Hormuz; at her work, she reincarnated Zeenat Vakil. It was the varnish that made her task possible, she explained: that thin film which separated the earlier picture from the later. Two worlds stood on her easel, separated by an invisibility; which permitted their final separation. But in that separation one would be utterly annihilated, and the other could easily be damaged. 'Oh, easily,' said Aoi, 'and if my hand shakes in fright, that's it.' She was good at finding practical reasons not to be afraid.

My own world had been in flames. I had tried to leap out of it, but I landed in the fire. But her life, Aoi's, had not deserved this climax. She had been a wanderer, and had had her share of pain, but how comfortable she seemed in her rootlessness, how easy in herself! So it was conceivable that the self was autonomous, after all, and that Popeye the sailor-man – along with Jehovah – had it just about right. *I yam what I yam an' that's what I yam*, and to the devil with roots and schmoots. God's name turned out to be our own as well. I am, I am, I am. I am. I am. *Tell them, I AM hath sent me to you.*

Undeserved as her fate was, she faced it. And, for a long time, did not let Vasco see her fear.

What did scare Aoi Uë? Reader: I did. It was me. Not by my appearance, or by my deeds. She was frightened by my words, by what I set down on paper, by that daily, silent singing for my life. Reading what I wrote before Vasco spirited it away, learning the full truth about the story in which she was so unfairly trapped, she trembled. Her horror at what we had done to one another down the ages was the greater because it showed her what we were capable of doing still; to ourselves, and to her. At the worst moments of the tale she would bury her face in her hands and shake her head. I, who needed her composure, who held on to her self-control as if it were my lifebuoy, was dismayed to find myself responsible for these jitters.

'Has it been such a bad life, then?' I asked her, piteously, like a child appealing to his headmistress. 'Has it truly been so very, very bad?'

I could see the episodes passing before her eyes – the burning spice-fields, Epifania dying in the chapel while Aurora watched. Talcum powder, crookery, murder. 'Of course it has,' she replied, with a piercing look. 'All of you . . . terrible, terrible.' Then, after a pause: 'Couldn't you all have just . . . calmed down?'

There was our story in a nutshell, our tragedy enacted by clowns. Write it on our tombstones, whisper it to the wind: those da Gamas! Those Zogoibys! They just *didn't know how to be calm*.

We were consonants without vowels: jagged, lacking shape. Perhaps if we'd had her to orchestrate us, our lady of the vowels. Maybe then. Maybe, in another life, down a fork in the road, she would come to us, and we would all be saved. There is in us, in all of us, some measure of brightness, of possibility. We start with that, but also with its dark counter-force, and the two of them spend our lives slugging it out, and if we're lucky the fight comes out even.

Me? I never got the right help. Nor, until now, did I ever find my Chimène.

Towards the end, she retreated from me, she said she did not want to read any more; but read it, nevertheless, and filled up, each day, with a little more horror, a little more disgust. I begged her for forgiveness, I told her (my nutty cathjew confusions persisting right to the end!) that I needed her absolution. She said, 'I'm not in that line of work. Get yourself a priest.' There was a distance between us after that.

And as our tasks neared completion our fear hung lower over us and dripped into our eyes. I had long coughing spasms, during which, retching and with streaming eyes, I almost hoped for an end to come, like this, to cheat Miranda of his prize. My hand shook over the paper and Aoi, too, often had to stop work, and drag herself off, chains clanking, to huddle against a wall and compose herself again. Now I, too, was horrified, for it was indeed a horror to see that strong woman weaken. But when I sought to comfort her, in those latter days, she brushed my arm away. And of course Miranda saw it all, her weakening and our estrangement; he revelled in our crumbling, taunting us: 'Maybe I'll do it today. – Yes, yes! – No, on second thoughts, tomorrow.' He did not care for my portrayal of him, and on two occasions placed his pistol against my temple and pulled the trigger. The firing chamber was empty both times, and, fortunately, so were my bowels; or else there would certainly have been a humiliation in my pants.

'He won't do it,' I found myself repeating. 'He won't, he won't, he won't.'

Aoi Uë cracked. 'Of course he will, you bastard,' she screamed at me, hiccuping with terror and rage. 'He's mad, mad as a s-snake and sticks n-needles in his arms.'

She was right, of course. This deranged, late-period Vasco had become a heavy user. Vasco Miranda of the lost needle had found many new ones. So when he came for us at the end he would have dutch courage running in his veins. Suddenly, with a great wheezing shudder, I remembered how he had looked the day after he read my piece about Abraham Zogoiby's venture into the child-care business; I saw again the lop-sided grin on his face as he gloated over us, and heard – with a dreadful new understanding – his voice on the stairs as he descended, singing:

> *Baby Softo, sing it louder,*
> *Softo-pofto talcum powder,*
> *Bestest babies are allowed-a*
> *Softer Baby Softo.*

Of course he would kill us. I imagined that he would sit between our corpses, cleansed of hatred by violence, and gaze upon my mother's unveiled portrait: united with his beloved at last. He would wait with Aurora until they came for him. Then, perhaps, he would use one last silver bullet on himself.

∽

No help came. Codes were not cracked, Salvador Medina suspected nothing, the 'Larios sisters' remained loyal to their master. Was this a talcum-powder loyalty, I wondered; did they go in for this type of needlework as well?

My story had arrived in Benengeli, and my mother, cradling nothing, looked out at me from the easel. Aoi and I barely spoke any more; and each day we awaited the end. Sometimes, while I waited, I interrogated my mother's portrait, silently, for answers to the great questions of my life. I asked her if she had truly been

Miranda's lover, or Raman Fielding's, or anyone's; I asked her for a proof of her love. She smiled, and did not reply.

Often I stared across at Aoi Uë as she worked. This woman who was both intimate and stranger. I dreamed of meeting her later, when we had escaped this fate, at a gallery opening in a foreign city. Would we fall upon each other, or walk on by without showing recognition? After the trembling, clutching nights, and the cockroaches, would we mean everything to each other, or nothing? Perhaps worse than nothing: each of us would remind the other of the worst time of our lives. So we would hate each other, and turn furiously away.

～

O, I am deep in blood. There is blood on my shaking hands, and on my clothes. Blood smudges these words as I set them down. O the vulgarity, the garish unambiguity of blood. How tawdry it is, how thin . . . I think of newspaper accounts of violence, of mimsy scriveners revealed as murderers, of rotting corpses discovered under bedroom floorboards or garden turf. It is the faces of the survivors I remember: the wives, neighbours, friends. 'Yesterday our lives were rich and various,' the faces say to me. 'Then the atrocity happened; and now we are just its things, we are bit-players in a story in which we don't belong. In which we never dreamed we might belong. We have been flattened; reduced.'

Fourteen years is a generation; or, enough time for a regeneration. In fourteen years Vasco could have allowed bitterness to leach out of him, he could have cleansed his soil of poisons and grown new crops. But he had mired himself in what he had left behind, marinaded himself in what had spurned him, and in his bile. He, too, was a prisoner in this house, his greatest folly, which trapped him in his own inadequacy, his failure to approach Aurora's heights; he was caught in a shrieking feedback loop of remembrances, a screaming of memories, whose note rose higher and higher, until it began to shatter things. Eardrums; glass; lives.

The thing we feared came to pass. Chained, we waited; and it came. When I had brought my story to the X-ray room and Aurora had burst through the weeping cavalier, at mid-day, he came to us in his Sultan outfit, with a black cap on his head, key-ring jangling on his belt, with his revolver in his hand, humming a talcum-powder shanty. It's a Bombay remake of a cowboy movie, I thought. A showdown at high noon, except that only one of us is armed. *It's no use, Tonto. We're surrounded.*

His face was dark, strange. 'Please don't,' said Aoi. 'You'll regret it. Please.'

He turned to me. 'The lady Chimène is pleading for her life, Moor,' he said. 'Will you not ride to her rescue? Will you not defend her to your last breath?'

Sunlight slashes fell across his face. His eyes were pinkish and his arm, unsteady. I didn't know what he was talking about.

'There is no defence I can make,' I said. 'But unchain me, set down your gun, and sure: I'll fight you for our lives.' My breath brayed loudly, making a jackass of me once again.

'A true Moor', responded Vasco, 'would attack his lady's assailant, even if it meant his certain death.' He raised his gun.

'Please,' said Aoi, her back to the red stone wall. 'Moor, please.'

Once before, a woman had asked me to die for her, and I had chosen life. Now I was being asked again; by a better woman, whom I loved less. How we cling to life! If I flung myself at Vasco, it would prolong her life by no more than a moment; yet how precious that moment seemed, how infinite in duration, how she longed for it, and resented me for denying her that aeon!

'Moor, for God's sake, please.'

No, I thought. No, I won't.

'Too late,' said Vasco Miranda merrily. 'O false and cowardly Moor.'

Aoi screamed and ran uselessly across the room. There was a moment when her upper half was hidden by the painting. Vasco fired, once. A hole appeared in the canvas, over Aurora's heart; but it was Aoi Uë's breast that had been pierced. She fell heavily against the easel, clutching at it; and for an instant – picture this – her blood pumped through the wound in my mother's chest. Then the portrait fell forward, its top right-hand corner hitting the floor, and somersaulted to lie face upwards, stained with Aoi's blood. Aoi Uë, however, lay face downwards, and was still.

The painting had been damaged. The woman had been killed.

So it was I who had gained that moment, so eternal in anticipation, so brief in retrospect. I turned my tearful eyes away from Aoi's fallen form. I would look my assassin in the face.

' "*Well may you weep like a woman*," ' he told me, ' "*for what you could not defend like a man*." '

Then he simply burst. There was a gurgling in him, and he was jerked by invisible strings, and the tides of his blood were unleashed, they poured from his nose, his mouth, his ears, his eyes. – I swear it! – Bloodstains spread across the front and rear of his Moorish pantaloons, and he fell to his knees, splashing in his own, and fatal, pools. There was blood and more blood, Vasco's blood mingling with Aoi's, blood lapping at my feet and running away under the door to drip downstairs and tell Abraham's X-rays the news. – An overdose, you say. – One needle too many in the arm, causing the insulted body to spring a dozen leaks. – No, this was something older, an older needle, the needle of retribution that had been planted in him before he had even committed a crime; or, and, it was a needle of fable, it was the splinter of ice left in his veins by his encounter with the Snow Queen, my mother, whom he had loved, and who had made him mad.

When he died he lay upon his portrait of my mother, and the last of his lifeblood darkened the canvas. She, too, had gone beyond recall, and she never spoke to me, never made confession, never gave me back what I needed, the certainty of her love.

As for me, I went back to my table, and wrote my story's end.

~

*The rough grass in the graveyard has grown high and spiky and as I sit upon this tombstone I seem to be resting upon the grass's yellow points, weightless, floating free of burdens, borne aloft by a thick brush of miraculously unbending blades. I do not have long. My breaths are numbered, like the years of the ancient world, in reverse, and the countdown to zero is well advanced. I have used the last of my strength to make this pilgrimage; for when I had gathered my wits, when I had freed myself of my shackles by using the keys on Vasco's ring, when I had finished my writing, to do proper honour and dishonour to the two who lay dead – then my last purpose in life became clear. I put on my greatcoat, and, leaving my cell, found the rest of my text in Vasco's studio, and stuffed the thick furl of paper into my pockets, along with a hammer and some nails. The housekeepers would find the bodies soon enough, and then Medina would begin his search. Let him find me, I thought, let him not think I do not wish to be found. Let him know everything there is to know and give the knowledge to whomsoever he desires. And so I left my story nailed to the landscape in my wake. I have kept away from roads, in spite of these lungs that no longer do my bidding I have scrambled over rough ground and walked in dry water-courses, because of my determination to reach my goal before I was found. Thorns, branches and stones tore at my skin. I paid no attention to these wounds; if my skin was falling from me at last, I was happy to shed that load. And so I sit here in the last light, upon this stone, among these olive-trees, gazing out across a valley towards a distant hill; and there it stands, the glory of the Moors, their triumphant masterpiece and their last redoubt. The Alhambra, Europe's red fort, sister to Delhi's and Agra's – the palace of interlocking forms and secret wisdom, of pleasure-courts and water-gardens, that monument to a lost possibility that nevertheless has gone on standing, long after its conquerors have fallen; like a testament to lost but sweetest love, to the love that endures beyond defeat, beyond annihilation, beyond despair; to the defeated love that is greater than what defeats it, to that most profound of our needs, to our need for flowing together, for putting an end to frontiers, for the dropping of the boundaries of the self. Yes, I have seen it across an oceanic plain, though it has not been given to me to walk in its noble courts. I watch it vanish in the twilight, and in its fading it brings tears to my eyes.*

*At the head of this tombstone are three eroded letters; my fingertip reads them for me. R I P. Very well: I will rest, and hope for peace. The world is full of sleepers waiting for their moment of return: Arthur sleeps in Avalon, Barbarossa in his cave. Finn MacCool lies in the Irish hillsides and the Worm Ouroboros on the bed of the Sundering Sea. Australia's ancestors, the Wandjina, take their ease underground, and somewhere, in a tangle of thorns, a beauty in a glass coffin awaits a prince's kiss. See: here is my flask. I'll drink some wine; and then, like a latter-day Van Winkle, I'll lay me down upon this graven stone, lay my head beneath these letters R I P, and close my eyes, according to our family's old practice of falling asleep in times of trouble, and hope to awaken, renewed and joyful, into a better time.*

# Acknowledgments

The words spoken by the Resident on pages 39–40 are for the most part taken from Rudyard Kipling's story 'On the City Wall', included in the collection *In Black and White* (reissued by Penguin, 1993).

The italicised passage on page 55 is for the most part taken from R. K. Narayan's novel *Waiting for the Mahatma* (Heinemann, 1955).

The letter from Jawaharlal Nehru to Aurora Zogoiby on pages 117–18 draws on an actual letter written by Mr Nehru to Indira Gandhi on 1 July 1945 and published, as Letter 274, in *Two Alone, Two Together: Letters Between Indira Gandhi and Jawaharlal Nehru 1940–64*, edited by Sonia Gandhi (Hodder & Stoughton, 1992).

The illustration of the 'Common Man' on page 229 is by R.K. Laxman.

The extract from the Ramayana on page 368 is taken from the verse translation by Romesh C. Dutt, first published in 1944; Jaico Books edition, 1966.

The extract from the Iliad on the same page is taken from the verse translation by Sir William Marris, OUP, 1934.